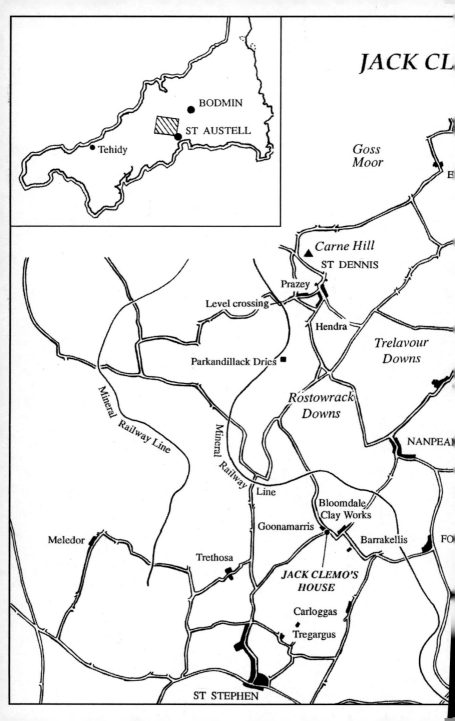

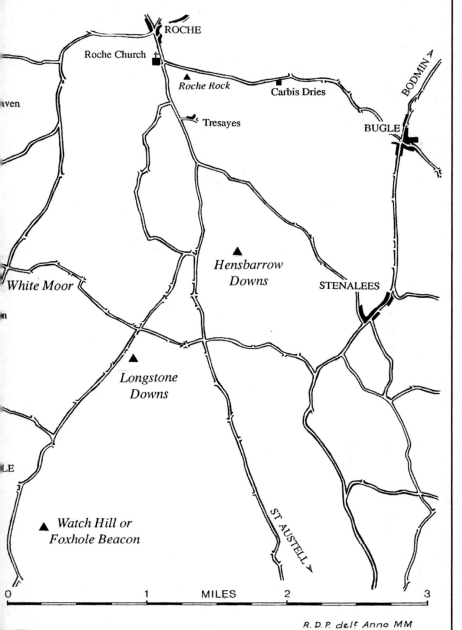

MO'S CLAY COUNTRY

ROCHE

Roche Church

Roche Rock

Carbis Dries

BODMIN

BUGLE

Tresayes

aven

Hensbarrow
Downs

STENALEES

White Moor

Longstone
Downs

Watch Hill or
Foxhole Beacon

ST AUSTELL

LE

| 0 | 1 | MILES | 2 | 3 |

R. D. P. del⁵ Anno MM

THE CLAY KILN

A novel by

JACK CLEMO

Edited by Donald R. Rawe
with an Introduction by John Hurst, M.A.

Pallid birth of my pain – where light, where light is aspiring
Thither I rise, whilst thou – Zeus, keep the godship and sink!

– ROBERT BROWNING

1

©2000 Ruth Clemo

ISBN 1 900147 20 3 Paperback
ISBN 1 900147 21 1 Hardback

Published by
Cornish Hillside Publications
St Austell, Cornwall

First edition 2000

Cover illustration by the late Jack Merriott with
kind permission of Mrs H. Merriott

Book designed by Ray Lancefield
The Design Field, Truro, Cornwall

Printed and bound in Great Britain by
Short Run Press, Exeter EX2 7LW

INTRODUCTION

'It's like being in a kiln, the way I've growed up... Penned in behind the walls and shutters, almost in the dark – not even a window to look out of..'

The central character of *The Clay Kiln* Joel uses these words to his newly-wedded wife Lorraine, as they explore and summarise their experience. Her reply indicates the way in which each has been brought to this point through similar patterns;

'...you've been fighting to get out – where you could see the pattern of things... I've been the same – through my childhood almost exactly like you; the slums were a sort of kiln'.

Jack Clemo's writing is rarely far from the autobiographical. Even when he moves in theme away from the constricted boundaries of the Clay World which dominate his fiction and his early poems to the ever widening range of subjects which mark his developing poetry he is never far from an awareness of the wonder that empowered him to escape from his own 'clay kiln'. Joel and Lorraine stand where Clemo himself and Ruth were to stand two decades later;

'...two more loves are freed,
Outside an age adrift and dark
...we find how disenchanted seed
Is changed to spirit's Cana-spark' (Wedding Eve, to Ruth)[1]

Humanly and artistically Clemo's is an extraordinary story. Himself penned in like Joel in the novel by an isolation that was both physical, as his deafness closed in, and temperamental, he turned in early 'teens to writing. Ever aware of a genetic inheritance that must be both overcome but also exploited he said to his mother

'What about if I was to write stories like-like they 'ockings?'
(Confessions of a Rebel p.69)[2]

This resolution had some immediate fruit – as he soon found a market for short dialect stories, which display, as well as a sharp humour, not often associated with this author, a sensitive ear for dialect and the characteristics of life in the clay world. The major outcome of the resolution, however, was long delayed. The first dialect story was published in 1930 – when he was 16. It was 1948 before the novel *Wilding Graft*[3] achieved publication.

3

'The struggle of nearly two decades, involving fifty-three rejections of my novels, including seven refusals of Wilding Graft was over '(*Confessions of a Rebel* p. 240)

That struggle was a remarkable story of tenacity. The place of *The Clay Kiln* in this slow and painful evolution is interesting.[4] Clemo worked for several years, and often simultaneously, on a variety of novels which never found a publisher. Three of these, at different times, Penance of the Seed (worked on from 1941-46), Unsunned Tarn (worked on from 1937-46) and Private Snow (worked on first from 1936-39 and then revised in 1945; this, in turn, incorporates some earlier material). All three were drawn together to provide the basis and structure of *The Clay Kiln* with fresh material added in 1950-51. Simultaneously, in the aftermath of the publication of *Wilding Graft* Clemo was working on another novel which had occupied him since 1938 which was eventually to achieve publication many years later in 1986 as *The Shadowed Bed*.[5] It is clear from *Marriage of a Rebel* that Clemo wished to continue as a novelist after the successful publication of *Wilding Graft* and that Mss were submitted, unsuccessfully, for publication. Gradually, however, it became clear to him that his success was to be found in poetry, and the writing of fiction ceases altogether. The Ms of *The Shadowed Bed* was taken up after many years in which he had written no new fiction). The extant Mss of *The Clay Kiln* indicate that the novel is almost, but not quite finished. There are gaps in the flow of the narrative. There are details, particularly of geography, which required checking. But, substantially the novel is finished. It is clearly from the same hand as *Wilding Graft*, though it does not display the technical assurance of *The Shadowed Bed*, which can be seen as the most mature example of Clemo's art as a novelist.

Clemo's vision of life in the Clay World is a sombre one, but in the last analysis, positive. Unredeemed life there is indeed nasty, brutish and (often) short; but, because it is life raw, and without illusions, it is life in which the essential nature of men and women is seen more clearly. And can, therefore, because more clearly diagnosed, be more readily cured. Its cure lies not in its prettification, but in its transformation. That transformation works itself out not, as in *Wilding Graft* on the self-discovery of one couple 'predestined to marriage', but two – Joel and Lorraine, and Gwen, Joel's sister and Euan. All come from

4

backgrounds in which, but for a touch of grace, they could have been dragged into the clay slime which appears to be their inheritance, or stifled in the clay kiln from which nothing productive can come. All by that touch of grace escape into the dynamic of Christian marriage.

It would have been easy for Clemo to have declined into the creation of Mills & Boon novels of the Clay World. There is, indeed, an element of the melodramatic in his writing, often surrounding his portraits of the hero as misfit. It can be seen, again, in some of the poems of this period such as Clay-land Moods – almost 'grand guignol' at times in its extremes of expression and gesture; but he is always pulled back by his earthy commonsense; his awareness that salvation is found, not in romantic gesture, but in the real lives of men and women together; and the reality of life in the Clay World.

Much of Clemo's vigour arises, in fact, from a deep ambiguity in his attitude to the Clay-land which both nurtured him and restricted him. There is, on the one hand, the constant awareness of the ever-present destructiveness of the industry's methods of operation. The 'clay-crabs tactics' which he had known all his life. Known that they had destroyed the farm on which he might have been born.

> As a young schoolboy I scanned the farmhouse
> With mild curiosity – then it vanished
> Swallowed by a clay pit...

He goes on to speak of

> the intense need to come to terms
> Make the wrecker seem not all malevolent[6]

It is that understanding he is moving towards in *The Clay Kiln*.

The novel is full of striking insights. Side by side with a full awareness of the crudity of the contorted lives led by many of the characters and the uncared for squalor of their environment, he also sees there a strange and original beauty. He speaks of its 'bleak lyricism... poignant beauty'. The fascination of 'the outcast soil moving softly and gently with its quiet menace to the rhythms of the breeding earth'. And he takes the vision further. 'The ubiquitous claywork scars added a harshness that was beyond Nature's – the ultimate quality of violent, calculated interference which belongs to God'. At the heart of Clemo's vision as a young writer is this paradox – that the intrinsic violence of the Clay Industry is nearer to God's purposes, to God's way of working on men and women, than 'in Churches nestling snugly in the fold of scented hillsides'.[7] And he pushes his vision further still. He sees clearly where surrender to genetic inheritance can take mankind. The awareness is on every page – from the harsh squalor tense with barely suppressed violence, of the opening scene in the Kruse's cottage to the eruption of violence which leads to Cal's death. That is the operation of the embracing of Predestination – God's purpose as opposed to Nature's. Clemo speaks vividly of the two ways as 'the two streams flowing in the opposite direction'. It is strong theology; but it is a theology so interpreted through his characters as to provide a convincing substructure for the novel.

By the time Clemo laid the Ms of *The Clay Kiln* aside his encroaching deafness had made him unable to hear speech for several years. Shut off from the sounds of the vernacular of the Clay Country (which he writes with such vigour and accuracy in the humorous tales[8]), barred from the daily tales of life around him, he turned away from the writing of a fiction whose springs had been removed from him. To his own amazement a new, almost unsought and uncultivated ability to write powerful and distinctive poetry, had come to him.

He had written a little juvenile poetry – which writer has not? – but it came to little. The new gift was to take him in 'the mercy of time's means' further and further from the Clay World. But the essential vision remains. The terror of the pull of the inborn nature; The wonder of 'amazing grace'. Clemo's theme is always that hard-won grace. In the end, even in a novel as sombre as *The Clay Kiln* he is a praise-maker.

NOTES:

1) in *The Echoing Tip* pp6-7; Methuen 1971: also in *Selected Poems* pp778-79; Bloodaxe Books, Newcastle-on-Tyne 1988.
2) Chatto & Windus 1949
3) Chatto & Windus 1948; reprinted in Cornish Library, Anthony Mott Ltd 1983
4) The Mss of the greater part of Dr Clemo's work have been deposited in the Library of Exeter University. A fuller treatment of the complex Mss situation with regard to the fiction is given in Hurst J S: Voice from a White Silence; *Cornish Studies* 3 pp125-43; University of Exeter Press 1995. The Ms from which the Clay Kiln has been prepared is not, however, the one in the University's collection. Though substantially the same it is not a photo-copy or carbon copy, and differs in detail. It may be regarded in some respects, as nearer to the final thought of the author.
5) Lion Books, Tring, Herts 1986
6) in *A Different Drummer* pp30-31; Tabb House, Padstow 1986
7) from Christ in the Clay-Pit; *Selected Poems* p21; original printing in *The Clay Verge*.
8) there is a valuable selection of these in *The Bouncing Hills*, Dyllansow Truran, Redruth n.d.

EDITOR'S NOTE

The main aim in judiciously editing this early novel of Jack Clemo's has been to make clear to the reader what was relatively obscure, and to improve the flow of narrative and dialogue from the occasional clumsiness of a young man who was, with his various disadvantages and disabilities, still an apprentice writer.

The theology-driven plot of *The Clay Kiln*, it seems to me, requires for its effectiveness an author of rather more proficiency than Clemo was at that stage, in the late 1930s and 1940s. It is not surprising that this novel found no acceptance at that time among London publishers. It must have appeared as outlandish a story a *Wuthering Heights* must have on first being considered by a publisher. But here is a book which, I am convinced, will add worthy weight to the growing corpus of modern Cornish literature.

It is a novel very much of its time: gathering clouds of war hang over the sombre, harsh landscape, with four characters doggedly, almost inarticulately struggling against the narrow values and moral degradation of those about them. It has certainly not been my intention to rid the text of Clemo's powerful, if egregious, often startling descriptions and observations; only where the writing appeared to our 21st century expectations difficult to interpret and, at times, jarringly unsubtle, have I dared to change the occasional epithet or phrase.

Historically, some of the terms Clemo uses appear puzzling: for instance, he refers to the secondary school which Euan Kella attended as the 'County School'; which was indeed the name by which St Austell (Poltair) School was known until 1947. I have changed this to 'Grammar School', since after that date the school-leaving age was extended to 15 and all pupils then went to either a Grammar School or Modern Comprehensive School. And in the original text Joel is summoned to appear at the local 'Police Court'; I have, for clarity, used the modern term 'Magistrate's Court'.

Jack Clemo may be forgiven for referring to stone circles and barrows as being sacrificial places of the Druids or Celts. I have (chapter 15) used the more historically correct term pre-Celtic. 'Iberian' (Chapter 3) has been left as it stands: Clemo apparently meant 'Spanish', meaning progeny of Elizabethan sailors from Spain;

but Iberian will satisfy those students of prehistory who hold that the short dark people still found among the Cornish are actually descendants of Neolithic immigrants from that peninsula.

Most of the other changes made have been purely typographical, to improve punctuation and narrative flow, and various typing errors have been rectified: work which any publisher's editor would be expected to perform. The author entitled this work The Dry Kiln. This has been amended to *The Clay Kiln*, which may be better understood today.

Donald R. Rawe

PUBLISHER'S NOTES ON THE TERMINOLOGY OF CLAY WORKING

The methods of clay working which were familiar to Jack Clemo have changed greatly over the years, although the principles of separating china clay from the other minerals by settling processes followed by drying still hold. To assist the modern day reader the following notes are written to explain some of the older terms used in this novel.

'MICAS'

The micas were groups of long shallow channels each about eighteen inches wide which were used to refine the mixture of clay and fine sand pumped to surface from clay pits. This mixture was allowed to flow slowly along these channels so that coarser particles settled in the channels. The fine clay flowed onto settling tanks to thicken before drying. The particles which settled were discharged via drains into local streams, or contained on flat ground in 'mica dams'.

'MICA CLAY'

In the separation using mica channels some coarse china clay settled with the fine sand. To minimise losses residues were often retreated to recover a lower grade of china clay known as mica clay.

'CLAY DRY'

A "dry" or kiln with its coal fired drying floor in a long shed-like building is partly described by the author. Thickened clay from settling tanks was brought into the dry using wooden bodied wagons running on rails which were laid temporarily in the tanks as they were emptied.

Inside the dry the drying floor was spanned by a travelling bridge which could carry a wagon and move it up and down the length of the kiln. This bridge was used to distribute clay from the wagons. Clay would usually dry after a day or so at the "fire end" of the kiln but might take several days at the "chimney end". The daily task of dry workers was to shovel dried clay into the storage linhay and replace it with wet clay. By starting early in the morning this work was often accomplished by mid-day.

SAND TIPS

Sand tips formed of waste sand, gravel and rock were, at the time covered by this novel, usually formed by inclined railways. A sand laden 'skip' waggon was pulled up from the pit bottom to be tipped on the edge of the pit. Conical pyramids, often called 'sky tips' were created as the tip grew.

At the top of the 'incline' a structure of wood and steel beams projected beyond the tip. This enabled the skip to discharge just forward of the tip. A man was stationed at this point to monitor operations and this was a job to which the youthful Jack Clemo aspired.

Some waste rock was moved within the pit along light railway lines, in hand pushed 'tram' waggons, to the bottom of the inlined railway for transfer to a skip waggon. At the top of the incline waste material was sometimes tipped into tram waggons. These were pushed along a horizontal set of rails and tipped to form flat topped 'finger' tips.

For many years now tips have been built as flat topped structures using conveyor belts or shovel loaders and dumpers. Such tips, when complete, are profiled and seeded to blend with the landscape.

Charles Thurlow

CHAPTER ONE

OVER Hensbarrow Downs the moon had cast a flurried brilliance which disclosed the near approach of autumn, for this was the last Sunday in August, 1938. Moonlight had fanned out over the eastern clay-range as dusk fell, and lit up the western slope of the dump behind the Kruses' cottage as Joel descended into the pit.

Joel did not look at the moon; the weird shadows slipping and breaking among the white cliffs made no impression upon his senses. Even the uncanny stillness, frayed slightly by the gurgle of water in the conduits and micas, did not seem awesome to him. The atmosphere was natural to the place; it was natural to Joel. His character had been moulded by these surroundings.

He descended by a gully that had been cut through the cliff face, reaching ground level just outside the low garden wall. This gully had once been the track of an inclined railway, but the rails and sleepers had been removed years ago and the sockets in which they had lain were densely covered with weeds and bramble. Stunted gorse and hazel bushes overhung the upper part of the cleft, the lower and steeper part being bare, strewn with boulders and deeply fissured by its exposure to rain.

Joel's movements were irregular, at times causing a slithering sound as he momentarily lost his foothold.

The pit was full of that harsh melancholy which makes this area of Cornwall so repellent to the casual tourist. A latent ferocity breathed forth from the mouldering hollows of rocks, as from a skeleton. The crags jutting in all directions, impassive to the play of moonbeams and shadow, might have been gravestones.

This place was indeed a tomb to Joel, for all his hopes had been buried here. It was to the pit that he had always come in childhood to brood alone over his grievances. In clefts of the rocks he had often hidden from his father, waiting with childish, impotent rage as he watched Zachary stagger past, shouting, peering into the empty wagons, pushing open the unlocked doors of the cuddies, even seizing a shovel that lay on the ground and waving it as he lurched about. Sometimes Joel had been caught and thrown upon the sand and beaten or had been forced to stay for hours, late into the night cowering upon a ledge along the side of the chasm. The pit was haunted for him with ghosts of his unhappy childhood, and now with adult burdens weighing upon him he still sought its bleak seclusion when human society became for awhile intolerable.

He crossed the pit bed, picking his way among the blasted stone and scraps of timber, the network of rails, the unloaded waggons; stolidly he moved between the huge masses of granite, gnarled and twisted shapes like pillars of some temple. He surveyed them gloomily as he passed, raising his head to glimpse their broad ragged summits.

Joel had never felt that this whole scene was artificial, the product of human industry, bound up with the complexities of modern civilization, affected by trade conditions and political manoeuvres in remote lands. He did not realise that these white crags that somehow solaced him as breasts of Nature had been hewn to supply foreign markets with raw material. In early boyhood he had unquestioningly accepted the sand-dunes and clay-beds as natural features. Since then he had seen the pit expand until it almost threatened the existence of his home; he had seen the refuse heaps rise higher until from almost every cone a flat sinuous ridge crept out over the downs; and daily noticing men at work in the pit and on the sand-tips he had know that they were responsible for these aspects of the landscape. But this explanation had never seemed real to him. The hubbub about his home during the daytime passed like a dream from which he awoke in the evenings when silence closed over the deserted workings and he recognized the vague, familiar idiom of the rocks that were scarred and impoverished as his life.

Reaching the far side of the pit Joel halted; he turned and glanced around the edge of a gaunt crag. There was upon his face a rapt brooding look, as if he awaited some message. His gaze lifted, his face was caught in the full stream of moonlight, tense and haggard. Its features if lit by happiness would not have been unattractive, but misery now puckered the low forehead, the swarthy cheeks; the grey eyes scowled, dull and defiant under thick brows; the passionate lips were gripped in. His clothing – an old tweed suit patched at knees and elbows, a soiled cap and unpolished shoes from which the soles were peeling off – was further proof that here was a man submerged and stagnating.

Just beyond the rim of the pit he saw dimly his home, the square block of granite; feeble lamplight dribbled through the window. Behind it the white pyramid of rock and gravel, piled two hundred feet high, squatted with its tip-beams smudged upon a cloud. Other clouds crossing the moon caused its rays to flutter, the broken flashes slipping down over the gravel folds, jabbing the cottage roof, the cliff face, the small greenish pit-bed pools. Standing with hands on his hips Joel looked upon his home, loathing it. He remembered, vaguely, painfully, the many Saturdays when he had left it to join the football team at Roche: the bus rides to neighbouring villages, the keen, wintry fields, the sureness and mastery of play that lifted him for an hour free of the squalid background. He could feel still the sense of release and achievement as his boot struck the ball. But the house had won, drawn him back from that brisk sanity into this wretched state of gloom, smothered him. He wanted now only to forget his early bid for liberation, to meet the future with a numbed fortitude.

Joel's eyes wandered slowly along the pit-head, like the edge of a bowl far above him in every direction. The walls of the pit were very high; they enclosed him there among the debris, the slimy pools and the torn crags which became blurred in semi-darkness for awhile as clouds covered the moon. Joel stood in the shadow and heard the scraping of thorn branches near the cliff top, the trees half buried in the spilled fringe of refuse but still alive. A hawk swooped overhead, seeking prey in the cornfields that interspersed the downs between the clay-work and the road. Joel shrugged, and crossing to a wooden waggon at the base of the new incline he sat down on its scarred edge. After fumbling in his coat for an almost empty packet and matches, he mechanically lit a cigarette and leaned forward, staring through the faint wisps of smoke at a plank lying as a bridge over a deep crevice a few yards in front of him. His mind dimmed fading to the verge of unconsciousness.

Suddenly he was roused. He glanced up quickly, towards the house on the cliff opposite. Moonlight had once more flushed the sky, now with greater brilliance, for the wind was rising and driving the clouds northward. Joel saw immediately that something was wrong within the cottage. The windows were dark, and from inside the thick walls came confused, ugly sounds: the howling of a baby, the cry of a girl, the din of raucous adult voices shouting each other down... Nothing unusual: just another fuss. But revolt flared in Joel, a fierce reaction from his drowse, surprising him. He rose with a muttered curse and strode back across the pit-bed.

When he reached the base of the gully by which he had descended, footsteps pattered near the summit of the cliff. Joel recognised them and knew that his ten year old sister Ruth was running towards the pit edge, down the garden path. Standing rigid and expectant, he frowned up at the cliff top, the half smoked cigarette gripped tightly at the corner of his mouth. He waited in silence, and from above there soon came, as he had anticipated, a call:

"Joel! Are you still down there?"

Ruth's voice, thin and panicky: poor little devil, so delicate and mixed up in these squalid affairs.

"What's up?" he shouted gruffly in answer.

"Don't stay down there. Come in – quick!"

"I'm coming," he replied, and began climbing.

A few minutes later, half-way up the pit side they had met. The gully was in shadow, but Ruth's bony shoulders and white pinched face cut starkly into a drift of moonlight.

"Don't be scared." He muttered as she seized his arm. "Just stop here wi' me till 'tis blowed over. I knew there'd be a flare-up before bedtime: they've been on at one another all day. I couldn't stick it no longer – had to come out and get a bit o' fresh air ... Why didn't Gwen come out wi' you?"

"She couldn't. You must go in."

"Why – is it Gwen's fault?" he asked uneasily.

"Partly – she egged on dad. You know she been upset for days – disappointed about Marvran not coming to see us. I s'pose".

Joel turned and looked confusedly back into the pit, the glow of the cigarette jerking sideways as his lips tightened. He was obviously gripped and shaken by associations that made the present family dispute remote, irrelevant. His mind seemed to lapse, folding in on vague emotions. Ruth tugged at his sleeve.

"Go in quick, Joel, and cool 'em down, else they'll be coming to blows."

Joel's mind freed itself from the momentary personal ache, and dimly recognizing the bafflement it steeled with exasperation. Squalor and strife were so common in his home near Roche, he had grown hardened to them; but occasionally an irrational bitter disgust broke through the shell of indifference which Marvran Creba's departure from the village had formed within him. Such a moment came now, sharpened by Ruth's reminder that Marvran was again near him, holding aloof. Passion blazed up in his eyes; his face was wrenched, ugly.

"Tis time somebody took a strong hand wi' that lot," he muttered. "I been too quiet with 'em since Gwen left school. It got to finish!"

In reckless haste he clambered on up the gully, digging his toes into the soil and seizing hazel twigs to assist himself. Ruth lagged behind, stumbling among the ruts, panting and tearful. Having reached the summit Joel pushed through the long grass to the garden wall and vaulted over it. He hurried across the black, ridged earth to the path, noting the cat perched on the mud bank at the corner, and glanced at the dark window and the low porch screening the doorway. On gaining this he threw his fag-end aside and passed from a scene of bleak tranquillity to one of stifling tension.

The kitchen was illuminated only by moonlight; the lamp had been overturned and lay on the table, the glass smashed and strewn about in fragments. A fire dwindled in the stove, and on top of the oven were a saucepan and a pair of bellows. In a pram at the foot of the narrow stairway the two-year old Pearl was struggling and whimpering. Beside the table, their backs towards the door were Joel's mother Sarah, a squat grubby little figure, and his eldest sister Gwen. The woman was clutching Gwen's shoulder with one hand while pointing at the floor with the other. Zachary stood facing them, his short wiry legs apart, his arms slightly extended, as if he were eager to come to grips with someone. His coat had been removed and his dirty braces were twisted over his shoulders; his shirt was ragged and smelt strongly of sweat. Behind him, close to the mantelpiece, crouched Arthur, the most dull-witted child of the family: a thin twelve-year old with pimply cheeks and frightened, callous eyes that looked bigger than his mouth.

As Joel paused on the threshold Sarah was shouting, her face jerking close the girl's: "Clean up that mess now – do 'ee hear?"

Gwen writhed irritably. She was a dark raw-boned adolescent, taller than either of her parents. She wore a soiled cotton frock which, like her bare, dusky limbs, caught the gleam of moonlight, though her head was in shadow. Her straight brown hair tumbled about her lowered face as she replied in smouldering, sullen undertones:

"'Tis non 'o my doing. Dad threw the stuff on the floor, he ought to wipe it up himself – or lick it up, as he would if 'twas a bottle o' beer he'd let fall and broke."

Zachary lurched forward, almost stepping into the clotted stew that, with fragments of a broken plate, showed dimly between the dresser and the table. "Do what yer mother tell 'ee – go on!" he cried hoarsely. "Scrape up that soup and wash the floor."

Gwen turned defiantly to her father.

"Why should I do extra work 'cause you've got such a beastly temper?"

"I couldn't eat that bloody muck. 'Twas near burnt to a cinder: you and your mother nagging and arguing when you ought to have been minding the saucepan."

"Well you and mother was lounging in bed all the morning when she ought to have been down here getting the dinner."

"I aren't going to bandy words with 'ee. You git on your knees wi' pail and scrubbin' brush, or something more than my tongue'll git busy."

There was an ominous deliberation in Joel's movement as he stepped into the room. He was looking steadily at this father.

"You'll have me to reckon with before that happens," he said, his voice hard and threatening.

He halted behind Gwen, and she glanced round with a motion of relief and appeal. Sarah also screwed about; a grin spread across her square sallow face, her dull bulging eyes leered craftily.

"No supper to-night, Joel," she greeted him in slow, thick tones. "Had a little upset here."

"I don't want none o' your excuses. Let Gwen alone!"

Sarah wrinkled her nose, scowling back at her husband. "She got to clean up floor first – han't she, Zacky?"

"Reckon so. I'll teach her to stand up to me! She got to do what I tell her".

"We'll see about that. She shan't as long as I'm here."

Zachary pushed past his wife, his small, partly bald head jerked forward on the scraggy neck. He was a shrunken man of epileptic tendency with a bristly moustache, black pig-like eyes and a face blotched by twenty years of heavy drinking. "Who's top dog in this house, I'd like to know?" he challenged.

"Lay a hand on Gwen and you'll find out," retorted Joel. The instinctive antagonism between father and son was evident in both of them, but in Joel it had a quality of disgust, the recoil of a finer nature from a grosser one.

"You always stick up for Gwen, whatever she do," Sarah grumbled. "Gettin' too fond of her, I believe. You'd make a good couple."

She thrust the girl roughly towards Joel; he put an arm protectively about her shoulders. Behind them in the doorway Ruth stood now, her ragged frock smudged against the dark garden, her face a white blob stung by the hair which she kept tossing back with her red bony hand.

The flurries of the wind were strengthening rapidly; its nosing currents could be heard as muffled snarls among the crags of the claypits. Gusts blew in through the open doorway, chilling the room.

Zachary, noting that Joel was in an ugly mood, decided that it was best to recant. He had no relish for violence when Joel was present; he had shrunk from it physically ever since, some three years ago, Joel had beaten him in a fight.

"S'pose you may as well wipe it up, woman," he said grudgingly. "Better'n leaving it there like this all night."

"Me? Not likely! 'Twill stop there till Christmas before I touch the blasted trade." Sarah stepped around Joel, lurching up to the girl in the doorway.

"You, Ruth – look sharp now! Go outside for scrubbin' brush and water. You go upstairs for a lamp, Arthur," she added, turning to the boy.

Ruth hurried out at once, past the window to the house corner. They heard the bump of a pail in the barrel, the splash of water. When she appeared, pail and scrubbing brush in hand, Arthur was seated on the table swinging his legs, staring vacantly at the baby. The parents were eyeing him threateningly, and Sarah was repeating her request in mutters that were scarcely audible above the renewed screams of the infant.

Ruth dropped the pail and crept timidly forward until she stood beside Joel. He glanced down at her, and she saw the glint of revolt now steady and determined in his eyes. He slipped an arm about her: the two girls were shielded, one on each side of him.

Joel spoke, tensely. "You party've gone far enough this week-end. We was here till after midnight rowing about Gwen, and now you're on at her again. You treat her as if she was still a kid instead of a girl nearly old enough to be married."

Sarah was measuring his mood, growing more docile; she stood back against the table and peered at him suspiciously. "What're you driving at now?" she muttered.

"Well, if you go on like this she'll be running off and getting married at the first chance."

"She always blab her secrets to you," remarked Sarah, her voice sinking to a whine of complaint. "And there's times when we'd be glad if some chap did take her off our hands. She's nothing but a burden to we. Here's Zachy been out o' work two year, yet we still got to maintain her. And what good is she at home? She'd never do a scrap o' work if she wasn't bullied into it. And what wi' her temper and laziness, and the dunce she always was at school, she'd never hold a job long enough to bring us any wages."

Gwen met her mother's eye with a mutinous flash of anger, but she felt secure under Joel's strong vibrating touch, and remained silent.

"Gwen's worth a dozen of your modern village maids" cried Joel fiercely. "She's in the wrong home, that's all. And so am I!"

"We been waiting a long time for 'ee to clear out of it," jeered Sarah. "Ever since you stopped your footballing you've been threatening to kick loose from we. But you'm still here."

"I shan't be here much longer, unless you mend your ways," Joel retorted.

Zachary slumped against the dresser, fumbling with his braces; his manner had become sulky and insolent.

"Mend our ways?" he repeated shrilly. "What's wrong with our ways, I'd like to know?"

"So would I," commented Sarah. "Me and Zacky do get along well enough, and the rest of 'ee could too, if we all pulled together."

"Joel's grip tightened on Gwen; an understanding glance passed between them. "We aren't all going to pull downward," he said.

Sarah replied with her back towards him, while moving up to the pram: "You and Gwen is getting' too high and –mighty. You ought to belong to a family like the Crebas up to the bungalow, so you'd have something to swank about."

The taunt brought a dark red flush to Joel's face; he glanced aside, out of the window, and it was Gwen who took up the challenge.

"And where'd we have been if those Crebas hadn't befriended us?" she cried hotly. "You've been sponging on 'em for the past ten years. Nearly all the clothes me and Ruth have had has been Marvran's cast-offs, and we hardly ever eat anything that hasn't got something in it you've 'borrowed' from Mrs. Creba."

"Well, they can 'ford to spare what we've had from 'em" observed Sarah complacently as she bent over the now quietened infant. "Eli may be only Joel's workmate there on the kiln, but there's money in the family. Mrs. Creba's sister married that Luke, the Falmouth business man, and tried to push Marvran up to high circles down there. And you'm getting' the same itch. You wasn't contented here after seeing the fine furniture in their bungalow, piano and wireless and electric gadgets everywhere, and the food laid out on the tea table, what you spied when you called in wi' Marvran on your way home from school."

"Joel hasn't been inside the bungalow in his life." Gwen protested. "He's never seen a set-up different from this one. But he knows there's something wrong with it."

Her passionate tone roused Joel afresh; he released her for a moment and flung out his arm.

"What's this house ever been to me?" he demanded. "It've blotted out all the life I might have had. It come between me and my school-mates, between me and my footballing; it even stood in the way…"

"Stood in the way o' your marrying some smart young lady, I s'pose you mean?" sneered Sarah, straightening to face him." I don't call to mind that we ever tried to stop 'ee getting married. We never heard you wanted to."

Joel looked sullen, half ashamed, as though the gibe reminded him of the flaw, the slackness in himself. He had often felt that the atmosphere of this home was akin to that in which he worked on the steaming clay-kiln a mile away. His home was only another kiln, with hidden heats and, on the surface, the soft slime of a primitive, enclosed world. His whole life was bounded by this ignoble idiom – not the finished clay, fit for the potter's hand, but horribly leprous, the undeveloped slack mud. And here in the cottage the leprosy pierced through to his soul, so that he went about the villages in the evenings and on Sundays with a sense of defilement, the white scabs of the kiln still clinging to him, though he had put off his soiled workaday clothes. His home had laid this stigma upon him. And now, as he took the full pressure of the latest scene that had formed on the surface of its obscene life – the half-dark room, the broken lamp, the soup clotted on the floor, and the human figures groping beast-like and mindless around him, submerged in their instinctive tensions – the tide of nausea mounted, overwhelming him. He repudiated the kiln-world, but the active menace was here, more close and stifling than he had ever known it. He must escape, pull himself free, or be sucked down and dissolved as an individual. The hard rock and fresh air of the clay-pit were not enough to arrest this fetid corrosion... He released both girls and stepped forward with clenched hands.

"'Tis no good arguing or threatening any more," he said in a new deliberate tone. "I've had enough this time. I better quit and finish with it all here"

The family stared at him, realising that a crisis had arisen, something more serious than the bad temper provoked by a spoilt meal. Zachary and Sarah recoiled from its impact, edging closer together until they stood side by side on the hearth.

"When? Asked Sarah blankly.

"Right now."

The woman's brows knit under the fringe of matted grey hair. She, like Zachary, was going bald, but she had a large bun of hair at the back of her head, secured with a broken comb. She rallied a little, attempting to treat Joel's decision with mockery.

"Dunno where you could spend the night – unless you went down to Olive Buzza's," she remarked, leering at her husband. "Anyway, you'd be back home again to-morrow, looking to we to fill your belly."

"I'll never look to you for anything again as long as I live," cried Joel recklessly. "I'll get lodgings in Bugle or Stenalees – somewhere near enough for me to bike in to work every day."

Gwen moved up to him, subdued and troubled at this outcome of her defiant stand; she touched his sleeve.

"But without your wages, Joel, we'd never manage..."

"I'll see to that," he said more gently. "You can come over to my lodgings every week and I'll give you what's needed. I aren't turning my back on you or the kids: I'm just getting clear of this house – going somewhere where I can breathe."

Gwen's face remained hard; her lip was bitten as she studied the tranquil moonlit scene beyond the window, Presently she confessed with a note of desperation: "I shan't stop here long if you go, Joel. I'll go off into service, and soon get somebody..." Her eyes clouded, brooding on some memory that still rankled in her. It was as if she recalled a recent emotional encounter in which she had been repulsed.

Joel cast a grim warning look upon his parents.

"Maybe they'll treat you better after I'm gone," he said. "I know they nag you partly to aggravate me – because they know I don't like it. They just wanted to see how much I'd stick, and now they've found out. But you shan't suffer by it, I'll see to that."

He strode forward again, very tense, pushed between his parents and Arthur, and began climbing the stairs. The family watched him ascend, heard him enter the back bedroom, then stared at each other, dazed and shocked by the sudden upheaval. Ruth fumbled for Gwen's hand, pressed close to her and started sobbing. They listened to Joel hunting about this bedroom, striking a match, opening a trunk: all his movements deliberate, purposeful. It was evident that this was no bluff: he was preparing to leave them.

Impatiently they waited for him to reappear with the bundle of clothes he had collected. But the minutes passed, the clock on the dresser struck the half-hour after nine, and still he did not return. A strange silence fell upon the whole cottage. Joel remained where they had last heard him, by the trunk near the small casement that over-looked the slope of the downs towards Roche. Probably he was standing at the window, and Gwen began to wonder whether he was reconsidering this impulsive action and might, once again, abandon his plan at the last moment.

The cause of his delay was at length revealed. The group in the kitchen were startled to hear the approach of someone whom Joel had been watching with lonely and bitter absorption; first the sound of quick, light, footsteps in the lane, then the click of the garden gate. A black Pomeranian dog appeared, sniffing about the porch, and behind the animal the slim moonlit figure of a girl cast a shadow towards the doorway.

Before the rest of the company had roused themselves to a normal mood of welcome, Gwen hurried past the spilled soup and the pail, with a cry of relief and amazement:

"Marvran!"

CHAPTER TWO

WHILE Joel brooded in the clay-pit, Marvran Creba had been alone in the grey, solitary villa on the outskirts of Roche village. Her brooding was hardly more cheerful than his, but the cosily furnished parlour, growing vague and shadowy as twilight deepened, was a more fitting background to her thoughts than the harsh, blasted scene amid which Joel reviewed his frustration. Her emotion was simple enough, but the memories associated with it were softly exotic: memories of Falmouth hotels, sub-tropical gardens and the amusements of a brisk seaport. The subdued dance music drifting from the radio on the sideboard fell about her like a remote echo of that palpitating world. She was aware of it only defensively, as something that must be kept at a distance, a lulling, detached sound like that of an ebb tide. She had to adjust her whole attitude to life, slowly and painfully, in the twilight, before exposing herself to the full wave of that returning thrill.

As the mantelshelf clock struck nine she rose to switch on the electric light. She stepped back then into the centre of the room, leaned for a few moments against a heavy round table, moving from this to the piano standing across a corner between the sideboard and the chenille curtain of the bow window. Mechanically, she drew the curtain and turned back past the settee. Halting under the glowing electric lamp she cast about her a dull groping glance. She looked tired, but her weariness was clearly the depression of a high-spirited, alert and adventurous nature. There was a hint of blunted vivacity still in her movements and in the rebellious twitch of her lips. She had obviously enjoyed good health, though her tall, slim figure had lost its buoyancy and the flat-cheeked face, fringed by thick, curly black hair, was pale and haggard, appearing alien in this setting unreconciled to it. She had never meant to live here again. After spending over a year at Falmouth and meeting Donald Pearce, she had dreamed of becoming the mistress of a stylish house at Falmouth or St. Mawes, the gritty moors behind her forever except when she motored up on an occasional visit to her parents. And now she was flung back again bewildered and mortified to the village twilight and solitude.

Her memory fumbled among the nightmare hours that had preceded her parents' arrival at their friends, the Lukes' home near Gyllyngvase beach, five weeks ago. She recalled her strained gaiety, as on the previous evening, boarding the St. Mawes ferry with Pearce, she told him the Crebas would expect him to call and be introduced, ending their doubts about his intentions. The nonchalant derision of his response had brought the sick dismay of realisation, and kept her sleepless until the dawn broke over Pendennis Point; she saw again the abandoned castle rising from the mist as part of her crumbled world. There had been her abject confession to her parents when, early in the afternoon, they arrived, meaning to take her home for a week's holiday. The embarrassed explanations of Aunt Ada, the malicious amusement of cousin Joan; Eli's flustered outburst of resentment. Her swift, hysterical decision to throw up her work at the nearby hotel and leave Falmouth; the hasty packing and the long, final journey to Roche.

The finality of the stroke was fully accepted now, though for days her body had been unable to submit, to feel the shamefulness, the prospect of stale barren evenings in which no man would kiss her. Pride had guarded her from the stark emotional reaction, but the knowledge crept through, nagging at her mind and nerves. She had been just another inexperienced country girl, naively misreading the attention of a sophisticated cad.

The memories passed over her and she emerged, looking now at the closed door. Her four-year-old pomeranian, Flush, was pawing at it, whining at the absence of the elder Crebas. They had attended evening service at the village chapel, where Eli was a steward and his wife, Hester, the organist, and had then gone to call upon a sick member of the choir, Mrs. Bassett, whose husband worked with Eli and Joel on the claywork dry-kiln. Marvran had been a member of the choir before going to Falmouth, but she was in no mood to resume any of her old activities. She seldom went down into the village, though she sometimes boarded a bus outside the bungalow and sought a few hours distraction in the inland towns of Bodmin or St. Austell. Here at home she helped her mother with the housework, complained about her nerves, and occasionally chattered with an unsuccessful attempt at gaiety.

She called the dog now, sharply, and as he bounded back into the room she dropped to her knees on the thick pile carpet. Her bare arm slid round him, her face nuzzled into his thick black coat. She began playing with him, rolling him over and keeping her hand just out or reach of the little snapping teeth, murmuring now and them a husky word of endearment. But abruptly she rose to her feet, crossed to the radio and irritably switched it off. The nostalgia behind the music had pounced afresh in the lapse towards tenderness as she caressed the dog. She sank into the arm-chair by the screened fireless grate, her white, slender fingers clenched, hardening herself. She frowned at Flush – who watched her in dudgeon from under the music stool – as if she were angry with him for having betrayed her to that momentary ache.

Her mind cast about for something outside the whole range of her personal orbit, and at length steadied as an unexpected flash of impulse replaced the strain. The Kruses! Several times during the past month Hester had urged her to visit them, resuming her part of the relationship that had existed between the two families since, at the age of nine, Marvran had confided to her mother that little Gwen Kruse was coming to school in rags and often without breakfast. Memories of the squalid clay-pit cottage had grown somewhat repugnant at Falmouth, contrasting with the elegance and frivolity of the hotel. But now, on a sudden veering of instinct, she felt a craving for fresh air, for a walk and another glimpse of the family whom she had not seen for nearly eighteen months. Their very lack of intelligence was an asset from the standpoint of her present mood. She shrank most from the embarrassed tones and glances of people on her own mental and social level: those who were genuinely sorry for her, or who veiled a secret satisfaction with affected sympathy. It was rather fascinating to descend from this level into the underworld in which the Kruses lived, and see what kind of irrational, sub-human reaction they felt towards her plight. Nothing they said could hurt her, for there would be no subtlety behind it, no understanding of her emotions. She would enjoy the sense of power and superiority, of having these creatures at her mercy, befriending or spurning them as she chose.

Hastily she got up and left the parlour, Flush leaping around her expectantly in the dark passage. She entered her bedroom, tidied her hair and freshened her make-up a little at the dressing-table, then fitted on a grey tweed coat and blue halo hat and moved out to the front door with more elasticity and self-confidence in her manner.

Flush raced ahead of her into the cool, shadowy garden, and as she closed the door of the darkened dwelling she cast a swift glance at the shrubbery, the well-kept lawn and the flower beds. The frail beauty of the moonlit wallflowers and chrysanthemums touched her poignantly, as if these cramped little plots had been salvaged from the colourful, exotic past. They looked incongruous here amid the drab clay-waste and the scrubby moors. But she did not linger to commune with them, but stepped briskly down the gravel path to the big white gate and followed Flush into the roadway. The dog barked shrilly for some minutes in his excitement at being in the open air, then grew quieter and nosed along the gutter, throwing a small black shadow upon the hedge.

Marvran watched him as she paused a moment, then peered back at the crossroads on the hilltop a hundred yards away. Moonlight glinted on the low roof of the school near the corner; close to it stood the church: a high, very dark tower, veiled by scabrous elms. The houses of the village were on the other side of the hill, invisible from here, and the road was deserted. There was a sense of elevation in the scene, especially when she turned east to pursue her journey. This plateau formed the backbone of Cornwall, nearly a thousand feet above sea level, and the landscape for miles around had a bleak, storm-bitten aspect. There were few trees and comparatively few villages between this ridge and the distant heights of Bodmin Moor on the skyline. The obelisk on Bodmin Beacon marked the position of the Cornish capital nine miles away, while beyond a flattish heath in the foreground lay the small clay-mining town of Bugle.

Marvran surveyed the whole countryside with distaste, her gaze centring at last upon its most arresting and stark feature: the weird schorl outcrop of Roche Rock which loomed up on a spur of downland quite near the road, so that she had to pass it as she hurried forward along the slope. An evil fascination brooded about those freakish crags as they snarled out under the moon. Despite the ruined mediaeval oratory on the massive central rock, the atmosphere of the place at nightfall was entirely pagan. The ancient Celtic gloom lapped powerfully upon the black stone, gripped and submerged the surrounding soil in a harsh drowse of barbarism that dwindled only when it reached the clay dumps. It was the cold, sadistic paganism of the North, with intimations of Druidical rites and blood sacrifices to the sun and moon. Marvran had always recoiled from it, loathing its dark pre-Christian vitality. She was a girl of solid practical sense, attracted by clarity rather than depth, and was irritated by the mystical undertones of the landscape.

It was a relief when she turned the next bend and glimpsed the huddled farmsteads and clay-dries at the foot of the hill, near which was the lane that wound up eastward past the Kruses' cottage. She was soon treading the rutted cart-track, absorbed in the fresh prompting of memories. Flush was often out of sight, nosing behind gorse bushes and scratching at rabbit-holes. Occasionally she called him, finding his company a welcome distraction. The stillness was broken only by their movements, the faint rasp of the wind and the plash of water in the micas nearby. Through the few stunted thorns on the hedge she saw the red roofs and tall smoky chimneys of drying-sheds, with clay tanks behind them, white scaly blobs amid the fields. These features reminded her of Joel, and she wondered vaguely whether he would be at home tonight. Her parents had told her that he had grown more surly during the past year, cutting himself adrift from his old mates in the football team, sometimes drinking at the public house but never relaxing to friendliness with anyone. She had received the news with indifference, though Joel had always stood a little above the other Kruses in her regard. His prowess as a footballer had made her feel proud of him, as of one whom she had encouraged. When she saw him in his shorts and jersey he no longer belonged to the sordid picture of his home life. But he had faded from her mind when she met Donald Pearce, who played golf and water polo and took part in yacht races. That vivid, adroit male world was now closed to her and she was stumbling back through a sterile land in which Joel was merely one among a number of stiff, crude figures that had no meaning for her except as curiosities.

At last she rounded the final bend of the lane where it became a hedgeless track over the sprawling base of the clay dump. She moved into the shadow of the dump and had soon come in sight of the Kruses' dwelling, which seemed to have sunk towards the pit since she paid her farewell visit there, the refuse encroaching at the back so that deep gravelly drifts were settling against the wall. She halted a moment, noting that Flush too had paused on the sand, watching her dubiously, his tail half dropped. The scene was almost unbearably repugnant after the lush beauties of Falmouth; but she forced herself on, forward to the small wooden gate. Before reaching it she saw that a lamp was burning in the back bedroom, its light faint but shining clearly through the uncurtained window. The downstairs rooms were dark. But the door was open, and she guessed from the deathly silence of the cottage that something unusual had occurred.

Flush trotted warily up to the porch, and Marvran followed him, her hands twitching nervously. She observed a movement in the dim interior of the house, and Gwen emerged very much agitated. She kissed Marvran impulsively.

"We thought you were never coming!" she greeted.

"It is a long time – I'm really ashamed," responded Marvran, somewhat embarrassed by the reckless undertones of Gwen's mood. "But it is good to see you looking so well. You have grown since I was here last!"

The two girls were now about the same height, and both stooped under the low door lintel as they entered the kitchen. When they were on the threshold Sarah crossed to the foot of the stairs and bawled sharply:

"Marvran's come, Joel – bring down the lamp!"

This request struck a note of practical normality that helped to dissolve the atmosphere of crisis. Arthur screwed about and set the overturned lamp on its base, pushing it back among the fragments of broken glass. Marvran steeled herself for unpleasant disclosures, standing beside Gwen near the pail of water. Ruth stole shyly up to her, and she bent to kiss the child, murmuring a strained, playful greeting. The group waited uneasily.

Joel was heard coming out on to the landing, moving stiffly and awkwardly, as though reluctant. He came very slowly down the stairs, carrying a small brass handlamp. He had no bundle with him, and had left his cap in the bedroom also. He still looked tense, but the tension was one of a different kind, less harsh, with a confused, almost bashful self-consciousness. He did not speak or glance towards Marvran, but stolidly set the lamp on the table, turning the wick a little higher and peering fixedly at the flame. His family regarded him with puzzled, uncertain fascination, and Marvran found it impossible to address any of them; they seemed remote, ignoring her presence.

It was Flush who drew their attention back to her. He had crept stealthily up to the clotted soup on the floor and began sniffing round it. Marvran had not immediately noticed the debris, and gave a sharp gasp, stooping quickly to pick up the dog, holding him under her arm and stroking his ears to hide her discomfiture.

"Let'n eat it, let'n eat it," cried Zachary, lurching forward with arm outstretched as if to seize the dog.

Marvran shook her head; she was rather pale. "The plate – he might swallow bits or cut his tongue on it."

Sarah leaned against the side of the dresser, her head grazing the banisters. "We had a mishap here just now," she explained in a suppressed tone. "Nothing to be surprised at: you know our ways, Marvran. Maid was jist goin' wipe it up."

"I see." Marvran's gaze slipped across to Joel; she wished to greet him, but he gave her no opening. He was still bent over the lamp, fumbling with the screw, his back touching the pram in which Pearl was sitting up, sucking her thumb and staring past him at Marvran. Joel's rugged face under the short black hair looked very masculine in its concentrated brooding power, the heavy bone of nose and jaw being prominent in the yellow light.

Zachary took a chair that had been set at the table and dragged it to the corner between the dresser and the stove. He sat down, his face twisted irritably. "How've 'ee come here this time o'night?" he demanded. "Goin' on for ten o'clock,' tis."

"Yes, I know – it's just an impulse. I felt I needed whiff of fresh air before mum and dad come in for supper. They're down with Mrs. Bassett. I shan't stay long."

"What 'ee been doing down Falmouth? Working in a hotel, wasn't 'ee?" Zachary scowled up at her over Ruth's shoulder: the child was timidly caressing Flush, who wriggled under Marvran's arm.

"Yes, on reception. Very interesting job. I saw all sorts of well off people."

"Well," commented Sarah with sour derision, "they wouldn't have looked at 'ee twice if they knowed your father do muck around in 'dry' wi' Joel. And it ha'n't done 'ee no credit to come back like this – as good as jilted, so all the neighbours is saying."

Marvran flushed, her eyes lowered as an abrupt sting of humiliation ran through her. She had expected such remarks from the Kruses but she had supposed that they would be made in a more normal atmosphere. She was oppressed by the sense that something dramatic and momentous was being concealed from her. This unnatural constraint was evident in the parents and in Gwen, but most of all in Joel. She knew that behind his sphinxish mask a struggle was going on. And the shadowy appearance of the room intensified the suggestion of mystery and hidden conflict. Moonlight still poured in through the window, vying with the glow of the little lamp.

"I wasn't jilted at all," she replied in a low tone but with a touch of asperity. "It wasn't serious – just a friendship. People always exaggerate these things."

"Your mother said it upset your health, anyway," mumbled Sarah. "You'm looking washed out – ha'n't put on any weight wi' all your fine hotel feeding. Been under the doctor, have 'ee?"

"Not exactly. My nerves are a bit jangled, that's all. Town life a little too hectic, perhaps, after being reared in small village. I thought I'd better come home for a rest."

Gwen broke in quickly, a troubled frown on her face as she turned to Marvran. "Do you mean to go back when you've picked up or stop around here?"

"I can't say how things'll shape. I've got to like town life, and don't want to get stodgy again. But probably I shan't return to Falmouth." Marvran brightened, smiling. "How are things going with you? you haven't started work yet, so mother tells me."

"No; they keep me slaving here, "Gwen answered, lapsing into sullenness.

Sarah blinked at her daughter, recovering something of he old nagging animosity towards the girl as she compared her dark passionate features with the refined pale delicacy of Marvran's.

"'Twas a pity you ever went to Falmouth, for our sake as well as you own," she grated. "Gwen felt left in the lurch and been working off her spite ever since. You'm the only decent maid she was ever thick with: they all cut her around village because she's our brat. She's getting a pretty handful to we".

Marvran squeezed Gwen's hand reassuringly, but made no comment.

Zachary took the poker from the ash-box and waved it excitedly. "Had another taste of her tantrums only last night," he said in his high-pitched, tremulous voice. "Give us the slip early in evening, she did. Me and Joel was back from pub and had our supper and still there was no sign of her. First time she been out so late; and when she come at last, after eleven o'clock 'twas, I'd have give her a taste o' something to mend her manners, only Joel was in one of his ugly moods too. We had a row over it, I can tell 'ee! Me and Sarah told her she wouldn't tread they stairs till she'd owned up where she'd been, but she wouldn't blab – not a word."

"No, we couldn't wring anything out of her," Sarah grumbled. "We don't know to this hour where she went or who she was with. Only 'tis plain from the sulks we've had to put up with to-day that she didn't get what she wanted."

Gwen bit her lip, but Marvran forestalled further heated exchanges between her and the parents. "Gwen needs a bit of freedom now she's nearly sixteen," she observed. "It might do her good to go away like I did for a while, for a change."

"She been wanting to go off in service somewhere." Sarah explained, snuffling as she wiped her nose with her apron. "Had high hopes since you come home, 't'would give her the chance, she thought, if you took to lending a hand here like you used to."

Gwen glanced at Joel, and with an agitated quickening of her breath she said, addressing Marvran "We shall need all you can do now…"

Marvran realised that the family were somehow threatened, and that the threat come from Joel… She looked at him again, seeking a clue. He had straightened, but could not move out into the room without squeezing past Sarah and Arthur. He stood rigidly in the corner behind the pram, absorbed and intent, staring around the kitchen. His gaze met Marvran's, and there was in both a sudden sense of intimacy, as though the discussion of their personal affairs had stripped them, left them naked and primitive to each other.

Marvran frowned as she replied to Gwen's appeal. "Of course I – I'll drop in now and then. And mother'll help as usual."

Sarah squinted at Joel, hearing the scraping of his shoes against the stairs. He had stirred, rousing himself, and was still looking at Marvran. His face was changed: less grim, its expression one of sadness softened by a vague yearning, as though his soul was arrested and challenged, shifting its foothold. Sarah lumbered across to Zachary and tapped his arm, slyly drawing his attention to Joel.

Marvran found the situation becoming intolerable. The menace had veered round, no longer objective but sweeping in upon her, enclosing her in its dark vibrations.

"Well, I must be going now," she remarked abruptly. "Mum and Dad will be wondering where I am. I'll pop in again one day of the week."

She hesitated, looking towards the pram where Pearl was lying back, comforted by the light, staring at her.

"Pearl's grown to a fine toddler while I've been away; haven't seen her since she was six months old."

She was confused, but fought back the emotional implications, deliberately forcing herself to the usual formalities of such a visit. She handed Flush to Gwen, stepped over to the pram and took the infant in her arms. Gwen and Ruth moved forward, regarding her stolidly as she spoke a few words of crooning baby-talk to the child. Arthur regarded her with resentment.

Presently, having kissed Pearl's cheek, Marvran laid her back in the pram. Joel was within a yard of them, pressed stiffly against the wall. He watched her, holding his breath, feeling his soul strike a fresh foothold, stand firm and expectant.

Marvran turned to him and extended her hand, smiling with a strained superficial friendliness. "You too, Joel: It's good to meet one's old schoolmates again. I hope things aren't going too badly with you these days."

Joel looked at her strangely, a flicker of a smile on his lips and gripping her hand he pressed it hard. His reply came quietly and with a crude earnestness:

"No – not so bad as you may have heard. I've chucked up any notion o' quitting the place. Don't take no notice o' tales o' that sort. I shan't be leaving here. Glad to see you… Goodnight!"

There was tense silence. Joel's family stared at him in astonishment as Marvran took Flush from Gwen and moved towards the door.

CHAPTER THREE

OLIVE Buzza was sitting with her father in the kitchen of their home, the last of a row of houses at Whitemoor flanking the roadway a mile or so south of Roche. It was early in an evening near the end of October, a lamp had just been lighted on the table, and the meagrely furnished room was cosy with the fire's warmth.

Seated on a chair at the table's side, Olive was leaning forward, comb in hand, titivating her hair before a mirror set against an earthenware flower-pot. Her hair was straight, light brown, and fringed a face very round, freckled but unhealthily pale. Her hands, plump and white, busied themselves about her head, patting the hair, and sometimes halting under her firm chin, propping it while she viewed herself in the glass. Her eyes, grey and small, roved occasionally from the mirror about the room, haunted, furtive, gloating. And yet fear marked her face, a shrinking, physical and mental, from an expected reality; fear at issue with craving and impatience.

Laying down the comb she straightened, glanced at her father. A smile twitched at her lips, expressing not quite pity, not quite contempt, certainly no affection. Her father was crippled, practically an invalid, having lost his right foot through a fall of rock in a clay-pit five years ago. The accident had come while Olive was distressed by the sudden death of her mother. Her childhood had been spent in the Pendeen district of West Cornwall, where Buzza had laboured on the small patch of clay-workings near Land's End, forty miles from the main Cornish clay area to which the family had shifted when Olive was sixteen.

Buzza was huddled now over the fire, morose and remote, hardly really present. Since he became disabled he had withdrawn morbidly into himself, losing touch with normal life, and lapsed into a soft sensuous drowse of rebellion. He was a short, flabby man with very dark, coarse skin, thick black beard and moustache, and cunning heavy black eyes. He looked as though he had Iberian blood in him. This ancient streak was common in the inhabitants of the coastal regions of West Cornwall. Olive had inherited her father's indolence and slovenliness of habit, with the restless impulses of hot Neolithic blood that seemed almost exotic on these bleak uplands. Buzza was unusually surly to-night: he had not spoken to her or observed from her behaviour that a visitor was expected.

Olive was roused from contemplation of that tragic figure by a sound, soft but noticeable: a rattle of gravel thrown lightly against the window panes. The man did not stir, but Olive rose, smiling unpleasantly, and crossed the little room to the doorway.

It was not yet dark outside; there was no wind. Everything quiet, fitly quiet. All the other houses, as she glanced along the row, loomed incurious, no one visible. She hurried past the window, around the house corner towards the back garden, where the bulk of the house screened her from the view of anyone watching from neighbouring dwellings or gardens. There was no gate there, only a field and outside the hedge, in the gutter a shadowy male form was standing.

"Charlie!" Olive, moving close to the hedge, grimaced. She leaned over the top, and the man outside, strained his neck, thrusting upward a thin pale face beneath a cap pulled low over his forehead. She returned his kiss, then fell back, waiting, her hands nervously clasped. The fellow climbed noiselessly up the hedge, and a minute later stood in front of her, very lean, very tall, a youth hardly yet out of his teens, smirking.

"You told me to come," he said in a somewhat effeminate tone. "I don't back out, Buzz."

"Good boy. Anybody seen you coming?"

"One or two in the village. Shouted out to me - they knowed where I was going. It don't matter." He looked at her feverishly. "I'm cold, Buzz. Warm me up."

"All right. Come here."

She drew back into the shadow of the house. He followed, and in the deep gloom she caught him, fiercely embraced his thin shivering body. There were no words for awhile; their desire groped, inarticulate. Olive goaded him with smiles, then slowly and deliberately set her lips to his. He was numbed, his flesh hard and cold from exposure to the wind, and some moments passed before the contact yielded pleasure. But he soon roused to her, and they gave heat for heat in a brief amatory duel until she mastered him. She let him go, leaned back against the wall, and frowned.

The youth peered into her face, limp and shaken by her mature, practised instinct, but his grin showed a male mockery still at work under his submission.

"You aren't looking too happy, Buzz," he remarked, taunting her.

Her response came with a bitterness that startled him:

"D'you think I'm ever happy? My God!"

"Anything gone wrong indoors?" he asked uncomfortably.

"No. He's no worse. Gets on my nerves – but he always did. I'm sick of it all, that's the truth". "

"How long've you been on this business?"

"Five years – ever since the old man got crippled. I don't feel safe: look at the future!"

"He might peg out, and you'd be left in a fix: that what you mean?"

Olive stared without answering for several minutes around the valley. The roadway dipped from this house to a narrow belt of moorland, a fringe of Goss Moor which curled about the rocky, high sprawling shoulder of Hensbarrow on which Roche and Trezaise were set. On the slope opposite stood Roche church, very black and grim, like a fortress amid grieving trees, and near it could be dimly seen the ragged skull-like bulge of Roche Rock. The whole landscape was unspeakably desolate, the horizons wild and fantastic with headlong descents. Westward the belt of moorland broadened, a flat drab expanse, treeless, with here and there a small tarn, and narrow hedgeless roads crossing it to the lowland hamlets. Along one of the roads from Enniscaven, the youth, Charlie Crago, had come to her now. And last week. And last month. He, one among many who crossed the moor, or crept down the hill from Nanpean, to share her bed as an hour's purchase... Olive shrugged, and turning back to Charlie she exclaimed with vehemence: "I wish to God somebody'd marry me."

He whistled, his eyes bright and jeering as they met hers. "Want me to propose?"

"Hardly, darling. It'd take someone tougher than you to give all I'd want of a man."

Her derisive laugh vexed him and he glanced aside, his brows knit angrily. He knew that she despised him, and sometimes he hated her for it. There was a sulky insolence in his tone when he next spoke.

"Well, I hear 'tis chiefly me and Cal Mannell who've had the favours this year. Why not try your luck there? Cal's nearly forty, I know, but still a bachelor."

Olive recoiled slightly, as though the reminder were unpleasant to her.

"Nothing doing in that direction," she said with dry malice. "Cal soon tired o' the sort of thrills he got from me. He's never happy unless he's breaking up marriages, or romances. The latest I've heard of him, he's trying to wreck Euan Kella's affair with that Skiddy girl – Lela down there at Nanpean."

"Why not get your own back by making a dive at Euan?"

"Not my line, Charlie. Grammar School chap, so I gather – only came back to claywork because his dad was killed: would have been at college or university by now otherwise. Fancy me marrying a bookworm!"

"Euan isn't much of a bookworm these days, I believe. One of his mates there at Rostowrack lives next door to us, and says he's a queer mixture – as rough as the rest of 'em in some of his moods."

Olive shook her head.

"He's engaged to Lela, and he doesn't interest me anyway. I'm serious this time. I want somebody my own sort – down to earth and not too much brains."

She was obviously sincere, and Charlie sobered, lounging beside her against the house wall. He cast about for some further suggestion, and presently nudged her.

"If you want a real tough guy," he said speaking now with genuine helpfulness, "I can put you on to one – and I reckon he'd be as keen as you to get settled."

Olive gave him a peculiar, questing look. "Oh? One of your chums?"

"Not exactly. Only see him sometimes at the claywork when our lorries have a job there. He's rough all through – no brains: used to be a footballer, but never had any maids after him".

"That's interesting. He lives around here?"

"Not far off. Chap called Kruse – belong to that family living on the moor, other side o' Roche Rock. You know who I mean don't you?"

"I've heard of 'em"

"Ever tried to pull in Joel?"

"Haven't given him a thought. I've had enough to amuse myself with around this way, only none of 'em be willing to splice it." She swept an arm towards the villages out of sight beyond the southern ridges and the flat moorland to the west. "And he keeps off women, you say?"

"Sure. Glum beggar – and lately it's got him down like the gripes. Something's bitten him. Wants a safety valve, see? I was there to the 'dry' last week – had a rush order three days following; and I noticed a difference in him. In his twenties, and I reckon he's getting fed up with his own company. But no decent piece o' skirt'd look at him, and he's waiting for some beauty to start things moving. 'Tis just your chance, Buzz."

Olive crossed to the hedge and stood looking along the road which, after scoring the belt of moor-land, slanted in a curve up the hill towards Roche. Charlie watched her closely, eyes narrowed, but her face told him nothing. Her breasts swelled quickly under the frock she wore, her hands were set lightly on her hips. Presently she inquired without turning round:

"When you say he's rough – d'you mean he's the sort who'd knock his wife about?"

"Depends how she behaved, I s'pose." was Charlie's sly rejoinder. "He'd be jealous – and woe betide the woman who tried to fool him! I shan't be running no more risks, anyhow, if you git Joel for keeps, so you'd better let me know in time if you mean to try your luck; I'll leave him a free field."

Olive shrugged. "I can't decide till I've seen him – you'll probably hear if it's love at first sight," she answered, and swung round with a glance that showed the undeflected immediate urge. "You're here now, anyway. Had enough?"

"Don't feel so. Hardly snug outdoors."

"H'm. Well, come along in".

At the rear of a drying-shed, inside one of the tanks of settled clay, Eli Creba and George Bassett were busily loading the wooden truck which stood between them on the line, surrounded by smooth drifts of the white slurry. The water had been drained off, the men shovelling the clay in damp, spongy clots, their shirt sleeves rolled above their elbows, caps pulled low over their eyes. It was now about eleven o'clock in the morning, and the day's shift was nearing its close. Owing to the nature of the work and the hot atmosphere of the drying-sheds, these labourers usually ceased toil at noon.

A road wound in front of the 'dry'; behind it a flat heath sprawled westward to ploughed fields ridged by a railway line crossing Goss Moor. The building was isolated, on the base of one of the many valleys which slope from Hensbarrow Downs, south of Bugle. No other sign of a claywork was immediately visible, the liquid clay being pumped to this spot through underground pipes from the main works half a mile away.

From inside the shed came a low hissing sound where clay was bubbling in the kiln, heated by a fire burning in the furnace at the far end of the building, the heat being drawn under the kiln by means of flues running the whole length of the shed. At intervals came also a dull muffled sound: footsteps on thickly- strewn clay-lumps. The footsteps of Joel Kruse, who was preparing for the return of the filled waggon.

There had been a long period of silence between the two, which Eli broke abruptly. He was a thin, short-legged, lively man with a sharp clean-shaven face that, as he began speaking, was half-hidden behind a spotted red handkerchief

"Trade's on the upgrade again, so it seem," he observed. "Last summer it looked as if we was heading back to the slump days when clay was lyin' in the pits with weed growing over it. But I believe the worst is over. If Munich have really settled things we may have another boom: it seemed likely a year ago."

Bassett's red beefy face lowered towards the truck as he drove his shovel under the slurry. A truculent, humourless fellow, he lived chiefly in the past, though still in his fifties.

"Nothing'll ever git back to what is used to be." He said, dolefully aggressive.

"Output was rising steady, till Hitler grabbed Austria."

"And who was better off for it? Only the inventors what turned out gadgets to throw men out o' work. When the markets is a bit brighter the companies put on extra machinery what do keep half the unemployed still out o' jobs." He lifted his shovel, glaring over the waggon at Eli. "What difference do it make to the workers? Wages stay low as ever, and if the pit men hadn't kicked up a rumpus they'd be still slaving on 'eleven pence a hour."

Eli, resuming work, nodded. "Lucky that didn't mean a strike – looked ugly at one time."

"Bosses wanted to save face, that's what 'twas. They'd had their lesson. We've only seen one big strike on the clayworks, back in 1913 – lasted six weeks, and bosses been quiet ever since."

Eli straightened. "I was in that strike," he said reminiscently. "I can mind the gangs o' men marchin' along here, goin' from one claywork to another. We wanted higher wages, and though the strike was broke by a parcel o' Welsh police hired down for the job, we did get our rise afterwards. Since then we ha'n't had much to complain of, and say what you like, you wouldn't go back to they old times that you d'talk so much about, back before the War."

"I would," declared Bassett, spitting over his shoulder. "Everything was better in they days – safer, and a man could tell what was going to happen next. And there was more spice to it : machinery have knocked the kick out of everything. Clay used to be dried outdoors in the sun, and then shovelled in barrels for the waggons to carry away. And women helped wi' the drying."

Eli glanced across the fields at a large flock of birds passing just then above Bugle, very high in the blue heavens, dark and swift, heading eastward towards Stenalees.

"I know," he grunted, "and that's the sort o' thing you wouldn't like to see come back,"

"Oh yes I would. My mother used to work in the 'air dry' from the time she was twelve year old. Long hours and only a few shillin' a week wages. No chance to think o' dollin herself up, or gaddin' around. And come evenings, after she got married, she'd be doin' her housework and cookin', unless she done it early in the mornin' afore she went to work. And there was the children to tend to besides – ten of 'em altogether. Ah!" Bassett screwed his eyes almost shut, as if visualising those past scenes. "Lively days they was – everybody glad they was livin'. Now they'm polished they'm more easy broke, and even then they"ll go around flaunting the pieces.

Eli did not contradict the statement. He had proof of its truth in the worry that gnawed at him: the plight of Marvran. He continued stolidly his shovelling, being careful to avoid meeting Bassett's eyes.

"That stuck up spirit," Bassett resumed, bobbing rapidly up and down as he worked, "is in all the maids nowadays, whatever they do. Whether 'tis earnin' their living' or fallin' in love. Or anything else, 'tis all done to be noticed. Education have taken the place of' work, and so people got swelled heads instead o' happiness."

Eli nodded, still thinking of Marvran, and his face hardened. He glanced along the flat heath stretching west, with only a few clumps of golden gorse vivifying its monotonous brown surface. A train was passing under the bridge at Bugle, and the engine whistled. Eli remained silent.

Bassett knocked his loaded shovel accidentally against the waggon, splashing clay on to his boot. "Here's these maids," he said, "takin' joy-rides in aeroplanes, hopin' Hitler'll take it to mean we're a tough country. People talk o' the guts they're showin'. 'Tis all jist swank. Tryin' to look big and get their mug in the papers. In the old days women had guts enough to slave and sweat year after year, and not expect no thanks for it. And they was happy."

"I dearsay, " Eli commented, dry and reticent as before.

Bassett's thick eyebrows lowered, and grasping the shovel he struck the waggon with it. "If married couples didn't agree back then," he continued in a louder, more provocative tone, "they'd fight it out and be all the more willin' to fill another pram afterwards – no squealin' and running away at the first pin-prick like they do now. Call it life in the raw if you like, but there was heart in it, Creba, real guts." He spat into his hands, rubbed them together for a few moments and resumed work with a personal thrust which he hoped would draw Eli into the argument.

"Reckon that's the trouble wi' your maid – wanted to pick up wi' some dandy down Falmouth so that she could make us look small. Some millionaire at the hotel – or a Pearce anyway. And so she come a cropper. Better for 'ee all if she'd bided quiet where she was reared…"

Eli threw aside his shovel and turned, gripping the truck; his mouth twitched, there was a rasp of anger in his tone. "That'll do, George. Waggon's full, isn't it?"

The pair got behind the waggon, near the back wall of the tank, Eli looking somewhat frail in contrast with this mate, who, touching six feet in height, was heavily built. Their combined efforts set the truck in motion along the iron rails that reached from the tank to the edge of the kiln inside the shed. It slid noisily through the opening, a low doorway, into the stuffy gloom of the interior.

The 'dry' was some fifty yards in length, and low-roofed; its outer side was the storage linhay, closed by wooden shutters swung between stone pillars and hinged, not at the sides like a door, but to the timber beams supporting the roof. Most of these shutters were now hanging down, and as the building had no windows the kiln, some twelve feet above the storage area in which dried clay-cubes were stacked, was deeply shadowed. Through the fetid steam the slurry on the kiln-pan glinted, bubbling whitely up like a leprous skin. On each side of the kiln was a footwalk; on the rims of this an iron rail ran the whole length of the shed, and on the track formed by the two rails, straddling the kiln, was a platform, which had been wheeled close to the opening through which the filled trolley entered. Joel was standing near it, a blurred brooding shape, one hand on a bar attached to the platform, the other set lightly on his hip. The truck was wheeled in upon the platform in the manner of a car boarding a ferry, and once it was safely mounted Joel leapt up beside the waggon, and the two men began pushing the platform, Bassett on one side of the kiln, Eli on the other. The pair were bent forward, though no great exertion was necessary, and slowly, with a low rumbling sound, the platform, bearing Joel and the loaded truck, rolled inward through the dense vapour until it reached the spot where the previous load had been tipped. On their releasing the platform Joel heaved up the body of the waggon, and soon its contents were spread about a foot in depth over the brick floor of the kiln.

"Kiln's nearly full; 'nother load'll do un," commented Eli.

Bassett was not to be side tracked from his subject. "What do you think, Joel? Don't have much to do wi' maids, do 'ee?"

Joel stared at Bassett in a stolid manner, as if he scarcely comprehended. He leaned slightly against the truck, and with lips tightly set, remained silent.

"I was tellin' Creba here what the trouble is with his maid," Bassett went on, his harsh voice ringin hollowly among the rafters. "Nothin' exceptional about her: all maids is the same nowadays, cryin' for some moon or other to brag about. If this maid had been able to come to claywork instead o' goin' to Falmouth..."

"Don't talk such rot, George!"

Eli's brusque advice roused Bassett, and waving a hand above his head he shouted: "I'm tellin' of 'ee the truth! She been down wi' the toffs for twelve months, and what've it done for her? Here she is, gettin' on for twenty, and nothin' to put her feet on. Better she'd gone to work sensible. If she'd been 'lowed to come here in the 'dry' like my mother used to – well, I don't reckon Joel would has gived up his footballing. And if she'd just been proud o' that, there'd ha' been something to show for it – eh, Joel?"

The jest brought to Joel's face a dark red, angry flush. Standing on the platform he glared into the kiln, hands clenched on the waggon's rim. Eli noted the reaction, and feeling uneasy he called across to his mate:

"Come on, Bassett, that's enough o' this! You'd gab all day long if we give 'ee the chance. There's work to be done. Push her back for next load. Off you git, Joel!"

Joel stepped on to the sidewalk and stood trembling slightly, while the dull roar of the retreating platform echoed amid the rafters scarfed densely with mist. He watched the men disappear through the opening, pushing the waggon again to the tank outside, then moved down the narrow track to the other end of the shed, and descended a ladder to the furnace. This was situated in an enclosure well stacked with coal; an open doorway faced the ladder. Between the furnace bars the fire glowed fiercely. The heat was terrific, and sweat streamed over Joel's cheeks amid the black and white markings of coal and clay. He opened the heavy iron door and shovelled more fuel into the furnace; and stoking the fire he let his thoughts, confused by Bassett's talk, drift hungrily to Marvran.

It had not been a mere coincidence that Joel dropped out of the football team just after Marvran went to Falmouth. But the sense of loss had been part of a general mood of deprivation. Although he was then twenty years old, he found no particular emotional focus in Marvran. During their schooldays she had been one of several girls for whom he felt a vague, inarticulate yearning; her vivacity attracted and challenged him. But there had been no mature development. He had obtained a job as 'kettle boy' on Hendra claywork directly he left school, and had been later employed at Rostowrack clay pit, not far away. He had seldom been at home when Marvran visited the Kruses. His growing sense of inferiority and shame had caused him to avoid such refined, decent girls. Even as a footballer he had concentrated on the game for its own sake, working with the team automatically, feeling no companionship. Marvran had sometimes watched his deadly play as centre-forward at Roche, Bugle and Stenalees, but he had remained as indifferent to her, as to the other spectators. Yet when she left the village he was aware that something vital had gone from his life. The subsequent news of her affair with Pearce had troubled and vexed him. And now, with her return, his indifference had broken up. The sight of her had touched his whole personality with vibrations utterly new to him. Suddenly in the midst of his reckless resolve to leave home, there had come with her mature bruised beauty a feverish urge, both sensuous and spiritual; the conviction that he must stay near her. And now he waited, not yet fully aroused, but conscious of the passion and gratitude as his numbed nature tingled towards recognition and acceptance.

Joel now stirred and moved back to the open doorway. He leaned against the jamb and surveyed the outer world with casual interest. The strip of road, the field hedge, the bare heath slope beyond: nothing impressive. A cart had just passed the clay-dry; he heard the crack of the driver's whip and the sudden quickening of the horse's hoof-beats beyond the near corner. The sky was filmy blue, with hardly a cloud; very cold, taut, and crisp. There had been hoar-frost in the morning when he arrived here, the chill vapour shuffling along the valley like a procession of ghosts, harried soon by flashing spears of light as the sun emerged above Hensbarrow. Clear sunlight still flooded the scene, mellowing all, and giving to decay a lustre and unique beauty. From the chimney stack at the other end of the shed dense smoke poured above the rusted corrugated iron of the roof. Joel watched it slide out over field and down-land, fouling the pure sky.

Back by the tank Eli and Bassett were talking afresh; hearing his own name spoken Joel listened, with eyes lifted to the top of the ladder, where the hot vapour coiled and writhed above the kiln.

Bassett's voice broke, thick and bawling: "Seen her here yesterday, walkin' to and from outside the 'dry'; she'd go up so far's the corner, then turn and come back. 'Tis Joel she's after, I reckon."

"Had'n't been up around this way much lately, have she?"

"Not since the fellows was here mending the road back in the spring. She was around here then nearly every day."

"I remember. That maid don't seem to pull up at all. But she was put in a nasty fix when her father was crippled."

"Lucky he is crippled," came Bassett's response with a guffaw. "He'd be creeping around else and spying through the keyhole – seein' what goes on there to his place in the evenings. Men coming in several nights a week, so I hear."

"I wonder old Buzza have let it go that pitch – though I don't s'pose he could do much to stop it."

"He don't seem to mind her carrying on – was always a bit loose hisself before this wife died. The money it bring in must make things a lot easier for'n too."

"'Twon't be so bad if Olive don't get catched sooner or later and find herself with a increase. She must be twenty-three or four now, and a maid can't go on like that for ever."

"Well, she ha'n't put on the brake yet, and it look to me that she got her eye on Joel: been outside here twice this week already. So the increase may come from that direction..."

Joel ascended the ladder as he heard them begin pushing the waggon back into the shed. His lips were compressed, and his eyes scowled. Olive Buzza! He'd heard of her: just the sort of woman they'd expect him to mix with. While Marvran – they'd never dream that he could think seriously of her.

CHAPTER FOUR

EUAN Kella hurried out from Rostowrack claywork to the roadway, his mind struggling back to contact with the earth that was in a mood similar to his own: stripped, bruised and defensive. The November sunshafts fluttered aimlessly, picking out the red haws of the thorn trees by the roadside, and the few shrivelled blackberries, dry as cinders, clinging to bramble bushes between blotched leaves that twirled like tiny shields as the wind smote them. Rooks flapped about the tree-tops, while from the gorse-matted refuse heaps the sturdy notes of robins fell dull and remote on Euan's ear. He strode on in grim detachment, a slender but firmly-built young workman, over the railway bridge at Goonamarris Slip, down the hill past Goonvean clay-dump and across the field to the isolated cottage in which he had been born.

He removed his muddy boots on the doorstep and put on the shoes set ready for him. When he entered the kitchen his mother, Rachel, was preparing tea. She was a short, dark, vigorous woman with a general air of bitterness and resentment that, during recent weeks, had sharpened with fresh fears about his impending marriage to Lela Skiddy. Being of an ardent, bustling nature, she felt that marriage alone could rid him of those dreamy impractical moods that so often swayed his mind and made their home life an unhappy clash of temperaments. She turned, and as he lingered at the doorway glanced at him. "Euan!" "What's up? Your face! You've been hurt?"

His response was a jerky nod; he remained tensely on the threshold. Presently he said: "Bit of a scratch. Nothing to worry about."

"Had a mishap at the works?"

"Not an accident."

"What then?"

Euan's smile was both whimsical and defiant. "We've had a fore-taste o' the war jitters at Rostowrack lodge, that's all."

"What d' you mean?"

"Me and Cal Mannell had a little argument"

"Came to blows?"

"'Fraid so."

Rachel dropped back into a chair by the dresser, obviously shaken. "How's this, then?"

Euan stepped forward and leaned against the table. He was calm, and stared into the fire as he replied moodily: "We quarrelled – these things will happen. Wasn't much of a scrap, a dozen blows or so. Cap'n came down as we were going to settle it in earnest. He cautioned us when the men blabbed; but I shan't be sacked, so you needn't lose any sleep over it."

Rachel was watching him closely, as she probed him further: "And the squabble – what was that about?"

He did not answer; and presently, at the tea-table, few words were exchanged. Rachel was tortured by renewing fears, he by doubts of his immediate duty. He must see Lela and get this matter cleared up one way or the other, know whether Mannell's story was true or not; but it might be advisable to wait...

The evening drew on, the flare of sunset faded, first from the valleys, then from the moors, and finally from the peaks of the clay-dumps where its last red waves set the electric wires gleaming like spider's webs against the sky and lay along the wooden tip-frames so that the iron fastenings breaking their dull grained surface were plainly visible from below.

The dusk thickened slightly after sunset but did not close in, for the full moon had already risen. The northern stars were exception-ally clear, Capella swinging up over Curyan, the Great Bear over St. Dennis, Vega over the north-western plateau around Meledor.

Across Rostrowrack and along the road that Euan had traversed that afternoon came Gwen Kruse. She had alighted from the bus at St. Dennis and hurried along the lonely, unfamiliar by-way. A woollen coat – a cast-off of Marvran's – gave solidity to her figure, while the spilth of moonlight tended to etherealize it. Odours of decay mingled about her with the thinned autumnal scent of gorse. The hedgeside trees were spilling leaves with every rasp of wind, casting in the gutters a gloom of funereal melancholy; but Gwen was to herself a sufficient reserve of happier moods. She tripped to the stile at the foot of Goonvean hill and crossed almost furtively the path to the Kellas' home. The house loomed gigantic, its shadow lying westward on the field and the few bushes shivering above the brook. Gwen stole to the gate, then reached the back door, braced herself and knocked.

Indoors, the lamp was now lighted in the kitchen, Euan sitting on the bench mechanically watching Rachel darn his socks. The tap at the door startled both of them; their eyes met in a swift glance of foreboding.

Euan rose, steeling himself, moved to the outer door and opened it. He gasped. It was Lela he had expected to see – Lela, come to reproach or reassure him about that business at Rostowrack. Instead he was confronted by someone whom at first sight he took to be a stranger, then recognized with obvious surprise. Gwen, too seemed confused and defensive as she inquired: "Please – where does Mr. Veale live?"

Euan replied stolidly: "Veale? His place is the farm, up the other end of the woods."

"I'm sorry," she murmured with a quick evasive glance around the garden. "I asked and was told he lived near the sand-burrow in a house standing by itself. I thought this must be it. I couldn't see any other."

Euan was staring at her, his heart swooping as realisation deepened in him. The present scene fused with memories: Rostowrack clay-work was again vivid in his mind, but no longer as the background of his sordid squabble with Mannell. He saw the rambling dunes on the escarpment above St. Dennis, Gwen strolling towards him along the cinder-track by the pit edge, bare-headed and bare-limbed, like a strayed dryad in the golden drowse of summer sunset...and the conversation they had had.

Restraint was forced upon him by Rachel's appearance in the back kitchen. Her face was grim, her hands clawed at her pinafore. "Who's that?" she demanded.

"Girl wanting to know the way to Barrakellis," Euan replied, stepping back a pace to give Rachel a clearer view of her.

Rachel's gaze travelled piercingly over Gwen's shabby clothes and her dark clear-cut features under the green beret, then centred on Euan. "Who is she? D'you know her?"

"Not exactly. Saw her once on St. Dennis downs in the summer. Called Kruse – her brother used to work at Rostowrack."

Gwen nodded. She was accustomed to rebuffs, and Rachel's severe attitude had no perceptible effect upon her. She cast a glance around at the garden, and said casually: "I'm going to try to get in service wi' Mr. Veale."

Amid the whirl of his own reactions Euan saw his mother's lips snap shut in a thin white line. She stepped forward until she was beside him, arms akimbo. "I dunno what put that in your head," she commented brusquely. "Veale isn't likely to want any maids muddling around up there."

The challenge of the words probed through to a latent perversity in Euan. Before he could check the impulse he had taken his overcoat from a nail behind the door and turned to Gwen, smiling tensely. "I'll go up part way and show you."

The look of amazement on Rachel's face contrasted strongly with the obvious relief that lit up the girl's.

"I'd be glad," she said in an undertone. "I've never been down this way before, and might lose myself."

Euan turned up the collar of his coat; his arm touched Rachel and she felt it trembling. "I'm not going up specially with her," he explained without looking at his mother. "I've got more serious business to attend to this evening."

Rachel's countenance was strained and pinched in the faint light. "You're going out Nanpean to see Lela, are you? Then... 'twas something about her that set you and Mannell fighting?"

"Perhaps," he said between his teeth, and stepped outside close to Gwen.

"We'd better hurry along...though Veale isn't often away from home in the evenings."

"I ought to have come earlier, I s'pose," Gwen admitted; "but I've been kept busy all afternoon helping mother."

He nodded. Rachel gave them a bewildered, hostile glance as they moved down the path into the field, then slammed the door.

The air outside was chill, and clouds drifting darkly under the moon. Moths were abroad, visible in brief, slipping patches of moonlight. Above the gloomy ravine of Tregargus an owl hooted.

Euan led the way until on the streamlet's bank they paused. Clayey water plunged among the boulders here, scurrying down past the house, bearing dead twigs and leaves from the coppice which arched its black, shaggy folds to the north-east. Gwen eyed with some hesitation the long narrow plank that spanned the water.

"It's safe enough," said Euan. "Take my hand if you're afraid you'd fall in."

He suspected that she had been awaiting such an offer; and as he gripped her hand she gave his fingers a squeeze, keeping close to him on the plank, her face bent towards him with something of the attraction he had seen upon it at Rostowrack.

Soon they were climbing up a rocky slope overhung by gorse, emerging on to open downland. The path here was rutted, narrow, edged by a linked succession of pulley-rods that creaked over tarred wheels, turned by the big water-wheel down by the wood. Gwen often halted, gazing curiously at these strange details, but Euan sensed a deeper motive for her lingering; and, indeed, was himself in no haste to part with the girl's company. He walked just ahead of her watching her furtively over his shoulder. She unbuttoned her coat, and he noted that her figure had ripened considerably since August. Her face, seen now by moonlight, had a stark beauty, revealing a nature that could never be content with the flippancies of adolescence, but seemed moulded for dark, tragic intensity. The solemnity of the earth lay upon her, breathing through full passionate lips, awake in those large, restless grey eyes.

Euan spoke first. "So you're going to try and get in service up here at Barrakellis?"

She nodded eagerly. "Yes. We heard Mr. Veale'd lost his wife a month or two ago, and was thinking of having somebody as he can't manage well on his own."

"It's true, I think," said Euan. "We get our milk from the farm… in fact, he asked mother if she'd be willing to come up there as housekeeper - thought I'd be married soon and leave her free."

"Is that true too?"

"Not exactly. He has a neighbour from Goonamarris to clean up every few days, but I should think you'd stand a good chance o' getting the job.

"I hope so. What sort o' fellow is Mr. Veale?"

"Quiet and decent: he'd treat you all right. Getting on in his sixties now. Fairly easy-going." Euan paused, then added with some reluctance: "That bloke Mannell I squabbled with this afternoon has been at the farm a lot since Mrs. Veale died. I don't think Digory like it, but he doesn't seem to have guts enough to tell people when they aren't wanted."

"Why – what's wrong with Mannell?" asked Gwen. "Apart from the fact that you're jealous of him I mean, of course. He can't be very young if he's thick with Veale."

Euan frowned down at the coppice, shaking his head. He never wore a hat, and his brown hair, rather long, fluttered untidily.

"Cal's middle-aged," he said in a curt, suppressed tone. "Illegitimate son of a village woman up here at Foxhole. She cleared out when he started working. She went to live in Plymouth – had another baby up there, then shifted over to the Scilly Isles, where she is still, I believe, with her daughter. I've never seen either of them. I don't think Cal's ever met his sister – and his mother's only paid one or two visits here, so far as I know".

There was a brief silence until the first kissing-gate of the path was reached. Gwen waited behind when Euan passed through, and as he turned to confront her on the other side she studied his face curiously. It was now bruised and puffed about the mouth and left eye, but even in its normal state it was a strange face, its sensitiveness and intellectuality somehow warped by a latent primitivism. The high forehead and deep brooding eyes of the thinker were contrasted with the willful, sensuous lips and the short, squat nose. He looked something of an oddity, and was commonly regarded as such. There was no studied revolt in his behaviour, but a kind of whimsical perversity was evident in many of his actions. Though firm enough in his spiritual anchorage, he was fundamentally unbalanced, alternately brilliant and dull, and he seemed to exploit moods to cause the utmost embarrassment to everyone. He would deliberately lapse into a clouded, semi-stupefied condition among educated people who expected him to show a keen intelligence – for he had won a scholarship to the Grammar School and would reveal depth and originality of thought in talking with his illiterate workmates. He was consequently regarded as a fool by those who shared his mental tastes, and as a snob by those who shared his emotional vitality. But the streak of violence was always very near the surface: not even Cal Mannell had been much surprised when his taunts this afternoon roused Euan to a fury of retaliation.

Gwen had sensed his strange individuality during their encounter at Rostowrack three months ago, and felt again now, more deeply, the qualities that set him apart form normal social life. She recognized him as someone congenial to her, a misfit.

She closed the gate and came out into the mottled twilight cast here by an overhanging bank.

"Did you lick Mannell just now?" she inquired.

"I don't know – we didn't finish!"

"Well, if he comes to the farm you may soon feel like fighting him again – over me instead o' Lela next time!" Gwen laughed teasingly; but as Euan remained tense she sobered, resuming with abrupt detachment: "Joel and Dad had a fight once, back when Joel was in his teens. It didn't last long: Joel knocked him flat on the garden before they'd had their coats off many minutes. That's all over now, though – years ago. I believe things have turned the corner for Joel."

"He hasn't cleared out yet, as you said he was threatening to?"

"No; I don't think he will – till he gets married."

"So there's a girl come into it now?" Euan smiled. "I said that was what he needed – d'you remember?"

Gwen nodded, standing close to him in the shadow. "It's Marvran Creba," she said quietly.

"Oh?" He looked surprised. "Lela told me she'd come back from Falmouth."

"Yes. That's why I'm free to get a job. She's helping a bit at our place again – minding the baby and tidying things up sometimes."

"And finding 'tis a convenient way to get to know Joel?"

"There's nothing like that, yet, and you can never tell – may not come to anything serious. But the first time she called last August – the day after I met you at Rostowrack – we was all upset: I'd been working off the way I felt after seeing you. She cooled us down, and both she Joel have been different ever since."

"Were they friendly before she went to Falmouth?" Euan asked as they moved forward.

"Not since their schooldays. It won't be easy going: she got messed up at Falmouth, though she'll live it down once the towny streak's pulled out of her. She'll see that simple fellows like Joel can be trusted. These town blighters can't – nor the girls either."

Euan shot her a queer glance, furtive and ironical.

"Lela's a village girl, I'm afraid," he said dryly.

"But she must have picked up towny ways: I know you were worried about her when I found you there on the works, mooning around after all your mates had gone. I went home pretty sure you'd had a tiff with your girl friend. She's got the modern streak worse than Marvran, I should think."

He sensed the jealousy in her tone, and was troubled by it. "I'm not fully acquainted with Miss Creba's private life – and perhaps not even with Miss Skiddy's." He spoke bitterly, and the twist of his lips was defiant and rebellious.

"Marvran's quite decent," Gwen put in after a moments hesitation; she was uncertain how to deal with him in this mood.

He remained silent, smouldering and casting about for relief. His glance flickered across to the massive wedge of Goonvean sand tip which filled the cleft of the valley northward and sprawled several hundred yards up the slope north-east. The row of tip-lights flared steadily along its summit, the white refuse spilled out as a skip appeared between the beams of the tip. His eyes narrowed with a sort of yearning, a strange fixedness of recognition and communion. They had passed over the woodland with indifference, but were held by the claywork fantasy. He knew the idiom of his countryside, the bleak lyricism of the flowing sand. There was poignant beauty now in the scene as the gravel poured out over the ridge, groping blindly down among the folds and ruts of the dune's face, settling into the furrows like grain, yet hostile to the mood of fertility. It fascinated Euan, the sight of the outcast soil flung nakedly out under the arc-lights, moving softly and gently with its quiet menace to the rhythms of the breeding earth. Gwen could not wholly interpret the look of absorption on his face, but she felt that it was congenial to her. She too had seen the unscarred country only in the distance and with distaste. She was earthy, but a natural background was inadequate and false to her.

She was earthy only within the bounds of her fate, and here with Euan she seemed already beyond it, outcast with him in the subtler illumination of the clay-tip.

As Euan roused afresh to an awareness of her, he also felt that he was being pushed over a frontier. Something in this girl had affected him powerfully. He had vaguely sensed her influence throughout the autumn. He saw so few girls that his encounter with Gwen at Rostowrack had caused an emotional disturbance, aggravating his uneasiness about Lela, and now his doubts about the latter were focused by the squalid inferences of Cal Mannell, he found in Gwen's coming a ready compensation that, with his erratic temperament, he knew to be dangerous.

"Have you told Joel about seeing me on the claywork?" he asked presently.

"No – haven't told anyone."

"Joel will remember me, I expect."

Gwen frowned at the tarred rods on pulley wheels that operated a pump and prevented her from walking beside him. "I hadn't heard of you before," she said. "Joel's never mentioned you."

"I worked up on the tip while his job was in the 'bottoms'. We weren't pally. But he must have heard enough... I got engaged while he was employed there."

Her counter-thrust came sharply. "Oh! You did? Well, I don't think you're going to add anything to it tonight. Do you?"

She had not misread the veering of his impulses. Her presence had made the prospect of going on alone to Nanpean seem a repulsive anti-climax. He had shrunk from it, and her challenge brought a hardening of decision.

"It'll probably be best to put it off for a day or two," he replied, keeping his back towards her. "I suppose we shall make it another sort of Munich, and I'm not in the mood at the moment."

Gwen stared, grasping his meaning but finding it remote. "Yes, I heard about that, "she said in the careless tone of one whose interests were strictly local. "Lucky they patched it up. We don't want another war."

"We don't," he agreed. "But Hitler and Lela Skiddy may both have to face something tougher than appeasement one of these days."

"I believe you just dragged in her name to throw your mother off the scent. You wanted to work off something –talk to another girl – a bit like I felt at Rostowrack."

He turned and looked at her, deliberately now. There was a glint of the old perversity in his eyes; but it was wholesome. Any flaw in him was like a cleft in a bare, wind-swept rock, not a wrinkle on a soft treacherous swamp. Gwen felt the hard strength of his character and instinctively trusted it. In a way it was like Joel's though much more subtle and complex.

"Yes," he admitted slowly, with a whimsical pucker of his mouth, "I do feel rather like a time-bomb tonight. Lela could touch it off in one way and you in an other."

"Which would you like best?"

"There'd be danger either way," he said, and left the matter there in ambiguity. But there was no repulse in his manner; though it could not be called flirtatious she knew that he was intimately aware of her, revelling darkly in the threat to his former loyalties.

They had soon reached the point where the path began slanting down to the flat pastures around Barrakellis farm. A broader view was disclosed here: the valley sloping up southward to Foxhole Beacon with the scattered houses of Carloggas beside it on the skyline, and away to the east the gaunt plateau of Longstone Downs rising towards Hensbarrow. Clouds still drifted across the moon and a cold flutter of gloom beset the autumnal land. Only the claywork lights gleamed steadfastly, some of them flashing through the fringe of the coppice from mica clay tanks on the other side of the road beyond it. There were other refuse-dumps along the hillsides, but they were derelict, their dead, stiffened surfaces emerging intermittently from shadow with a brief baleful glitter.

The path widened as it left the humped downs, and Gwen stole up at last beside Euan. He kept one hand in his pocket, the other hanging loosely, and as suddenly it grazed hers he felt the quick, fondling movement of her fingers. Instinctively he responded: they walked on in silence, their clasped hands sometimes gripped tightly together, sometimes relaxed as they caressed each other. Euan looked tense and obstinate: he knew what he was doing and the effect such behaviour might have on a wayward adolescent. He peered stealthily at her, and saw that she was flushed, her eyes rapt and brooding, her lips pouted, naked and passionate, he whole face lit with a startled joy and wonder. Yet he did not feel guilty; he was not trifling with her. He still had the sense that this fusion was predestined, a part of the patterned ascent from the debacle to which his fate head led him this afternoon, and he accepted this apparently random and undisciplined contact with a blind, fanatical, even religious trust.

She was aware of his regard, and presently her glance swept round to him; she smiled with full, quite vulnerable understanding. He noticed for the first time that the inside of her lower lip was swollen and discoloured. The questioning look in his eyes caused her to flounder into confession. She pointed. "Dad did that, two days ago. We had an argument while Joel was at work, and he hit me in the face." Her voice was unsteady, deeply emotional. "No wonder I want to get clear of our home, is it?"

Euan squeezed her hand convulsively. "It's a wonder you've stuck it so long," he said. "You're too old now to live with a brute like that."

"Yes; I was sixteen last month…You've lost your father, haven't you?"

Euan nodded.

"He was killed over there by the engine-house" – he pointed to a roof and stack visible above the fields on to which Goonvean sand-dump spilled out. "Oiling the workings in the shaft and slipped on the ladder. Three years ago now."

"Did you get on with him all right?"

"Better than I do with mother. He was more my type – liked to think things out: read a lot, and used to preach in the chapels around here – a Methodist 'local'."

"Ah. That explains why you're so different."

"Partly, perhaps – though before he died he'd begun to fear that Lela was turning me into a pagan. It wasn't that, of course: she'd only complicated the religion I was brought up in, and set me working to fuse it with the emotions of a lover." Euan had bent his head, and seemed lapsed in dreamy absorption as he continued:

"Took my starting point from Browning:

 'Where is the use of the lip's red charm
 Unless we turn, as the soul knows how,
 The earthly gift to an end divine?'

I didn't stop there – I came to see that the natural soul doesn't know how, and found my solution in theology, not poetry. But Lela didn't understand any of it – didn't want to. She wanted the mere human feeling, the moment's pleasure for its own sake, without any mystical 'clap-trap', as she called it. And I told her that her so-called 'adult' outlook was a sham because it started with the childish simplification of leaving out God. And so we've bumped along for three years, having more debates than kisses, and getting on each other's nerves."

Gwen disengaged her hand; it became a fist as she frowned at him. "Why on earth haven't you broke free?" she demanded.

"Well, I'm a stubborn devil for one thing – I hold on. I've sacrificed a good bit for Lela, and don't want it to be all for nothing. Dad had set his heart on my studying for the Methodist ministry, but Lela said she'd throw me over if I took a step in that direction. So I didn't. Which side I'd have come down on if father'd lived I don't know; maybe I should have finished with her by now, and been in a pulpit. I did want to preach – I still do sometimes."

"Your nearly did at Rostowrack," commented Gwen with a nervous laugh; "though it only put me in a temper. I didn't like being lectured by a fellow who'd worked on a claywork with Joel."

"But it might have proved useful," Euan murmured, as his hand closed over hers again.

"How?"

"Well, you seemed to think all chaps were alike – that a girl only had to act in a certain way to get a certain response. You found there were exceptions."

"I always knew there were cranks in the world, of course," said Gwen teasingly.

"But you'd never met one before?"

"Not one like you. But you're nicer to-night."

"'Nice' is the last word I would apply to my present feelings."

"Towards Lela perhaps; but you are nicer to me. Last time you just wanted to get away from me, but now… I didn't expect you to come out for a walk, much less get this far."

"Well we're nearly there now," he said, perversely twisting her words, for he knew she was not thinking of their approach to Barrakellis.

The farm was in view, about two hundred yards ahead: a tiny smallholding with plashy meadows in front of it and a couple of stony fields behind. Several gaunt elms fringed the dwelling, above a more exotic growth of wanly spearing pampas grass. A faint gleam of lamplight played among the blunt, feathery stems near the window. Euan pointed.

"Looks snug, doesn't it? Very sheltered little place. Veale's at home too – I thought he would be."

They halted on the path. He still caressed her fingers, and they both vibrated under the stimulus of the touch.

"I'd better not go further up with you," he said with obvious reluctance. "It might spoil your chance if Veale saw us together."

"You're very thoughtful."

Lingeringly their hands slipped apart; Euan stepped back a pace on the turfed verge of the pathway.

"Well – good luck! I hope this'll mean the start of better times for you."

"It will, if I get the job." And looking him steadily in the face she added; "I shan't be in there more than a few minutes. Won't you wait here till I come out?"

Euan peered towards Nanpean village, the lights of which caused diffused glow along the hillside a mile off, under Longstone Downs. There was an almost malicious glint in his eyes, as if he was enjoying some secret retaliation against Lela. Yet tenderness was there also, and the malice sank behind it as he turned, smiling. He laid his hand on Gwen's shoulder.

"Yes, I'll wait, Gwen," he said.

CHAPTER FIVE

THE sudden collapse of Joel's resolve to leave home did not lead his parents to form the suspicions he had feared. The incident was similar to many that had been staged in the cottage in recent years, and they had come to regard his threats with the amused tolerance accorded to the whims of children. Joel was impulsive, and on the spur of the moment was capable of any extreme, irrational revolt, but the fever soon spent itself and he lapsed into his usual sullen resignation.

True, the matter had gone to more serious lengths this time. Joel had really intended carrying out his threat, and but for Marvran's appearance would have left the house and slept elsewhere, probably in some claywork lodge. But the diversion had given him time to cool, had checked the riot of his emotions, and by the time Marvran left he had regained mental balance. Zachary and Sarah asked no questions, but with sly grins and glances they assured him that his joke was much appreciated. Events in the house returned to the ordinary rut; the squabbles, the drunken orgies, the crushing of the gaiety and innocence of youth in the lives of the two girls continued.

And Joel was changed. In manner and in habit he had made a definite break with the old brutish ways. He no longer visited the public-house; he no longer spent hours alone in the clay-pit. He listened eagerly to every detail concerning Marvran which was let fall over the meal-table. Marvran was visiting the cottage once or twice a week, in the mornings, so he never saw her there. But in the evenings he was close to her, waiting, watching, on and about Roche Rock.

That mysterious pile stood a hundred yards north of the Crebas' bungalow. Near the summit of the Rock, thirty feet from the ground, was the walled enclosure of St. Michael's chapel, reached by an iron ladder affixed to the northern face of the crag. From this chapel another shorter ladder gave access to the ruins of a cell of which nothing now remained but a few crumbled arches and breast-high fragments of wall. Screened by these, Joel could see the dwelling clearly, while remaining invisible to anyone who might be looking towards the Rock. As dusk fell he was almost always there; and often glimpsed Marvran in the garden or outside the doorway, in the path. He watched for her, crouching motionless as the grey crags, watched until he saw her appear; and then he gazed and smiled oddly; his eyes glowed and he trembled with expectancy and desire. There was nothing in this of the airy flamboyance of first love; the feeling itself seemed a wintry growth of grey stoic intensity that neither possessed nor wanted colour, fragrance or softness. At its highest reach it made him vaguely aware that a Mood had broken in upon the darkened kiln-world of his fate, a Mood capable of releasing him; and he groped towards the particular balance of passivity and resolve that would give it freedom.

He came to the Rock early on the afternoon following Gwen's visit to Barrakellis. Her success brightened the background of his thought: she would start work at the farm in the New Year. It seemed that both he and Gwen had reached a point in their struggle where circumstances were beginning to turn in their favour. He felt relieved, hopeful, puffing with stolid enjoyment at a cigarette as he climbed the knoll. The air was dry and frosty, wan spilths of sunlight probing through grey haze and flickering over the Rock, which now in the daytime seemed merely an oddly-shaped natural formation.

Reaching the end of the path Joel began clambering over the low fringe of crag, leaping across fissures, from ledge to ledge, until he drew close to the perpendicular body of the main pile. He tossed his cigarette stump aside, pulled his cap further down over his eyes and glanced up. Bulges in the rock face showed black and gigantic, some of them moss-grown with ivy here and there. Cautiously he stepped around the northern side, where isolated crags reared to twice his height and the ledge along which he moved sloped steeply upward, turfed, to the foot of the ladder. Seized by an impulse to be immediately amid those ruins, always charged for him with the presence of Marvran – she must often have been there – he began the ascent, racing up the almost perpendicular ladder. Gaining the top, he swung himself on to the uneven floor of the enclosure.

The chapel was not large, about three yards in width and was shadowed by the ruins of the cell above it. One wall was higher than the others, and towered over the ruins, forming the pinnacle of the Rock, and its topmost window was inaccessible. Joel was panting from his exertion, flushed, his eyes bright as he glanced swiftly about the deserted sanctuary. But he crossed at once to the second ladder and was soon on the exposed ridge of the pile, surrounded by the mass of the roofless and the ruined archways. He felt a momentary dizziness at seeing the ground so far beneath, to which a false step might send him hurtling. Recovering, he stole to one of the thick archways on the eastern side of the ruins, and crouched behind it, looking across at the dwelling. Smoke oozed from its chimney, a waft of sunlight glinted on the roof. Marvran's home! She was within it, he felt sure; she never went anywhere. His parents had said only yesterday that she still held aloof from social contacts – didn't even attend the chapel. Joel was relieved at this news; when she resumed her old habits there would be danger. Other men, decent, respected, having every advantage over him. Before then he must move, deepen their relationship, make sure of her...

He sat, arms clasped about his knees, and stared moodily around the screening parapet at the walls behind which Marvran's bruised spirit sought healing. But soon he grew cold; there was a strong draught from the many openings; and crawling to the ladder he descended to the more sheltered area. On a bulge of the wall he again seated himself, and peered up at the tiny window through which only the sky was visible, tossing sun-shafts into the grey interior. And again he brooded.

Suddenly he was startled by a sound of voices from below. He grew tense, listening.

"I say, Marv, I've got a little secret for you. I didn't mention it in there with your parents because I wanted to spring it on you just between ourselves..."

Joel leaned against the chapel wall, holding his breath. The voice was strange to him, with a crisp town accent, and after a moment's reflection he realised that the speaker must Marvran' cousin, Joan Luke – daughter of the family at Falmouth who had introduced Marvran to the hotel job. They had come up on a visit, apparently.

"Oh?" Marvran's response sounded tired. "Anything special?"

"Very special. Have you forgotten Don Pearce yet? Daresay you've found another by now, more to your taste…"

There was a tense silence, then Joan spoke again, lower, as if confiding her news close to Marvran's ear:

"He's going to get married – engaged a fortnight ago."

Marvran's reply came, dull and suppressed. "Well, if he is he is. It's no business of mine."

"But can't you guess…?"

A longer pause, then Marvran's voice, still cool but a trifle bitter: "If he wants you he can have you, I suppose. I saw how things were heading before I left, so it isn't much of a surprise."

"I can see you're jealous, though! You always were at Falmouth when Don took me off for a dance."

"It doesn't matter now. Falmouth means nothing to me any more. I aren't going to talk about it, so there!"

"Wouldn't you like to hear the details?"

"Not much. Oh go on. If you're going up!"

There came a thud of a foot on the lowest rung of the ladder, then a squeal from Joan.

"No, I can't – I should lose my head. You lead the way Marv. You're used to it aren't you?"

"Of course. I've been up scores of times when I was a kid."

Yes, they were coming up. Joel heard the rapid thudding of Marvran's feet; Joan's slower, irregular, just behind. He forced himself to be calm, standing now at the foot of the second ladder, facing the top of the first. His fists were clenched, he watched with a fixed stare for the appearance of a head over the rim of rock against the skyline. His muscles tensed; he feared she would hear his breathing which broke harshly from between gritted teeth.

He heard an exclamation of alarm escape Joan.

And Marvran's voice: "Don't look down – you'll be giddy."

Then again the only sound was the ring of their shoes on the ladder as they mounted higher. Joel pressed hard against the rough rock, shuffled around by it until he no longer faced the ladder, but stood beside it, in shadow.

Over the top of the ladder appeared a blue beret, jaunty above a flushed face. Quite close to him Marvran exclaimed: "Here we are –

easy to get inside. You can get a view from the top. There's nobody else...Oh, I beg your... Joel!"

She had glimpsed him, and was surprised at the confusion which welled within her; confusion bubbling from a fount opened afresh by Joan's news. Her mind was fevered, shaken by the sly revolting image of Pearce. She was trying to understand that he was going to marry Joan... he whom she had once believed would one day be her husband. Renewed hatred of Pearce swirled about the stripped elements of her nature, her defensive womanhood. And rising from the froth and sputter came a grim male form: Joel. It seemed idiotic that he was there, for no reason – just an accident; but distinctly embarrassing. So much so, that she stepped back to the opposite wall, leaned there, palms pressed against the cold ragged black stone. Her chin was turned towards her left shoulder, her lips parted. She felt that Joel also was perturbed in some way; he must have heard them speaking at the Rock's foot, must know that the man who had played with her was going to marry another...

Joan stepped from the ladder into the chapel: a weakly-looking, flat-breasted blonde, stylish in a fur-trimmed brown coat and grey halo hat. She stared from Marvran to the stranger who, with head dropped forward, was peering intently at the floor, his mouth set grimly.

Joel did not glance at Joan, but becoming aware of her presence he roused himself, and, keeping his eyes lowered, shuffled to the outlet.

"Excuse me," he mumbled. "I'm sorry. Didn't think nobody'd be coming. I'll go down."

He swung himself to the ladder and dropped from their view below the level of the rock.

Joan waited impatiently until he reached the bottom, then clutched Marvran's arm and challenged her with a whispered question: "Who's that chap?"

Marvran attempted a giggle. "Called Kruse – lives in a shanty up there among the clay-dumps. "Crazy, isn't he?"

"Looks so. My dear girl! However you came to throw over your chances at Falmouth for a place where all the men are half-baked..."

"They aren't all like him. He just belongs to a terribly poor family – riff-raff of the district."

She moved forward to the top of the ladder, wishing to glimpse Joel again. Joan followed her to the narrow ledge, slipping an arm about her neck over the brown coat collar. The two girls peered down at the sprawled base of the Rock. Marvran was still breathing heavily, her face pale, agitated.

Joel was in sight, climbing over the fissures and stumps of crag, making towards the lane that led to his home. He walked with frequent lurches and stumbles, his head bent, in a daze.

"Look like a fellow walking in his sleep," Joan commented. Her small blue eyes met Marvran's with a mocking private innuendo as she added: "Is he married?"

"No."

"Courting, I suppose?"

"Not yet, but... Oh, never mind!" Marvran shrugged irritably, casting about for some association that would free her from this emotional strain. She hit at once upon a relevant memory, and seized it with forced eagerness.

"Funny!" she exclaimed, glancing back at the rocky chapel floor which had been worn smooth by the feet of countless sightseers since the monks knelt there in their medieval devotions. "I came on him here like this once before."

"Recently?"

"No – before I went to Falmouth. The summer after I left school, the day they held the Gorsedd here." Marvran's hand swept the general foreground. "There were crowds everywhere, filling the roadside and all the fields and downs between here and Roche school. Looked like a carnival, only a bit dull – all the Bards were dressed alike in blue robes. The ceremony was boring, just jabber in Cornish, a foreign language to us moderns. We just ate ice-cream and pretended it was a fete or something. When it was nearly over some of us girls began climbing round the rock; and we found Joel Kruse sitting up there" – she pointed through the cavity at the rear of the chapel – "behind a pillar. All by himself glowering at the crowd as if he was the spirit of the place – a very insulted spirit, by the look of him."

Marvran spoke rapidly, vivid in the momentary sense of release. Her cheeks had flushed, her eyes held a glint of her old vivacity, though it was brittle, feverish.

"What did you do then?" asked Joan as they edged once more into shelter.

"Ran down again. Dad was coming back there from work – he didn't care much for the Gorsedd, though. Too quiet and too bogus, really. All those modern bourgeoisie – pretending they're Druids or Bards. We just laughed – all except Krusey. He stayed glum till the football season came round. But dad… you know his great love, don't you?"

She was still defensive, but had almost escaped to superficiality. Joan watched her, subtly aware of the struggle, rather amused.

"I seem to remember that his idea of Heaven is your annual Band Festival here at Bugle," remarked Joan slyly. "A score of brass bands blaring all day long."

Marvran nodded. "Yes – loves it," she said. "I'm sure I got my taste for a bit of liveliness from dad. Mum's just the opposite."

"Does he still play his trombone – or has he hung it on the willows in mourning over your eclipse?"

The brief silence was painful as the stab recalled Marvran to the present. She moved close up to the wall, hiding her face from Joan, and answered in a low, more defiant tone as her hand clawed at the rock:

"He still practises – getting ready for the summer, when he'll be off in the bandsmen's bus, going to carnivals and Sunday School treats. He's in his element marching around the villages at the head of the processions – but he's such a little fellow, he does look comical in his uniform!"

She checked a gurgle of hysterical laughter, and abruptly darted forward and began ascending the ladder to the ruins. "Come on! You want a view, don't you?"

A few minutes later, on the summit, both girls were clutching nervously at the arch behind which Joel had screened himself just before they left the bungalow. They were again following his movements. He had reached the narrow path winding down to the lane, and was pushing savagely along it, his clothes caught at times by trailing brambles. He did not look back or aside until he arrived at the stile. On this, however, he paused glancing about dazedly, as if sensuous connection with the outer world was something new and bewildering to him. His gaze soon focused on the Crebas' bungalow; he stared at it, erect and motionless on the stile.

"What's he seen there?" inquired Joan in a puzzled whisper.

"Nothing," Marvran replied shortly. But she bit her lip and stole back to the top of the ladder, suppressed and vulnerable. There was piercing revelation for her in Joel's attitude. All that she had felt while with him in the oratory just now returned, free from the brief pitiful counter-thrust of trivial memories. She remembered, too, the look in his eyes when he told her at the Kruses' cottage that he wouldn't be leaving home: strange, as if she had had some part in his decision.. And now, halting on the stile, he showed the same groping tenacity, staring at the home to which she must return with the new knowledge, newly wounded. She gave a writhing shrug of exasperation.

"Oh, come on Joan – let's go down, This place seems haunted to-day, or I'm in the wrong mood for it…" She hurried into the chapel and swung herself on to the outer ladder, a brown smudge against the grey-black rock face. "I'm vexed about this. Why did you have to tell me now?"

Joan came leisurely out from the shadow, fingering her diamond engagement ring; she smiled with playful malice. "About Don?"

"As if I wanted to hear anything more of him! Don't make a to-do about it indoors, or I'll leave the room and stay out till you've gone!"

Joan narrowed her eyes again to observe Joel. He had left the stile and was moving slowly up the lane towards this home. But he was peering at the Rock; obviously he had seen them.

"No doubt our talk on that subject would be as boring to you as those Bards," she said with measured irony. "But by that time your cave-man might be back on his perch here for a third meeting. Third time lucky, perhaps?"

CHAPTER SIX

HEAVY rain-cloud had sagged over Goss Moor all day, causing the cottage lamps at Enniscaven to remain burning for several hours after dawn. At nightfall the clouds were still intact, as if intending to reserve the downpour for Christmas, now only two days ahead. But the moorland tracks were miry from earlier showers, and Charlie Crago, cycling along one of them towards Roche, found the journey uncomfortable. There was little wind, but the cold air chilled him as he nosed over the dark heath. He was often jolted as the machine bumped into stones and puddles, the water sometimes splashing upon his shoes and spraying out over the scabrous foliage in brown jets that glinted momentarily in the glow of the headlamp. The track was a mere footpath, and he was taking it chiefly to avoid passing the Buzzas' home. He was in no mood to invite temptation to-night. During the past week he had received a profound shock, his first experience of the swift incalculable menace within life, and though its effect would soon wear off he felt at present decidedly repelled by the thought of Olive. The bleared lights of Roche on the hilltop reminded him of Joel Kruse, and he felt relieved that, if his recent hint led to serious developments, Olive would not be inclined to molest him further.

Last Sunday word had reached the Cragos from Tehidy Sanatorium, to which Mrs. Crago had been removed a year ago, that her condition had taken a grave turn. On Monday the family had gone down to the sanatorium, and found her facing the last struggle. Yesterday the fatal news was brought: his mother had died just before dawn. This ill-timed and unexpected bereavement angered Charlie, and also burdened him with disgust for the easiest mode of compensation that offered itself. Sensual pleasure had slunk for him like a stale, futile ghost into the meanest background, among the eternal debris. He didn't wish even to be reminded of its living form, its jests, its laughter, its caresses. Drink was a surer remedy, being less natural – less, one might almost say, of an interference with God. Charlie was on his way to escape the gloom of reality at the Roche public-house.

The inn stood half-way up the main street of the village, not far below the Church. The bar window was brightly aglow as Charlie drew abreast of it, and dismounting he set his bicycle against the wall with a sense of relief bordering on bravado. There was no one else outside, and he swaggered to the door with long strides and a deceptive air of familiarity. He was not much addicted to liquor: a fortnight had passed since he last touched it, and he knew that a very little would be sufficient to land him in difficulties. But tonight he did not care; he was recklessly resolved to drown out the suggestion that life was such a serious business as his mother's dying eyes and words had implied.

His hand was on the door knob when it was abruptly turned from within, and he stepped back to make room for an emerging couple: a wiry short-necked man wearing a muffler and pulling on a pair of heavy leather gloves, and a girl in a rain coat and crimson beret, tall, slim, and with a cool vulgar elegance in her movements.

Charlie recognized them and greeted the man sardonically: "Lucky I aren't Euan Kella, or you'd be spending a merry Christmas in hospital, Cal!"

The girl, who was Lela, tittered. "And I might be spending it in a coffin. You can never tell."

A scowl darkened Charlie's face. "You've heard about me mother?"

"They was jist tellin' of it in there," replied Cal, jerking a thumb towards the bar window. "Our mothers have done their damnedest to spoil this Christmas for us, Charlie, so we got to work it off somehow."

"What yours isn't gone too, is she?"

"No such luck! She's still lively enough to spring a bombshell – hit me two days ago. Got a letter saying she's leaving the Scillies; can't stick it there no longer. Didn't give any details, but I reckon she've got in some scrape or other – drunk and disorderly, p'raps, or up to her old Plymouth game again"

Charlie stared, his hollow face maliciously twisted. "So she's coming back to live with you there at Carloggas?"

"Threatenin' to – and there's no way I can shake her off. She said if I was married she wouldn't come, knowing 'twould be a cat-and-dog life; but I can't risk that – not with Olive Buzza, though she asked me to marry her last September. And as for Lela here - she still got her big date wi' me sparrin' partner at Rostowrack!"

Charlie stepped across to Cal's motor-cycle, which stood close against the lower wall, and examined the headlamp. Suddenly he turned under a fresh thrust of curiosity. "What about your sister over St. Mary's: she flittin' back wi' Sue?"

Cal's laugh was brittle and jeering as he replied. "No good settin' your hopes there, old sport! Lorraine's stayin' put. Got her job in Hugh Town; she'll be glad to be rid of her mother, so the letter said. She's a queer specimen to crop up in our family – over twenty, and ha'n't been in a single scandal yet. Quiet, moody sort – like Lela's young man, I should judge."

"Well, you'll be taking on a handful wi' Sue around here again. Arriving soon, is she?"

"Week after next, unless the boat goes down. I'm hoping 'twill. No more snug little larks with maidens at the shack once that old cat d'take over. Me and Lela's goin' back there now; may be our last little fling in that bedroom."

Charlie shrugged, and without any further word went up the step and entered the public-house. Cal and Lela stood for a few moments undecided, then Lela moved out the pavement, looking up and down the deserted street.

Cal joined her and slowly they strolled up towards the lonelier section of road outside the churchyard. There, under the black forms of moist elm boughs, they halted, and Cal scanned furtively the whole length of the hill, down to the crossroads. The wide street with its garish lamps and mean blocks of houses was more like a town thoroughfare than a country road. Few villages in the clay district possess charm or beauty; there is a general utilitarian drabness, except where the sand-cones tower close to the cottages and give a fantastic Alpine touch to the scene. But the upland village of Roche was particularly grim and inhospitable. Its inhabitants were held by some Cornish historians to be a tribe apart. There was no apparent difference between them and other clay area villagers, but the place itself had a depressing aspect, as if it were a mere remnant of a lost pagan world. Its chilly gloom was pagan, despite the church tower on the hilltop. It was the atmosphere of the Rock seeping down among the dwellings and becoming void of significance in its transformation from the natural to the civilized form. The village was little more than a junction, its shops, garages and dour granite houses huddled about two crossroads from which lanes wound out over the plateau, south, east and north-east. The eastern one, in which Cal and Lela stood, was the most cramped and squalid. And they seemed to belong to it, to be part of the pagan dereliction that brooded here. Cal nudged the girl teasingly.

"Feel scared o' going back Nanpean way, or no? We may pass Euan down there somewhere."

Lela paused, lighting a cigarette, the flare of the match showing her face to be pale, hard and defiant. It was not a well-moulded face: the nose was sharp, the mouth too near it and naturally thin-lipped. But her red artificially curled hair gave a certain vividness to her appearance, and a kind of slack flame played about her features.

"If we do, so much the better," she replied. "'Tis time the storm broke. Since that fuss at Rostowrack our meetings have been enough to make me scream: Euan been tensed up so, afraid to bring it to the point."

Cal lit his cigarette at her match, then remarked, "Should think you'd break it off without waiting for him. People's beginnin' to treat the affair as a laughing-stock."

"I'll have the last laugh, though. I'm just pleasing myself. He still fascinates me – the sheer oddity of the fellow, with that violent streak in him. I don't believe there's another chap like him in Cornwall."

"Poor lookout for Cornwall, if everybody in it was like him," commented Cal.

"'Twould be a rather weird place – and dangerous too. But he's no fool, say what you will. He knows so much about the modern way of life as I do; he's lent me scores of books about these advanced ideas of conduct, like Lawrence's novels, and books on sex. But he just reads 'em and goes his own way."

Cal bent irritably and spat into the gutter. "He ha'n't never been able to get you there with him, though; you've gone your own way too, from the start. Can't see what's kept him hangin' on all these years."

Lela smiled. "You don't understand him. He's a queer mixture, sensitive, but not a bit refined. His natural taste is for the low type o' girl that – that gives his conversion ideas something to work on, see? No ready-made ideal for him! He wouldn't find Olive Buzza as repulsive as a decent little go-getter like Creba's girl up here." She flicked her cigarette towards the Crebas' bungalow. "'Tis sophistication he hates most in women and I've got precious little of that. I'm just a village girl with a bit of intelligence, still crude enough, despite going to Grammar School. And that's what he likes in me. Only he wants to use it for his own mystical ideas, and I won't let him."

"He'll have to practise on somebody else soon – he must know that now," remarked Cal after a pause.

"Yes. I think he's got the hunch that you were telling the plain truth at Rostowrack when you bracketed me and Olive among your latest doxies. He knows he's lost the game, but he's clinging on blindly till the final wrench comes."

"You'm ready for it, o'course?"

"I shan't jib. I'll fling the facts in his face and tell him not to be a damned fool."

Cal glanced at the church tower looming black and melancholy through the shaking elm boughs. The gloomy silence of the graveyard made him recoil towards the living tang of sensation. A broad, froglike grin grew across his face as he turned to Lela. He hunched his shoulders, pulling up the collar of his raincoat: an awkward, almost deformed figure, not as tall as she. There was something cold, spongy and reptilian about him, but also a powerful male fascination.

"What'll yer ma say?" he said. "She must have heard the talk about us carryin' on."

"I suppose so, but she hasn't mentioned it. Mother just isn't interested in my affairs. I've always had a free hand, ever since she separated from dad when I left school."

Mannell edged restlessly, his senses stirred to impatience by Lela's provocative, shadowy form. "Well, we can't stop here all night. Time we was spinnin' home to Carloggas, me darling."

Lela followed him in silence, smiling cynically and feeling, as he did, the menace of the churchyard and the pagan darkness of the village.

CHAPTER SEVEN

FROM the top of the sand-hill overlooking the Kruses' home Olive Buzza watched a grotesque scene taking place below. The pinnacle was narrow, the apex of a pyramid, and she stood between the rails of the inclined railway, screened by a thick wooden beam of the tip's framework. It was now mid-afternoon of Boxing Day, and Olive, well wrapped in a grey tweed coat, had been on the sand-hill nearly half-an-hour.

At the rear of the Kruses' cottage the entire family were grouped, puppet-like in the shadow of the dump. Olive could not distinguish their faces, but her eyes centred on Joel, who lounged by the house corner.

Zachary was the chief person concerned in the incident. He stood, legs wide apart, between his wife (who held Pearl in her arms) and the older children, swinging at arm's length a sack and thumping with his fist some object that writhed an wriggled inside. From remarks occasionally dropped by one or other of the family Olive gathered that the cat had been taken with fits, and that Zachary was stunning the creature prior to drowning her in a near-by-pool. His fantastic movements caused Olive a deal of amusement, but the crafty smile which flitted about her round, colourless face told that her design was serious. She waited impatiently for the act to close, and her body writhed, made restless by the riot of desire within her. Her thick lips twitched, her hands clawed at each other, prodded her breasts, sometimes pressed hard over her belly.

A piteous cry broke from the cat as Zachary paused for a moment to gain breath; she squirmed and tore feebly at the sacking. The man made a rush forward and swung the creature violently against the wall. She was then quiet and Zachary slung the sack across his shoulder, staring across at the children with a vacant triumphant leer.

"Comin' down?" Olive heard him ask Joel. "Got to make sure she do go to bottom. May need your help."

Joel nodded sullenly, and he and Arthur stepped forward as Zachary lurched towards the sand-hill. The female Kruses moved slowly into the garden. The three males strode in silence away from the cottage. They were hidden for several minutes from Olive's view, close to the sand-dump's base; then, seeing them emerge west of the dump, followed their progress down the rutted cart-track leading towards Roche Rock. Zachary and Arthur led the way, Joel, following behind, hands in pocket, shoulders hunched.

On reaching a bend of the path near the road the trio paused beside a small slime-coated pool. Zachary swung the bag from his shoulder, allowing it to dangle against his leg. The cat made no motion.

"She be quieted right enough, "Zachary announced shrilly. "Now, we must git a stone pretty big…Got the string, Arthur?"

The boy fumbled in his trousers pocket and handed a length of dirty cord to his father, while Joel began searching for a suitable stone. The place was strewn with boulders, but most were deeply embedded in the soil, or too small to be of service. At length, however, he found a fragment of rock about ten pounds in weight and carried it across to Zachary.

With trembling hands the man held the sack's mouth wide open. The bag had been tied once already, in the middle, and thus the boulder could not come in contact with the stunned creature lying below.

"Drop un in there," grunted Zachary. "Then we'll tie the bag on top."

Arthur stood close beside his father, gaping with fascination as the sack was weighted and tied. Zachary then raised his burden, dropped it, and swayed.

"Too heavy," he muttered.

In silence Joel took the bag, lifted it level with his shoulder, and flung it into the centre of the pool. Olive heard the splash and shrugged with an amused titter. She saw the three figures silhouetted against the sombre downs, looking intently at the tarn's surface.

Zachary was leaning forward, both arms extended towards the water; Joel stood erect, hands set on his hips, – his face grim and pale; while Arthur was squatting on his heels, mouth wide open.

Presently Olive saw the trio stir and move back towards the cottage, now in single file. She waited in a fever of suspense until they reached their abode. She believed they would go in, all except Joel; she had heard that he seldom stayed indoors during the day-time; and when he was a safe distance from the house – she would trap him! No fear of being spied upon to-day; none of the clay-works was active.

At the corner of the cottage Joel paused, and as she had hoped, Zachary and Arthur went in. While Olive watched, however, Gwen appeared, hurried through the gateway and approached him. The girl caught his arm and leaned close, whispering. Joel nodded, and a minute later the pair were moving along the tortuous narrow path between the clay-dump and the pit, over the rude bridges, towards the east.

Olive gnawed at her lip in sudden dismay as frustration pounced back on her. Gwen had obviously suggested that Joel should go for a walk with her instead of joining the company indoors. There would be no chance of getting him alone now…Olive stepped a few paces nearer the edge of the dune, watching intently. The pair strolled slowly through the desolate scene. They walked side by side except where the path was so narrow that they were forced into single file. They appeared to be silent, glancing moodily into the pit which they were skirting, or across it at the low flat refuse-heap on the ridge opposite their home. When they reached the foot of this dump they halted for a few minutes and then began climbing up through a broad gully. Olive followed their movements until they gained the summit and became tiny blurred shapes on the white gravel. They had not glimpsed her, and she stole back behind the beam.

Joel and Gwen lingered near the brink of the dune, flushed and breathing heavily as they faced each other. There was an awkward silence, which Joel broke at length.

"Now, what did you want to see me alone for?"

Gwen's eyes dilated. She looked inflamed and suppressed in her scarlet jumper. "How d'you know I had any reason?"

"I noticed something in your manner. You aren't a kid now, to just want to go for a walk with your big brother. What's behind it?"

She shrugged, glancing away towards the tip-frame that loomed up like a gallows at the far end of the pile. "I'll tell you d'rectly. Let's go further in – 'tis cold here."

The two went on, keeping to the rails which scored the centre of the dump in a straight track to the tip. There the tram waggon stood under the naked, slanting prongs of the rails that bore the big skip from the clay-pit. Close to it was a rough shelter built into the cone of refuse, its stone walls roofed with corrugated iron. The hut had no window and the wooden door-posts sagged beneath the gravel and boulders that weighted the roof. Gwen's face softened with uneasy reminiscence as she and Joel drew level with it.

"D'you mind how we used to play Indians here, Joel – me and you and Marvran and one or two others? Seems a long time ago, doesn't it?" She pushed open the rickety door, surveying the interior. "The two seats is still here. I'm going in." She moved into the hut, squatting on the bench in the far corner. She crouched there, half-hidden in the gloom, only a bright gleam in her eyes clearly visible.

"Come in here, Joel. You're tired aren't you?"

"Not particularly."

"Well, I am. Come in and sit down with me."

Looking harassed and wretched Joel entered the cuddy, bending low, his bulk filling the entrance and causing an almost complete darkness until he had seated himself opposite her.

"Well? You got something to tell me?"

She touched his knee, much agitated.

"You aren't enjoying this Christmas, are you?"

"Why shouldn't I be?" he asked gruffly. "It's as good as most. We know what to expect – no parties or special doings like other people have."

"No, but… you know what happened on Christmas Eve, don't you?"

"Of course."

"What?"

"Crebas' girl came over with nuts and stuff, and decorations. Our party wouldn't let her put 'em up. I don't see why they should: our beams is so low, 'twould only get in the way."

"You didn't see her then; you was out on the sand-burrow sawing off the pulley frame to burn. But I heard the saw stop as Marvran left the house, as if you was listening, hoping she'd call to you. And she didn't."

"It was raining," he said defensively,

"But when she came yesterday with the fowl and Christmas pudding, you was there. And still she didn't speak to you. It wasn't like Marvran at all."

Joel flushed, biting his lip. "She's still upset about that Falmouth business, I s'pose," he said.

"But 'tis her you're worried about, isn't it?"

He hesitated between the instinctive recoil and the urge to share, on this issue too, the life he and Gwen had lived apart, aloof from the rest of the family.

"Don't go bothering about me, Gwen – I aren't worth it," he replied with a forced smile.

"You are. Don't put me off. We've been through so much together...I've got a right to know, haven't I?"

The reminder softened him, but he continued to hold her back from her probing intimacy. "Well?"

"You've been so different lately. I've wanted to get you alone and have a talk. You seemed happier during the autumn, but since I got the job at Barrakellis – you've closed up...Would you rather I stayed at home?"

He sat tensely near the door of the cramped hut, looking out over the clay sand that stretched frost-white to the horizon.

"No, 'tisn't anything to do wi' that,' he murmured. "I'm glad you'll soon be free."

"Then it must be Marvran?" Gwen had leaned closer and caught his arm, her face partly hidden by the tumbling brown hair. "Did you meet her somewhere in November?"

Joel's will seemed drugged as he floundered towards confession. "I seen her on Roche Rock one day – only for a minute. There with her cousin – Lukes' maid."

"Ah! So it all links up as I thought. All your moods ever since August they point the same way. That Sunday, when you were getting your things ready to clear out...it was Marvran who pulled you up and made you change your mind, wasn't it?"

"I'd backed out several times before – you know my moods," he said, rallying a little against the emotional pressure.

"But 'twasn't the same. I saw the look on your face when you told her you'd be staying on here. So did mother and dad and they've noticed the change in Marvran 'specially yesterday. We've all got our suspicions, though of course I haven't said a word."

Joel's hands fumbled about the ragged wood of the bench; he frowned at the gravelly, tar-splashed floor, glancing quickly aside as a robin alighted on a boulder just beyond the threshold.

"What suspicions?" he asked at length, mechanically.

Gwen pushed her cold, eager face close to his.

"You're in love with Marvran, aren't you?"

He stared at her, rather dazed under the sense of betrayal and commitment.

"I s'pose 'tis that," he said. His mind veered round and steadied among the crumbling defences; he gripped her wrist almost violently. "You haven't dropped any hint to Marvran herself, have 'ee, that I'm feeling anything for her?"

"You know I wouldn't do that, Joel. I'm just wondering what's to come of it. Will you try to start something serious when I've gone down to the farm?"

A full discussion was now inevitable, but Joel found it impossible to meet the challenge while enclosed in the mouldy cave-like shelter. He rose clumsily and stepped outside. Gwen followed him, and a few yards from the cuddy they halted and faced each other. The girl first spoke.

"I don't want you to hurt yourself. And you will if you aren't careful. You see. Don't you?"

"I've thought it all out, everything. But there's a chance, there must be, or I wouldn't feel things for her."

Gwen toed the gravel, her eyes stark and rebellious with pity for him. "Tisn't your fault, Joel. It's our family. You'd have been one of the most popular chaps around here by this time if 'twasn't for them. If you'd been able to live up to what was put in the papers so often – 'brilliant work by J Kruse, the Roche centre-forward' – you remember? I used to be proud, and so any girl would be if she didn't know what Marvran's known all along.."

"Yes – yes, it's true – she has. But if she looked down on us felt like – like a little snob – I mean, she wouldn't come at all, would she?"

"She's sorry for us, just like her mother. But it's one thing to be befriend a poor family, and quite another to think of marrying one of 'em."

Joel peered haggardly out over the bleak moorland, to which the ubiquitous claywork scars added a harshness that was beyond Nature's: the ultimate quality of violence, calculated interference which belongs to God. And wherever the scars went deep into the bowels of the earth, the furnace fires roared and the clay heaved in the kilns. His hidden symbol was there. He felt again the leprous touch, the defilement.

"Don't say too much!" he muttered." I've been through hell, Gwen, these last few years. You know some of it, but not everything, because you aren't in love yet."

Gwen caught at this opening and after a moment's struggle she brought it out: "How d'you know that?"

Joel stared. "What, have you got a secret too?"

"I can't tell how it's going to shape out any more than you with Marvran. But I believe it has come to me."

"Some fellow down where you're going in service?"

"Yes. Called Euan Kella. I don't know if you remember him. He works at Rostowrack, where you got that job four years ago."

Joel scratched beneath his cap, frowning. "I've near forgot that crowd," he said. "But I think I mind the name. Euan… is that the quiet bookish bloke used to work on the tip?"

Gwen nodded, then fearful lest he should follow up with some question about Lela, quickly forestalled the fuller awakening of his memories. "I saw him first the evening before Marvran came to see us, that Sunday, there on the clayworks above St. Dennis. You can guess the foul mood I was in over Marvran, but he didn't take it as most chaps would."

"I see. And when've you met him since?"

"The day I went down to see Veale. I called at the wrong house first, where Euan lives, and he came up the moor with me to show me Veale's place." Her hands clenched, she gulped, and her mood broke to full stormy confession:

"And I felt it again deeper; and now it's pulling me to pieces all the time. I know what you suffer, Joel, to see Marvran as she was yesterday. And I'm in a worse fix than that."

"How?" Joel's eyes were probing her, and suddenly they widened; he gasped, his face flinching under the stab of realisation. "Ah, yes…wasn't he the chap who got engaged while I was working there – her father killed or something?"

"That's it. The affair's still dragging on; but I feel sure he won't marry her, any more'n Marvran married Pearce. He hinted that much to me. And when I start work next week I'll have a chance to see him any day. And something's going to break. I know it."

Joel sighed, forcing a wan smile as he stepped back a pace.

"Well, we can't stop you, Gwen. But it don't look too promising, do it?"

"No – not for either of us. But I've got to hope, or I'd be going headlong the way Olive Buzza went."

This reference, reminding Joel of yet another threat, the talk of Eli and Bassett in the 'dry', the dark alternative for himself, almost unnerved him. His face showed torture for a moment, then with a passionate gesture he cried: "Don't do that, for God's sake! I feel just as desperate about Marvran as if God's playing some damned trick, sending her back in the nick o' time and then letting her turn cold and put me in a worse hell than I was before! But I'll stick it for your sake as long as I can. Don't let me see you cave in first!"

"I'll try not to." Gwen passed a hand shakily over her forehead. "You know I wouldn't stand in your way o' your happiness. And – and you won't interfere between me and Euan, will you?"

Joel calmed himself, shrugging uneasily. "I may go along and see Kella sometime," he muttered. "I'd have more peace o' mind if I knew what he's really up to. But I shan't meddle or drop any hint even to our people."

"No, don't tell them… They must be wondering where we've gone by this time. Ought to be going in, didn't we? I'll have to get tea soon."

Joel nodded, and she followed him with lagging steps to the wide, deep gully west of the hut, by which they would descend.

On the sand-hill behind the Kruses' house Olive Buzza moved stealthily down the zigzagging path facing the moors of Hensbarrow.

Her cheeks were flushed with frustration and she scowled over her shoulder. She saw Joel and Gwen returning and wondered what had occurred between them further in on the dump.

"If only that bitch hadn't been with him!" she muttered.

CHAPTER EIGHT

AS Hester Creba approached the Kruses' cottage late in the morning of the eighteenth of January, she was greeted by a sound that was familiar to all who passed the dwelling: the loud rasp and snarl of angry voices. She halted on the path, thinking that another family squabble was taking place; but after a few minutes' listening she realised that the trouble was not of the usual sort, and not a bickering of the Kruses among themselves. A voice, which she recognised as that of Reginald Chegwidden, the Captain of the surrounding clay-works, gave a crisp, acrid flavour of intelligence to the dispute. Hester moved close up to the house wall, not wishing to interrupt the scene, but curious to know what fresh crisis had arisen.

In the kitchen Zachary and Sarah stood in their ragged, dirty apparel, with faces on which the blankness of dismay and stupefaction was being broken up by sullen and dangerous flickers of resistance. They were alone with the captain, who had paused just inside the doorway. He was a stout middle-aged man, wearing a heavy tweed coat; occasionally he tapped the bare floor with his walking-stick. Beneath a black bowler hat his grey eyes scanned with distaste the room and its dishevelled occupants.

Zachary was pounding the table, on which lay a skinned rabbit; his fist was smeared with blood that had trickled across the board when Sarah cut the animal open to prepare it for dinner. He spoke belligerently, though his voice quavered from shock and was thickened by recent drinking.

"They talk o' trade picking up and things improving, the bloody liars! What do it mean when you go behind the scenes? Families chucked out o' their home. And what for? Why should the likes of we have to pay for it, I'd like to know?"

Chegwidden coughed, smiling blandly, but his gesture and tone betrayed irritation. "You've been given six months' notice; that's ample time. The company are keeping on the lookout, and you'll be informed as soon as they find a suitable place for you."

Zachary kicked the table leg savagely.

"We won't go – we won't go, Cap'n. Let 'em blow the bloody house up under us!"

"You'll have to be reasonable, Mr. Kruse. The decision has been made and I'm afraid there's no alternative left. You couldn't safely live here when work is resumed on this side of the pit."

The Kruses scowled at each other and for some moments there was silence. Sarah chewed her lips anxiously. Zachary clawed at the lapels of his coat, leaving a stain of rabbit's blood on one of them.

"We been in this house twenty year," he protested at length. "Come in from Stenalees just after Joel was born. Missus have had four other children up in bedroom. And now you talk o' pulling the place down! And what for? So as you can swell yer profits and pile up yer money."

Sarah pressed both fists against her apron and stared at Chegwidden with a sour, primitive defiance.

"What've us done to be kicked out? We paid up our rent all right..."

"That has nothing to do with it. The pit must be expanded to cope with the increase of trade. The land belongs to the company; you know 'tis the usual thing to demolish where old houses stand too near a pit which is still being worked." The captain stepped further into the room, flicking his thick fingers. "For some time this cottage has been hindering our operations. We can't blast along the whole south cliff because of the risk of stone falling on the house."

Sarah lurched heavily to the table and peered out across the pit. A waggon rumbled up, and the dull clang of tools could be heard far below, with the steady splash of water, the hose-jets softening the cliff face.

"We d' always stay indoors when bell do ring for blasting, even when 'tis on t'other side," she observed, seizing on a momentary distraction. "And a nuisance it have been, 'specially of a showery Monday when I got our clothes on the line. Rain 'll start and I want to go out and pick in me clothes, but no! there's the old bell ringing!

Blast may go off any minute, and I got to stop indoors and glaze through the window, watching me clothes get soaking wet again because I can't chance having me head cut abroad wi' they flying rocks." Sarah's hand clenched on the blood-stained knife as she turned to Chegwidden. "'Tis no comfort to live here, cap'n, but 'tis our home, all we've ever had, and folks like to keep their own home."

"I can quite understand your feelings, but this sort of thing is happening throughout the area. You're no exception, and the move will be in your own interests."

The finality in Chegwidden's tone reduced Zachary to a mere whine of complaint; he slunk back against the mantelpeice.

"You can't fool we like that, Cap'n. We know you only picked on this house because our family live here…"

Chegwidden turned and stepped over the threshold.

"Good day!" he said curtly, turning to go.

Hester had by now moved away from the cottage wall, and disappeared around the corner of the sand-hill, on her way home, as the Captain opened the garden gate.

Before Joel reached home to learn of the claywork company's decision he had been met with a piece of news that perplexed him and disturbed his balance of mind. At the end of the lane Arthur was waiting, having just arrived there on his return from Trezaise, where he had been playing football, today being Saturday. His clothes were tattered, much too tight, and he looked like a small scarecrow as the wind fluttered the garments about his bony frame. On seeing Joel he raised a hand and shouted:

"Hi! Joel! Got somethin' to tell 'ee."

"Well?" asked Joel impatiently: he had been thinking of Marvran, and the crude jarring upon that aching beauty was very unwelcome.

Arthur sniggered. "I seen a bloke jist now," he continued. "Over Trezaise way. Stopped a lorry there and called out to me."

"Who was that?"

"Charlie Crago lorry driver he is; lives down Enniscaven. You know him, don't 'ee?"

"Haven't taken much notice. He comes there to the 'dry' sometimes… What did he want?"

Arthur stooped for a stone, and rising, threw it at a pair of bullfinches perched on a hawthorn tree further up the lane. "Charlie asked me to let you know he'll be waitin' around next Saturday night. Good news, he said, that you'd like to hear of. I thought he'd maybe heard of a job somewhere what you could git if you moved off. You told 'em at the works you wanted to go, didn't 'ee?"

A suppression was immediately apparent in Joel's manner: he clenched his hands as he moved slowly forward.

"Yes."

"Thought that's what 'twas," said Arthur. "He's all over the place wi' the lorry, and he may ha' picked up news of some openin' miles away. Would 'ee take it?"

Joel glanced up towards the Crebas' bungalow, smiled slightly, and answered: "No fear o' that!"

Arhthur's hands wound with difficulty into his trousers pockets. "It may be somethin' else," he admitted dubiously. "He didn't say. But you'll go and see him, I s'pose?"

"Reckon it won't do any harm. When did he say – Saturday?"

"Yes, nine o'clock in evening, there to the corner o' Roche hill, below the Council houses."

"I'll remember."

But, hearing the news with which his parents greeted him, Joel quickly dismissed Arthur's information as trifling and irrelevant. The proposed demolition of the cottage came upon him like a stroke at the heart, maliciously and cruelly timed. If the transplanting of the family would lead to a new domestic tone, a fresh beginning, it would be tolerable. But he knew that the same routine of muddle and brutishness would be pursued elsewhere; the new home would soon be as squalid as the clay-pit dwelling. Zachary and Sarah would find their own level in the new district, and bring to a fresh circle of neighbours the dank, outworn qualities of rural life. And Marvran! He was chilled, appalled, as he thought of the personal menace. If he lost touch with her he knew that he, too, would slip back; the earthy roots would bind him again, and more grossly. He could still cycle to Roche in the evenings and hang about in the hope of seeing her; but the pattern of ripening intimacy as he had cherished it seemed irretrievably broken.

Joel felt that he could not stay in the house lest some member of the family spoke of Marvran, yet during the afternoon he was too stunned to make any exertion. At tea-time the unfamiliar absence of

Gwen – for she hadn't been at Barrakellis a week yet – aroused memories of their talk on the sand-hill on Boxing Day. That fellow Kella! How would this turn affect her relations with him? Were Kella and Marvran the tools of Providence, or mere mocking shadows on the kiln?

From these sombre musings he was jolted as Zachary drew his chair close to the fire and remarked: "Best go out for smutties, Joel – ha'n't got no firing in to light up to-morrow morning."

Joel nodded, rose dazedly to his feet, and without a word left the house.

A wheel-barrow was turned upside down in the garden path, and taking this he set out along the track he and Gwen had followed on Boxing Day. Reaching the bend he forked slightly to the south, heading for the open moor behind Trezaise. The 'smutties' (burnt furze twigs) were plentiful on the downs; many clusters of the charred gorse met his eye, black and ugly blobs amid the sure brown of natural foliage. Children lit fires here in winter, and the dried sticks were widely used for fuel by the poorer families in the neighbour-hood. Joel pushed his barrow towards the thickest of these clumps, not far from the worn path that crossed the expanse from Trezaise to the clayworks.

There was a keen wind, a tang of frost in the air; a grey-white bar hung over the horizon, tinged slightly with a hue of saffron westward where the sun had set. Clouds in the sky appeared like black sheep turned out of the heavenly fold and quarrelling among themselves, joined together and then separated for the next angry rush. Winter moths occasionally crossed Joel's path – mute erratic shapes that faded into a faltering ebb of light. The houses of Trezaise loomed starkly on the southern rim of the moor; between them the few trees rose as sentinels, very tall, weirdly bare, jarred by the blustering wind. On one side stood Roche Rock, on the other Roche church: dark testimonies of stone, older and more rude than the cottages or trees. Ahead of him the downs rolled desolately, with only the grey silent sand cones breaking the flat surface. The crackling of twigs and bracken under his feet, and the creaking of the barrow-wheel smote strangely sharp upon the stillness. Joel's eyes were fixed gloomily ahead, on a point always just in front of the barrow. He did not glance about, but was obsessed with the bleak inner world of his emotions.

Change – nothing but change and disruption still for him, it seemed. And he had been so sure that the stage was set, here at Roche, for his release from the stifling, clay-heated destiny that must be his lot while he stood alone and unloved. In a few months there would be only a bare cliff-face where he now lived. The garden would be dug away, its soil crumbling into refuse. He saw in his mind's eye the excavators scooping up the low hedge, the path, lifting the rubble of the dismantled house into lorries that would dump the surface material somewhere on the moor until the clay ground had been reached. Before summer had passed the machines would come, the destroyers. And dourly he accepted this as necessary. If the clay-pit was to expand the house must go. And as far as he was concerned the whole blow of the decision lay in its threat to separate him from Marvran. He might have welcomed the move if she were still at Falmouth. She must be told, and then…!

Joel dropped his barrow and set to work, snapping the brittle twigs close to the ground, holding them in the crook of his arm until he had a bundle and then crushing them into the barrow under his boot. He worked rapidly, almost feverishly, finding some relief in the brisk exertion.

The barrow was nearly full when a shrill yelp just ahead of him drew his eyes to a small black Pomeranian dog that had come stealthily close an begun racing round and round, excited by the sight of a wheelbarrow piled with sticks and a man bent in such a ridiculous posture. Crouching a moment in the bracken, hind legs stiffly erect, nose on the ground between flattened fore-paws, the dog surveyed Joel with impudence. Joel recognized the animal and bit his lip as the reminder stabbed afresh, but he did not straighten. He flourished a twig, and immediately Flush, for it was he, bounded sideways, resuming his shrill derisive barks; a moment later he was behind Joel, in the same position, peering expectantly at him. No encouraging movement came this time, and Flush growled softly, challenging the huge stooping figure to turn round and be mocked again.

Joel continued his work, reaching for more twigs; he had not glanced beyond the dog. His thought was too sombre to let him relax at the playful mood of an animal, and his senses were dulled by a cloud of foreboding.

Then suddenly the voice penetrated – clear, though a trifle strained:

"Good evening, Joel."

He seemed scarcely to have heard, but straightened and looked round with a slow groping tenseness. He knew who was there; Marvran, within a dozen yards of him, on the path, her face so greyly shadowed that the bright mouth with its thin smear of lipstick was somehow pitiful. His eyes wandered over her; he said clumsily:

"Ah! You, is it?"

"Yes. Out for a stroll with Flush – lovely weather, only a bit rough. You're busy!"

Joel was conscious of deepening shame as he realised the impression he must have given while she approached – a mindless thing, bent to the scorched earth. He glanced at his clothes and hands, at the wheelbarrow: coarse and dirty, they showed her the level on which he still lived, submerged in the brutish routine of his home. She must remember the glittering sophistication of the Falmouth hotel, and all this must seem to her so contemptible. He forced a smile and said in his confusion: "I look a fright, don't I?"

"Like a chimney sweep." She laughed, nervously, then sobered. "It all helps, though, when you can't afford to buy firewood. We're in the coldest part of the winter now."

Joel's face was indeed streaked with long waves of smut, and gradually a dark red flush spread about the black marks. His gaze centred on the dog, who, with nose thrust daringly between two spokes of the barrow wheel, was kicking bracken into the air with his hind legs. The conflict in Joel's mind became unbearable. He stepped forward, knocking his hands together to remove some of the smut, and a minute later stood on the edge of the path, close to her. She had not stirred, but regarded him questioningly.

He stared at her; something was struggling through his face, trying to become articulate. He made a fumbling gesture with his arm. "You've heard. I s'pose?"

"What?"

"Your mother was due to visit us this morning. Haven't she told you?"

"Nothing special; though I thought she seemed a bit worried when she came in. She couldn't have stayed more than a few minutes at your place. What's happened?"

Joel smothered a bitter laugh.

"They want to turn us out," he said.

Marvran stiffened, her face paling a little.

"Out of your house? Who?"

"Claywork bosses. Want to bring back the pit where the house is standing. Got six months to quit. Pretty thing, isn't it?"

The bright mouth was even more pitiful now as it thinned and wavered under the shock. Her eyes, too, were helpless, cloudy black pools disturbed by the heave and turmoil of her emotions. Her face looked a tragic mask in the tumbling wind-blown frame of her black curls. She drew back and said in a stifled, almost dismayed tone: "You'll have to go"

Joel tried to probe behind the mask, but could sense only the running confusion. "I s'pose so," he muttered.

"How terrible for you – so sudden. If it means losing your job…"

Again he laughed, and glanced back at the dim melancholy clay-dump looming above his home. "I wasn't thinking about that." He stepped nearer, and she sensed a new, rousing intimacy. She couldn't move, but merely stared at him, quite passive, as he continued: "You don't need me to explain anything. You've seen what's happened to me. I know you have. And now this has come."

Marvran suddenly realised that something here was alien to her and must be rejected. He saw the slow change, the features tautening, hardening.

"Perhaps it's for the best," she said dryly.

He was stabbed by this and replied with a sharp challenge: "D'you mean that?"

"Well, if you're going to move somewhere else, it's better not to tie yourself into knots here."

"But I can still hang on to what I want here," he said with dogged persistence. "'Tisn't as if we had to leave the country."

"Don't be absurd. It's bound to mean a new start for you – in every way. Perhaps you ought to be thankful."

Joel looked at her, perplexed. He noted defiance now in the red, firm line of her lips. There was a coldness about her. She had become distant, unlike herself. The mask baffled him, and having no weapon but his sincerity he blundered into further challenge: "Aren't you going to do anything?"

"What can I do about it?"

"You know what you can do all right!" he said.

Marvran's mouth relaxed, its curl rather grim, because of the hurt to herself in resisting him. She edged back to the fringe of bracken, her clenched hands bulging her coat pocket.

"This decision seems to be a stroke of luck," she commented. "It's come to check things before they go too far. Get me out of your mind, Joel: In a few months you'll be gone, probably miles away, and we may never see each other again."

She was not regarding him, but Joel watched her steadily. His passion was beating up, savagely against the barrier she presented now.

"'Tis your pride, that's all," he broke out at length. "It got to be knocked down, and there isn't no time to be lost... Listen to me!" He stepped forward and, forgetful of his smutted hands, caught her arm. "Are you going to throw away your life?"

She was startled, a little afraid of him. Her lips were drawn in, her body was tense, shrinking. "Let me go!"

He gripped her harder, knowing the crisis was upon them, the ordeal of proof and recognition.

"No. I've seen too much for that. I been wondering for weeks what to do about it but couldn't bring meself to say anything to you. Now this has pulled me up sharp, and we got to face facts."

"If only you'd face them, you'd let me alone." She struggled, but his grasp of her did not loosen.

"'Tisn't facts you're thinking of," he said. "Only tricks and lies – stuff you ought to have left behind down Falmouth."

Marvran sighed, glancing away across the moor. Flush was racing towards one of the low, rambling gravel-heaps in pursuit of a rabbit. But the sight of his urgent little body, with its tranquil domestic associations, brought no relief to her lips; she scarcely noticed, so much stronger was the grim power of the exposed landscape.

The bleak, frost-tanged dusk was pushing more darkly along the horizons; the ponderous creeping clouds seemed to drip gloom, and the wind to vex it, till the clay-range awoke to its communion with

cloud and wind. The veiled stretch of the heath with its sinuous mon-
umental dunes grew alive with forces that threatened her, fused with
Joel's heavy, stifling vitality. Her eyes swept over it, fastening at
length upon the faint blobs of light that gleamed from the cottage
windows of Trezaise. She turned back to Joel, curt in repudiation.

"I know it's no good arguing with you. You're so crude in your
outlook. You can't help it, of course, brought up as you've been..."

He flung her arm aside. "That's right, go on like the rest of 'em
and say I'm to be pitied. Whatever may be the truth about how I've
been brought up, I'm right in this business and you're wrong. And
you know you're wrong. Because you aren't being natural."

"Then why waste any more time on me?"

"I need you – that's reason enough, isn't it? I'm looking to you for
everything, and you try to stand away and look on as if you didn't
care what happened. But you do care you know you do."

"I'm sure I've never given you any cause to think so."

"I can read what your feelings are," said Joel bitterly. "That afternoon on Roche Rock and Christmas Day... Why wouldn't you speak
to me? I know what it must mean. It began that night you came
visiting us after you came back from Falmouth five months ago." He
frowned at a wanly glimmering puddle a few yards further down the
path, then added in a subdued tone: "I've stayed on here because o'
you. I meant to quit that Sunday and should ha' gone if you hadn't
pulled me up."

"Well, I'm glad if I've been that much help to you."

Joel knew that her flippancy was defensive, and that the thrust
and flux of her emotions was painful to her. He was baffled by her
mood, but was aware that she found something equally baffling,
equally obstructive, in him. But in him it was not a mood; it was his
whole nature which set her against him. He saw in her eyes that she
was searching him, probing for a quality more sensitive, flexible,
nearer the mood into which she had been schooled at Falmouth. But
he could not adapt himself to her need; he could not reach to where
she was. He offered his simple devotion from the other side of a
chasm which he could never cross, and which she could cross only on
a bridge of humiliation.

Joel moved back a few paces, stooping over the gorse, then
straightened with a dead twig in his hands. "I can make some

allowance for you being a bit stiff wi' me these days," he said, his voice hesitant and persuasive as he tried a new line of approach. "I know what you been through – 'twill take a good while for 'ee to feel easy wi' any man after that. I'd be patient for a year or two if there was something to wait for, if you'd only let me know how I could help, while you was fighting through to the old free way we had in our schooldays."

Marvran shook her head, still looking fixedly at him. "There'd be nothing to wait for. And if I'm fighting through, it isn't towards the sort of thing I knew before I went to Falmouth. That's behind me for ever."

"'Tis still alive for me," he said, snapping the twig with his twitching fingers and tossing the pieces aside. "More alive now than 'twas then; that's why I had to speak out before 'twas too late."

She seized on this and roused, though her figure was growing more cold and shadowy in the fast-deepening twilight. "But, it is too late, Joel," she said, edging restlessly into the path. "We could talk till midnight, but it would be no use. There's no common ground between us. We can't really touch..."

"We used to," he murmured.

She smiled at his naivety. He was probably thinking of some childish game in which they had held hands.

"I mean, of course, in mind and heart," she brought out falteringly, looking away from him in the direction Flush had taken. "We seem to be made of different stuff. You're as grey and heavy as the clay of your kiln; I like a fellow to show he's alive, and have a bit of colour and gaiety about him."

"You've proved what that sort o' fellow does to you," retorted Joel with a touch of his old brutal candour.

"Never mind that. I know what I can accept – nothing that's in you."

He pondered this for a moment, the sultry heat spreading up over his face again.

"Don't you want love?" he asked then, tensely.

"Not love in the raw."

He could not comprehend her. He intended only an honourable courtship and marriage, yet her words seemed to imply something dubious.

"I aren't always so rough as I look now," he said, bewildered. "I'm sure I could get in a football team again, here or wherever we shift to."

"And you think that would give a little extra polish to your love-making?"

Marvran forced a laugh, and he felt that she despised him. There was irritation as well as a dull hopelessness in his manner as he responded after a pause:

"I can't make you out, Marvy. What's got into you?"

But protests were unavailing; he realised the fact of total frustration and was silent, biting his lip.

"Well good-night!" said Marvran abruptly, and with a vague gesture of farewell she stepped along the path towards Trezaise. She held herself erect, but her movements were strained, unnatural.

Joel watched her fade into the general gloom of the moor and cloudy skyline, then shuffled back to his wheelbarrow. He heard her call Flush, her voice thin and shrill in the wind, and soon the dog raced back past him, quite close, without a glance or bark of recognition. Joel took the barrow handles, and the grating wheel and the piled black furze twigs preceded him across the downland under the indifferent stars.

CHAPTER NINE

JUST south of Barrakellis lane, filling an area of the downs between the farmstead and the roadway, was an old mica clay site, long abandoned and now densely over-grown with bushes and bramble clumps. It was difficult for a stranger to cross it without mishap at this hour of twilight, as the concrete refining channels and settling tanks had not been filled in, and some of them were five or six feet deep. No water remained in any of then, but scraps of timber with long nails jutting from the rotten wood had been thrown into many, and a fall might involve serious injury.

It was into one of the round tanks that Gwen had fallen as she hurried across this site, taking a short cut from Barrakellis to the corner of the road below Foxhole Beacon. Its bottom was moss-grown and she was unhurt, except for some scratches on the leg where brambles trailing down the side of the wall had ripped her stocking. She climbed up out of the hole with her lip bitten vexedly, and stood for a minute brushing dead leaves and spots of clay from her coat, peering about with a slightly dazed look. All was silent save for the faint brush of a rabbit which had been frightened by her approach and was scuttling among the undergrowth towards its burrow in the old clay-pit.

Gwen appeared strangely forlorn amid the bleak shadowy landscape, the chill tones of autumn sunset draining her figure of warmth and solidity. Just behind her the sun seemed to rest like a red ball on top of the earth-dump, rayless in the bluish frosty haze that was sliding down upon bar after bar of golden and yellow light which only a few minutes ago had coloured the western sky. The whole background was remote from the girl, withdrawn, leaving her to the beat of tides outside the normal wash of sensation.

Gwen had returned here from Roche last Wednesday in a mood of reaction that had caused her a deepening misery over the weekend. She had hardly slept at all on Saturday night; hour after hour she had tossed in her bed, tortured by the possibilities that lay in the latest developments at home. Now that her family were under notice to quit Roche, anything might happen. Joel would certainly make an open declaration of his love for Marvran, if he had not yet done so; and as Marvran was nineteen they wouldn't have to wait. A sudden collapse of her unnatural resistance might lead to an immediate marriage between them; and the contrast between such joy and her own frustration was growing daily unbearable to Gwen. No use reminding herself that she was nearly four years younger than Marvran, that this feeling of desperation was ridiculous at her age. It would have been, but for her family background and the fact that the love for Euan which had broken upon her was one of those intense passions which, whether they end well or tragically, are sure to make all safer levels of experience insipid. Her nature had become as incompatible with the superficial conduct of good citizenship as that of a young prostitute. Though not consciously anti-social, she was aware that no Kruse in this district could compete with respectable girls for the friendship of decent men. In Euan she had seen her only way of advance, a by-path of lonely blossomings and secret fruits, and that way appeared still closed to her.

Gwen had settled in fairly well at the farm, apart from this emotional tension. Digory found her a capable worker, efficient in cooking the simple Cornish fare required here: pasties, currant 'obbans', seed and saffron cakes; and she was making progress at milking and general dairy jobs. The routine was usually bracing; but this afternoon, by a grotesque irony, her obsession had received further edge from a commonplace incident of farm life that was now taking her with all haste to Foxhole.

She had resumed her journey and almost reached the road, picking her way cautiously, when she was startled by a rough voice calling from beyond the hedge: "Hurt yourself, my dear?"

Glancing quickly to the road she saw the head and shoulders of a woman who was standing in the ditch, pressing aside with her gloved hands the bracken on the hedge top. The figure was gaunt, clad somberly in black, and the face, turned towards the sun, showed dark and sardonic. Gwen had never seen it before, and she answered almost mechanically: "Not much – just cut me knee."

"In a hurry to git somewhere, no doubt," the woman commented, stepping back as Gwen scrambled over the low hedge and dropped into the lane a few yards further up the hill. "I know what it feel like, my dear – was young meself once, and playing the same game on this very downs though there wasn't no clayworks here then."

Gwen stared, her manner hardening defensively. "No," she said with a cool touch of scorn; "I aren't out after a chap. Going up to Foxhole to phone for the vet, that's all."

"Vet? You come from the farm down there, do 'ee?"

"Yes; Mr. Veale's. His cow's took bad."

"Having a calf, is she?"

"Yes, and it – it don't seem to be going well, so he's having the vet in to help."

A scowl had clouded the woman's face; her eyes were narrowed upon the chimneys of Barrakellis rising tall in the darkening valley. "H'm. I was just goin' down there meself. Any neighbours there wi' Veale?"

Gwen nodded. "Len Truscott's come since tea-time. They're both busy down in the cowhouse now."

She was studying the stranger's face, and suddenly illumination struck her. "I think I know who you are," she said hesitantly and with an obvious sense of recoil. "Sue Mannell?"

"Yes Cal's mother. You can see the resemblance, I expect."

"A little."

"Have 'ee seen Cal down Barrakellis yet?"

"He called once, week before last, but I don't think he'll be there again."

"I felt there was something wrong, "said Sue, moving forward with brisk familiarity. "He didn't want me to call down for some reason. In fact we had a little tug o' war just now, and he's gone off in the sulks, because I got me own way again. He can't stop me visiting me old friends. But I must put it off till things is more convenient."

"Yes, I should, now."

"Don't want to be in there wi' two old men wi' such delicate events happening. I couldn't help on that job, though if 'twas a maid there instead of a cow – you, for instance what had been took a bit sudden, I could ha' lent a hand while we waited for the doctor. I've done a bit in that line for one or two maids while I was up in Plymouth. But you don't look as if you'll be needin' any such help yet awhile."

Gwen ignored this banter and half turned, inquiring coolly: "D'you know Mr. Veale well?"

"I remember'n from the time he was younger'n you be – mind him as a boy there on the same farm. But we wasn't thick after our schooldays: decent, steady-going' chap Dig was as he growed up – picked in wi'cobbler Truscott's daughter and settled down respectable, while I was going headlong to ruin, as they called it. He can't have much in common wi' Cal if he's still the same man."

"I don't think he has."

"He and Cal have squabbled, no doubt. Cal wouldn't tell me exactly what 'twas about, but if you'm living there – I reckon I can guess!"

Gwen flushed hotly and made to hurry on, but Sue was at her side in a moment, touching her sleeve and grinning with malicious enjoyment. "Whatever happen to Cal there's sure to be a maid behind it somehow," she confided. "And if he get a hard knock one way there's nice little scores elsewhere to tickle him. He've had one this week-end; you've heard, I daresay?"

"No, nothing special."

"Well, he come home from work in high feather this afternoon. Another of his workmates ticked off fine – chap he've never liked much – floored him wi' the little game Cal been practising ever since his mother showed'n how."

Gwen's heart was fluttering wildly, and she had paled, though she kept her voice tolerably firm for the sharp demand: "What chap was that?"

"Fellow living down near Barrakellis, I believe. Called Kella – Evan or some such name."

It was what Gwen had guessed, the news she had been awaiting for weeks; her swift pulse of relief almost betrayed her into indiscretion. But instinctively she knew that this woman was not her friend, and, keeping her hands clenched in her coat pockets, she forced herself to remark with seeming unconcern: "Oh! I hadn't heard. He's really finished with that Nanpean girl?"

"Finished all right. They split last Saturday, so Cal's telling. She owned up that she and Cal've had high doings up there in the cottage, so o'course no self-respecting chap could go on with her."

She glanced eastwards past the stacks and kilns of a brickwork to the tangle of railway sidings and clay-dries in the valley below Nanpean. Several trucks were being shunted over there, and the clang and jangle of the buffers fitted Sue's mood. Her voice had a rasp in it, though she spoke jestingly.

"I dunno what Kella will do next. I was pulling Cal's leg tea-time, saying he ought to advise 'n to emigrate."

As Gwen stared in perplexity Sue pointed away to the west, where the sand-heaps loomed like the wreckage of ghostly ships along the horizon.

"Over, to Scilly Isles, I mean," Sue explained. "You know I got a daughter on St. Mary's, I daresay.

"Mr. Veale said you had," replied Gwen vague and indifferent. She again moved forward, but Sue also turned, and the pair began ascending the hill together Gwen walking in the ditch and frowning at the clay-smeared road.

"Called Lorraine, she is," continued Sue aggressively. "Twenty year younger than Call; and no two people couldn't be more unlike each other. Lorraine have got her mother's good looks, but nothing of her mother's spirit, I'm sorry to say."

"Born up the country somewhere, wasn't she?" asked Gwen, still vague, following her own thought under the mechanical surface response to Sue.

"Plymouth, my dear – Barbican; that's where she came from. One o' these war babies. Her dad was a soldier, though he went off to fight before she was born and I never saw no more of him. I had to rear the chiel meself as best I could. 'Twas pretty slummy, and a more tiresome job than bringing up Cal; I was only seventeen when he was born, and hadn't been worn down and pushed from pillar to post like I was when I got to Plymouth."

"How long have you been on St, Mary's?" Gwen inquired.

"Nearly nine year. 'Twas a sudden move – one o' the few times when I've acted like a good mother. I'd come on Lorraine one night in Drake's Circus, looking a bit lost, She was a big plump maid, nearly thirteen, so I thought 'twas time we quit Plymouth or she'd soon be on the streets. And I needed a change meself: city life wasn't what I was brought up to. I like a bit o' fresh air. As I didn't want to bring her back here close to Cal, with all me old neighbours slinging mud at her, I gived in when she asked if we could go over Scilly to live as far away as she could get from they docklands."

Sue cleared her throat, scowling at the corner where she and Gwen would part, now only fifty yards ahead. The sense of general frustration nettled her; there was a hard scorn in her voice when she resumed: "And there the maid is still, like a thing split in two pieces – half of her wanting life in the raw same as she got used to in Plymouth, and half wanting the flowery dreams and sweet little ways what fit in wi' Scilly. And as she can't find both in the same man she's just stuck – ha'n't had no chap at all yet, beyond a few casual friends. So you can see now why I'd give the hint to Kella."

Gwen looked up quickly, her face blank, puzzled. "Not exactly," she said.

"Well, he do seem to be split very similar," commented Sue, her eyes probing the girl. "Part of him hankering after the book-learning and polish he was trained for, and part only wanting to muck around in the clay-pit and have another go at Cal like he did last November. So if he and Lorraine was to meet they might soon be two, as the saying is. I'd be tickled if he did take the hint and got Cal for a brother-in-law one day. But I reckon 'tis doubtful."

Gwen relaxed, her swift, cryptic smile answering the jeering twinkle in Sue's eyes. "Yes, I think it is," she agreed, guarding herself, but poised without tension now that she was being rid of the woman' company. They had reached the corner where a by-lane forked back to Carloggas under the shaggy hump of Foxhole Beacon.

Sue paused for a moment, lifting her gloved hand in farewell.

"I'll see 'ee down Barrakellis soon," she called as Gwen hurried on into a gloomy section of road that had been cut through the soft rock of the Beacon.

The remark was ignored; not until Gwen reached the top of the hill did she glance back. The sun had disappeared; earth and sky alike had taken on the hazy stiffness and passivity of the winter frosts an incongruous setting for the hot, vivid palpitations that had broken so suddenly upon her numbed spirit. She saw that the hill was empty, though there was a slight uneasiness in the knowledge that Sue had only temporarily been turned aside; her parting words held a menace, as though her design was to break up the present order of things at Barrakellis.

But Gwen's true mood evaded this threat as she peered beyond the farm towards Euan's home. The shadow of Lela had gone from it, and the sordid details didn't matter, only the fact that Euan was now free, that the passion she had felt welling in him during their walk across the downs could now flood nakedly to her, unforbidden, and lift her to the heights of communion. To-night she could think without pain of Joel's possible marriage to Marvran, confident in the belief that Euan would soon seek her out.

CHAPTER TEN

JOEL had been so disturbed after his encounter with Marvran that he almost forgot the meeting with Crago. Charlie was not at the clay-tip during those few days. There was nothing to remind Joel of the mysterious summons, except a craving for relief from the nightmare thrown around him by the other, darker news. He set out on Saturday evening in a dull mood, seeking only a temporary stimulus such as he had previously found at the public house.

Towards nine o'clock he was striding grimly through Roche. His hands were in the pockets of his thin, clay-smeared raincoat, his face was sombre under the low-drawn cap. He spoke to no one, looked at nothing as he moved from shadow into the glare of street lamps, and again into shadow, on past faintly lighted windows, houses from which laughter at times smote out. He passed from the village into silence, darkness. The roadway sloped, grew narrower. There was no view except straight ahead, where across the valley he saw the claywork lights east of St. Dennis, blurred by the drizzle. His brain seemed fogged and deadened; he moved mechanically, neither braced for an encounter nor curious about his meeting with Crago.

Drawing near the corner where Charlie had promised to be waiting, Joel slackened his pace somewhat, as if warned subtly of danger. His eyes narrowed, scowling as he approached the bend of the hill. Before he reached it a movement by the hedgeside caught his attention, a solid grey figure stepped into the road and swung slowly towards him. Joel halted and stared in bewilderment.

The girl drew close; he saw vaguely her pale, puffy face, and as her eyes met his he felt a strange magnetic fascination thrill through him.

"Joel?" asked her soft wheedling voice.

"Yes," he muttered fumbling stupidly at his coat. "Why, who... what d'you want?"

The girl laughed quietly. "You expected to meet Charlie?"

"Isn't he coming?"

"He couldn't manage it tonight... You guess what it means, don't you?"

Suddenly Joel comprehended. "So Crago didn't mean to come! He was just your tool?"

Olive was studying his face, which was tense with shock, though not clearly visible. "I had to go carefully, she said. "Thought you mightn't turn up if I let you know I'd be waiting."

Joel took a step sideways towards the ditch; he glared in dark impotent anger. "Well?"

"I've been up around the 'dry' where you work," Olive continued slowly, several days. I didn't dare to be too bold, or people would have warned you off. I've never seen you there, so I thought this was the best plan."

She came nearer, her eyes warily searching him.

"You look a tough chap all right – exactly as Charlie said, she commented. "Just in my line. I'm sick of these delicate little fellows – they're dried up in no time. You're a real man, and that's what I want."

Joel was still dazed; he leaned weakly against the damp hedge and let her proceed.

"Shall we begin to-night or d'you want time to think it over?" Olive laughed, laying a hand on his sleeve. He tried to wrench his arm away, but it was already pressed against the hedge and she did not release it. She squeezed his hard muscle possessively. "It's all right Joel. I'm just what you've been looking for, aren't I?"

Joel stared at her, and out of his stupor a flash of memory stung him to an awareness that this situation must be handled more effectively that the one Marvran had thrust upon him last week. That encounter among the charred furze! The contrast with this present duel was torturing. He saw Olive, the smouldering, heavy face and body, eager to yield herself to the naked, inflamed heave of his blood-consciousness. He remembered Marvran: aloof and frigid, burdening him with her ambiguous silences, her quick reserves and repulsions. Yet the true fire burned behind that mask, while this potent freedom was but a counterfeit. The paradox was baffling, but blindly he clung to it; loathing bristled in him.

"Reckon you're too late," he muttered.

"Oh no. I'm not going to take that. Charlie told me you aren't fixed up with anyone – never had a real love affair. And I can see you haven't."

"Crago don't know everything about me." Joel pushed her from him with a lunge that sent her staggering into the middle of the road. "I don't want you. Get away."

She eyed him narrowly.

"You don't mean that, dear. You're a little bit scared... are you? You needn't be." Her tone grew gentler, caressing. "Come on now there's nobody to see. Just let me know I can expect developments."

Joel still tussled with the two images, the mental and the actual, too bruised to make any gesture of resistance as she stepped again to his side.

"I've heard o' your family. We're both off the beaten track – no decency or anything to live up to. Why should we care? We can do what we like and nobody'd care tuppence. You know there's no other girl who'd look at you."

Dully Joel said "Why not? I've never played wild like you have. People remember me back in me teens when I was in Roche football team... And even since I quit 'tis only been the drink and – I've chucked that now."

"Trying to get respectable enough for some high-class young lady? Poor Joel!"

He laughed at her taunt, but could think of no rational argument or retaliation. Between his will and all such weapons lay the dead weight of the mental image, Marvran's repulse.

Olive sensed the struggle in him; she spoke more urgently, leaning so close that her hair brushed his ear.

"Take your chance, Joel. Don't waste thought on those little prigs. You're a man. And I'm a woman; and I like you. You're the sort that mean business. And I mean business too."

Joel trembled. The images clashed, bitterly wounding him. Here was a woman who wanted him, and met him on a level he understood, while he loved a woman who wanted him but protected herself from the desire, fearing it, waiting for him to use the tools she understood – the delicacy and elasticity of approach that were so utterly beyond his range.

Olive sensed the need in him and resumed. "I know your type, Joel. You want a girl to lead you all the way and not leave you guessing about what she feels."

"That's about it," he agreed, despite himself.

"Somebody warm and comfy to make you feel safe, and not give you problems to work out, eh?

"Yes, I s'pose I do," he said with a groping surprised glance at her.

"Well, you won't get that from 'decent' girls these days, even village girls. They couldn't make it clear to you, the way they put out their feelers. They'll drop all sorts of subtle hints that a slick fellow could pick up. But simple straightforward fellows like you – you wouldn't twig a thing, or get a step nearer anything serious. You've found that already, I expect."

He did not answer, but the clenching of his hands confirmed her suspicion. And as she glanced towards Roche she gave an abrupt start, her thought focused.

"I wonder…is it Crebas' girl who's upset you?" She turned back to him with a new jealous urgency. "I've heard about her come home from Falmouth a mincing little snob, pretending she knows the world. She lives nearest you – went to school with you, I expect, didn't she?"

Joel remained stubbornly unresponsive, breathing heavily, his eyes staring past her, very still.

"Used to be a sort o' Lady Bountiful to your family, believe, and if she's taken up that role again I can guess what's happened."

The words seemed to reach him from a distance; he was dully aware of their penetration and of himself responding with a shrug of irritation: "Never mind she!"

"Try to forget her, if she's hurt you." The voice was coming nearer, breaking him open with soft, dark thrusts. "Her sort's no good to you. Even if they felt anything for you there'd be no way in - you couldn't master the tricks…"

Joel shivered, lurching away from the hedge, which was becoming wet as the drizzle turned to sharp rain. Olive followed him, but he evaded the full personal revelation.

"Why must girls be like that?" he asked. "Isn't there no middle way between all this slick play-acting and – your sort?"

"Not nowadays. We're supposed to be civilised, you see! You won't find anyone simple and direct and virtuous; so it seems there's only me if you're going to get what you want."

He was stubborn again, reaching for the old foothold. "But you couldn't give me what I want," he protested, his voice hard and thick as he clumsily buttoned his coat collar against the rain. "I seen something different."

"In Miss Creba?"

The irony was almost too much for him, but it struck an illumination. "It come wi' she, but ...'twasn't in her," he said.

Olive frowned. "You've been imagining things – put her on a pedestal. Of course."

"No, 'twasn't any fancies like that," he replied, his eyes catching the pale glint of the claywork flood-lights, and smouldering with emotions that puzzled her. "'Twas something deeper – something you wouldn't have a clue to."

Olive was aware now of the difference in him. She became puzzled for a moment.

"You're getting tied up inside yourself, brooding like this," she observed slowly. "You need to be pulled out o' yourself the way I could do it."

"How'd that mend matters if you can't give what I'm after?"

"But it would be final – permanent; not just an hour's pleasure. If we got married..."

Joel laughed derisively. The prospect was so grotesque, yet the sense of her surrender, the rude female power exposed and vulnerable to him, struck through to the male nerve. He felt an odd thrust towards mastery, relieved from the strain Marvran imposed upon him. But with this, and soon overwhelming it, was the knowledge that this potent freedom was not his victory but only a means of escape from the unequal contest for the true life he had glimpsed. And as Olive again caught his arm he felt the rage of his frustration return upon him, the necessity of choosing between these alternatives – Olive's lure or the resistance of the subtly guarded, subtly challenging virginity of Marvran.

Olive noted the crisis point; she slipped an arm suddenly round his neck, pushed her face forward and kissed him. "There! Come on. We'll go back home now if you like, and talk it over. 'Tisn't far."

There had been a moment of black-out under the kiss, but as the sensation died out along his nerves it touched off the explosion of anger. "I'll give 'ee something to lay off that!" he spluttered, his voice almost inarticulate with fury.

Olive cowered away from him, raised her hand to protect herself and gave a low cry.

Joel approached her, a brutish male mass in the darkness. She saw the glint of his eyes and the bared teeth as his arm jerked up to strike.

Around the corner at that instant came two dimly moving forms, a pair of lovers, clasped together in watchful silence. Joel slunk back at once into the hedgeside, breathing hard, and glared as they drew nearer. Olive stood by the hedge opposite, and as the couple passed the girl addressed her cheekily:

"Good night, Buzz!"

Joel recognized the speaker as a St. Dennis baggage. Her companion was silent, but Joel, peering closely at the tall wiry figure, had a strong suspicion which Olive immediately confirmed.

"Wish I was so lucky, Charlie," she said with strained flippancy. "'Tis hard work here."

Crago laughed.

As the pair receded into the darkness Joel lurched out from the gutter, and stumbled away uphill towards Roche.

When Marvran returned from her eventful walk over the downs, her parents did not at once observe any fresh sign of emotional disturbance in her. They had been discussing the forthcoming eviction of the Kruses, and this had distracted them from their normal concern about Marvran. They hoped that she too might be diverted from personal worries by this news, and mentioned it in her presence several times during the week-end. They were perplexed when on each occasion she soon rose and left the room in a state of suppressed agitation.

Marvran knew that she was approaching another crisis, and she bore the mounting tension in secret. In a way it was a relief that no-one guessed her predicament. It seemed fantastic that such a complication should have arisen so soon after her return from Falmouth.

Her instinctive gravitation towards Joel was as embarrassing as her break with Pearce, and almost as painful. The pressure was relentless; there was no relaxation to mere friendship or neighbourliness in any of their meetings. They were always swept into confused, passionate depths of significance. Even at Christmas, when she had ignored him during her visit to the Kruses' home, the sense of baulked intimacy troubled her. She had been fretted into keen self-reproach by the memory of Joel squatting on the bottom stair in the kitchen, very quiet and withdrawn, rather pathetically waiting for her to notice him; at length taking Ruth on to his knee and stroking her hair, groping for comfort in his sick disappointment.

Their encounter on the moor had brought their relationship into the open, and Marvran was aghast to find the problem so much deeper than the social gulf between their families. She and Joel were alien types; if they were to fuse one of them must absorb the other. She feared the strong male life in him, knowing that it could destroy her superficial individuality. And because that individuality must be safeguarded she felt more remote from him now, hardening in rejection of his values, while desperately craving the full release.

While Joel fought his duel with Olive an atmosphere of crisis broke within the bungalow. Supper proceeded quietly at first, almost in silence. The three Crebas looked troubled, and the electric light in the kitchen cast about them a fantasy without cheer. Marvran had eaten little, and kept her eyes lowered except for an occasional glance of peculiar hardness at one or other of her parents. They sat opposite her, facing the window, the curtain of which was not drawn.

Eli at length pushed back his tea-cup and stretched himself, then with a puzzled frown at his daughter he commented abruptly: "Time you was visitin' they Kruses again, Marvran. You need somethin' like that – keep it up till you'm on your feet proper."

Marvran glanced from Hester to her father, clearly on the verge of an outburst. It came. "That lot! I should think you'd got them on the brain. It's all I hear of."

Hester, who had not yet finished her supper, said gently. "They won't be here much longer, Marvran; we ought to do all we're able. 'Tis a bad job for all of 'em – dunno where they'll find anybody who'll do for 'em like we have; and left to theirselves, goodness only knows where they'll get."

Marvran leaned across the table. "If only we'd left 'em to themselves!" she cried bitterly, launching a reckless charge at both parents. "It's all your fault – this muddle I've got into! What did you ever mix with those Kruses for?"

"Why, my dear!" exclaimed Hester, astonished. She controlled herself. "I know that Zachary and Sarah aren't exactly pleasant company…"

"I don't mean them."

Hester's dark eyes searched the girl through her steel-rimmed spectacles. Her pale sensitive face puckered under her thick greying hair.

"Something's upset you," she observed. "What is it?"

"Can't you guess?"

"It surely can't be anything to do with Joel?"

"I'm afraid it is."

Eli gave a start, leaning back in his chair with arched brows. "What've he done to upset 'ee?"

Marvran said with biting irony. "Fallen in love with me; that's all."

The parents exchanged a swift glance; silence fell upon the room. Flush, who had been gnawing a bone under the table, left it, crossed to the hearth and looked with head cocked questioningly at the three seated figures. In that sudden stillness he was unheeded.

Eli spoke next, his sharp red face screwed into an expression of grotesque incredulity. "Joel struck on 'ee?"

"It seems so. He started making advances to me last time I saw him."

"But – you haven't even been close friends," objected Hester.

"I know. He – just blundered into it."

Eli shifted his feet on the floor; at which movement Flush, fearing for the safety of his bone, darted back under the table.

"A fella like that!" muttered Eli, breathing hard, and glaring from his wife to Marvran. "He ought to know better – decent maid like you.! I shall tackle him at the works about this."

"No, don't dad, for goodness sake! It'd spread all over the place. Besides, you can't argue it out of him; he hasn't got the intelligence to understand. Keep quiet and it'll die out - they've got to leave". Marvran drew herself erect, very pale, but relieved that the confession was now made. "You see, don't you, why I can't go on visiting that family?"

"Of course." Hester passed a hand unsteadily across her forehead. "I never dreamed that such a thing...It can't be helped, anyhow; and if you keep out of his way till they've left, there'll be no harm done."

Marvran made no comment, and for a while silence again brooded tensely in the room. The parents sat stiffly, hands gripping the table's edge. Feeling Flush against her leg Marvran stooped and stroked him. Flush growled, warning her that the brush had been quite accidental. She felt lonely and repulsed, strangely naked and vulnerable, with an itch of resentment against the whole cramping situation. When she straightened up her face was dark, feverish, her voice almost desperate.

"But I can't go on in this rut! It'll drive me crazy – one thing after another. Don't you think it's time I tried to get back to normal again?"

Eli was staring through the window, his mind on practical issues which he had recently discussed with this wife. He nodded slowly as he turned to Marvran.

"Would 'ee like to git another job somewhere?" he asked hesitantly. "You've nearly run through your savings; been home here for six months."

"I know; I shall have to do something soon. But I can't go back to Falmouth, and I don't want to go off to a strange town; and as for a job in a poky little village shop – it'd be too deadly dull after the hotel."

Eli frowned at his empty cup. "The real truth is I s'pose, like Bassett d'say at the 'dry' – you need to git settled," he said with awkward delicacy.

"Well, I can't do that while I stay cooped up here. I don't want any more of these crude village ways, like Joel's – so horrible, the way he came up and grabbed hold of me..."

"He went that far?" said Hester, shocked.

Marvran nodded. "He was half cracked, I should think. He'd just heard about having to quit the place, and it upset him. Acting like a great brute..."

Marvran spoke excitedly, half-laughing, half-crying, in a state bordering on hysteria. Eli reached out and caught her shoulder.

"If thing's is got to that pitch," he said firmly, "the sooner you get in wi' your old decent pals the better. Joel would take the hint, I expect, if he saw 'ee havin' a good time wi' a crowd he couldn't join."

Marvran braced herself; she rose and pushed her chair close in against the table. "I shall look up some of my old school chums in the next few days, and get some dates fixed," she said. But her tone revealed a nature stung and bruised, and her casual manner was unconvincing.

CHAPTER ELEVEN

ON the morning of the first Thursday in February, Charlie Crago arrived with the claywork company's lorry at the 'dry' where Joel worked. He arrived in time to prevent a minor crisis on this particular kiln, and unwittingly to precipitate a major crisis on that inner kiln which was Joel's emotional battleground.

The day was dark and thundery, with a biting wind that chilled the four men working in a row along the front of the bleak, cold shed, tossing dried clay-cubes into the vehicle. Eli, Joel and Bassett were now engaged in the loading, as they had been forced to suspend their normal activities. There was no fire in the furnace and no slurry had been brought in from the tanks for several days, the storage linhay being already stacked full. This condition led Bassett to utter many dark prophecies, and in his truculent perversity he seemed almost resentful that the arrival of the fresh order had prevented the works from closing down.

Noting his unusual silence Eli spoke abruptly, with a somewhat strained force. The proximity of Joel was disturbing: he realised now that Joel's moodiness was due to his preoccupation with Marvran, but he had followed her advice and said nothing. However he believed Joel guessed that Marvran had revealed his secret to her parents.

"Good job you've come, Charlie," he remarked, standing on the extreme left of the group and vaguely outlined against the shed's dim interior. "If you hadn't hustled along this week to take some 'o this off us we'd ha' had to say good-bye to our wages for a bit. We've been busy down around the pit bottoms this last day or two – not a scrap o' work to be done here."

Charlie shook his head, looking very lean as he stood high up, hunched under the roof on the pile of white blocks.

"Tis somethin' of a cut-back" he admitted. "Same all over the district. Output's dropped be thousands o' tons since December."

"Fact is," observed Eli, who was working beside Bassett, divided from the other two by a stone pillar, "We had a bit of a boom two year ago, and now we got to pay for it. There's a whack o' clay in stock what ha'n't been got rid of. But I reckon things'll level up again when that's sold out."

Bassett frowned; he threw a cube with such contemptuous vigour that it fell into the road on the other side of the lorry. "Not a bit of it!" he shouted, his fat red face jerking to and fro in emphatic dissent. "There's another slump comin' – I've seed it on the way. Slumps do always come when people start braggin'. Worst days for clayworks is yet to be. What can 'ee expect? Near everthing's done by machinery, and trade agreements aren't no more dependable than women, now Hitler's upsettin' our markets in Europe. A boom couldn't come nowhow, and you moonshiners got to eat yer words. I told 'ee of it, but no! you would have it that things was buckin' up, better and better, till all of us'd be rollin' in money and out-swankin' the Cap'ns." He turned to Joel as he stooped for more blocks.

"That pit there be Kruses' place is back to half-time...isn't it, Joel?"

Joel nodded glumly, squatting back on his heels to dislodge some cubes that had become jammed.

"If things is goin' smash," continued Bassett, intensifying his familiar aggressive tone, "what're 'em turnin' 'ee out for? Cap'n said they must pull down the house to make room for expandin', but if things go on at this rate the works'll soon be shut up."

"I wouldn't say you'd have to leave if that happened," Eli remarked; leaning over the clay his voice was muffled and uneasy. "Everything's uncertain at the moment, but I aren't expecting' the down-grade to go that far."

"Hope you stay on, Joel," said Bassett; not that he desired Joel to stay, but he was forced to take the opposite view to that which he felt latent in Eli's speech. "Now your family seem to be settlin' a bit smoother – Gwen in decent service – you could level things up and get more chummy around here. Try and join the football team again, old buck; we've missed 'ee pretty bad this last two seasons. You used to draw the maids' eyes when you was in shorts and jersey out on the fields, and could again if you got back your old form."

A dull flush burned beneath the clay powdering Joel's cheeks; he straightened with a lump of clay in each hand, turning his back to Bassett.

"That's all behind me and finished with," he muttered.

No further word was spoken for several minutes. The men ducked and straightened with swift, silent movements; the clay blocks flew, alighting with soft thuds amid the pile which already half filled the lorry, while the fine dust was blown in clouds, sometimes across the road, sometimes into the men's faces, causing them to shut their eyes. Their heavy breathing showed that they worked whole-heartedly; now and then a cough from one or other of them told that the dust had got into his throat.

Presently, throwing up a block which knocked against the roof, Charlie stepped back and winked around the pillar at Eli. "Your maid's beginning to open up anyhow, isn't she? Not exactly in the ladies' football team yet, but on the way to it. Been to a dance or two, so I hear."

"Yes – going down St. Dennis to-night to pictures," mumbled Eli, glancing again uneasily at Joel. "Can't keep her in wi' we old fogies."

Charlie whistled, leaning against the pillar to light a cigarette. "I was meaning to go there meself this evening wi' some bit o' fluff," he said musingly. "May be able to see who Marvran do take up with. I bet she'll set her cap somewhere after being off duty so long. Got to make up for lost time. Pretty piece too – I mind her. She won't be hard up for what she want." He looked slyly back at Joel – a glance which was ignored. "We'll all get paired off in good time," he said. "Joel won't need to turn footballer again. He's leading the way already – he and old Buzz..."

"What?"

The word came from Eli, and in a moment a thrill of drama had swept through the group. All four men stood erect in tense attitudes.

Bassett's japing eyes fixed Joel with a long probing stare, and a low chuckle escaped him. "Now we'll hear something worth listenin' to," he observed mockingly. "I told 'ee what 'twould come to wi' she hanging round the 'dry' so often."

"You'm right," began Charlie, but before he could enlighten them a hand fell on his shoulder like a vice. Joel was there; he looked dangerous, and said between his teeth: "You'd better keep that bitch out of it."

Crago hesitated for a moment, twisting about to face Joel, pale and defiant; then he shrank back and commented with a sickly grin: "Huh! He wants to keep it hushed up. All right – anything to oblige."

It was a turn of things as critical as it was sudden, and throughout the remaining period of loading the men were silent. From Eli's expression it could be seen that he had received a shock and was seriously disturbed. It was clear that Charlie knew something which, confronted with Joel's threat, he was afraid to tell. Could it mean that Joel had realised that his love for Marvran was hopeless? Or would this lead to further complications? More apprehensively than ever Eli watched Joel's face: dark, sullen and impassive.

Behind that mask Joel's mind, stung by jealousy, aware of looming dangers, had made a decision.

A thunderstorm had broken upon the district when, towards ten o'clock that night, Joel entered Roche. He had walked the four miles to St. Dennis earlier in the evening and, hidden in a cottage gateway just below Robartes Road, had seen Marvran arrive at the cinema among a group of her old school chums. He had stood for a while watching the building with a fixed rebellious stare, then returned over Carne Hill in a glum mood of frustration.

It was not that he objected to Marvran having friends or taking recreation with them. He had tasted crowd emotions himself, even popularity, in his early passion for sport, though always there had been a difference, a stoical reserve and bitter irony which at least isolated and paralysed him. But it was the motive underlying Marvran's resumed social contacts that worried him now. He knew that her presence her to-night was a direct result of his making advances to her nearly three weeks ago. She was clutching at these gaieties to escape, not so much from him as from her feelings for him, feelings that threatened the role she had chosen for herself. Her heart bruised still with the humiliation of that Falmouth affair, he knew she was in no immediate danger from men. But why on earth need she cheat herself, take the meaningless friendship of these young fellows when she might have the love of the one man who cared for her and whom she, by instinct, wanted?

The storm grew with Joel's revolt and was at its height by the time he reached his native village. The streets were deserted; lightning ripped through the steady flare of their lamps, while the thunder, almost directly overhead, crackled and roared as the clouds let down torrential rain.

Joel paid little heed to it, but hurried up the hill, anxious to reach home, for a clammy dampness had penetrated his thin clothes to his skin. As he turned the corner opposite the church he kept close to the ditch, and bumped without warning into a crouching figure who at once let loose a stream of maudlin abuse.

Joel recognized Zachary, and the bitterness of his position rebounded more darkly upon him. Marvran free and superior, polished in communal life; his father here, drunk, outcast! The gulf between them! He asked sharply and with disgust: "What the hell's wrong with you, you fool? Take hold of my arm and get along with you."

Zachary shrank back as he grew aware that the intruder was his son; he knew this mood in Joel too well to maintain his belligerent temper against it. He became cowed and sullen, peering up at Joel resentfully, but making no resistance as Joel dragged him from the gutter and led him forward over the brow of the hill. They had soon passed the Crebas' bungalow, and Joel stared rebelliously at the lighted parlour window. Its serenity mocked him, and roused him to a fiercer sympathy with the savage elemental world beyond it; the shrill whine of the wind against the outer crags of the Rock, its moanings within the cell, the blurred boom of thunder receding northward over Bodmin Moor. He walked in silence, irritated by Zachary's frequent lunges and mutterings, moving more slowly when they turned into the lane and began ascending the dark slope of the heath. The thorn trees beside the hedge were flailing madly, their fibre strained almost to breaking point by the heave and buffet of the gale. Near the Kruses' cottage sand from the dump was being blown about like hail, stinging the men's faces as they approached; Zachary kept his sleeve drawn across his eyes, whimpering. The rain had eased a little, but so severe had been the downfall that thin streams were goring new channels down the sides of the dump and the clay-pit in which the storm water leats were flooded and could be heard gurgling and splashing in remote depths.

At the garden gate Joel shook of Zachary's arm and hurried ahead of him up the path. He was quite near the porch before he realised that the door was open and that Sarah was standing on the threshold. She greeted him excitedly, her usual stolid manner dissolved by the impact of crisis. "That you,' Joel?"

"Yes."

"Where've 'ee been so long? Not down pub, have 'ee?"

"No, not to-night," came the tense reply. "Where I've been's my own business. What you waiting here for? Any damage done?"

"Better come in and see," answered Sarah, starting slightly and scowling into the darkness as the swaying figure of her husband loomed up behind Joel. "There's a hole tore in the roof – rain beating in already: soaked Ruth's bed and made a pool on the canvas."

Joel peered up at the low eaves, near which some loosened slates were rattling. He seemed to be measuring his strength against a general onslaught of calamity.

"'Tis a devil of a night!" he muttered.

Zachary clutched at the porch, rendered frantic by his impotence and isolation. "Wha's marrer 'ere?" he demanded in shrill, quavering tones. "Wha's marrer?"

Sarah glared at him, her hands clenched, her body stiffening with rage.

"Just like you to git home drunk on night like this! May have to work to stop the place from fallin' to pieces. Damn lot o' good you are when a man's needed about the house."

She retreated back indoors, Joel following her in glum silence. As he entered the dark kitchen he remembered that August evening when he had come in from the clay-pit and been nauseated by the heat and slime of this underworld. Calm summer moonlight had softened the room then; now there was only the vindictive flicker of lightning, the winter storm. His life was certainly darker and more stricken now than it had been then. The impact of beauty that had arrested his flight had worked cruelly to increase his dereliction. If only he had left home before Marvran arrived, and taken lodgings in Bugle or Stenalees. He might have been courting some decent girl by now; perhaps been back in a football team. He would have escaped the tension of being torn between Marvran and Olive. But he was still here, more than ever sealed and ravaged by his fate.

118

Slowly Sarah groped her way up the stairs, and as Joel came after her he caught a faint gleam of light from the landing. A lamp was burning in the front bedroom, which was used by the parents. There was a strong draught: Sarah's thin grey hair flapped about her head, even her clothes fluttered as she stepped, red-faced and panting, on to the upper floor. Joel felt a spatter of rain on his cheek, slanting out from the girls' bedroom in front of the stairs, the door of which was open.

Zachary climbed nervously behind Joel, sometimes crawling and holding rigidly to the banisters. His maudlin appeals and curses were unheeded.

Sarah shuffled into her bedroom for the lamp, jerking her hand towards the girls' room. Joel saw that Pearl was squatting in a stupefied condition on the parents' bed, and passed on at once into the damaged apartment. Arthur stood just inside it, wearing only his trousers and a ragged shirt; he peered at Joel vacantly, his eyes dilated, fear-ridden. There were no carpets on the floor, no curtains to the widow, and the roof sloped so that in the far corner none of the adults could stand upright.

Sarah soon lumbered out from her room, and Zachary, staggering at that moment on to the landing, clutched at her sleeve in desperation.

"Wha's up? Wha's up?" he kept repeating hoarsely.

Sarah pushed him from her, and without answering she entered the back room where Joel and Arthur waited for the lamp. Its light, as Sarah raised it, showed that the window was intact, but a dark gash was observable in the roof, several slates having been ripped off. Some had been whirled into the clay-pit, while others, falling between the rafters, had crashed through the plaster ceiling and made a heap of debris near the bed. Ruth was huddled in the corner, partly screened by a tin trunk, trying to escape the raindrops that were blown erratically by the veering gusts of wind. She was half naked, her underwear being in rags, clinging damply about her frail, shivering body. She looked up at Joel with a numbed appeal out of the rigor of coldness and fright.

Sarah placed the lamp on a cane-bottomed chair as Zachary limped into the room, and for several minutes the family took in the squalid scene, grimly accepting it.

"Lucky Gwen isn't here," remarked Joel abruptly, his thought groping back among memories of Gwen that steadied him against the sense of disaster. "But we can't let Ruth stay like this all night. She can have my bed – me and Arthur'll sleep downstairs; but she must change her clothes first."

"Her others isn't dry from the wash yet," grumbled Sarah. She stepped across and fingered the child's nightdress. "Um; this is brave'n wet, might catch cold sleeping in it. She'll have to have the one Gwen left her what used to be Marvran's – too big for her, but 'tis all we got." She scowled up at the rotten beams, her manner hardening.

"Always some blemmin' nuisance. They let the place go to wreck and ruin and then talk o' turning us out! I'd like to make the bloody bosses live here!"

Joel turned with a sudden steeling of resolve; there was a challenge in the situation that fitted his mood. At least it was something outside the confused heat of his emotions, something against which he could match his physical strength.

"I'd better go out now," he said, forcefully, "and search around for a bit of stuff to patch the roof, else the hole'll spread right across and none o' the bedrooms won't be safe to sleep in. I'll bring in a ladder from the works and a few sheets o' galvanise if I can find any. Hendra works is closed down this week so nobody's likely to notice anything been took, and I don't care a damn if they do."

The family stared at him, wondering at his fierce truculent tone; but they made no comment. He left immediately, hurrying downstairs and soon slamming the outer door behind him.

CHAPTER TWELVE

MARVRAN expected to be alone on the following Sunday evening while her parents were at chapel. She was in no mood to go with them and hear the gossip of the neighbours, crudities of village life rooted in primitive drives of instinct. Events were converging to release her from the stifling earthiness of such a world. For several months it had threatened her through Joel, but its pressure had been dwindling for some weeks, and seemed now to be finally blunted by the shock of learning, earlier that day of Joel's possible downfall at the hands of a prostitute.

The news had come suddenly, while she was keeping up her defensive battle, struggling to settle afresh into the normal happy mood of youth. She had returned from a dance at midnight, feeling that Joel was again a distant, uncouth image, almost as remote from her as when she lived at Falmouth, yet still aware of a fascination and a peril that might sweep her back unless she maintained her resistance. But in mid-morning, while she and Eli were in the garden, he had mentioned the incident at the clay-dry last Thursday when Crago had linked Olive's name with Joel's.

"Wouldn't let Charlie speak, he wouldn't," said Eli. "That must mean he got something to cover up..."

This revelation had at first left Marvran amid a flux of uneasiness. The situation was personal for her, accusing and challenging. She knew that if Joel had not already fallen, she alone could save him; but perhaps her repulse had sent him to Olive immediately, in the bitterness of his despair, and the fact that she had belied her true feelings in rejecting him further disturbed her. But as the evening drew on the fever passed, and she felt a new hard clarity of independence.

Marvran was not by nature a primitive. She had always possessed something of the artificial dignity that belongs to the more refined strata of village life. Her grandparents, Hester's people, had kept a prosperous drapery store at Bugle, and that side of the family had bequeathed to her a social tone which, but for her common sense and the warm, simple heartiness of her upbringing, might have become snobbish. Even before she went to Falmouth she had not been a raw undisciplined country girl. She had refined the spirit of the soil by singing in the chapel choir and at local concerts, and trying, though unsuccessfully, to become carnival queen of Roche. She was not a sensuous, smouldering creature, not earthy or capable of those odd, irrational whims of devotion that mark the true peasant mentality. She could never have turned to the old Celtic superstitions, or felt anything but repulsion towards the gods of blood-intimacy whose influence still brooded about the Rock, and who were considered by some villagers more worthy of worship than the civilised gods of intellectual advancement and material comfort. She had not, indeed, worshipped these modern gods, for she was still comparatively une-ducated; but she approved of them, unthinkingly, moving with the progressive elements of working class society which she felt to be superior to the earthy, primitive values represented by Joel and Olive. She could not accept the prospect of a liaison between those two as a challenge; her instinct was to recoil from it in disgust, to retreat and hide from such fumbling monstrosity until it had passed over her like a thundercloud and left her free to steal out again into the brilliance of her role as an adult citizen.

Memories of Olive, whose early scandals she had heard of before she left school, broke upon her with an obscene personal clarity at odd moments during the day; her fascinated glances at the lighted bedroom window of the Buzzas' home when now and then she passed it on a winter's evening; one or two glimpses of Olive in the summer twilight entering or leaving claywork huts or creeping behind hedges or towards knots of woodland with some stray lover. The crudity of these affairs had stiffened Marvran's pride, so that Olive had come to typify for her a quality of life infinitely remote, paltry and ludicrous. But now it was close and loathsome, a vivid pal-pitating thing that breathed upon her and threatened to smother her.

She ate little at tea-time, and as soon as she was alone in the bungalow, curled up in the fire-side armchair in the parlour with

Flush on her lap, trying to blunt her emotions by reading a thriller borrowed yesterday from a friend with whom she had attended the dance.

The detective was hot on the scent, having just discovered a poisoned cigar stump, when Marvran's interest was diverted by the knowledge that Flush also had detected something. He had stiffened, jerking up the book as he stood erect on her thighs, ears cocked, and before she could restrain him he had leapt on to the carpet and trotted to the closed door, growling softly.

As she watched him she heard the gate click. A knock came upon the outer door, but as she made to rise it was opened; muffled footsteps sounded in the passage.

Flush's barking became frantic, and as the parlour door was pushed inward he bounded out, snarling for a minute before a muttered word from the visitor led to recognition. This was the man who had playfully waved a stick at him on the moor! Flush wagged his tail and began frisking about the big, restless feet.

It was indeed Joel who had entered. He wore a heavy overcoat, and a scarf wound clumsily around his neck, partly hiding the jaw as he came in with his head bent. His face was stiff and reddened. The weather had changed: there was an icy north wind and a threat of snow. And as he glanced up from the dog he sensed the wintry atmosphere in Marvran also: the same chilling repulsion she had shown on the downs, but sharper now as she had moved further into an alien world and, being more remote from him, was less troubled by ambiguity. She rose, pale and startled, the book slipping from her hand to the floor, but her confusion was entirely hostile as she greeted him.

"Why are you here? You've no right to intrude..."

"Wait a minute. 'Tis nothing to be frightened about."

He shut the door and turned, setting his back to it. They faced each other across the room tensely. After a brief pause Marvran spoke again, her voice curt but with a tremor of fear in it, fear of the rude male strength suggested by his rough gypsy-like appearance. "I can't understand why you should want to see me again. I thought that meeting on the downs had shown you it was all a mistake, if you'd ever fancied anything serious about me."

The words confirmed his intuition, and with a slow awkward gesture he waved her protest aside. "I came about something else," he said evasively. "Our roof was all but blown off Thursday night, with that storm."

"Well?"

"I patched it up as well I could – working on it till nearly midnight, nailing on galvanize. But Ruth got wet - rain blowing in on the bed – and she been took bad."

"Caught a cold?"

Joel nodded, moving forward into the room and groping with one hand until it fastened on the edge of the table.

"Pretty bad – she isn't strong, you know. Reckon she'll pull through all right, but she'll need nursing"

"And you want me to come there and help?"

He flinched and murmured in an apologetic tone while watching Flush settle himself on the hearthrug: "There's nobody else – except your mother, perhaps. Her own mother can't do much, only mess around."

Marvrn noted his heavy breathing; she pondered for a few moments, running her fingers through her mass of black curls, tossing them loosely on the neck of her frock. "This is just an idea of your own, I suppose?" she said then pointedly.

"No. Ruth's asking for you. 'Twould be rough on she if you didn't come."

"But if she's really ill no doubt Gwen could get leave for a day or two to come home and nurse her."

"Yes, I expect she could," he said, "but I don't want to ruffle things for her just now. There's reasons…"

Marvran raised her brows, questioning him. There was a fresh animation in his manner; his eyes had a softened, brooding upon the fire.

"What reasons?" she asked.

"I been down that way this afternoon," replied Joel, evidently finding relief in telling her. "Went down to see the chap she's got stuck on. One o' my old work mates at Rostowrack; good fellow he is, and it give me fresh heart when I found he was serious and not playing with her. If 'twasn't for seeing him maybe I shouldn't have called here now – wouldn't have had the heart; but it lifted some burden off me to know Gwen had found the way through, and I – I thought I'd try once more."

"I didn't know Gwen was courting," Marvran observed in surprise.

"She isn't – nothing open yet; but things is shaping very helpful there at the farm. Veale seems to have got stuck on a woman just come back from the Scilly Isles: She's been at the farm a good bit, and now he's off in the evenings sometimes at her place, so Gwen and the chap – Euan Kella he's called – find it convenient, as he lives close by. I want to leave it to run smooth for Gwen – 'tis time she had some happiness – and I'd rather not bother her about Ruth."

Marvran stooped to pick up the book, laying it on the mantle shelf. "Well, I'll see if mother can take the job," she said with a touch of irritation." I'm certainly not going to; this is obviously a crude attempt to get me in your company under your own roof. It would only make for talk – and now I know what your feelings are it's better for all concerned that I keep away."

The light went out of his face; he answered huskily:

"I can't help loving you. How's it my fault?"

"I'm not going to invite scandal, or make myself a laughing stock among my friends, just to humour some sentimental whim of yours. Pull yourself together, Joel!"

The flash of anger roused him and he lurched free of the table, his arms outstretched, almost touching her hair.

"I wish you'd pull yourself together!" he said grimly. "You're just trying to get away from yourself again. I saw you at St. Dennis Thursday evening."

"So you're following me about?"

"I had to find out if it 'twas true – that you'd started to go that way again," he replied more quietly. "You've proved already that 'tisn't safe to go along blind with the crowd. You get that you'd do anything to make 'em notice you – wreck your life with play-acting rather than face a few sneers from your friends, as you call 'em. Everybody looking on, wanting you to copy their tricks. And deep down you want to love, but what chance has it got?"

Marvran sank back into the armchair, her eyes strained, haunted. As the shock of his arrival passed, her mind took the full weight of the other shock. Olive! Her father's remarks! She looked up at Joel, warily searching him from the core of disgust. The element of personal jealousy was very faint, a brief sting in remote depths that had almost congealed. And with a numbness of neutrality there came a greater inflow of confidence. She knew he could not penetrate to her reaction, and, freeing herself from the sense of intimacy, she condescended to him. She could lapse into the crude working-class familiarity when she was rid of any thought of him as a lover. It was only her emotions that were so sensitive, so subtly guarded, recoiling from the touch of his unsubtle sincerity. She answered him with blunt derision:

"I've got a right to live my own life, Joel, without any advice from a stick in-the-mud – even if he did used to think he could play football!"

"I know," he admitted flushing hotly."I haven't been mixed up in all this putting on airs. My footballing wasn't that: I never cared about the crowds, whether they cheered or booed. But you do care, and it's messing up your life. I can see it all the plainer for being outside it; and I know you're on the wrong track because you – you make me pay for it."

He was coming close again, heavy and stolid. She could not bear it, that raw, exposed simplicity. The sudden cold flicker in her eyes checked him, threw him back. Then her retort followed, hard and flippant:

"That's easily remedied, if I can judge from what I've heard lately. Haven't you come to the wrong house tonight?"

He flinched, but evaded the full implication. "What d'you mean?"

"Well, if you want someone to nurse Ruth, wouldn't it be better to get someone who may one day nurse you?" The words hurt her a little but she forced them out, deliberate in her repudiation on him.

Joel had stepped back towards the settee in a pitiful confusion, as one betrayed.

"Nurse me?" he repeated blankly.

"Yes. As your wife."

He understood then and looked away from her, fumbling to loosen his scarf, as though it was strangling him.

"You've heard about Olive Buzza, I can see what 'tis,"he said in a low voice.

"Dad did mention it. And really Joel, I think it's a good opening. There's always the chance she might mend when she's once settled."

Joel winced under the sneer. He turned again to study her face, now visible to him for the first time in the glare of electric light. It appeared quite different from the face he had seen in the faint lamp-light of his home, in the daylight shadow of the Rock and on the twilight moor. Its features had been subdued then, with a hint of mystery. But now they were too sharp, even theatrical. She had more lipstick on her mouth than when he last saw her, and it gave her an almost garish artificiality. Her bright, pitiful mouth had appealed to him on the downs, moved him to tenderness, but the present scarlet blob in the pale, flat-cheeked face merely marked her as a creature not of this world. And as he looked at this aloof, cold mask it seemed to separate from his memories, become naked and hideous, unknown to him. The girl he had loved was not there. The old image was quaking, dissolving within him, and with its disintegration all his trust and desire were sucked out of him; they had grown brittle and shallow, so that he could examine them and wonder at them. He was numbed in to a new, strange loneliness, standing there with the girl who was passing, fading from him. He could no longer reach for the little spark of life in her, somewhere beyond the enigma of her repulsion. The disguise was too alien at last.

"I come here to know about Ruth," he said doggedly, yet with curious indifference, an emotional deadness, as though the matter were now impersonal.

Marvran had lifted Flush on to her lap; she glanced up from her restless ruffling of his thick black coat. "When did you say you wished me to call – to-morrow?"

"Please. They're having a doctor for her to-morrow morning if she isn't better, and they want you – or your mother if you won't be bothered – to come in the evening and do what he says is needed."

"Well, I could hardly have managed it to-morrow even if I'd been willing. I forgot for the moment, but…" She straightened with a freshening of interest "You've heard, I expect, that we're having a special St. Valentine's Eve dance in one of the Carbis clay-dries next Saturday night?"

Joel nodded gloomily.

"Your father and Bassett been making fun of it over on our kiln," he observed. "Seems to be the latest craze. You'll be going, no doubt?"

"Of course. And I've agreed to meet some of our crowd at Roche to-morrow night to make final arrangements about decorations and such like. Roy Chegwidden's taking charge of that side of it – getting a hundred Chinese lanterns and fairy lights fixed along the beams, and the carpenters are rigging up a bandstand just inside the furnace wall. It won't look much like the sort of place you work in, by the time Roy's finished with it!"

Joel was surprised to find in himself a sudden rush of jealousy whipped up by this remark. She had set before him a concrete male image, and though her face was dead to him he was aware of her in the body for a moment, disturbingly. She looked very graceful and feminine, slumped in the chair; the soft yellow frock emphasizing the mould of her breasts as the weight of the dog pulled it down. He moved towards her with a rising violence of emotion.

"It's linked up all right, hasn't it?" he cried with bitter mockery. "Chegwidden comes into our home to order us out – and then his son goes home and asks his Dad if he can have the clay-dry to help Miss Creba get going again among her equals – when I'm safe out o' the way!"

Marvran answered coolly. "It was natural that Roy should organize this dance, as his father's the captain of those clayworks. We had to get Mr Chegwidden's permission."

Joel felt the whole situation close in upon him, intolerable in its irony. He thought of the life that awaited him in the dry kiln, the leprous symbol he had hoped to escape when he had come here tonight, heartened by Euan's assurances. And Marvran, absorbed in anticipation of the Valentine's dance, had taken his tragic symbol and turned it into a token of her release from him. Colour and gaiety would welcome her in a setting, which to him meant only grey fetid gloom and sullen stagnant mud. He threw out an arm in a despairing gesture, savagely reproaching her.

"Didn't I suffer enough while you was down in Falmouth," he said, "without having to go through this now you've come back? If I felt anything for 'ee before you went away, I'd got over it by last summer. Why did you come and give me that hope again, and now you let me down worse than ever? I wish to God you'd never darkened our doors."

Marvran shrank from the passion in him, and glanced nervously at the clock on the mantleshelf.

"Yes," she replied quietly, "I've told mother it was a mistake for us to interest ourselves in your people. I've done nothing to blame myself for. I never gave you any encouragement, either before I went to Falmouth or after I returned."

The reminder was so true that he had no argument against it on the human level. He was forced deeper, into the muddy, unexplored bedrock of his consciousness. He grappled and floundered, submerged beyond the mere personal relationship.

"I know you didn't," he confessed, still speaking in a harsh constricted voice. "'Twould be easier to bear if 'twas only you that was cruel. But 'tis life and God – how they've used you. I told Gwen last Christmas 'tis all like some damned trick o' the almighty, I feel it even more now."

"That just shows you're getting morbid."

"Yes – yes, I knew you'd say that. But I can see 'tis no good to bandy words. We can't go on to work out any future – and I don't even want to, now."

She glanced up at him, her black eyes wide and startled. "D'you mean that?"

"Mean it? What else can I mean when you're what you are?"

As Marvran studied his wretched face she realised that his feelings and outlook were other than she had supposed. What, she wondered, had he really sought in her? Was it merely carnal love, or the physical affirmation of some mystical faith that had struck root in his simple soul? Whatever it was, it perplexed and repelled her. The gulf between them was now unbridgeable. He had no clue to her need, and she had no clue to his.

"Well, it's a relief," she murmured, her voice mingling with the snowy rasp of the wind outside. "I don't mind your coming here tonight if it's convinced you that you must find – someone of your own kind." He had begun groping towards the door; she added in a firm practical tone, "You can tell your people to expect mother to-morrow, possibly in the morning. She'll do what she can about Ruth."

The outer door closed heavily and Joel's footsteps receded, stumbling down the dark path.

CHAPTER THIRTEEN

EUAN was the first labourer to arrive at Rostowrack clay work on the following Tuesday morning. It was half-an-hour before sunrise when he left his footprints on the hitherto untrodden snow on the road at Slip and crossed the moorland track to the sand dune. There was a weird, sickly light in the sky, laggard flakes blunting themselves like arrows against every feature of the solid lower world.

It was nearly a year since Euan had walked to work through a snowy landscape, and the man he had then been seemed traceless as the snow that had irritated him on his journey. The earth was again winter-bound; when he passed close to broom and hazel bushes he felt that hardly any life remained in the harsh brittle stems; the patches of grass not yet buried in the snow were like ugly deposits of frayed ribbon and stiff colourless hair. But winter had no place in his mood. Reaching the humps of gravel washed down from Rostowrack dump he halted, peering fixedly through the blurred dusk around the clay work. It was no longer merely the place where he earned his living; every fresh contact with it brought a more vivid association with Gwen in the knowledge that she had first challenged him here by the pit. The incident which had once disturbed and perplexed him was now recognised and accepted as the decisive impact of the unfated pattern of life in which he believed. Even before he broke with Lela he had been awed and impelled by the possibility of this fulfilment. During his walk with Gwen to Barrakellis he had realised that with her he could touch a unity and wholeness of experience which had hitherto been denied him. After his mother Rachel had gone to bed that evening he had stayed down in the parlour, reading Browning and marking with the date a line in Ixion:

'Out of the wreck I rise past, Zeus to the Potency o'er him.'

130

Zeus, the natural god, the Fate that decreed the course of man's life inside Nature: Lela had represented that to him. And beyond it stood the Christian Potency, the predestination that destroyed fate and created pattern. He believed Gwen to be an instrument in the hands of that higher Power; he regarded his ultimate marriage to her as a pinnacle from which he could look down upon the sunken godship of his fate. He could not react or anticipate in any other way. And he wondered now whether Gwen's sympathetic response to his unusual vision was the result of the struggle she and Joel had waged against the carnal primitivism of their home. Though he and Joel live mentally in different worlds, there was a kinship in their spiritual situation. They both seemed to be creatures of circumstances, yet they were aware that their fate was not the whole of their experience. They recognised a conflict between their natural fate and that divine predestination which infiltrated through cracks in the normal routine and effected strange transformations on this side of a vast and terrifying frontier. Euan, with his wide reading in theology, could fit the changes of his life into a coherent system of thought, while Joel and Gwen simply felt as concrete events the moves and counter-moves of these striving forces, and sought a faith that would cancel the apparent triumph of tragic doom in their lives. For Gwen the way to it was now open, and in convincing Joel of this Euan knew that he had strengthened the young fellow's hope for Marvran. Gwen had told him that Joel was still baulked in his advance towards love, but Euan did not know enough of the inner story, or of Marvran's character, to give any detailed guidance. He had let the facts of his own victory speak for themselves.

From the time he repudiated his fate by turning finally from Lela, the new pattern had been unmistakable: incidents that seemed trifling or irrelevant had drawn him towards the fusion with Gwen. Sue Mannell's designs at Barrakellis had soon resulted in Veale's spending at least two evenings a week at the Mannell's cottage. Then Rachel had caught a cold which developed into influenza and kept her indoors for a fortnight. Euan had fetched the milk from the farm in the evenings, and though he did not stay long he always went indoors if Gwen was alone: the sense of intimacy deepened as they deliberately challenged and roused each other. The open declaration had come last week when he told her that Rachel was well again and would be calling for the milk in the morning as usual. He had asked whether he could come to the farm at nightfall.

"Yes – and you must," Gwen had answered determinedly. "I'll draw the shutters when Mr Veale goes out, then you'll know that if the windows are dark I'm in here – waiting for you…"

He had returned home in a daze of joy that evening, clutching the filled jug and staring across at the tip-lights on Goonvean clay-dump. They burned steadily as on the night he had first walked with Gwen; the white refuse poured out beneath the crossed wooden beams. And within himself memory was pouring soft jets of sensation down through his nerves, warm pulsations that settled like grain into the clefts of his soul. These thrills, the tremulous after glow of Gwen's first embrace and her young, clean kisses searching and fastening on his mouth fused perfectly with his mystical apprehensions, and threatened the gross earth in him which Lela had tried to nourish. He hoped that Joel too, would find release and fulfilment as the mask fell from Marvran.

The clay-pit was still gloomy when Euan strode forward past the engine-house and began descending the steps to the pit bottom. He held on to the wooden rail and moved carefully down the pit-face, testing his foot-hold on slippery patches where the cliff dropped from the path in a sheer precipice. Reaching the bottom he strolled along a waggon-track, pushing under a hazel tree that crouched over the frozen settling-pool. He saw vaguely the two waggons standing ice-bound in the water, and the sluices half open between the sand-pit, in which refuse was collected, and the pool itself. With a shrug he ventured out upon the snow-frilled plank bridge that spanned the pool and mounted to the broaded path above the sand-pit. Yesterday it had been frozen hard, but he knew as he trod upon it that under the splashing of water from the hose and the trampling of feet it would soon become slushy, reducing the risk of accident.

Euan was relieved: he felt cold, however, and picking up a shovel he turned back down the slope and broke the surface of the ice in the pool, which was comparatively thin; he tugged for several minutes at the waggon that stood within reach of the bank, but could not get it free of the stiffened mud. He scrambled up to the path again and kicked his way through the snow to the main lodge: a square stone hut near the foot of the ascending incline-track. The door was unlocked and he pushed it open. The interior was still dark, but he knew its contents. There was a pile of chopped sticks beside the grate, and a little coal; on the bench lay a newspaper and a box of matches.

Euan pushed a sheet of paper on to the grate-bars, strewed a few sticks upon it and set light to the fuel. The wood was soon crackling, the flames leapt with a ruddy glow, reflected on the black window like brandished swords. Euan's shadow swooped gigantic across the hut, and as if to escape some ghostly presence he went to the doorway and looked out for a minute before returning to put coals on the fire.

The submerged, bleared scene was awesome. The pit-bed could be traced as far as the grim barrier of a rock island veined deeply with snow, the crevices and crags looming like folds of ice, unearthly. The rails were buried and the rows of little trucks seemed forlorn, purposeless, dwarfed under the rocks. The impression was oddly spiritual in the mind such as Euan's; he had the poet's faculty for perceiving common objects as symbols, concrete images of his thought.

As the firelight gradually flagged in the lodge, Euan stepped back into it and laid coal on the grate. He then sat down on the bench and waited, rubbing his hands together and sometimes stamping his feet to keep warm. He wore a cap today because of the weather, and beneath its peak his deep-set, dreamy eyes scanned the brightening pit, watching the shadows dissolve and pass to a static of bleared daylight. This wave held each snow-gripped detail rigid with an unreserved menace that was most potent in the gaunt square bulk of the excavator hunched by the island, its scoop half-raised like a beak ready to pounce, and also in the many whitened pipes that zigzagged across the pit at various levels, like dead snakes.

He was roused at length by the sound of a laugh; a hoarse, croaking noise that broke the silence of the pit, as though something reptilian and obscene had awakened in it. He recognised the voice as Cal Mannell's, and his face hardened. He still shrank from the daily contact with Cal, the gross, spongy body that had known Lela's as he had never know it. He recoiled to the protective image, the secret bond with Gwen, and this made him more guarded and enigmatic than ever here among his mates. As he rose he heard them chattering as they came down the path. There were three others besides Mannell in this first group: Gumma, the elderly driver of the excavator,

Yabsley, who manipulated the hose, and Neale, the teenaged kettle-boy.

Yabsley was the first to appear in the lodge doorway; his plump, bow-legged figure stiffened as he saw who stood inside it. "Hullo! Euan's here already," he exclaimed in surprise.

"Don't blame me for that – warm yourselves up!" retorted Euan with a stained grin. "Fact is, I got here a bit early and couldn't stand around in the cold, so I lit the fire myself, about ten minutes ago."

The other three labourers were soon on the threshold, completely shutting out the light. They looked at Euan suspiciously.

Neale, a short, red-faced lad, pushed into the hut and examined the fire critically, prodding it with his boot. The rest of the group seated themselves on the benches, their hands stretched towards the blaze, and proceeded to gossip, recalling incidents of past years when clay-labouring was more closely affected by the weather. Cal and Euan merely listened, ignoring each other.

"Aye, the old times was rough," commented Gumma at length, as the talk veered from external working conditions to general standards and manners of living. "Few things was done without a drop o' beer in my younger days. I mind when I was waggonin', back before the war; a tough lot they waggoners; and they had one trick what made their lives pretty excitin'. The rules was o' course, that they wasn't allowed to stop nowhere between the clayworks and ports: they worked to a time-table, puttin' through so many loads a day. But 'twasn't no uncommon thing to see a empty waggon comin' back from Par or Charlestown all by itself no driver to be seen anywhere. He'd dropped in at some wayside pub and sent the hosses on ahead: they knowed the way back to claywork. And when driver'd had his pint he'd go runnin' across fields, takin' every short cut he could find, to catch up wi' the hosses and waggon before they got near home again. People used to laugh to see they waggoners rushing like mad, in a proper sweat o' fear lest they shouldn't overtake the hosses in time. But 'twasn't put a stop to till some of 'em got too bold and took more beer than they could stand. One or two waggons got back to 'dry' wi' nobody in charge: driver falled down somewhere, rolled over in a field in his haste and had to be picked up-sacked afterwards, o' course. But it just shows what a change have come over folks' habits and tastes this past twenty or thirty year. Even people's sins isn't so rough as they used to be."

Yabsley removed his cap and brushed the snow from it contemptuously into the fire.

"Sin's no better for bein' polished, Mr Gumma," he said with sober conviction. "That's where the moderns have got slipped up. They thought with the help o' this eddication they could polish their sins and make 'em look brand new, and that'd take away the stink. But that's where they're wrong, see." He peered meditatively back through the doorway, his round face puckered for a moment, then as an illustration occurred to him he dealt a sharp tap to Euan's knee as he was sitting opposite him.

"Take Charlie Crago, for instance," he resumed, looking past Euan to Gumma. "He's the modern counterpart o' they waggoners you tell about – going to and fro with his lorry. Now, a lorry isn't a intelligent animal like a hoss is – can't be sent on by itself while Charlie has his pint on the sly; and I s'pose you'd call that a sign o' progress. But when you size up Charlie's private life you find 'tis the same as theirs was: drink and women. So the hoss has become a lorry, but a swine drove the hoss and swine still drives the lorry. That isn't my idea of progress."

"Ah! But Charlie isn't a eddicated man," Gumma objected, stroking his grey moustache and speaking in his sour, dogged tone. "Cal here isn't either: both roughish men what ha'n't moved wi' the times."

Mannell, who sat nearest the door, pushed his head forward and glanced maliciously at Euan. "What about Euan's young lady, though? She've moved wi' the times all right."

"Yes, that maid seem to ha' got in with a pretty fast set since she split with Euan," muttered Yabsley. "So bad under her smartness as the old rips they waggoners used to carry on with." His large blue eyes warily probed Euan, who had stooped to push an empty pitcher further back into the corner so that he could stretch his legs to the hearth. "Euan was took in over that maid's polish, that's where 'twas. Polish! 'Tis the curse o' this age: say what you will, Bill Gumma; say what you will, old man. Scientists and school blokes been at it year after year, polishin' politics and morals wi' new-fangled theories and quack jargon – even polished God wi' their new theology, thought He was too rough. And what've 'em got for their pains? A headache in politics, a heartache in religion, and a bellyache in their morals, that's all!" He turned to Neale, who sat between him and Mannell, and nudged his arm.

"There'll be more o' such bellyache on view soon by the look of it," he went on after a few moments' deliberation. "Not exactly polished, I admit…"

"Where to?" asked Neale curiously.

"Up around Roche. Olive Buzza's runnin' after our old workmate Joel Kruse now, so I hear. You won't know Joel: used to work here while you was goin' school. Anyhow, she got a good chance o' getting him wi' what happened yesterday. Have 'ee heard of it?"

Euan straightened, his face eager with fresh interest, but the question was addressed to Gumma, who stared over his pipe, shaking his head dourly.

"No, ha'n't heard anything o' that blighter for twelve months or more," he grunted. "Seem to ha' vanished in thin air like a man buried alive. He haven't kicked a football nor married a maid, and he can't expect to be talked about if he won't do one thing or the other."

"Well, he've done something else now," commented Yabsley. "Got to appear in St. Austell magistrates court this morning."

Euan looked startled and incredulous. "What's he pulled up for?" he asked sharply. "Nothing very bad, took some galvanised sheets from clayworks last week, it seems, He'll get off with a fine, I daresay."

There was a brief silence in which Euan's face clouded with perplexity and concern.

"Sure 'tis true?"

"No doubt about it, old man. I saw his workmate George Bassett last night, and he said the police was waiting for Joel when he got home from the 'dry'. Everybody in Roche knowed of it before bedtime."

Gumma rose and lurched forward, spitting in the fire. "It don't surprise me," he said. "Joel was always a shifty beggar: even on the football field he was glum looking, as if he was playing more to spite somebody than to give us our money's worth. I never took to un; I was glad to see the last of 'n in the lodge here."

Mannell wriggled closer to Neale; his face, caught between flickering firelight and the snowy background, looked sinister, the eyes wide with a feverish obsession. "Thass a bit o' good news for me," he observed, chuckling. "Olive Buzza isn't the only one who'll find it helpful."

Euan remained cool, but he felt a bristle of antagonism. He guessed Cal's meaning; Gwen had told him that on his first visit to Barrakellis after she began working there he had tried to put his arm round her and made an obscene jest.

"Got plans around Barrakellis as well as your mother?" asked Yabsley, puzzled by the latent seriousness in Cal's tone.

"You must wait and see, old sport. That kid won't be able to put on such airs now her brother been in court and wi' Olive on his trail too. She'll see where the Kruses belong, and maybe when Ma goes down Barrakellis to live, Gwen'll come up to Carloggas instead o' going back home to Roche."

A spasm of resentment on Euan's face gradually relaxed into an ironical smile; he glanced with mocking reserve at the gloating figure on the opposite bench. But he was worried about Joel and made no comment on Cal's insinuations.

When Joel emerged from St. Austell magistrate's court that morning, snow swirled thickly over the town. The numbness within him was matched by a general cold torpor in the world outside. As he came out into the cramped Fore Street his footsteps were muffled, soundless, as though he moved in a padded cell. Few pedestrians were about on the narrow pavements; buses were running late, and those which had come in from the clay villages were almost empty. Business was practically at a standstill except for the custom of local residents. Something had gone dead. The tall shops loomed fantastically through the speckled flurrying mist. Tradesmen's vans groped by, driven by men with strained, pinched faces. And behind him in the court-room he had just left, there had been figures equally distorted: police officers, magistrates, and a number of people in the body of the hall whom he hadn't looked at. The only person in court who had stabbed out distinctly from the fog of his mind was the pompous Captain Chegwidden, who had given evidence identifying and valuing the sheets of corrugated iron that Joel had taken from the claywork on Thursday.

For Joel the whole reality of the scene focused on this man:

Chegwidden's presence linked this humiliation with the central catastrophe. Last night Marvran had been with this man's son, making
arrangements about the Valentine dance. Chegwidden represented
the hostile world of normal, superficial life from which Joel was
excluded. When asked to plead he had glowered steadily at the
captain and answered with sullen defiance:

"All right. I done it. Get all this business over!" He was already
bruised by the knowledge that everything was ended between him
and Marvran; the indignity of being fined merely emphasised the
sense of finality. It was his fate pouncing back in the full power of
release from the challenge of his allegiance to the higher level. It
sealed him as a victim, a man who must accept his place in the underworld.

The memory of his past talks with Euan were dim and remote
now, then bitter when it penetrated into consciousness. He remembered vaguely that Euan had spoken of the conflict between fate and
predestination, and that he himself had been aware of this struggle, if
only in the crude recognition that the impact of some events were different from that of others. The feelings inspired in him by Marvran's
return last August were wholly separate from those of his normal
workaday life spent between the squalid cottage and clay-kiln. The
two experiences were not the bright and dark threads of the same
pattern; they were fiercely contending forces, and he had realised
from the outset that one must destroy the other. But now he had seen
the triumph of fate over predestination: in Christian terms, the
triumph of Nature over Grace. The vision had crumbled before he
could build it up into a clearly defined faith. He had lacked an essential clue – that of Marvran's love, had she frankly expressed it.

He moved wearily along the street, hating the town, for it
reminded him of Falmouth, the brisk clarity that had taken Marvran
so far away from him that she could never find the way back. Even
though the place was now sluggish and deadened, he was stung by
the alien refinement. The people who passed him on the pavement
scarcely seemed to be fellow humans; they clicked by like robots,
either ignoring him or casting a disdainful, supercilious glance at his
shabby clothes and sombre, stiffened face. He felt isolated and submerged, a fugitive; about half-way through Fore Street he turned
down a steep alley leading to Duke Square, drawn instinctively to the

shelter and seclusion of the high, bare walls, the dingy atmosphere of neglect.

No one was visible in front of him, and because of the snow he did not hear the footsteps of the thick-set young woman who turned the corner a dozen yards behind him and followed him stealthily. The first intimation of Olive's presence was a soft tap on his arm when he paused by the wall for a few moments, intending to light a cigarette.

"Did you see me in court?" came the almost whispered greeting.

Joel turned, pushing the cigarettes back into his pocket. He stared blankly at her round damp face, noting the snow on her hat and coat. He did not reply:

"Well, I was there. I heard last night you'd been nabbed – though tis a miserable charge. Be more fun if they'd run you in for visiting a disorderly house, wouldn't it?" She laughed quietly.

Joel shrugged, peering aside as he commented bitterly: "I ought to have expected this, I s'pose. It fits in wi' the rest."

"Sure does," said Olive. "I want to help you: nobody else will."

Her small gloved hand squeezed his arm; as the truth of her words pierced through to him Joel slumped back against the wall, which was gaudy with huge coloured posters, the wet paper drooping raggedly at the edges.

"You paid your fine in court?" she asked.

"Yes; it only means two quid out o' me. They might as well ha' sent me to jail while they was about it."

"But you'd have missed a lot then. I'm glad you're still free."

Joel remained silent.

"I think something's gone wrong," she observed, studying his face now for the first time in daylight. "Marvran Creba's behind this somehow, isn't she? Did you pinch that stuff just to work off your devilment?"

He shuffled his feet in the snow, flushing.

"I was upset about her Thursday night," he admitted. "But it don't matter now. Even if I hadn't been found out, 'tis too late to hope anything more o' she. I've found her out since then."

"I knew you would. When girls like her get their pride punctured and have to climb back on their pedestal, a fellow like you doesn't stand an earthly. Have you quarrelled, or what?"

"Worse than that," he muttered, rousing and hardening. "'Twas about Ruth. I went to the bungalow Sunday night to ask if she'd come and nurse the kid."

"And she wouldn't?"

"No: she said I ought to ask you instead. Just a sneering little snob, she was. I can imagine what she's saying today and tomorrow I got to go back and face her father there on the kiln."

He spoke jerkily, reluctant to confess, yet finding relief in unburdening himself to one who seemed knit to him in the web of fate.

Olive was still caressing his arm, smiling.

"Don't worry, Joel: you can be a match for the whole beastly pack of 'em, magistrates and all if you'll let me help."

"How?"

She moved closer, warm and solid in the fluttering white haze. She wore no make-up; her full, naked lips seemed incongruous here, as remote from the artificial town background as he was, and strangely powerful.

"Your sister'll need all the money you can spare this week, won't she?"

"She'll need feeding up," he said. "But I can manage. Me wages isn't bad, only it all goes down the drain when mother gets hold of it."

"Well, listen." Olive pushed her face towards his, watching the cars and the few pedestrians passing the top entrance of the alley along Fore Street. "I'll make good your fine if you'll call down for it one evening. This is just the chance you need to break the ice. You thought you were a bit too good for me, but that excuse won't hold water now. We're on pretty much the same level, so we'd better chum up."

Joel was fully open and receptive now, vulnerable; he had no protection, no hope or aim for the future. There appeared to be only one course left him: to accept his fate, let the kiln slime suck him down with Olive. Yet it was still not simple, not just a matter of instinct. His emotional hunger was no longer a mere brutish appetite; it had become a spiritual problem. His soul was awakened and thrills of the body meant little to him in themselves. He required that physical pleasure should affirm truth – otherwise it would be little pleasure to him. And as Marvran had aroused the hunger without revealing the truth, he was in a strange confusion of flesh and spirit, on a borderline where Olive could not satisfy him. He stepped out from the wall and passed a hand wearily across his forehead, lifting the solid cap.

"I dunno, I'll see about it," he mumbled. "I don't want your money, but I – well I've pretty well had enough of all this…"

She brightened with a vague smouldering of possessiveness. "That's what I felt and the way's open now. I'll be expecting you – say next Friday? Any time after dark. Just toss a handful of gravel to the window. You know which house ours is, don't you? Last o' the row from Roche side."

Joel nodded and turned from her, lurching a few paces down the alley.

"You're going back right away?" asked Olive.

"Yes – straight up to station to wait for the first bus. You better come on a later one, else people'd be talking." He raised his hand clumsily, glancing back over his shoulder. "Well, so long!"

"Cheerio till Friday!" Olive called in response. After watching him disappear she moved slowly up into Fore Street, smiling to her self as she lowered her head against the fluttering snow.

CHAPTER FOURTEEN

ON the following afternoon Sue Mannell and her daughter Lorraine were strolling up the cliff-path east of Hugh Town, the capital of the Scilly Isles. Though the path was narrow they walked some distance apart, and the lack of genuine affection between them would have been obvious to any onlooker. The girl occasionally turned and glanced over her shoulder, a slight frown on her dark, mature face. She was of medium height and solid build, but with the powerful breadth of bone rather than the soft fullness of flesh: there was a starkness and rawness in her appearance, the indelible mark of her experiences as a slum child in Plymouth. She wore a fawn coat, unbuttoned, showing a red pullover and grey skirt. Her thick chestnut hair was almost hidden by a blue spotted handkerchief wound about her head and tied under her chin. Sue was slightly the taller, lean and gipsy-like; clad sombrely in black clothes, she moved as a funereal figure in private wintry tones. There had been no snowfall on the islands, the air was mild, and they had no need of brisk exertion to keep themselves warm. The drowse of spring was already here, with the scent of the flower harvests.

Reaching the cliff-top the couple paused, and then struck in across a strip of turfed ground towards the grey round tower that dominated the headland. The sun, fighting through cloud over the Outer Isles, beyond the Bishop Rock light-house, touched them with a pale glimmer and gave mellow emphasis to the broad remote seascape and grey shapes of the outer islands now disclosed to their view.

Hugh Town lay below, hardly more than a village: a few tangled streets of Victorian shops and houses, with one or two hotels on the northern side, facing the long arm of the pier that stretched across the harbour, parallel with the lonely islet of Samson which rose like a tiny volcano midway between St. Mary's and Bryher, two miles off. The town was built on an isthmus from which Garrison Hill, the head of St. Mary's, bulged westward, while the body of the island, on which the couple now stood, sprawled behind. Its two beaches showed like sickle moons with their backs to each other and a medley of roofs squeezed between them. The houses on the southern side fronted the sea at Porth Cressa, though protected by low sand-dunes that were fretted with stalky grass and bushes. In one of these cottages Sue and Lorraine had found lodgings nine years ago – a house occupied by an elderly widow, Mrs Rescorla; and there they had lived together until Sue returned to Cornwall six weeks ago.

The present scene was perfect in its realisation of a mood of sober tranquillity, but the two watchers by the tower were obviously ill at ease, aware of discord, of something final and irrevocable in the setting and drama of this afternoon.

It was Sue who expressed the cause of their tense unnatural bearing, her voice grating as she turned to nudge the girl's arm.

"Well, maid, I s'pose this is the last time I shall see these old islands – and after the welcome I've had today I wish I'd never seen 'em at all. I might as well have finished with 'ee for good when I left here at Christmas."

Lorraine shrugged, answering in a subdued tone: "I hardly expected you'd be back again so quick – though 'tis no great surprise really. You always would throw away money on any whim that came into your head."

"And it upset your hopes, eh? You was hoping you'd never see me again in this world."

"Not exactly that. But you couldn't expect me to be sorry you'd cleared out, in the circumstances."

"'Twas a bit nasty, I admit, to lose your mother in such a way. I'd been fed up here for months, and 'twould have been better for you if I'd left quiet and peaceable instead o' being bundled out like that. But for me own part I don't regret it, 'specially when I think o' the time Mrs Danning had in hospital."

Sue glowered back eastward past St. Martin's towards the mainland twenty-five miles away, screened in wintry haze, the sea pulsing greyly near the horizon, though blue in patches of sunlight around the isles.

Lorraine stepped closer to the tower and said with a hint of bitterness: "If you were so proud of it I wonder you didn't tell Cal in your letter last Christmas – let him know the real reason why you were shifting back there."

Sue's black eyes twinkled. "You don't know Cal as well as I do, Lorraine. Can't never tell how he may take anything. Might ha' turned ugly, thinking I'd only make trouble for'n. 'Twould have gived quite a wrong impression, for I'd had enough excitements here and in Plymouth to last the rest o' me days. I meant to settle in sober and respectable – be a credit to the parish in me old age, as I scandalled it so much when I was young. I knowed Cal wouldn't have no bother wi' me, and 'twas best to say nothing o' the uproar till I was safe under his roof."

"You told him then, I s'pose?"

"O' course: it all come out when we got to yarnin' o' one another's scrapes, all free and open as a mother and son should. But his eyes popped when he heard I'd been summonsed and had to fork out so much. Assault and battery: he couldn't recognise his mother in that description. He took a more sensible view than you, though – said I'd done the right thing in givin' that woman Danning something to mind me by."

"You told him 'twas all her fault, I expect."

"And so 'twas. For years she'd been the ring-leader o' the scandals about me, and when she said to me face that morning that I was setting an example o' disgrace to the whole island well, I just catched up the pitcher what she was filling at the tap – first thing that came handy and scat to her with it. I didn't care if I broke her arm or cracked her head abroad. And when I found I'd done it, broke her arm and sent her to hospital, why I felt 'twas a good day's work, well worth whatever I had to pay for it. But I don't want no more such doings."

Lorraine was on the step of the tower now, between two of the massive buttresses, shadowed in the grey niche of stone. She was looking hard at the gaunt restless figure of Sue against the sky, and spoke with curt deliberation.

"I certainly hoped you'd act a bit different in Cornwall. Not that it could hurt Cal as it's hurt me, but for your own sake…"

"Ah, of course! Think a lot o' your mother, don't 'ee? For her own sake she must improve and not go brawlin' and fightin' like she was still in the slums." Sue came forward and patted her daughter's shoulder, her malice fashioning brittle humour as she continued: "You needn't have worried about me, my dear. I'd made up me mind to be quiet as a lamb back there and leave Cal to do all the dirty work. Two such people in one house is a bit much."

"Really?" said Lorraine coldly.

"Yes: if you'd been a wildy-go like Cal I might have set a different example here. You know why we left Plymouth before you finished your schooling, and if you'd broke loose here I might ha' turned as solemn as even Mrs Danning could wish, and started to lecture 'ee for the good o' your soul, as they call it. But you been stuck so glum and moody year after year that I just had to liven things up a bit to mind me of old times."

Lorraine sighed, moving again out on to the turf, crossing now to the low wall of granite boulders ridging the slope that dipped to the harbour. She gazed towards the flower fields, still golden with daffodils, stretching to Holy Vale, the low-lying centre of the island, then northward to where, six miles off, across Crow Sound, St. Martin's lay blurred and thin like a faded leaf adrift amid the sun-spilths and sea-dashes. She brooded upon all this beauty in silence.

Sue continued with a sly wink: "You ha'n't been so lonely since you been here without me, I bet; ha'n't suffered no hardship in no way. You can manage well 'nough on the wages you git from Ford's shop though you may not need 'em much longer. Me and Cal may have to send over a wedding present before you can send one to either of us."

Lorraine's full lips compressed. "I don't think you need fear that expense."

"Well, you'll find openings enough if you rouse yourself a bit and let folks know I'm out o' the way for good. P'raps you'll see what sort o' respect they've had for 'ee all along, only couldn't show it till now. But after this split today it looks as if me and Cal will be kept guessing."

"I shall answer your letters, of course," said Lorraine grudgingly. "But I'm well in my twenties now, and there won't be any of that sort of news for you and Cal to snigger at."

"Git along! You aren't too old yet." Sue peered more narrowly at the girl's face: not thin, yet almost haggard, a hand denting her cheek as she watched the vast Atlantic rollers shouldering in upon Samson. "If you'm really fed up here too," she resumed tentatively, "p'raps..."

"I shan't go back to Cornwall."

"Not even if Cal wanted 'ee to?"

"No."

"Shan't I tell'n you'll be over to visit us when we'm settled respectable? You haven't seen one another yet."

"That's no loss to either of us."

"And seems I aren't no loss to 'ee either. Want to wash your hands o' the whole family. I wish I hadn't come here visitin' 'ee today. I thought you'd prick up your ears when you heard o' the surprising turn things have took since I went back wi' Cal. Now I've got in thick wi' a decent steady old widower like Digory Veale, and Cal's aiming to splice up wi' this maid Kruse, – Veale's servant there to Barrakellis farm – I felt you'd be glad to see how virtuous we'm getting' in our old age. Thought 'twas too good a piece o' news to waste postage on. But I might as well have saved the fare, and left 'ee knowing no more about us."

"Yes; people's plans miscarry sometimes," said Lorraine cryptically; she had stooped, stroking the ferns along the boulders of the wall, her back towards her mother.

Sue's hands clenched, her face reddened venomously. "You think I come here just to show off and try to make 'ee feel small – just for spite and malice? Well, I won't bandy words. I should ha' knowed better than to try and make peace between me and such a cold, sulky devil like you always been."

Sue flounced out towards the road that crossed the island: merely a rough lane, passing from open downland into the shelter of low hedges to the east. She turned on the rutted gravel, and as Lorraine glanced round at her she pointed down to where, in a flurried stain of sunlight that reached the breasts of Samson, the white sleek hulk of the Scillonian lay moored, its one funnel oozing smoke, at Hugh Town quay.

"There's the boat waitin' – getting' up steam now," cried Sue with a burlesque pathos that had defiance in it. "In another hour or two I'll be sailing on her back past Land's End; and these is the memories I'll take with me. But I don't care a damn for it all, now I've struck it rich back in Cornwall."

Lorraine's gaze was diverted for a minute by a group of flower pickers approaching from Peninnis, clambering over a stile a quarter-mile off as yet; then she faced Sue, her tired irony flecked with irritation. "D'you think I'm surprised to hear you're fishing for another home? I never expected you and Cal to get on together for long."

"Well, Digory won't be very proud of his step-daughter when I tell'n how she've served her mother; and I can guess what Cal's language will be. Gwen Kruse may not be showing him much encouragement, but I've more hope o' the comfort o' me old age coming from she than from you."

"You may be right," said Lorraine dryly. "But I pity Mr Veale, and I pity Gwen Kruse, if anything does come of this."

"I shan't tell 'ee what come of it. I feel I don't want to speak another word to 'ee, nor write another letter."

"Please yourself."

With bitten lip Lorraine stepped out into the high-way several yards ahead of Sue. The presence of the hurrying islanders behind them caused her to detach herself from the sense of drama; she turned with a casual inquiry.

"You'll want some tea before you go back, won't you?"

"Just a bite there in the tea-rooms," replied Sue. "No good showing me nose at the lodgings: I'd only git the door slammed in me face."

Slowly and stiffly the pair descended the cliff-path and skirted the beach. Lorraine lagged behind her mother as they entered the built-up area, her eyes down-cast so that she might avoid the hostile glances of the townsfolk. Soon they had crossed the isthmus and were on the broad concrete pier. Overlooking this, almost opposite the moored steamer was a long low building, arched up like a Noah's Ark, its doorway reached by steps from the jetty. It contained the tea-rooms which during the summer months were crowded with trippers who arrived by sea or air from Cornwall. Few tourists were about at this wintry period, but the place was noisy with the clatter of footsteps and the scrape and bumping of crates of flowers being loaded into the steamer. Gulls screamed as they flapped up past the grey house roofs and out among the craft that rode sleepily the blue waters between the pier and the beach.

Sue paused a moment till Lorraine was abreast of her in the shadow of the building. "Coming up to the tearooms with me?" She muttered.

"No thanks, I'll say goodbye now." Answered Lorraine in a hard suppressed tone. She went straight on, heading blindly into the cool streets, her hair blowing free and her emotions loosened, torn by a sudden sick feeling of homelessness and banishment.

CHAPTER FIFTEEN

IN the kitchen of the Buzza's home, softened by faint lamp-light, Olive sat restlessly before a dwindling fire, her eyes darting from the clock on the mantelpiece to the man who was hunched sphinx-like and aloof, at the table. On the white cloth amid the unwashed tea dishes stood several beer bottles, most of them empty, from which Buzza had been drinking at frequent intervals for an hour or two. His puffy fingers jerked and clawed at the cold glass, he peered steadily at the bottle before him, lapsing into a fuddled state in which he was unaware of Olive's presence. She felt his morbid brooding energy in the room, and though she was accustomed to it there was an unusual galling oppression in it this evening, as if that squat, impotent figure were an image projected by her own frustrated mood.

Tonight was Friday; it was past eight o'clock, and still there was no rattle of sand on the window, the signal of Joel's arrival outside. Her intuition told her that she was wasting time in remaining passive and expectant: Joel had not promised to come. He was different; entangled in some obsession which only her direct attack would cut away from him. She had weakened it at St. Austell on Tuesday, but when he had gone back among the familiar scenes he would be tethered afresh, irresolute.

Had they been alone together in some remote spot on Tuesday, instead of in a town street, she might have turned his rebellion into a sensual channel and drawn him to her in the swift, brutal release of despair. That would have rid him finally of the emotional over-tones of his faded hope for Marvran Creba. But nothing less than his full surrender in the body would free him, and unless this was achieved soon it might be too late.

She brooded on the memory of Joel's sullen face in the magis-

149

trate's court, his reckless admission of guilt, the bitter hungry look he had given her when they parted. Her hands clenched slowly with the thrust of desire; the craving became intolerable, and abruptly she rose, feverishly spurred to action. She moved across to the stairway and took her coat from a nail above the banisters. The movement roused Buzza; he scowled at her.

"Going out again?" he asked testily.

"Seems I've got to," she replied, turning as she pulled on her coat.

He watched her with drowsy resentment until she snatched up a small grey hat from the stairpost and drew it over her short yellowish hair.

"Been expecting a customer?" he inquired.

"No – somebody more important."

"Isn't the blighter coming?"

"Doesn't look so. I must go and find out what's wrong. I'll have to try and fix things wherever I find him – probably shan't bring him back here tonight. I may be out late, but you'll be safe enough here. Have a nap in the chair when you've finished your beer."

Buzza's voice took on the plaintive whine of the confirmed invalid: "I don't like being left alone, Olive, you know I don't."

Olive opened the door leading into the passage. "It can't be helped. If I hit the bull's eye this time you'll soon have a son-in-law for company. Time you had one, isn't it?"

Buzza's face was fear-ridden, the face of a very sick man, as he raised the bottle shakily to his lips. "I shan't live to see that," he mumbled.

"Don't be too sure." She spoke with irritation, and a minute later closed the front door behind her, sealing the cripple in the silent house.

Brilliant moonlight flooded the outer world, glinting here and there on drifts of snow that remained by the hedges. The road had thawed and was now slushy. The air was not cold, but the recent frost had left a crispness and clarity in the atmosphere, contrasting with the heavy, clogged soil and the confused thrusting of twigs and stems released from the pressure of the snow. But Olive was in no mood to observe this natural transformation: briskly she crossed the open valley and began climbing the hill towards Roche, keeping to the centre of the road to avoid the worst patches of mud and the blobs of snow in the gutter. She was tense, alert for the sound of approaching footsteps, her hands clawing at the inside of her empty pockets.

She had not brought the money to replace Joel's fine; she knew he would not accept it. The issue between them must be stripped of such irrelevancies. Yet as she passed the spot where she had first encountered him she felt uneasy: that incident had shown that the mere crude appeal as between male and female would not succeed either. But her task was far less difficult now; and once she had brought him to intimacy, she believed he would be willing to marry her without delay. Her father was in a critical state, the doctor said. He ate little and slept badly; sometimes he had attacks of giddiness and often complained about his heart, which was diseased. It was unlikely that he would survive until the summer: she and Joel would soon have the house to themselves.

Olive anticipated their life together with an excitement that was new to her, apart from her usual emotions. Her feelings for Joel, though selfish and lustful enough in the main, had in it elements of real tenderness. She felt protective towards him: he was in some ways like a child. And there was also in him a rare strength and nobility which put her off a little. Sometimes she wished to destroy these qualities and pull him wholly down to her level; at other times she wished to find the clue to his superiority and to share it. Joel fascinated her; he was distinct from all the men she had known hitherto. She had despised them; but there was something in Joel which she respected. His heaviness and greyness gave him a singular clarity. All that Marvran had found repellent in him attracted Olive, because she judged him from her uncomplicated instinct. And around this core of basic recognition and respect they could build a tolerable marriage. It would not be simple; there would probably be a good deal of brutality, a hard sensual fight between them before the true balance was achieved. But she would trust him in all his moods, depend upon the rooted male element so honest and exposed.

Olive entered the village without meeting anyone; her thought was recalled to the present as she passed into the lamplit streets. She had to decide whether to wait around here and make inquiries, or go straight to Joel's home. She paused for a few minutes outside the public-house, listening. She heard George Bassett's voice in the bar with other voices known to her, but not Joel's. The air was colder here

151

on the hill and she shivered, moving on up the ill-lit, gloomy road, her feet chilled by the slush.

As she reached the corner near the church gates and stood hesitating, she glimpsed a man approaching from Trezaise: a small but energetic figure in dark raincoat and trilby. She soon recognised him as Eli Creba, and an unpleasant grimace crossed her stiffened features. Thoughts of Marvran jabbed her again, whipping up malice and jealousy.

Eli was obviously surprised and flustered to see her there, but he came on with short dogged strides, the melted snow splashing about his feet. His eyes narrowed upon her, and as she stepped deliberately towards him he addressed her sharply:

"Where you off to Olive Buzza?"

Olive's laugh was brittle, derisive.

"Not looking for you, anyway."

"I reckon I know who 'tis," said Eli; his lean red face poked up into the moonlight, aggressive and suspicious. "Seen Joel Kruse this week?"

"What if I have? She demanded.

"I heard you was in court Tuesday," he observed, halting on the corner and spitting sideways into the snow.

"Well? Has Joel dropped any hint at the 'dry'?" She was serious now, anxious for some clue, but Eli remained stubborn and hostile.

"Hardly spoke a word to us since Monday," he muttered. "Me and Bassett thought you'd be taking your chance now he've disgraced hisself."

Eli licked his lips, peering across the downs towards the Kruses' cottage. It was evident that Joel's entanglement with Marvran had humiliated him, that he was fretted by a deep antagonism towards the young man, almost a fear of him, and in his overriding urge to protect Marvran he had no scruples about aiding Joel's downfall with a timely word to Olive. He lurched nearer to her, his arm jerking out, pointing past the bungalow.

"I seen Joel half a hour back, when I was leaving home," he said in a suppressed tone. "Heading across the fields down Carbis way."

"Your daughter wasn't with him, I suppose?"

There could be no doubt of Olive's relief, but her insolent, provocative manner caused Eli's face to darken angrily and brought a rasp into his voice as he continued: "In a ugly mood, Joel is – may be up to some mischief now he've been in court and come a real cropper. I had half a mind to tell the police to keep a lookout on that 'dry' down here – where they'll have the dance to morrow night. Joel's a spiteful beggar when he get the wind up; might put a match to they decorations if he got inside, and burn the place down to stop the decent young folk enjoying themselves there."

Olive smiled mockingly, gliding back into the shadow of the school yard wall.

"I don't think you need to set the police after him again." She said. "Better leave him to me: he needs to be taught a lesson the way I can do it."

Eli grunted but made no further response; he strode on with a shrug of disgust, kicking his way through the soft mire and casting a long shadow upon the whitish road, for the moon was sinking westward, shedding its full crisp gleams from above the coast. Olive slowly followed him, watching until he disappeared inside the gate of the bungalow, then hurried past it, scowling as she heard Marvran's voice indoors greeting her father. The physical presence of Marvran, so close to her, so near Joel still, yet withheld from him and no longer desired, brought upon Olive the fierce pang of possessiveness, with the gross sense that the issue must now be fought in an underworld. Joel, like herself, was cast out from decent society; they would be like lepers groping for one another, revelling in their submerged, closed passions, down there on the clay kiln.

The Crebas' home was the last dwelling on the hilltop, and when she was beyond it she felt that she had escaped from civilisation and was descending into a dark barbaric land. The scene confronting her now was even grimmer than when Marvran had surveyed it on her journey to the Kruses' abode last August. The distant tors loomed icily, and the dwindling froth of snow clutched at the stiff fields like a sickness, a kind of leprosy. And while surfaces were gripped in the numbness of winter, the ancient elemental flow of cruelty was running with a stronger pulse in the soil. Olive felt its savage power and released herself into it, letting the pre-Christian magnetism pull upon her blood. She looked dreamily at the Rock, the ragged fangs of black stone arching and bristling above the snow-tufted knoll. It reminded here of similar outcrops on the moors behind Zennor: she often remembered her childhood when she crossed this plateau. There was the same prehistoric gloom and ferocity here as in that western part of Cornwall where her nature had been moulded and aroused, though this region lacked visible relics of the ancient Bronze Age tribes, while the Penwith area was littered with bee-hive huts, cromlechs, and other tokens of pre Celtic sacrifices and burial. It was the lawless feel of the land, not its remote human associations, that fascinated Olive. She fed on it greedily, her mind consciously closed in upon the male image.

She passed the lane which led to Joel's home, giving only a brief glance up towards the clay-dump. She was sure Joel had not returned there; she believed she knew where to find him, and pursed her lips hungrily as she reached the foot of the hill and saw, beyond a few smallholdings, the stacks and low roofs of Carbis clay-dries. The pout of her mouth became a contemptuous curl as she thought of the young crowd who would swarm along this road tomorrow night and fill one of those sheds with noise and revel. She felt that there was more dignity, if less innocence, in the present situation: she and Joel drawn by their fates to the lonely silent kiln.

When Olive drew abreast of the first group of clay-work buildings she paused, wary and furtive. Everything was very quiet, no one in sight on the road or around the farmsteads. The cluster of clay-dries seemed deserted. She turned in along a cinder-track that wound past several of these which were either still active or too dilapidated to be used as dance-halls. She had learnt from village gossip which shed had been selected for the dance: the last of the group, at the end of the path where a flight of steps led up to a concrete block of settling-tanks now empty and coated with frozen slime and grass. Snow remained on the cinder-track, which was sheltered by stacks and walls; there were even frills of ice where clayey water had leaked out. Olive's footsteps were muffled, except when her shoe crunched a large cinder; she advanced cautiously, holding her breath, alert for the least movement or sound. Her figure glided as a dim blob on the snow, for the moonlight did not penetrate this narrow passage.

When she neared the towering pillar of the stack outside the door of the converted 'dry', there came from the other side of the stack a sound that made here heart swoop up in assurance – the slur of heavy shoes grazing the stone. She knew Joel was there, even while the bulk of the stack hid him from her view, and edged forward on tiptoe, her trembling under-lip dented between her teeth. She moved towards the clay-splashed wall of the shed, and soon glimpsed him.

Joel was slumped against the base of the stack, a cigarette clamped in his mouth, his gaze fixed on the frozen clay-leat that ran close to the tank wall. He was obviously exhausted, for though he started and jerked up his arm as he grew aware of her intrusion, he lapsed back almost at once to a stolid acquiescence. It was as though he had expected her to seek him out. His face looked pale and drawn as he stared at her; the eyes were very tired and somewhat reddened, probably from lack of sleep. He took his cigarette from his lips and straightened. "So it's you," he said dully.

Olive smiled and sought to rouse him with a jest that conveyed the intimate undertones of her mood. "Got any matches left?"

"Matches?" he repeated in bewilderment.

"If you have you'd better hand 'em over to me. I've been sent instead o' the police to make sure you don't set fire to the decorations in there."

Her laugh was rather unpleasant and Joel's face darkened, though he still leaned against the stack. "Who sent you?" he inquired.

"Your prospective father-in-law at least, I suppose he must be that, as you didn't keep your appointment with me."

He puffed at his cigarette, shrugging. "I wasn't in the right mood," he said. "So much been on my mind this week."

"Your sister better?"

"Yes, pulling round now – still in bed, but out o' danger."

"That ought to be a relief. What's held you off tonight? Is it just Marvran – or have you heard you'll have to shift before you're ready?"

The fear of Joel slipping from her grasp through being suddenly removed to a new district had shadowed her mind, and she spoke with genuine concern, frowning at him from the low shed doorway.

He confirmed her suspicions with a glum nod, pushing a hand into his raincoat pocket as he stepped out on to the snow.

"That's part of it," he admitted. "We had word Wednesday. 'Tis all fixed up – first week in March."

There was a brief silence; she was taking the measure of the threat, searching his face. "Where's it to be – far off?" She asked then.

"No; only down to Curyan – house standing by itself near the end o' the row overlooking Nanpean."

Olive's hands fluttered; she almost clapped them as the sense of security returned and strengthened in her. "Even closer to me than you've been at Roche! I can see why you're uneasy!" She swayed forward, her round face glowing. "Will you keep on your job at the 'dry'?"

He shook his head. "I'll have to find something nearer Curyan. Shan't be sorry, either – time I had a change."

"Naturally – with Mr Creba there, and this dance tomorrow night. It'll make you sick of such places." She pointed at the gaunt, squat building. "Have they finished decorating in there?"

"Dunno – I haven't been inside."

He was very grey and reserved, but seemed docile enough. After a moment's hesitation she urged: "Let's go in and see – or is it locked up?"

"Door's locked here, but I expect we could get in down other end, around by the coal yard."

"Well, it'd be a bit of shelter – and it must look interesting, they way they've fixed it. I s'pose it'll be like an old-fashioned barn dance. Quite a novelty. And it does suit the village; far better than the Institute or the stuffy church rooms."

Joel eyed her warily, suspicious of her motive, yet finding comfort in her warm friendliness. For some moments he waited in indecision; then with a confused beckoning gesture he led the way past the tank steps and along the front of the shed, between the railway lines that were overgrown with weed and partly buried in snowdrifts. Olive followed him past the row of swung awnings, dark wooden shutters that creaked on rusty hinges; the white stone pillars loomed rhythmically out of the twilight upon the field of their vision. They did not speak until Joel turned the corner at the far end of the building, stepping down behind a low wall into the little yard where coal had been stacked when the kiln was active. He moved jerkily across to the small door leading in to the furnace. As his hand lifted the latch he nodded, glancing round at Olive as she came inside the moonlit enclosure. "We can get in here," he said.

He opened the door and went in, reluctantly, as if forcing himself. Olive was soon with him in the grimy furnace room, and when she closed the door they were in total darkness, as there was no window or opening in the thick walls. But within a foot of the door a flight of stairs ascended, guarded by a rail, and Joel at once swung on to the steps, the red tip of his cigarette being the only clue to his position.

"Wall's black wi' coal-dust, mind not to rub against it," he mumbled.

Olive gave a soft laugh, fumbling for the rail and climbing heavily behind him. "It doesn't matter much," she replied. "I don't aim to be queen of the ball!"

There were about a score of steps, and then they were on the level of the kiln, facing the door that opened on to it. This door had no lock, and the bolt had been drawn on the inside, but there was a hole through which Joel pushed his finger and after some minutes he worked the rod free of its socket and heaved his shoulder against the door. It would only open half-way, as a platform had been erected just beyond, but there was enough room for him and Olive to squeeze through. When they had entered the shed they paused, scanning the strange, fantastic scene that now confronted them.

The long kiln-pan stretched away, a broad tiled floor above the storage linhay guarded by the massive white pillars. Moonlight filtered in through this, spearing between the wooden doors; but the main illumination came from the opposite side, in big square patches through the openings leading out to the slurry-tanks. The whole kiln was a flickering chequer-board of faint light and dark shadow, and the rafters loomed low down within the track of the moonbeams, so that the tint of coloured paper, Chinese lanterns and streamers, was here and there disclosed. A ladder stood on the platform, where a row of benches had been set ready for the band. The silence was rather ghostly, and when at length Olive broke it her voice sounded stained, hollow. "Isn't it sweet!" she exclaimed. "Think what it'll be like while the dance is on all the lights twinkling up there and dance music blaring here by the furnace wall, and the linhay whirling with little dummy figures. Show how bored they must be always wanting some new kind of thrill. Not like us, Joel; we can be content with one sort, the sort they're afraid of."

Joel seemed not to hear her. He stepped to the edge of the kiln and sullenly took in the incongruous details. His eyes were narrowed to mere slits, and Olive saw that his mood was changing. It would not be so easy to deal with now that he was being challenged by a scene that had such bitter personal associations for him. Outside he had been passive, inclined to drift, yielding to her, but he was stiffening definitely under the silent impact of the kiln.

Presently he turned to face her. There was a hard glint in his eyes; his voice was level and ominous. "This is where she'll be tomorrow night," he said. "Dawdling round wi' fellows like Roy Chegwidden and fishing for bloody compliments! And she'd be here just the same if the blinds was drawn down at our place. 'Tis no thanks to she that Ruth's getting better." He held his cigarette at arm's lengths, his body tense as the fierce memories stung him. "Ruth cried her heart out on Sunday when I told her Marvran wouldn't come. She couldn't make out what had changed Marvran so, for she used to be warm-hearted: our maids loved her before she went to Falmouth. But now… Matters o' life and death is nothing to her now compared wi' a bit o' Valentine foolery. That's the sense of values she's got. I'd rather have yours, Olive."

Olive glanced aside, across the platform. She felt uneasy, for though there was a rough brutality in his speech there was something else also: a hint of spiritual depths she could not penetrate. He was still simple and unsubtle, but his simplicity differed from hers, not only as man differs from woman but in something more radical. She could not define it, but it was there, and it obstructed her.

"Good", she murmured, responding to the surface affinity. "I warned you it would end like this."

He looked steadily at her, blowing tobacco smoke across a moonbeam that slanted a yard in front of him, leaving his features in shadow, indistinct.

"I know why you've come," he said with hard realism. "And I'd take what you're offering if 'twould give me any happiness. I've had precious little so far, and now Marvran's let me down so bad I feel I deserve some."

"You do", Olive put in quickly. "You deserve all I can give you now and always."

But he shook his head, turning away from her. "Twouldn't work; not as I am this evening. I been knocked around too much this week, what wi' that court business and the news about shifting to Curyan.

'Tis like a nightmare, set off by what I run into at Crebas' bungalow last Sunday."

"But there's only one way out, and the sooner you take it the better."

She had moved forward, rousing and persuasive. He had made some concessions, but was not surrendered, not yet close. And he drew back even further from the point of intimacy.

"'Tis no good, I can't Olive; this isn't the mood. I couldn't get any pleasure, do what you might. Me feelings is gone numb: I been freezed up all this week wi' the ice in she."

"No wonder. I know what a terrible knock you've had. I hate her for what she's done to you."

"Yes – yes, you do understand a bit," he said with a furtive glance at her face as it came whitely into a moontrack. "And I'm thankful for it too. But it goes deeper…"

Olive sighed. She had to accept it for the present, the partial triumph. "It's true one isn't always in the right mood," she admitted, "and if you aren't, it'd only make you sicker than ever. I won't press things while you're half stunned with all the devilry that's being heaped on you. But I can hope now, can't I – for something definite?"

"It seems so," he answered gloomily. "Everything's pushing me that way. A few weeks and I'll be living within a mile of you, all my life here broke and ended."

"You wouldn't have wished to stay, with that girl still at the bungalow."

"No, I don't want to see she any more, nor hear what becomes of her. I wish to God she'd married Pearce and spared me this trouble." He stared at his cigarette as he flicked off some ash, growing more agitated. "Yet when she come home first I was thankful – thought I saw the way plain: and as if God had a hand in it. You don't know what a breaking-point I'd got to last August. And she did help, Olive – she did lift me up. 'Twas a new world I seen when I hoped for her."

Olive's hands clenched; a blind jealousy swept in upon her deepening tenderness. She felt an itch of rage against Joel, the powerful, virile figure so near to her, the starved instinct shown nakedly in his face. He and she were so much alike in physical texture that they might be expected to come together automatically, on the mere pull of their nerves and blood. They had little intellect to inhibit them, no social standards. Yet there was this other element, his irrational obsession with something that thwarted her designs.

"Don't rake up that now, only to hurt yourself," she murmured, rather coldly.

"True, it don't help," he said. "But I can't keep back what I feel about it." He stepped down onto the tiled kiln-pan, his emotions rising strongly so that he continued speaking more to himself than to Olive. "If only I'd spoke out before she went to Falmouth – or if she'd learnt her lesson down there and come back seeing things in the right light… But instead o' that" – he jerked his arm around at the shadowy building – "here's her world; the kiln, cold as ice no clay and no fire, but just acting and playing safe. That's the taste God's put in her, and after keeping me waiting all these years I should think He could have done a better job."

The rebellion seethed in Joel now. He began pacing the kiln: a strange, tormented figure moving in and out among the moonshafts. This mood was a little nearer to Olive, and she entered into its dark spirit.

"Never mind God," she said bitterly as she stole across to the sidewalk and paused by the first pillar. "He's served me some dirty tricks too – taking mother and letting Dad get crippled, just when I was trying to go straight. It's no good to think serious like that or try to make sense of anything. Just take what's offered, Joel – and you know what that is from me."

Joel halted and looked at her, rather pitiful in his craving for support. "You still mean it serious, don't you?" he asked.

"Yes I do – honest, Joel. I aren't Marvran Creba, or God either, to play with you and fool you. You could take me to register office next week if you wished."

He frowned in silence for a minute, then roused. "Nothing so hasty as that," he said. "I don't know how long it'll take me to get warmed up to things again. "'Twould be useless for anybody to live with me as I am now: all freezed up – like this 'dry' – and the ice going so deep because I seen the pattern o' what me life could ha' rose to…" He stubbed out his cigarette and tossed the fag-end over the sidewalk onto the floor of the storage linlay which was to be used for the dancing. "Only last Sunday afternoon I met Euan Kella, and he was telling what God had done in clearing up the mess o' what seemed to be his fate. It helped me to get a fresh grip and trust what God was doing when He sent Marvran back. And then I was pitched into this! Faith may have worked all right for Kella, but it've turned out different for me – damned different."

He had concealed all reference to Gwen: another sign that he could not share with Olive his real, true self which had fought so loyally beside Gwen in recent years. Olive was aware only of the turmoil behind his words; the mention of Euan seemed irrelevant and she ignored it. She edged down the sidewalk towards him, stretching out her hand to touch his shoulder.

"Poor Joel, you are tortured tonight," she said soothingly. "Try to be quiet. Think of the times I'm going to give you. Don't fret yourself about that little hussy and don't get yourself frozen stiff with thinking about God. He'll melt like any other iceberg when we get together."

Olive saw from the dark glow on his face that her impiety gave him a sense of fusion, drew her to him more powerfully than the mere sex appeal. He seemed to be regarding her in a new light, as one whose flame could apprehend the Almighty in the fascinating and terrible heats of self-justification. Compared with this the mere animal lust was a dull matter; even Olive felt the keener tang of the spiritual anarchy. She descended onto the kiln and stood in front of him, smiling.

A sharp struggle tore at Joel; he breathed heavily and a tremor of passion ran through him. Abruptly he put his arm about her and pulled her close – but only for a moment: he released her at once with a swift revulsion of feeling and lurched aside, reddening with anger and disgust. "Better go home now," he mumbled in a thin strained tone. "You can't do any good here. Go on home, Olive."

Olive was smouldering with the brief release of desire in him, but she could not mistake the new dangerous note of finality. She must be content with the knowledge that his restraint was weakening. She sighed and stepped from the kiln, lingering by a pillar, one hand resting shakily against it.

"Well – all right," she faltered. "Don't be afraid: I shan't pester you – if you don't keep me waiting too long. I shall expect you to take the lead before you go to Curyan."

He did not reply, but stood dazedly on the kiln, watching her fade into shadow and pass around the platform to the door. She waved to him and called a hesitant "Goodnight!" as she squeezed through.

When she had gone down the dark steps and he heard the lower door click shut behind her, Joel moved wearily across the kiln and seated himself on the edge of the sidewalk, under a pillar. He leaned forward, awesomely alone as in the nave of a cathedral, with the faint rays of moonlight playing through the vast empty spaces.

The blind, hot emotion now welled up slowly, breaking up frozen surfaces that had gripped him all this week. At length he felt tears against his hands, saw them splash down upon the floor. The irony was complete now, and brought him to a rare moment of self-pity, a spasm of fanaticism in which there was both exultation and bitterness.

"I'm leaving my mark on the kiln, though she'll never know," he murmured chokily. "My tears and not my sin!"

The kiln darkened around him; a cloud had covered the moon. Above him the Chinese lanterns and paper streamers swayed slightly as the cold night wind crept in among the rafters.

CHAPTER SIXTEEN

FROM a ridge of the Nanpean – Roche road, at Whitemoor, Rachel Kella glanced impatiently over a scene on which a break low in the southern sky had permitted March sunlight to be thrown in lifeless straw-coloured bars. The landscape to the extreme west and south was composed of rich farmland, wooded dales, the criss-cross of country lanes along natural declivities and swellings of the soil. But to the north and east the features of the clay district gave to the view a harshly aggressive character in its sudden and prolific outbreak. Over every slope and about every hamlet sprawled the crisp gleaming waste sand of the clay-pits. Impressive against any background, they were most majestic on the wild hedgeless plateau spreading into Hensbarrow Downs to the east, and undulating northwest to the bleak tableland around Black Cross: areas seldom visited except by the labourers at these remote pits and desolate dunes.

Rachel, familiar all her life with this type of landscape, gave no special heed to it. She moved briskly over the brow of the hill and down the steep, winding lane leading north to Roche. The road was flanked by squalid dwellings, many of them converted railway carriages; below, in the neck of the valley, a few granite cottages gave a more appropriate touch to the picture.

Rachel's interest was centred on these houses; and as she approached them she was surprised to see a small, middle-aged man pass from the gateway of her sister's home near the end of the block and move away with an odd, stealthy air. He seemed cowed and dejected, glancing over his shoulder as if fearing that his visit to the cottage had been observed. He raised his hand several times to his grey trilby, and when he reached the strip of open moorland below, a swarthy tongue of Goss Moor that licked between the shadowing hill, he began poking with his walking-stick at the ferns and gorse bushes that fringed the hedgeless track. He headed westward across the flat heath towards St. Dennis, and was lost to Rachel's view before she drew abreast of the row and strode vigorously up between the shrubs bordering the Webb's front garden.

Her black eyes, narrowed against the sun, lit next, with darkening fascination, upon the adjoining house, the last of the group. She noted the rough stone walls, the bedroom window, open, with a rug hanging across its lower sash, the blotchy green paint on the closed door. Her dark, full face, red and sweating under her felt hat, expressed a shuddering aversion. She never enjoyed calling at her sister's home. After the complete isolation and rural freshness of her own abode, the taint of a vicious slum atmosphere that reeked next door to the Webb's was disturbing to a woman of her turbulent and embittered virtue. And today she was more than ever on the defensive, her nerves strung taut with suspense concerning Euan. Every suspicious movement, as of the stranger leaving her sister's house, every spot that reminded her of the warped havens to which struggling youth might be forced, broke upon her with sly, shrill insinuation.

Without knocking at the Webb's door she lifted the latch and entered. The passage inside was dark except at one point where sunbeams pulsed in whitish, smoky bars from the parlour. A sound of flicking cloth told her at once that her sister, Ellen, was busy dusting the furniture in that room; a moment later, as Rachel stumbled over the cat asleep on a pile of carpets by the partition, Ellen appeared in the parlour doorway: a mild complacent soul, bearing little resemblance to the restless, fiery figure of the younger woman. Somewhat taller than Rachel, not quite so stout, and of a fairer complexion, she was always happier, and her face showed it.

"So you'm come, Rachel!" she greeted in a slow, comfortable voice. "All clear back home?"

"Yes; Euan'll manage to get his own dinner today when he comes in from the claywork. He'll be up at Barrakellis all afternoon helping Veale to clear the clay-stream."

"Oh! What've happened there?"

"With all the rain we've had this week, part o' Veale's pasture's fallen away through the night – a great mass of the bank slipped down into the leat, and it've stopped the water-wheel."

"And Digory seen Euan on the way to work, I s'pose – told'n about it?"

"No; Euan doesn't know about it yet. Veale asked me when I went up for milk early today if Euan could come and help; so I've left a note on the table. Good news for him, I think." Rachel's mouth twitched ironically.

"Do Euan go up to the farm often?" Ellen inquired.

"I can't say how often. He's out in the evenings more than he used to be, but beyond that…"

"You've still got your suspicions?"

"I have – but I shan't say nothing to Cal Mannell… It can't be kept close much longer, if there is anything going on." Rachel followed Ellen into the fire-warmed cosily-furnished parlour, frowning heavily when the two again stood face to face.

"That note of mine will puzzle Euan, I expect. He'll be wondering whether I really do suspect some affair with Gwen Kruse, or whether I'm deliberately encouraging him to go to the farm."

Ellen nodded. "Plenty o' mysteries around Barrakellis lately," she observed.

Rachel continued to stare at her, hard and quizzical. "You've had one visitor here already this morning, it seems!"

Ellen's small pale mouth dropped open; her face looked somewhat foolish, as if she were uncertain whether the fall of her jaw had been intended to express astonishment or amusement. "That fellow you jist seen leaving here?" she said at length, casually.

"Yes. I didn't know what to make of it. Quite a stranger to me. Who was it?"

"Crago, from over to Enniscaven," replied Ellen, moving to the window and peering out with her hand on the cold glass. She was framed by the red curtains, a subdued figure, wearing a white pinafore over her grey blouse. "First time he been here; we only know un by sight."

"What's he come here after? Seemed fishy to me slinking off as if he felt half ashamed of hisself."

"Well, he didn't come on very pleasant business," remarked Ellen, turning slowly, her blue yes now shadowed. "Worried again about his boy Charlie; he's always off late at night and sometimes don't get home from work till supper-time. He called over to ask if we'd seen Charlie hanging round Buzzas', in next door, lately."

"One of Olive's customers?" suggested Rachel in a hard, jerky tone of disgust.

"He was last year. Olive got'n down pretty bad; made a proper nuisance here. He'd stop his lorry outside when he was passin' carryin' clay to the docks, and drop in a minute. Sometimes Olive'd come out to the lorry instead and they'd spoon up in sight of anybody that might be lookin': neither of 'em didn't care."

Rachel seated herself with abrupt energy in an armchair beside the grate, her lips twitching, her hands plucking at her brown costume. "Calf love, I s'pose, on Crago's part; or was he old enough to know better?"

"In his teens then. Bad job for his family – a decent lot. Old Crago seemed broke up about it, wondering where the disgrace is goin' to break out – or where 'tis goin' to stop."

"Did you have any news for him?"

"Not what he thought. I told'n that affair wi' Olive was played out months ago: ha'n't seen Charlie around here since Christmas. Must be some other maid he've falled for now."

"Olive gone quieter since they broke?"

"Not yet: one less don't trouble she. She don't go smooth wi' none of her fancies. Indeed, there was another rumpus in there only last night."

"Oh! Who was it this time, anyone you know?"

Ellen took her her duster from the head of the sofa and moved nearer to the mantelpiece.

"Yes; but a very different sort o' business from the usual thing that goes on in there," she answered stolidly. "If it'd come to anything I wouldn't ha' mentioned it. But as 'twas…"

"What happened?" demanded Rachel.

Ellen sat down in the vacant armchair, stroking her pink cheeks meditatively.

"Me husband was outside just after dark," she began, "locking up the coal-house where he'd dumped in a few sticks from the sand-burrows, when he heard footsteps coming down the hill – Olive in front and some man a yard or two behind her. Tom thought first that he was drunk as he seemed all stupefied, comin' after her like if he didn't know what he was doin'. "Twas good moonlight and Tom seed 'em plain as they got to gateway and went up the path. The chap looked real stewered, but Tom saw he wasn't drunk; and havin' recognised him he wasn't much surprised. He come in feeling there'd be something funny about it, and so it proved. Once they'd got indoors the fellow seemed to come to hisself. We heard Olive go back to stairway and begin climbing up; but the man didn't follow, and after a minute she come down again. We heard her ask him what was the matter, but he didn't make no answer at all. He was still standing out in the passage from all we could gather, and Olive soon begun to get rattled started to laugh and jeer at'n, and then we heard the door open and the chap went stumbling out to roadway and up the hill; no harm done and nothing more likely to come of it."

"Rather strange, certainly," commented Rachel. "Who was it?"

"Gwen Kruse's brother Joel," Ellen replied hesitantly, dropping her duster on the cat, a plump tabby which had just come in from the passage and begun rubbing itself against her leg. "They say Olive been mad after'n for months wanted to pull'n in so they's have to be married. It seems he's still holding off – puttin' up a stiff fight agin his family influence, that chap. But it look as if he's badly in need of a decent maid to settle down with."

The room had darkened while Ellen was speaking: the firelight flickered out more prominently as the sunshine became smothered in rain-clouds bellying overhead for a shower. The trees along the valley stood abject and rigid in the transformation, shadows deepening upon them and over all the visible earth while the horizon brightened: a weird effect, darkening in Rachel the chill sense of foreboding caused by Ellen's news.

"No doubt that's at the bottom of it," she agreed in a hard, suppressed tone.

"Strain got too much for a minute – Olive catched him off guard. I don't think anybody's likely to hear of it. Joel will be too ashamed to mention what happened, and Olive's too vexed at the way it fizzled out. I shouldn't pass on what I told 'ee."

A scornful grunting sound escaped Rachel as she turned to watch the sombre changes of shape and tone beyond the window. "'Tis hardly my line – and I got no hope that Euan would profit by such a moral lesson. I may even hear yet that he's been in next door!"

This was a mere flash of bitterness, as Ellen knew, but she protested mildly: "You can't believe he'd ever stoop to that, Rachel. Mind, the boy have done some queer things since his father died. His affair wi' Lela Skiddy didn't bring him much credit, specially when he lost his temper wi' Cal Mannell at the claywork. And he haven't darkened these doors since he left school, as a nephew might be expected to. But I don't believe he'd bring a real scandal on the family."

"He might do anything – so far as appearances go," observed Rachel. "It isn't that he'd act shabby – if he's making up to Gwen Kruse it's because he means to marry her. He hasn't any taste for low life, but he seems fascinated by something that looks low but really isn't – from his high-minded standpoint. Always on the danger-line, looking about like a fanatic, quite sure he can't come to any harm."

"He've got no practical sense at all, that's the trouble. He just couldn't see that he was climbing down when he had to give up his school career to go to the clayworks. Apart from being upset about his father's death I think he welcomed the change. And he'd bring me somebody like Kruses' girl and really expect me to take her as a daughter-in-law, and be as proud as if she came from the highest circles in Cornwall."

Ellen straightened, her dark bulk scarcely distinguishable in the gloom that now flowed in on the parlour from the floundering mass of rain-cloud.

"Well, the Kruses isn't much lower than the Skiddys, come to that," she remarked. "There don't seem to be many decent families about these days; wherever you look there's looseness going on. Even Barrakellis farm quite apart from what Euan may be doing there isn't so respectable a place as 'twas when Bessie Veale was alive."

"It certainly isn't," said Rachel grimly.

"If Sue Mannell get in there for good… But somehow I can't believe a steady-goin' fellow like Digory'll let a woman o' that sort twist him round her finger."

"He still goes up to Carloggas after her, anyway and he've changed a lot these last two months; got shifty and grumpy. He knows what his neighbours think of him, and do keep out of their way. I hardly ever stop at the farm to talk these days. Sometimes I don't see either Veale or Kruses' girl, I find the filled jug waiting on the table. The girl's as sly and uncomfortable as he when I do meet her – got a guilty conscience too, I s'pose!"

Rachel's glance turned to the window. The shower had come, the first drops splashing and blurring the panes. The centre of the sky was black with lowering cloud, but the horizon east and south remained as a whitish rim, a narrow slit letting in light that played across the landscape and gave the shapes of trees and hedges a strange dark boldness.

And suddenly, following the slam of a door, a grosser mass intruded beyond the garden wall: the short, full figure of Olive Buzza, dressed in a grey coat and scarlet hat which struck like a flame upon the wan skyline and then rose against the rain-cloud as she stepped further out into the road. She stood for a few moments hesitating, her face lifted irritably, screwed up at the rain, then marched off down the hill towards Roche.

Rachel watched with intent, haggard fascination, half-rising from the chair, her hand trembling slightly as it groped to the sideboard. Ellen also got up, in time to see Olive disappear below the shrubs of the garden.

"Wonder where she's goin' now?" observed Ellen, turning stolidly back to resume her dusting. "You can see she's worked up: that business last night must have been the last straw. She won't know where to try or what to do next. But somebody'll have to pay, and pay pretty dear, 'fore that maid's quiet again."

CHAPTER SEVENTEEN

THE white gates of the level crossing were closed beyond the tangle of sidings that frayed off among the drying-sheds of Parkandillack claywork. Joel Kruse paused by the wire fence that divided the main railway track from the sidings and stared at the nearer gate a few hundred yards ahead, now a grey smear in the gathering darkness, the red lamp burning on top of it. The sight of the barrier seemed to jolt him into a vague consciousness that every step in this direction was taking him further away from home. He blinked at it, half stupefied, aware that something had gone wrong with him, that had he been in a normal state he would now be at home having tea instead of wandering aimlessly.

He had been walking for half-an-hour along the railway line from the wharf of a china stone quarry at Goonamarris Slip, where he was now employed. It was a mineral railway, used only by outgoing trains carrying clay and china stone from the pits, and incoming trains bringing coal and other supplies from South Wales and the Midlands. It formed a vast hoop hinging on St. Austell and enclosing practically the whole of the mid-Cornwall clay district. Joel had now reached its north-western corner, Parkandillack claywork being the last inside the bounds of the rails before the track swung out upon Goss Moor and nosed across a flat, bog-infested waste to the next ridge of clay-bearing land just north of Roche.

Joel felt that in more than a geographical sense he had reached a limit. The landscape with it blurred, clammy pyramids, bristling stacks, rust-red 'dry'-roofs, and the railway line boring along the valley, sometimes over a bridge, sometimes under one, mirrored the confused, fantastic quality of his mind. He leaned for a few minutes again at a post of the fence: a burly figure in clay-smeared corduroy trousers, raincoat and cap, but looking as if he had aged a good deal, the broad shoulders slumped, the face bony and haggard. He was much agitated, physically and emotionally tired out. He had slept little last night and had eaten nothing since the mid-morning 'crib' at the works.

When the other quarrymen returned home at noon, Joel had stayed behind on the wharf, and as soon as they disappeared he had climbed down into the quarry. All the afternoon he had remained there, sheltering in the tool-shed during heavy showers, moving out to sit on stone-heaps when a few gleams of sunshine pierced down. The place reminded him of the clay-pit outside his old home, but he had never endured in that pit a mood such as this. He felt unable to go back to his new home until he had mastered the crisis that had broken upon him in the past twenty-four hours. But when dusk began to close in he had still reached no understanding, no decision. He had scrambled wearily up to the railway line and headed westward, hemmed in between the palings, becoming almost panicky as the countryside darkened around him.

Now, however, confronted by Prazey level-crossing, he realised that it was time he took a grip on himself. His parents were probably not worried by his failure to return home for dinner or tea; they knew his vagaries, knew he was upset about Marvran. He had often missed a meal at weekends recently, taking long, lonely rambles. But they would be anxious if he did not arrive for supper.

He moved on jerkily along the track, his head bent, fascinated by the gleam of the wet rails and bleared light on the barrier. Pools several inches deep lay between some of the sleepers, and his boots often slipped, splashing into them, but as his feet had been drenched by the quarry puddles he felt no fresh discomfort. His sense impressions were blunted; he was preoccupied with the inner sickness, the hot shame and bafflement. He slunk along like an outcast, glancing furtively aside as he passed some cottages under the embankment, so near and low that smoke fumed from their chimneys on a level with his face. He hardly noticed it; it was the grime within, in his brain, that was suffocating.

Recent depression had probably toned him for last night's debâcle. Since his meeting with Olive in the clay-dry he had lived almost in stupor, in a faded consciousness. The bustle of shifting the furniture from Roche to Curyan, settling into the new house and taking the new job, had reduced him to a vague sense of general dis-integration. His whole world seemed to be breaking up. He was freed from the literal dry-kiln and now worked in the open air, but within him the clay that had begun to take pattern under Marvran's touch was running slack and formless again. The vision she had inspired was dead and remote, part of another life. Yet he could not seek out Olive and try to find reality in her; she had become even more starkly an impersonation of his natural fate, the slime of the kiln. The thought of Gwen had also deterred and steadied him, though it was very painful in contrast to his own frustrated state. As far as he knew, the secret courtship at Barrakellis was progressing without a hitch. He had seen little of Gwen since his final break with Marvran, but it was clear that her happiness was shadowed only by her concern about himself. She guessed that his hopes of Marvran had collapsed, and had probably heard the rumours that linked him with Olive.

The cloud had weighed heavily upon him when he left home last evening. He had roamed round Curyan Vale for an hour, until moonrise, then strolled up the ridge to Whitemoor and the huddle of clay-dumps on the plateau dipping west of St. Dennis. In mid-evening he had entered a claywork lodge on Trelavour Downs, intending to sit on the bench for awhile, brooding. Just inside the doorway a small can of tar had been left by the workmen, and in the gloom he had kicked this over, splashing tar on to his trousers. Irritation at this mishap had further deadened his mind, and his actions became mechanical. He was stooping over the bench, scraping the tar off his trousers with a piece of stick, when suddenly there came the sound of footsteps and Olive Buzza's voice greeted him from the threshold:

"So it's you at last! I saw you slip in here..."

He did not recall any conversation, only that Olive had glided in and caught his sleeve, and that the contact, the warmth of her had completely sealed off his consciousness and volition, so that like one hypnotised he had followed her across the downs to the road below Whitemoor and thence to her home. The whole memory was nause-ating, and he shrugged irritably now as he reached the level-crossing, angry with himself and impotent.

Joel stumbled out between the white posts into the road and

turned eastward. The great bulk of Carne Hill loomed ahead of him, the lights of St. Dennis twinkling along its southern and eastern slopes. The nearest way to Curyan was through this village, but when he gained the crossroads on the fringe of it he headed away from the streets around the dark northern base of the Carne. It was only a month ago that he had come to St. Dennis and watched Marvran enter the cinema, and the recollection was too painful in the glaring, lurid light of the catastrophe that had since overtaken him. He turned away to protect himself. And even in the lonely lane he kept close to the hedge, his footsteps muffled in the mud of the gutter. He wished to return home unrecognised. The precaution was fortunate. As he approached the tiny hamlet of Enniscaven, half a mile further on, he glimpsed at the top of a farm track a moving blob which closer scrutiny revealed as a pair of lovers. The man was tall and thin, like a wavering black stalk, the girl rather podgy; and somehow they did not look like a normal couple. The man showed a reluctance and the girl hung on to him with a sort of fierce possessiveness. Joel, halted, peering steadily through the dusk, and was soon convinced that something similar to that incident on Trelavour Downs last night was being enacted here, and that one of the persons was the same. He realised that the man was Charlie Crago and the girl Olive.

Joel's pulse hammered violently; a wave of confused recoil went over him. He had been weakened by cold and hunger as well as by emotional strain, and this fresh shock was a severe tax on his nerves. He leaned against the dripping foliage of the hedge, his hands clenched, holding his breath. He could not go on past them and his eyes darted round, seeking some way of escape.

Between him and the farm lane, was a long, narrow strip of waste land outside the field – an enclosure that had once been used for storing tree-trunks and sawn logs. It was still littered with scraps of wood and piles of wet, mouldering sawdust and shavings, and near the lane was the broken body of a lorry that had belonged to a timber merchant, now stripped of its wheels and engine. This fascinated Joel, and a strength returned to his limbs he found himself moving almost involuntarily towards it. He passed through a gap in the low outer wall, picking his way carefully among the logs, and along by the field hedge, screened from view by the lorry. Stealthily he drew nearer to the couple, and before he had got half way across the timber yard he heard Olive's voice, tense and urgent:

"You can guess why I've come, Charlie."

The man's weak voice, shaken by a consumptive cough, answered sulkily:

"Afraid I can't. Thought we'd said good-bye months ago – had enough of it."

"You're mistaken, my old boy – can't get off as easy as that. You've damn well got to do something about this."

"About what?"

"You're a bit dense tonight, Charlie. You must know I've failed, after all these months. With Joel Kruse."

A pause followed, during which Joel crept close up to the lorry and crouched behind it, his hand trembling on the rear mudguard buckled against the hedge.

"I thought it didn't look too hopeful," Charlie murmured at length, "when I saw you with him that night on Roche Hill."

"It got better after that. The night before the Valentine dance in Carbis 'dry' I felt sure I'd got him. He was broke up about Marvran Creba – had been in the police-court and knew it was no good looking to her again – or to any other decent girl. He definitely promised... But the weeks went on and nothing happened. And last night – it misfired again, worse than ever."

"Got him down around Curyan this time?"

"Never mind where, I didn't get him, that's all. It made me feel mad and I had to work it off somehow this morning. Went up Roche meaning to see Marvran Creba and ask her what the hell she'd done to Joel. But she wasn't in: I only saw her mother and didn't stop talking long on the doorstep. Mrs Creba assured me there'd never been any understanding between her daughter and Joel that Marvran hadn't visited the family for two months, and she was sure Joel would get over his disappointment now he'd shifted to Curyan." Olive's laugh grated with dreary mockery; her tone grew more smouldering and intense as she continued: "I came back feeling flattened: the bubble's burst. It's no good going on after this. I'm really fed up with him. Never saw such a fool. I don't know what he wants: Marvran's no good to him, yet he won't come to me either. So it's time I switched off and now it's your turn. After all, it was you who put me on this wild goose chase."

Charlie's reply was sullen, rather jeering, but it conveyed only a superficial resistance: "I didn't know there was another girl in the running. Tisn't my fault if you wasn't quick enough on the uptake."

"Joel isn't my type really, no more than those others you mentioned – Cal Mannell and Euan Kella. And you know this game's played out. I've just got to get married. There's only you left, Charlie – you owe it to me..." her voice dropped, wheedling and coaxing, as Joel had heard it last evening, but more assured and intimate.

"You know you want to, Charlie. You have all along... only you was a bit scared: just a little boy, you know, and it took you out of your depth. But you've got tougher since: I've heard things... But you needn't stop amusing yourself because you marry me. I don't promise anything extravagant; only we'd be safe and have the right company..."

Joel heard the sudden smack of her mouth on Charlie's, the confused slur of his feet as she pressed him back against the hedge; and he bit his lip, hot tides of shame racing up afresh in him.

"There!" said Olive as she relaxed her embrace. "It'll be all right... And I've been thinking: why not let Roche parson do the Job, if he'll agree to? Gosh! Wouldn't it be a scream especially if we could make it a double wedding!"

"Eh?" Charlie seemed dazed, responding mechanically.

"With Miss Creba and Roy Chegwidden, perhaps!"

"Ah! Yes, I her they're getting' thick – off dancing together a lot since that Valentine affair. May not be anything serious, though."

"I think it is. She'll be eager to show Mr Kruse how fast she can work among her equals around here, if not at Falmouth. And I'm in much the same mood."

"What about your dad, though?" Charlie mumbled. "I don't want to live there while he's above ground."

"Dad's weakening fast – the next attack'll finish him, so doctor says. It may come any day between now and summer. And then we'll be spliced: a real top-hole wedding, all in the newspapers. 'Marriage solemnised, etc., parson officiating, between Miss Olive Buzza, daughter of the late, etc... and Mr Charles Crago, son of the chapel steward of Enniscaven. The happy couple are well-known and highly respected throughout the district.' About as true in our case as in any other, old boy - let'em rip!"

The mockery and defiance of her manner was almost frightening to Joel. She had not reached this pitch last night, and it was probably fortunate for him that his stupidity had turned her mood to derision instead of whetting such passion as was now broken loose in her and thrown upon Charlie.

Joel had no wish to stay here longer. Obviously something more than words would close the scene, and these crudities of village life were the last things he ought to contemplate if he were to regain emotional balance.

Stiffly he rose and stole back to the end of the timber-yard, then climbed the hedge, lying close against the grass and bracken, and rolled over, clutching at the foliage as he slipped down into the field on the other side. It was now almost dark, and without fear of observation he crossed the fields to a gate opening into the lane several hundred yards below Charlie and Olive. Within a few minutes he was in another field, heading eastward, near the group of cottages called Enniscaven, whose windows, lighted by oil lamps of varying brilliance, looked out directly upon the vast tract of Goss Moor. Behind these dwellings Carne Hill towered up, a bleak, ragged tor on this northern side, retaining much of the savage spirit of pre-Christian times, when it had been a Celtic stronghold.

Joel struck out upon the road again on the fringe of the hamlet, and passed through it with freshening consciousness. Now that he knew Olive was not at home he could follow the road all the way to Curyan, past the Buzzas' house. The short cut across the clayworks and open downs was dangerous after nightfall unless one carried a lantern.

He could not dismiss from his mind the talk he had just overheard, but Charlie's surrender helped to throw into relief the one salient fact to which he had clung all day, pitting it fiercely against the sense of final, irremediable disgrace. Olive had not touched him; he had escaped without even a kiss from her. He paused now and then and lifted his arm, staring at the raincoat sleeve, soiled with fresh mud from the quarry stone and the waggon. Olive's hand had rested there last night, first at the lodge and then inside her home, in the dark passage as she led him along towards the stairs. All the clothes he was wearing now, except his boots, had been under Olive's roof within the past twenty-four hours. They clung about him with a clammy defilement; but his body had not been harmed. It was still as whole and intact as it had been three weeks ago when Olive left him alone in Carbis clay-dry. Apart from the one kiss she had given him by the roadside at Roche last January, he had not even known the pressure of the girl's lips. Yet his mind was bruised, and he knew he could never recover the almost sexless apathy in which he had hardened himself to live while Marvran was at Falmouth. He felt wounded somewhere deep in himself, in his basic impulses and the vague religious emotions that had been released by the brief glimpse of beauty beyond his kiln-world. He was now rid of Olive, his fate through her had fallen away from him; but the predestination through Marvran was also a spent force: he was quite indifferent to rumours of her attachment to Roy Chegwidden. The battle had passed over him and receded, leaving him numb, vacuous.

Presently he caught the gleam of lights on the slope that straggled down from Whitemoor. He paused and lit a cigarette – the last he had on him, as he had smoked half a dozen in the quarry this afternoon. The cool, strong taste was stimulating, and he approached the Buzzas' home with a freshened step. When he turned the corner and made to cross to the opposite ditch, he was brought momentarily to a halt, staring.

No light shone from the window of the house, but a woman was standing at the gate, a dark lean figure in the glow of lamplight streaming from neighbouring windows. As he moved jerkily into the shadow, she came towards him.

"You live here in the row?" she inquired.

The voice was harsh and rasping, that of an elderly woman. The speaker was unknown to Joel, but he was somewhat relieved by the prosaic challenge that edged him from personal fever. He took the cigarette from his lips and answered stolidly: "No, I belong up Curyan."

"Ah! Well, I just come from Curyan meself," the woman responded. "Been up wi' Lela Skiddy and her mother all afternoon, and when I heard 'em telling that Olive had been rather down in the dumps lately, I thought I'd stroll down and try to cheer her up a bit.

She and Cal used to be very thick at one time before I came back from Scilly."

Joel now realised that the stranger was Sue Mannell, and an instinct warned him not to reveal his identity. He knew that Gwen disliked Sue, and that Veale had been forced to check Cal's overtures to the girl as soon as she began working at Barrakellis.

"Yes – yes, I mind hearing of it," he said with reserve.

Sue pointed up at the blank window above the shrub-tops. "I wonder how many nights that was Cal's bedroom," she remarked sardonically. "He won't tell me much about that affair. Reckon it got a bad taste in his mouth somehow. I dunno what'd he'd say to me if he knowed I'd come here now to rake up his old scandals. But I thought it might put fresh heart in Olive to be minded o' they old times. And if she didn't want to hear about Cal, there's plenty of amusin' tales to tell o' me old Plymouth days: I used to know a lot o' maids like she up there. And when she tired o' that, we could have some fun tellin' about me lousy little snob of a daughter, Lorraine."

"I see," Joel muttered, preparing to move on.

"But it seems Olive's gone off somewhere," continued Sue. "That's why I spoke to 'ee – thought you might know where she's gone if you lived here."

Joel made a confused gesture, the red glow of the cigarette jerking between his fingers.

"I can't say where she spends her evenings," he replied, taut and defensive.

Sue stared at him, perplexed by the unnatural restraint in his manner. She was about to make more personal inquiries to satisfy her curiosity when her attention was suddenly diverted.

The Webb's front door abruptly opened and Ellen appeared, hatless and wearing a white pinafore. A glance showed that she was much perturbed, and on sighting the couple in the road she called tremulously: "Have 'ee been in next door?"

"No – only knocked and didn't get no answer," replied Sue, astonished at the sharp greeting from a stranger. "Olive's flitted – working hard on some new customer, I suppose."

Ellen raised both hands as she came out through the gateway. Her face was now seen to be pale and twitching.

"Just like that maid to go off and leave her father in the house by hisself! I reckon she've done it once too often."

"Why, anything up?" asked Sue, frowning.

"Yes; something's wrong in there. I just been upstairs for scissors to do a bit o' sewing – me husband being off for the evenin' – and I heard old Buzza in bed groaning and trying to call for help. Another heart attack, most likely. I must go in and see if anything can be done."

She moved past Sue and up the path. The door was unlocked and pushing it open she entered the dark passage. Sue hesitated for a minute, then followed her, leaving Joel in the road. He too, however, felt the pull of drama and soon crossed to the gate, leaning against the stone post, and blinking dazedly after the women as they disappeared.

Their footsteps sounded on the stairs, then a spurt of a light flashed in the bedroom, causing Joel to lift his eyes with a startled fascination. Just so the light would have flared last evening as Olive led him into her chamber…

A period of chilly suspense was unbroken till Sue came down and reappeared in the doorway. She was much sobered; her voice muttered with irritation. "Bad job this: look's as if the man's dying," she announced.

Joel staggered: he was less prepared than Sue for this unexpected denouement, though it was a fitting close to this strange day of lurid, elemental shadow. He rallied and stepped back with a wrench of his whole body. "Dying?" He repeated.

"Seems like it. Somebody must go for doctor."

The request met Joel's immediate need of physical exertion, a break from the sense that he was drifting in a remote dream-consciousness. He felt that he moved under a destiny, unresisting. "All right," he said in a fresher tone. "I'll call in up here at Whitemoor on me way back and ask 'em to phone the St Dennis doctor. I'll go straight on to Curyan then – shan't come back here."

With a clumsy flick of his cigarette in farewell he hurried away into the darkness.

CHAPTER EIGHTEEN

THE train from Penzance on the afternoon of the last Saturday in April brought Lorraine Mannell to St. Austell station. During the past week she had been shaken by momentous news, and had reached a decision which, a few months ago, would have seemed to her fantastic.

Since the previous Sunday she had received two telegrams and a letter from Sue, the first stating that her mother's affair with Digory Veale had suddenly collapsed and that she was now alone at Carloggas cottage; the second, that her brother Cal was dying as the result of an accident at the clayworks. Both telegrams had contained an urgent request that Lorraine should reconsider her former resolve and come back to Cornwall. The proposal had at first burdened Lorraine with aversion and dismay; had she been the cold, spiteful girl her mother thought her, she would have ignored it. But, though she sometimes sulked and was petulant, she could never be callous. She knew that under this double stroke of adversity her Mother's plight was desperate. Sue was now over sixty, probably shunned by respectable neighbours, and could not manage alone. She had always been robust, but as the frailties of age crept upon her she would need someone about the house. Lorraine had therefore decided that once again she must share her mother's life, now in a district quite unknown to her, but about which she had often felt a deep curiosity. It was the scene of Sue's birth and downfall, and something of its hard mysticism had passed to Lorraine through the gross Cornish veins of her parent.

Having agreed to the new plan, Lorraine found her reaction to it become more tolerant, even hopeful. Whatever the change meant, it seemed well-timed. The monotony of island life had grown tiresome during the past two months. She had heard nothing from Sue, and the sense of being isolated, cut off from the currents of the world, was depressing. She had tried to deepen her friendships with a few St. Mary's girls, and even with one or two young fellows, flower growers and fishermen, but still felt at a dead end, with no prospect of advance or achievement. These people did not understand her. She had realised finally that, although it would not be difficult for her to find a husband among the islandmen, there was none with whom she could attain the smooth unflawed self-exposure which she craved.

There had been no orderly development of Lorraine's nature. Had she remained in Plymouth she would probably have sought to escape the festering conditions of her home through an early marriage, as Gwen Kruse was doing in similar circumstances. But the transition from slum life to an exotic island background at the dawn of her adolescence had caused a warning and confusion of impulse. All her experiences had marked her deeply: she was sensitive, burdened with the need for communion, both spiritual and sensual. She had responded with vague, but intense, emotions to the religious influences that occasionally touched her. Some of Sue's neighbours in the Barbican area were Catholics, and Lorraine had attended Mass a few times with her playmates, becoming awed and fascinated by the mystery and transcendence in the ritual. She had been equally stirred at Salvation Army street meetings. Thus her memories of Plymouth were a mosaic of sharp contrasts: prostitution and prayer, drunken brawls and religious conversions. But her own home life had been entirely submerged in the darker elements.

As she had approached her twenties, with the fresh island images jostling those of her childhood, she felt that the two phases must be fused in an experience that would preserve what was essential in both. Plymouth had instructed her in human wickedness; the flower fields had taught her the goodness of the earth. There had been tones and evocations in each world that appealed to her, but in neither could she find satisfaction. She did not recoil fastidiously from a career of vice; she turned from it on spiritual grounds, and because her insight had gone deep enough to affect her physical reactions. And for the same reason she could not accept the higher paganism of Nature, the awareness of divinity in mere creation. Memories of the

Mass and the Salvationist meetings had led her to more complex levels of worship.

At first she had found a sort of rapture in the flooding colour of the daffodil harvests. In contrast to the cramped, stifling alleys she had known, there was a sense of spiritual release and potency in the broad seascape, the salt winds blowing in over the isles, and the sight of the moon lifting its white flare above Land's End and the black, floundering waters. But the vision had faded, inadequate. In some of her moods it even repelled her: it was too gentle and relaxed, too remote from the raw, fierce heat in which she yearned to be vitalised. The monotonous rhythm of fertility grew wearisome; she wished to get beyond it to an experience that was redemptive rather than creative, a stormy, purgatorial re-fashioning of the slum dross.

She felt expectant now as she turned back towards the Cornish clay-lands, for there indeed both her worlds were merged in a fantastic microcosm. Beauties of the open countryside, yet everywhere the sense of something gritty, enclosed and ignoble; and out of it all the clean white clay, the form and pattern created beyond the refuse and the roaring kiln fires...

The railway journey from Penzance, through the soft luxuriant Hayle Valley, the bleak and scrubby tin-mining area around Camborne, past Truro with its stabbing cathedral spires, and up through the dozen miles of rich agricultural land to the clay-bearing plateau, was poignant to Lorraine with reminders of that other journey nine years ago, that westward flight from Plymouth. She had been a precocious adolescent then, a wild creature palpitating with quest and desire; and now she was coming back past the unchanged landmarks, mature, yet loveless still. The goal was elsewhere, and as she neared St. Austell and saw here and there the white cones of the clay-sand tips in the distance, her heart quickened with ripe, aching recognition.

Sue was awaiting her on the station platform: a tall angular figure in black clothes, looking somehow forlorn and stricken, but as defiant as when the girl last met her. When Lorraine alighted, carrying a suitcase in each hand, she stepped briskly forward, her thin lips grinning, sardonic, as also were the black sparkling eyes.

There was no demonstration of welcome; the formalities of affection had long ago been dropped between these two. She had little knowledge of the girl's real nature: even as a child Lorraine had learnt to protect herself from the impure flame of her mother, who had seen only the frigid mask behind which Lorraine's passionate and enigmatic soul brooded over her secret quest and the mystery of the evil that surrounded her. Sue greeted her with a jeering gusto: "So you've turned up, maid! Wasn't sure if you'd find some way of dodging it at the last moment maybe grab some Scillonian chap and wire back that you was getting married and couldn't come."

Lorraine lowered her brows, thick and dark above large pellucid brown eyes set wide apart. "Well, I'm here – though it isn't exactly pleasant in these circumstances."

"No. I little guessed Cal would throw us together like this again. It've give me a scat too: all the week I've felt as if I'm in one o' me bad dreams." Sue eyed her daughter more closely as they began climbing the wooden floored bridge to reach the exit on the other side of the line.

"You'm looking a bit tired, cheel. Did 'ee have a rough crossing?"

"Rather choppy after we passed the Wolf and around Land's End. But it didn't upset me like when I went over."

"Your stomach as well as your sulks is got stronger now, I suppose. I can just see what I shall have to put up with! I don't look forward to living with 'ee again after the row last February and it may have spoilt some o' your plans. But 'tis no good blaming me for other peoples' doings." She bit her lip as though to check an outburst, and the pair were half-way across the bridge before she resumed in a low tone, bending nearer to Lorraine: "So poor Cal's gone, I've got to tell'ee. Pity you couldn't git back in time for the funeral. I've come straight from it."

Lorraine took this news stolidly. "Many people there?"

"Crowds – surprised me. But p'raps 'twas the tragic circumstances; I rather think so."

The five miles bus ride to Foxhole was endured in silence except for occasional questions from Sue about Hugh Town affairs and brief replies from Lorraine. Several villagers known to Sue were on the vehicle, and she did not wish to discuss family matters in their hearing. She noted that Lorraine was the object of general scrutiny and a certain amount of whispering among the local passengers. Her stark, wayward beauty set her apart from the other girls on the bus.

She wore no make-up, and her sombre brown coat and grey velour hat were shabby. But her long chestnut hair fell loosely around her shoulders, thick and gleaming in the warm spring sunshine, and the eyes of the men were attracted to her. There was an elusive dignity about her – elusive because it was not suggested by her features. Her deeply tanned face had nothing of classical perfection in its mould: the nose was short and blunt, with wide nostrils, the cheek-bones were broad, the mouth and chin heavy and obstinate. It was a powerful rather than delicate face, and the element that dignified it was both blame and shadow, a sultriness of hunger. She sat quietly, huddled a little in her seat, her eyes narrowed upon the strange land-scape, in marked contrast to Sue, who kept wriggling and peering about.

The Mannells alighted at Foxhole Post Office and moved out along the lonely road towards Carloggas. The mineral railway line burrowed under it at one point, and Lorraine gazed along this with curiosity as they passed. Near it stood a small farmstead, at which Sue pointed mockingly.

"That's where you might have growed up, if you'd had a decent father," she observed.

"Is that where you were born?"

"Yes, me old home, where Josh Trudgian from Karslake, Cal's dad, used to hang around, till I gived in to him in one o' they barns. I never dreamed this would be the end of it," she added with a bitter glance into the northern valley in which lay Nanpean churchyard.

Lorraine's fascination grew as she looked at the dwelling, but its associations were hostile to her, and she was relieved when it was screened from her sight by the green hump of the Beacon. They had soon entered the defile through which the road dipped before winding into the wooded dale, and here Sue roused from sullen reflection on the origin and fate of her son.

"Nearly home now, maid," she said. "Two or three minutes' walk down the lane here. Quietest place we've lived in so far – no next door neighbours. 'Tisn't anything to swank about, I can tell 'ee – not so grand as Mrs Rescorla's rooms over to Scilly."

"I didn't expect it would be," replied Lorraine bracing herself under the weight of the suitcases.

"'Tis nearly so bad as our Plymouth lodgings, though."

"Well, I can put up with it."

Lorraine spoke with cool deliberation, yet her sense of expectancy was blunted, and she recoiled when presently Sue indicated the Mannell's home. It was a cramped little cottage of rough granite, with only one chimney above the low slate roof and small grimy windows. It stood close to the roadside but at a much lower level: the roof and bedroom windows alone were visible as the couple approached it. A flight of nearly a dozen steps led down from the gateway to the tiny front garden that was over-grown with long grass, nettles and large coarse dock leaves.

Sue opened the rusty iron gate and Lorraine followed her down the steps, shrinking as she noted that the blinds were drawn over the windows. The house had no back door; Sue, taking a key from her pocket, strode up the cobbled path to the front door and unlocked it in silence. As she pushed it open a cloud of smoke caused her and Lorraine to draw back with averted faces.

"There!" cried Sue vexedly. "'Tis always like it when wind's blowing over Beacon: fire won't catch without filling the place with smoke. I blanked it in before I went to funeral, and put on the kettle for a dish o' tea: need it, I thought, after such a long journey. You can stop here a minute while I go in and open the windows – soon be cleared then." She advanced into the clouded passage, coughing and with her eyes shut, groping for the kitchen door.

Lorraine dropped her suitcases and leaned against the wall a yard or two away from the threshold. She bit her lip, chilled with dismal irony. Her eyes probed across the garden to the valley beyond, craving some assurance, but she felt only the gritty repulse of the refuse-heaps and the bristling, smoke-puffing stacks. The sunlight had withdrawn and the landscape seemed to lapse towards winter. The sense that this was her goal now seemed a vain fancy, and she ached with a swift, piercing nostalgia for the soft flower fields and the blue flooding sea.

There came from indoors the sound of Sue opening the window frames in the back room, then she shouted from the passage: "You can come in now, cheel. I've let out the worst of it and rolled up the blinds to give us some daylight. You'll have to get used to a bit o' smoke here: me and Cal have sat in it till it got so thick we could hardly see one another across the room. 'Tis no wonder that when he got the maidens here they bolted upstairs so quick."

Stiffly, with a sigh of weariness, Lorraine carried her suitcases into the passage. The parlour door was shut and Sue led the way straight into the kitchen. It was a narrow, untidy room, sparsely furnished, the paper peeling from the damp walls. The table standing under the window was laid for tea with a few plates of home-made buns and cake. Sue flung off her outdoor garb and bustled across to the stove where, amid the grime from a choked fire, a kettle was singing hoarsely.

Lorraine glanced about the squalid room, feeling a chill menace as she thought of Cal's coffin passing through it a few hours ago. She dropped the suitcases beside a chair, removed her hat and coat and hung them on the stair-post, then turned to face Sue, her features hard with reserve and fortitude.

While filling the teapot Sue tried to dissolve the oppressive atmosphere with a sardonic jest. "This is your dream come true at last, cheel, so you can't complain. Just the place you wanted to come to before your temper got soured."

Lorraine answered stolidly: "I never thought of coming here till I had your wire."

"Well you got a shorter memory than me. I mind what you said that night I come across 'ee in Drake Circus when we talked about shifting off somewhere. You had a fancy for coming back here where I was reared till I told 'ee how Cal and the neighbours would treat 'ee, and you changed your mind for Scillies instead." Sue stepped forward, holding the teapot, and nudged Lorraine, her grin baring her dentures. "Ever thought what you'd have been by this time if we'd stayed up Plymouth? I wonder pretty often. You'd have had plenty o' love to look back on."

"What you call love, perhaps."

"Ah, yes, I forgot your superior notions for the moment," remarked Sue in mock apology. "I don't suppose you'd call it love, for a couple to go off to blanket fair without saying their prayers. But the Plymouth chaps call it love – and so do Scilly ones, I believe. Or have some fellow over there showed 'ee his soul since I left?"

"I've gone on since you left just as I did before," replied Lorraine quietly.

"Thought so. But you won't be able to drivel on like that here forever, wi' me getting older, and sudden deaths started in the family. You'll have to find a job first, though, before you start husband-hunting."

"Naturally, I'll have to get work," Lorraine admitted.

Sue put the teapot down on the ragged tablecloth, peering sourly out at the gooseberry bushes fringing the garden, so near the window that they almost blocked the view of anything beyond.

"Cal didn't leave any fortune, worse luck," she grumbled. "Only enough to bury him, so you must bring in some money for us next week. I don't think you'll have much trouble: people's hearts is touched just now, and somebody'll take 'ee on, out o' pity."

"I want to get in to a village shop if I can," said Lorraine. She took a chair from beside the dresser as Sue beckoned her, and set it at the table. Sue moved back to the hearth, watching the girl more tensely, and after some hesitation she observed in an altered tone:

"I'm afraid I got another nasty piece o' news for 'ee... But put a cup o' tea inside 'ee first, and sample me buns there. No funeral spread, as you and me is the only mourners, but there's a good dram o' saffron in they buns, baked Tuesday, and the seed ones isn't too new neither, nothing to upset your stomach. 'Twill help to steady your nerves a bit."

Lorraine could eat little, but the tea was welcome, bracing her. Then Sue leaned across from the hearth bench and tapped her shoulder. "I said on me first wire that Cal was sinking fast, didn't I?"

The feverish suppression of Sue's tone made Lorraine apprehensive; her eyes widened, staring. "Yes. It was... an accident, warn't it?"

"Well, had to have me little joke, but now you'm here I needn't cover up the facts any longer." She straightened with a dramatic gesture and said deliberately: "Cal drowned hisself, that's the truth, up near the clay-pit where he belonged working. Went headlong into a pool o' water the Monday night 'twas. His body wasn't found till Thursday. I didn't know definite what had become of him when I sent me wire and letter, though I felt he'd done for hisself somehow."

Lorraine's face had blanched, she sat rigid and stark-eyed, her fists locked under her bosom; but the immediate sense of horror soon flagged as bodily fatigue blunted its force. Her tone was dull and mechanical as she inquired: "But why should... he do that?"

"Got tangled up over the maid Kruse I told 'ee about," responded Sue. "I don't want to rake up the hard words you spoke there by the tower, saying you pitied Veale and Gwen Kruse and had no sympathy for me and Cal. But I can see now that Cal was to be pitied for the state he was in when he got struck on that one."

Lorraine stared, her hand reaching for her teacup .

"And then," continued Sue, "I was making me pitch for Veale." "Cal was never too strong in the wits where women was concerned: he'd get nasty if he was crossed when his passions was up. And he'd had some brave scats these last few months, on top o' me coming back to spoil the fun here. He falled out with a maid called Lela Skiddy, and then one of his latest little tarts got married – Olive Buzza. A month ago that was – pretty little story behind it too." Sue drank noisily, her head bobbing out from the shadow, then resumed with a smirking relish:

"I was getting thick with Olive – one o' they girls we used to know so well up Plymouth. I called down to see her one night about six weeks ago and found she was out after a customer – and her old dad indoors by hisself, dying. I stayed till she come home, and when she heard the old man was dead she went straight back to the chap she'd roped in that evening, and wanted to sleep at his place. O' course, his family wouldn't allow it – decent chapel-going folk and there was uproar till the chap, Charlie Crago, walked out and said he'd never darken his father's door again as long as he lived. He stayed with Olive till they went to register office, though the marriage don't seem to be turning out well. I hear she and Charlie 've come to blows already – seen 'em down funeral just now, and they both had bruises showing. But all that helped to unsettle Cal, and made him mad to git Gwen Kruse."

Lorraine sipped at her tea, looking about the room with increasing distaste, realising the fetid moral atmosphere again threatening her. "And Gwen started going with someone else, I s'pose?" she asked.

"Started? Goodness knows when she started," cried Sue. "The fact is it come out all of a sudden that she'd been married. Last Saturday it was; spliced up with a chap called Kella, Veale's nearest neighbour down by the woods. And to make it worse, 'twas Cal hisself who forced 'em to marry so quick."

"How's that?" Lorraine demanded, frowning.

Sue scowled at the stove as another cloud of smoke belched out from it. "As I told 'ee over St. Mary's, Kruses' maid didn't show him no favours-could hardly expect it, he being nearly twenty years older than she. He went down farm several times when Veale come up here, but always found the doors locked and the shutters drawed. It didn't sweeten his temper, but he thought Gwen was in by herself; never guessed Kella was with her. Anyhow it soon brought 'n to boiling point, and he started banging on the door and shouting to the maid to let him in. She got real scared – afraid to go out alone in the evenings: she knowed what he'd do to her if he catched her in a field or a lonely lane. So she and Kella decided the only way they could stop the nuisance was to come out open, and git married." Sue's eyes flashed. "Kella must have gone to work Monday, thinking there'd be murder attempted when he broke the news. He and Cal had a fight last year about Lela Skiddy. But the news seemed to scat Cal sideways; his workmates say that after hearing Gwen was married he was like a man stunned, – just glowering at Kella as if he'd gone silly. And when the other fellows had gone home he must ha' stayed behind and had a last look round, and then went over to the pool."

Sue had given this information soberly, but her face now loosened afresh with malicious humour. "So you see there was some point in what I said about him sinking fast."

Lorraine looked at her mother, fascinated by the sheer callousness of the woman's speech and tone. It was familiar, though: this perverse cynicism had been in Sue as long as Lorraine could remember. The coarse face now grinning above her in the smoke-dimmed kitchen was the same as she had seen four months ago in Mrs Rescorla's parlour when Sue had come in dishevelled after her assault on Mrs Danning. It was the same image that rose, confused and terrifying, amid the memories of Plymouth – the impress of Lorraine's child mind of her mother's feverish, gloating face as she recounted some misfortune that had befallen a neighbour whom she hated. The gusto of Sue's lusts and loathings was impressive, and Lorraine preferred it to the tepid quality of natures that were subtle or merely nice; but she was aware of the evil in it too, and had shielded herself from its dark energy. Even now she felt the need to keep it at a distance.

"Where've Gwen and her man been living since they married?" she asked after a pause.

"Down Barrakellis farm. I s'pose Veale want 'em to stay there for a time to keep me off. But he needn't be afraid I'd darken his doors again." Sue struck the table with her fist. "He must have known for weeks that they two was planning to marry, and could have nipped it in the bud by taking me to register office and kicking Gwen out. But instead o' that…"

"It looks as if he found their courting rather convenient," remarked Lorraine, with a touch of sarcasm.

"Well, I did try to force the pace a bit, thinking he was faint-hearted. But when I found out what a double game he'd been playing – encouraging they two on the sly, while letting me and Cal believe there was still hope for us – I felt the whole width of Cornwall wasn't enough distance to put between me and that lousy lot."

Lorraine sat very still, an arm lying along the back of her chair. She glanced between the fluttering white net curtains of the open window, beyond which the green dome of the Beacon frowned massively up among smoky thundercloud and pulsing hot sunshafts.

"It's a pity you live so close to them," she commented.

"Yes, I'm getting to hate the sight o' this place here, wi' Cal gone – and the parlour still stinking wi' Veale's farmyard clothes. If I could shift I would, but there's no chance of it at the moment. I've got to get some freedom and fresh air around the villages."

"Found one or two neighbours like Mrs Danning?" Lorraine suggested, her manner defensive and ironical.

"Better'n that, I should hope," replied Sue as she rose, knife in hand, to slice the saffron cake. "I been out Nanpean pub every evening since Monday: some good company there, Lela Skiddy and her mother in partic'lar. A pair something like me and you, living alone together."

"Isn't the mother married?"

"Was once, but been separated from her man for years. Lela got a aunt up Plymouth too, Mrs Kessel – live near Barbican where we used to be; just my sort, by all accounts. They've promised to bring her over to see us when she's down this way again."

"Do they know I'm coming back today?"

"Sure. Lela dropped in here Thursday evening to offer her

sympathy when she heard Cal had been fished out, and I showed her your telegram, agreeing to come. She want us to come up to their place tomorrow, but I didn't say yes definite – thought you might be too tired or in one o' your sulks." Sue chuckled, munching at her cake as she sat down. "Lela'll be a grand help to 'ee if you get thick with her. You need to knock around wi' a crowd o' maids like she, and loosen up a bit before you'm fit for a husband."

Lorraine remained silent, her eyes half-closed against a fresh flurry of smoke that swirled about her, drifting slowly out through the window to dissolve among the thorny fruit bushes.

CHAPTER NINETEEN

EUAN and Gwen had paused on a bend of the hill just above the Kruses' new home at Curyan. The drowse of Sunday afternoon brooded around the cottage, which was now empty, Zachary and Sarah being at Nanpean gossiping with neighbours, the children at play in the fields. Ruth and Pearl could, in fact, be seen squatting in a field lower down the valley, picking daises. The immediate surroundings were gentler and softer than those of the old clay-pit house, but the higher levels of the landscape were as barren and austere as those flanking Roche. Beyond the green hollow of Curyan Vale with its scattered farms the plateau of Longstone Downs arched to a broad, desolate horizon from north-east to south-east. A few white sandcones were tilted upon it like vast fools' caps set incongruously on the skulls of primeval giants buried there. Spring had now diminished the savagery of the pent prehistoric atmosphere of those gaunt ridges; but a grim despotism belonging to winter, night and dissolution lurked in the southern valley, in the churchyard where Cal Mannell had been interred the previous day, and shadowed the mood of the young couple. There was upon them the stillness of full sensuous liberty, the new, awesome knowledge of a bride and bridegroom, but nothing of the carefree gaiety of a normal honeymoon. They were conscious of being apart, outside conventional life, thrown on a deep, satisfying integrity that was disowned or ignored by their fellows. Their faces, puckered against the sun, looked serious, though from a distance they appeared to be an ordinary pair of lovers. Euan wore a brown tweed jacket and flannel trousers, Gwen a blue halo hat and grey tweed costume which she had bought a fortnight ago and in which she had been married. The need for secrecy had forced them to marry at St. Austell register office, though they would both have preferred a church ceremony with that element of mysticism that was so fundamental to Euan's nature.

Gwen peered regretfully at the grey little dwelling they had just left. "I wonder where Joel's gone all the afternoon," she observed in a disappointed tone. "I did hope we'd see him today. After that talk we had with him here Wednesday, I feel sure there'll be big developments."

Euan glanced past the cottage, down the narrow road that wound into the vale among small groups of houses and then mounted the northern hill-slope to Whitemoor. It was very rural, with thorns, elms, and sycamore trees shading the low stone hedges; cows grazed in the pastures between the lane and the scabbed, craggy moors. Euan found the Vale somewhat alien to him: though he lived now on a farm he was still unreceptive of the mood of mere fertility, loyal to the rarer poetry of the clay-tips. The rush of sap and colour, the song and dash of birds among the trees and over the sun-flushed soil, had no power to stimulate him except in the superficial appeal to his senses. "Your mother said Joel's still 'cracked' which doesn't tell us much," he commented dryly.

"No, she wouldn't understand him," replied Gwen with a touch of impatience. "He must feel more than ever that he's in the wrong home. 'Tis odd that such people should have such a son – and such a son-in-law!" she added teasingly, nestling against him.

"They do seem a bit bewildered and I don't wonder. But I'm grateful to 'em for letting us marry – and even for leaving us to ourselves most of the time when we call up here. It may not be very civil, but it's better than having the door slammed in our faces, as we should if we called down at my home." He spoke bitterly, though Rachel's implacable hostility to the marriage was not unexpected.

Gwen's sharp, olive-dark face remained clouded for a few moments as she watched some white butterflies scudding from clump to clump of the campion blossom by the hedgeside. "I wish our marriage wasn't shadowed by so many things, right at the start," she murmured. "There's the shock about Mannell, your mother turning against you and – this terrible worry about Joel. That bothers me most, naturally."

"I know it does – and I'm with you there, as in all else," said Euan with deepening earnestness.

"I hated to hurt him by telling him I was going to be married so soon; and he was so unselfish about it. He said it seemed one of us had to be disappointed and he was glad it wasn't me. But he was really broke I could see it in his face completely baffled at the way things had turned out. I'd felt so sure me and Joel would win through together... Not that I feared he'd take Mannell's way out of his troubles, though he's suffering more than Mannell ever did."

"Yes, I believe he is," Euan responded. "I hadn't realised Joel was such a rare fellow till I met him again this year. At Rostowrack he seemed just an ordinary chap, a bit surly – the sort of fellow you find playing in a village football team. But he's got more soul in him than any other working man I ever met."

The haunting call of a cuckoo, one of the first to arrive that year, stabbed up from the vale while Gwen answered: "He always had. Even before Marvran came home from Falmouth there was that streak in him – I won't say religious exactly, but it was something near it; only 'twas smothered by our home life. When Marvran got him free from that, it opened out; yet – see what bitterness for him now!"

Euan frowned, stepping back into the gutter and breaking some grass stems from the hedge, his mind probing into its theological current. "This is the big test for him, it seems to me," he remarked after a pause. "Will he still believe that what's brought him into this dark patch was predestined, and take the leap of faith into the heart of it, holding on there till he sees how it fits the rest o' the pattern? Or will he give up and think it's all a mess of fate – driven to Olive Crago or someone of that type?"

Gwen roused against the humiliation, biting her lip; she pushed her arm further through Euan's and drew him out into the road, from which they could see the ridge of Whitemoor above Olive's home, half a mile off. Her small grey eyes, that had been dreamy as she brooded over the scenes of Joel's adolescence, now flashed in rebellion.

"I don't believe Joel will sink like that – I can't believe it," she cried passionately. "T'is the very thing he loathes most. I mind how upset he was last Christmas when I told him I might get like Olive if you let me down... In fact, I think she grabbed Charlie Crago because she saw she couldn't make any headway with Joel."

"Very likely that's true," Euan admitted. "I feel he's got past the crisis there, as he did with Marvran, and worked clear, out of danger. Everything depends now on the way he uses the knowledge these experiences have burnt into him. He knows he can choose whether fate or predestination is to control him. As I told him that Sunday on Foxhole Beacon, we can't change the course of either of those currents – they're both irresistible; but we can make the leap of faith from one to the other: from fate to predestination. And I made it clear that it must be Christian faith, because predestination works only inside Christianity; fate only works outside it."

Gwen's eyes softened as they turned back to his intense, oddly-moulded face. It looked more attractive now that the strain of frustration was gone from it; there was a steady, serene glow behind the bony features. But he would never look or be normal; he would always remain himself, an exotic among the working class, almost friendless and content to be so, reaching happiness through oblique channels of spiritual insight of which the common people knew nothing. Gwen could not get over the wonder of it, that a man with such a vision should marry her. And though he was intellectually so much her superior, he always made her feel that she was his equal in everything that was essential. He recognised the dawning soul in her, and the pull of her body was a rapture that strengthened with every contact. She satisfied him because she was not naturally his, nor his fate.

"You must have preached to Joel on the Beacon as much as you did to me at Rostowrack," she observed with a strained little laugh.

"It didn't put him in a temper, anyway. He was so desperately in need of guidance, and glad of any hints I could give him. I told him we're all born in the stream of fate, which bears everything in it towards tragedy. But close beside it, or above it, is the other stream of Christian predestination which bears everything in it to ultimate triumph, despite the dark patches. And sometimes a bit of spray from it comes over into the stream of our fate. We feel the different tang of the experience as it splashes in. It reminds us of God."

Gwen nodded soberly. "I felt like that about our walk to Barrakellis," she said, "and I'm sure Joel felt it about Marvran's first visit last August."

"Yes. I think he did get a taste of God through Marvran. It made him yearn more than ever to get outside his fate, out into that other stream where the beauty and wonder come from. But it was clear to me that Sunday he hadn't made the necessary 'leap of faith.' He was still bogged in the old stream – and the tang that had 'invaded' it was getting fainter."

They strode forward in silence for a few minutes, up the hill to the west. The Kruses' cottage was soon hidden from them, but they seemed reluctant to enter Nanpean village, and halted again at the next field gateway.

"You've helped him a lot, he really does admire you," Gwen stated, leaning both arms on the rough wooden bar. "And 'twas plain on Wednesday he was coming round to your sort o' beliefs. Our wedding had pulled him up – made him see he's got to stop drifting if he wants to get where we are."

Euan had climbed the lower bars of the gate and stepped out on to the hedge top, his shoes flattening the long grass. He stood erect, outlined against the blue sky, peering moodily down at the bottom street of Nanpean, to the south-west of Curyan Vale, which lay in a harsher, industrialised fold of the hills, flanked by railway sidings, clay-dries, an electric power station and a small loading wharf. His gaze centred with grim fascination on the churchyard, across which the shadow of the little church edged in sharp, leaping patches, tracing on tombstones and sward the outline of the pointed slate roof and the tiny arch supporting a bell on its southern tip. Euan seemed caught up and fused with something elemental that flowed with the sunshine to challenge the dark clay, the grave of Mannell. Gwen looked up at him, but her thought remained stubbornly within the bounds of the old life at Roche, the ache at the loss of Marvran's friendship.

"You really don't think there's any hope, do you Euan," she asked hesitantly, "that Marvran'll come back to Joel through some last-minute miracle?"

Euan roused, turning to glance at her. She looked very young, lounging by the gate tall, but rather gaunt in figure, the wedding ring still appearing strange to him on her dusky hand.

"No, I don't" he replied firmly. "If God intended that kind of miracle He'd have set Joel praying for it. But Joel says he can't pray for it; he doesn't even wish it. He seems to have found that she isn't what he wanted after all, and he's just gone dead to her."

"That's the queer part of it. He loved her so deep – it must have gone deep, or it would never have changed his life as it did – and yet it died out so quick. He couldn't have seen her more than half-a-dozen times between her first visit and that night he went to tell her about Ruth. The whole story was in those few meetings. Some people say he was faint-hearted to give up, almost at the first snub."

Euan shook his head, scrambling back on to the gate and vaulting down beside her. "No, it wasn't that," he commented. "I think what he was really after was that 'tang' – the whole breadth and depth of it interpreted through a girl's love. With that hunger in him, how could he go on chasing a fluffy little empty-head who seems to live only for dances?"

"I do feel now that Marvran was unworthy of him. She's decent enough, and she'll make a good wife for somebody like Roy Chegwidden. But Joel needs something more than pleasantness in a wife."

"He does; he needs someone more like his sister," Euan declared, as he slipped her arm through his and moved with her out into the roadway.

From here the road broadened south-westward, passing over the brow of the hill as a street, the last on the Nanpean to Curyan Road, with pavements and blocks of solid newer houses on each side. As Euan and Gwen came in full view of this street they saw the pudgy little figure of Sarah move from the pavement into clear sunlight and hurry towards them. She waved her hand, and they responded with brief, perfunctory gestures, strolling on in silence and watching her approach. Sarah was hatless, wearing a greasy pinafore over her blouse, but though slovenly she looked unusually cheerful. A simper creased her square, blotchy face, her small grey eyes glinted with relish, almost gloating as they wandered over Gwen, recognising that the girl was no longer a virgin.

"Going back farm now?" she greeted, obviously relieved that they had left the cottage.

"Yes; Mr Veale will be needing his tea," replied Gwen coolly.

"Have 'ee seen Joel?"

"No, he isn't come yet."

The three halted in a group by the roadside where white hawthorn spray scented the hedge and cast soft foamy shadows around them, like dark bubbles. Sarah slowly turned around, scanning the ridges of moorland.

"I expect he's out on the moors somewhere, or in a clay-pit like he used to be up Roche, squat down in a corner and sulking because you got all the limelight." She stepped up to Euan, tapping his sleeve with uneasy familiarity, the yellow stumps of her teeth showing in a grin.

"You've put Joel's nose out of joint fine, Mr Kella – you and Gwen between 'ee. There he was, the silly chap, thinking he'd soon have his photo in the papers, smiling coy at Marvran over the orange-blossom, wi' a article telling how the well-known Roche footballer had married the famous daughter of the trombone player in Bugle band. A real Society match! Instead he's pushed out in the cold, and his sister gets the limelight!"

Sarah's gleeful manner caused Euan to smile, though somewhat ironically. "The talk'll soon die down," he said. "We'll be glad when it does."

"Me and Zachy's enjoying it while it last, anyhow," retorted Sarah. "Twas worth leaving Roche to tumble into this. It've bucked up Zachy no end; he was moping and drooping near so bad as Joel when we shifted, but now why, he's lord o' the pub: all the men eyeing him envious – their daughters couldn't tell such a tale. And old Sue Mannell this past week glazing at'n across the bar as if she could throw her beer mug in his face. 'Tis all meat and drink to the poor old fellow."

Gwen shrugged and began edging away, but Sarah caught her arm restrainingly. "You've upset all that Mannell family," she continued in a lower tone, peering warily at Euan. "I spied 'em come down to Skiddys' half-a-hour ago – Cal's mother and the maid, I s'pose 'twas she – the sister that come back from Scilly Isles yesterday. Dark, wild-looking young thing: something like you, Gwen, only a bit shorter and not so skinny. She didn't look very pleased at being over here; and she must know by this time 'twas your doings."

Gwen glanced along the street in distress. "Well, t'is nothing to gloat about," she said, clutching tightly at Euan's arm and pulling him away. "We want to forget that side of it."

Sarah mumbled a grudging farewell and passed on. The young couple advanced into the built-up area, tense now with the fresh reminders of the disturbance they had unwittingly caused in the lives of others. They were soon in sight of the Skiddys' home, a fairly large detached house with a square stone porch. Beyond it the road narrowed again between fields, then wound amid refuse-dumps northwards across the fringes of Rostowrack Downs. Neither Gwen nor Euan spoke as they walked through Curyan Road with the scent of spring flowers fanning out from the colourful gardens. No one else was visible, but they knew that wherever they were observed there would be animated talk of their marriage, with the usual innuendoes. As this was not Gwen's native village she was not much concerned about the gossip of these strangers, except for its effects on Euan.

They were nearing the end of the row, abreast of the large bare chapel, when suddenly Gwen roused with a quick gesture of relief. "There's Joel!"

Euan too, had noticed the dark heavy figure appear around the corner west of the fields, at the edge of a track that led over the downs. He and Gwen paused by the stone gateway of the chapel, watching Joel's approach. He had not glimpsed them; he came on slowly with head bent, staring moodily at the ground, but it seemed to them that the old listless despair was gone from his step; there was a new power and assurance in his movements. He kept close to the hedge, but the sunlight played full upon his grey clothes and bronzed face, suggesting a mellow strength that had nothing of the wrench and twist of agony or defiance in it.

"I believe he's got there, don't you?" Gwen whispered.

"We'll know for sure when we speak to him," replied Euan, and they walked on down past several isolated dwellings and shops. They expected Joel to hear them and glance up. But he seemed to have lapsed into a dense absorption, plodding forward at a steady pace, his hands in his coat pockets. He was soon near the Skiddys' home, moving free of the field hedge into the broad open space between the house and the road.

As he drew level with the house the front door opened and a girl emerged from the porch, a solid brown figure, hurrying blindly out into the glare of sunshine. She looked tense, rather lost in the strange environment, as if she had left the place in anger or disgust. There was a stark appeal of bruised loneliness in her face as her eyes swept the outer scene. She saw the young couple approaching the corner, but it was on Joel that her interest centred at once. He had not been disturbed by the sound of the door closing, and as she darted towards the road he almost collided with her; only a quick swerve on her part kept the way open for him. She seemed to recognise that he too was preoccupied, questing in a solitary world, and looked searchingly into his face.

"Good afternoon," she murmured, somewhat confused.

Joel glanced up with a start, and as their eyes met there was a sudden flash of intimacy. Euan and Gwen realised as they halted in astonishment that something remarkable had occurred: a magnetic fusion, like lightning struck from the touch of two densely clouded natures. They heard Joel mumble a word of greeting; he stood rigid watching her as she passed out into the road and headed down the main street. His expression reminded Gwen of the look that had softened him in the clay-pit cottage when he came down stairs with the lamp on Marvran's arrival last August; but it was more mature, with a deeper assurance. On the surface he was startled and dazed; he remained where the girl had surprised him, staring after her. Before she disappeared beyond the railings of the inn yard on the corner, she turned and glanced quickly back. Joel raised his hand, automatically; only when she was gone did he rouse and make fresh mental contact with the familiar setting, the broad stretch of Curyan Road leading to his home.

His manner revealed another kind of shock as he grew aware of Gwen and Euan. It was the return of normality, the everyday contracts, and he appeared to recoil from it as one jealously guarding the stillness of a rare, transforming moment. But awkwardly he forced himself away from the view of anyone who might be regarding him through the Skiddys' window, on to the pavement outside a small shop a few yards further up the road. Gwen waved to him and hastened forward with Euan.

"Joel!" she exclaimed. "We've been waiting for you all the afternoon. Are you all right…?"

Joel seemed almost bashful as his gaze slipped from Gwen to Euan. He knew that they had seen his brief, emotional contact with the girl. His lips twitched into a sheepish grin. "I'm right enough now," he said.

"You know, you ought to look where you're going, and not go bumping into people!" Gwen's attempt at teasing was followed by a swift impulsive challenge as she stopped in front of Joel, lowering her voice. "D'you know who that girl is, just come out from Skiddys'?

Joel half turned, scanning the road where Lorraine had disappeared. He breathed heavily. "Haven't seen her around the village before."

"'Tis Cal Mannell's sister, just back from Scilly. Mother saw her go in there, she and Sue."

Joel frowned for a moment, his mouth slightly open, hardly able to comprehend all that was implied in the disclosure. "Mannell's sister?"

Euan nodded. His mind was alert, darting among emerging possibilities, though he too was startled by the abrupt encounter he had just witnessed.

"I like the look of her," he said with subtle deliberation. "She won't be another Sue or another Marvran Creba."

The silence of the group was profound, with a deep, naked understanding; then Joel replied tremulously, laying a hand on Euan's arm: "B'lieve you're right. I found me clue again, Euan. I haven't been through all this for nothing – 'twasn't all false, what I glimpsed when Marvran come back."

CHAPTER TWENTY

THE entrance of another customer was not welcome to Lorraine. She had been cooped up nearly all day in the stuffy little drapery store, while sunshine of heat-wave intensity drilled down along the stony slopes of Carne Hill. The houses of St. Dennis looked scabbed and flaky, simmering in the unsoftened glare. Lorraine felt tired and stifled, moving heavily among the hanging fabrics, peering through the window to the distant hazy skyline towards Goss Moor. She knew that from that height an occasional glint of sea flickered out there, the Atlantic some fifty miles north-east from the Scilly Isles. These glimpses had made Lorraine ache with the sense of transition, but she no longer wished to be back on St. Mary's in the captivity of probation and adjustment. Superficially she was cramped here at St. Dennis, but the deeps of her nature were freer than ever before.

She worked alone in the shop, which was the smallest of its kind in the village, standing several hundred yards above the tangled streets that clotted the southern and western hillsides. The store formed half of a double house, its owner, a Mrs Tamblyn, living next door and sometimes entering the shop to check up on Lorraine's efficiency as an assistant. From the upstairs window one looked out across the churchyard, past the dark squat tower and the cluster of ragged, wind-bent trees, northward over six miles of flat moorland with scarcely a house in sight. The shop stood like a tiny, ineffectual outpost of civilisation on the edge of a grim primordial world of absolutes. But not even the cemetery could depress Lorraine: it reminded her of that other burial-ground at Nanpean which she had visited only once, but with no sense of personal loss. Cal's grave had seemed at first a malign magnet drawing her back from life to deadening servitude; now it was merely a spot of corruption, brushed from the star of her destiny as it rose.

She had been employed here for a fortnight, and the feeling of strangeness had worn off, though customers still found her aloof and enigmatic. Working in this drapery store was less pleasant than selling fruit in Hugh Town. A pair of shoes or a coat could not be purchased as quickly as a pound of apples, and the extra time required to get the customer fitted was often a trial to Lorraine. But she must earn her living somehow, and this job would do as well as any other to tide her over until she was settled in a home of her own.

She knew instinctively that the waiting would be brief: the pledge had been given her. And she had needed it to offset the oppressive defilement of the Mannell's cottage. She felt that vicious atmosphere increasingly, as gossip brought to her mind the details of Cal's squalid career. The hours of darkness burdened her with intimations of those nights when he had brought home some loose woman: no-doubt the very bed she slept in had been occupied by local lights-o'-love.

All these reminders of the slum dross, the old menace that lurked within the clay-world, served to wring from Lorraine a more unreserved acceptance of the challenge she had received. She was old enough to know fully what this challenge implied: she was now mature not only physically but also in her beliefs. From the time she had sensed that the wine of love must be drunk either as a toast to vice or as a sacrament, that there was no middle course of satisfying adherence to the mere conventions of decency and order, she had used this knowledge almost perversely to isolate and protect herself. She was aware that evil forces had barred her off from normal life, but instead of trying to break through the barriers and become normal she had wished only to erect other barriers that were good – spiritual and sensuous truths suggested by the Mass and the Salvationist meetings. These gave her the unique thrill of being apart yet not inferior, free to indulge herself in the secret spasm of mystic otherness. And because this ultimate good must not be recognised as such by the outside world, she had cherished the dubious elements, nourishing the lure of her femininity which could draw to her, in physical beauty or squalor, the lurking nebulousness of the male world.

Yet it was always behind that barrier of goodness, a clean virtue and loyalty, that she brooded on the ambiguous flame. She had ceased to notice the gross barriers of ignominy and degradation. She felt herself the equal of the average unstained girls who enjoyed the common gaieties of youth. But she had other guides and must follow them. They had now brought her to Cornwall, to the Skiddy's home on the Sunday afternoon nearly three weeks, ago, to the encounter with that strange gypsy-like young man whose image had gone with her every day to the routine of the St. Dennis shops, as the authentic end of her search. She had no doubt now that her goal was here among the clay-dumps and the kilns.

The scrape of footsteps and the opening of the glass panelled door caused her to glance up from her musings, tidying her hair as she moved down behind the counter, her brows knit in momentary resentment. The new customer was a rather short, stout woman in her late twenties, wearing a blue halo hat and cream frock, her round puffy face reddened and glistening with sweat. She strolled close up to the counter, studying Lorraine's face curiously, her coarse hot lips parted with secret relish.

"What can I do for you?" said Lorraine coolly.

The woman ignored the formal, businesslike approach. "First time I've seen you, I think," she greeted in a tone of dry friendliness. "I heard you'd started working here. Not from your mum though – haven't met her since Cal was buried."

"Haven't you?" Lorraine was vaguely hostile, realising that this was probably another village slut who had carried on with Cal.

"No. Still, I knew your brother and – I expect your mum's mentioned me to you. Olive Crago."

Lorraine did not appear greatly impressed, though her eyes smouldered, her lips hardened defensively. She stood a little stiffly behind the counter, her white blouse shadowed against the drab background of shelves and boxes.

"Yes, mother told me about your marriage. Are you needing anything?"

"Dance frock, if you've got one nice and cheap. Now I've settled down I reckon I'm respectable enough to start dancing. I've never danced yet, see."

The statement was true, though it might appear incredible to one who judged Olive's reputation by urban standards. She had been a village prostitute of the old-fashioned type, never bothering to wear smart clothes or jewellery, or even using make-up. It was the sheer animal pull of her personality that had made her fascination so powerful to the village men. Standing now near Lorraine she looked decidedly plain with her bulging freckled face and squat, slovenly figure.

"Me and Charlie are going ahead fine," she continued, with a grin. "P'raps you heard we had a scrap or two, but that's all behind us. We aren't going to fall back now. No reason why we should, is there?"

"Not yet, perhaps."

"And there won't be. Things have been different ever since Cal's funeral." Olive leaned forward, her voice low and ingratiating. "I went there in a beastly mood, hoping I'd see a fellow to work it off on. But he wasn't there – only Cal's coffin; and it seemed to jolt me to my senses. I knew I had to make a fresh start, right away, while the mood took me. Me and Charlie stayed in Nanpean pub till it was coming in dark, and then I got him to go over to the pool where Cal drowned himself, and we went in to the hut where the body was taken. We needed a good purge, something different, and it's still holding us…"

Lorraine was fascinated by the morbid, feverish sincerity in Olive's tone, but she remained curtly practical, turning towards the stairway at the far end of the shop.

"Well – if you want to see dresses, they're upstairs."

The repulse nettled Olive, but reluctantly she followed Lorraine up the hot, dusky flight of steps to the upper storey where fantastic coloured shadows were cast by rows of hanging costumes, gowns and frocks.

The display of elegant drapery was an incongruous setting for these two women, both of them too genuinely passionate to care much about fashion and style. An appropriate background for either needed more sombre and primitive tones. There was a fundamental affinity in their physical texture, suggesting solidity and a kind of indolent strength rather than slickness or subtlety. They were women for whom love, in the very different senses in which they understood the word, was the one reality, the one prize worthy of effort. It was this divergence of attitude towards desire that struck them apart, into antagonistic worlds. The contrast between their natures was not simply that between the spiritual and the sensual; nor was it a mere difference of ethical standards. It was essentially religious, and could be more adequately expressed in Calvinistic or Pauline terms than in those of the contemporary moralist. The values here contrasted were not transient but universal, timeless.

They faced each other guardedly, aware of the struggle. Lorraine flicked her hand along a row of gleaming sun-warmed dresses. "Take your choice," she said.

Olive followed this up, close and intimate: "You made any choice yet? Got a boyfriend?"

Lorraine's brow darkened and it seemed that she would refuse an answer, but after a moment she brought out irritably: "I'm not likely to get a 'boy' at my age."

Olive laughed. "Well, if you want a bachelor, nearly as old as me, I can give you a good tip. If that girl Kruse, Mrs Kella I mean, hasn't put you in mind of him already."

Again Lorraine's face changed colour; her heart thudded and she lifted a hand to her throat.

"Who's that?" she asked, almost choking.

"Her brother Joel. Lives near the Skiddys' at Nanpean, where you and your mum go. Seen him yet?"

"Yes, I...I think so, but I haven't seen him to speak to."

"Well, that'll come in time." Olive stepped nearer the window, peering out as the churchyard gate clanged behind an entering group of mourners. Then she turned back to Lorraine, smiling unpleasantly.

"I nearly got him early this year, but he slipped through my fingers. He's a bit cracked, you know but that's only his decency. Fighting too hard against his home life. He tried football first, but it didn't satisfy him – he needed some high-class young lady. When I tried to break in, he was mooning about a little snob who'd given charity to his family – Marvran Creba. But he couldn't get anywhere with her. I thought I had him in my hands once in a clay-dry where she was coming to dance with her friends and forget him, and once when I actually got him inside our house. But he pulled away in time to spoil the fun."

Lorraine stared, her hands gripping the dress rail as if for support.

"Yes. Turned tail and bolted almost at the bedroom door, and hasn't shown his nose near me since. I've seen him climb over hedges to keep a safe distance from my place, even in the daytime."

Lorraine was roused now; her personal hostility flowed frankly out and slapped at Olive in a wave of sarcasm. "So Cal wasn't your only failure?"

Olive's lips curled; she struck back: "Me and Cal had our successes, my dear."

"Almost as short-lived as yours and Charlie's, though, weren't they?"

This stinging taunt jabbed deep into Olive and flung up the gust of rage that had itched in her when she glimpsed Lorraine downstairs. She lurched forward, pushing her hot, reddened face close to Lorraine's.

"If Charlie ever fails me again you're welcome to have the damned little fool," she snarled. "Him and Joel Kruse too, if one isn't enough."

Lorraine's smile was steely. "One'll be enough," she said, turning to adjust a frock which Olive's movement had set swinging. "And when I find him perhaps I'll let him be your dancing partner now you're so innocent."

The soil was gradually cooling with the advance of twilight that evening as Joel entered Rostowrack Downs. He had come in along a track from Nanpean, appearing as a dark smudge on the base of the main clay-dump, which on the western side had been washed into smooth white packs of gravel, ridged like a glacier and now quite hard to the tread. He seemed puny against the wedge of rock and sand that pierced up behind him into the soft, pale-glowing sky. But the massive stillness of the pyramid was in harmony with his slow, deliberate movements.

This plateau was now almost as familiar to Joel as the similar patch of industrialised moorland around Roche. He felt the whole scene fused with his own spiritual struggle, the element of squalor being here too as he recalled Euan's brawl with Mannell. The tragedy that had followed Gwen's marriage had caused him to penetrate further west along the downs, to the flooded quarry where Cal had drowned himself. Joel had, in fact, been returning from the quarry on the Sunday afternoon when he first saw Lorraine, and since then the pool, had held him even more powerfully, but with a new, richer fascination.

He did not come here now to brood over his bafflement; his

thoughts were turned to the future. The impact of Lorraine was in some respects like that of Marvran eight months ago, but the human appeal was differently toned and focused because of the spiritual convulsion that had shaken him during the interval. Lorraine's challenge was a vindication of the faith to which Euan had led him: not a brief glimpse of predestined life that would have to fight a losing battle with the alien tide of his fate, but something stronger, nourished by the whole flow of his new destiny as a believer.

After he lost Marvran he had been tempted to think that faith and predestination were the same thing, the general inexorable routine of cause and effect within Nature. Euan had renewed in him at a higher level the sense of dualism, disruption and re-creation which alone could give him hope. He had been helped by Euan's image of predestination and fate as two streams flowing near each other but in opposite directions, though the stream of fate still appeared to him as a sluggish clay oozing and bubbling over the kiln-bed. The important thing was that he had escaped his fate, whatever metaphor he used to describe it. These vigils on Rostowrack Downs were not a repetition of those he had spent on Roche Rock last autumn.

He was once more cherishing the lure of a girl's face, the starved womanhood that had leapt out like a flame; but the face, the flame and the cherishing had arisen on the other side of a spiritual frontier. The flash of illumination that had struck him when he glimpsed Lorraine had stood the test of sober thought; everything he had heard of Lorraine during the past fortnight had confirmed Euan's judgement of her. Joel was saturating his mind with the associations of Rostowrack, adjusting his outlook to the startling new pattern; he was now near the point where he would make a deliberate effort to seek further meetings with Lorraine.

He passed from the white base of the pyramid and turned west, away from the claywork, moving into flat, open downland where he became at times scarcely distinguishable against the tawny foliage and blobs of bushes. It was clear from his manner that he was intently watchful; his eyes darted wherever there was a break in the shadow, the rustle of a bird or rabbit in the undergrowth. When at length he came in view of the scene of Mannell's suicide he paused, taking the impact of the sordid, sinister details.

Down by the low bank of earth which had been thrown up from

the quarry, a hundred yards away, he saw the lodge; a small oblong hut of rough stone. He noted the granite wall beyond the mound, following the rounded edge of the quarry. The gap opening on to the St. Dennis road was close to it; he altered his course over the uneven ground, approaching the lodge. Sheets of corrugated iron lay rusting amid the ferns and bramble clumps behind it, having been blown from the roof during the winter storms; the gaps they had left showed raggedly above the blank, windowless wall that faced the moor. The two windows of the building fronted the bank; the door, too, was on that side, as if to welcome such burdens from the pool as it had received three weeks ago. The hut seemed to have connived in that tragedy, to be brooding, enclosing something still, though the body had been taken away.

And suddenly Joel's heart swooped as he became aware that the lodge had enclosed another body, and the one he desired – Lorraine's. She appeared now visible above its roof as she slowly ascended the bank. He halted and gazed incredulously, but there could be no mistaking that solid figure. She was bare-headed and wore a short jacket which flapped loosely in the brisk night wind. She moved in a curiously, aimless way, as if she had been pacing to and fro, up the bank and down to the lodge, many times since she arrived here.

Stealthily Joel advanced, picking his way carefully in the fading light. She had not yet seen him; her back was towards him now; but the crackle of a twig, the stab of his shoe against a stone or fragment of corrugated iron, would reveal his presence. If she saw him without immediately recognising him she might hurry away before he could reach her.

Lorraine passed over the brow of the bank and stood motionless, a hand tethering her hair, sharply outlined between the ruddy western sky and the featureless dark mass of the mound. She was absorbed, looking south along the road that led to Carloggas.

Joel reached the corner of the hut and leaned against it for a few moments; he bowed his head as if in prayer, then crept along the side wall to the front of the building. Only a few feet separated the hut from the base of the knoll; then he was screened under the dense growth of gorse and hazel that matted the whole slope, except where a path slanted up through ferns. But she heard his movements behind the thicket and turned with a start of alarm, watching rigidly until he emerged against the open doorway of the lodge. He raised his arm in greeting, and as recognition flamed through her she came swiftly to the top of the path, her vivid acceptance shown in her outstretched hands and confused little gasp of astonishment.

They stared at one another in silent fascination as Joel climbed up between the fern clumps. Their faces were too deeply shadowed for them to read the emotional play of each other's features, but since they had both wanted such a meeting as this there was no sign of tension or reserve in them, only a surface flutter of nervousness as the joy flooded in. When he was close to her she murmured with a quick heave of her breast: "I'm glad it's you."

Joel glanced past her as a nightjar whirred up from behind the quarry. "We aren't strangers," he said.

Her dark eyes searched him, the glowing mask of his face turned sideways under the low-drawn cap. "You're Gwen Kruse's brother, aren't you?"

"Yes – Joel," replied, his gaze veering back to meet hers. "I hope you don't think too bad of her because o' what's happened."

Lorraine shook her head, slipping her hands into her coat pockets and frowning down at the lodge. "No, I don't blame her at all. I'm glad she's safe with Euan. It's strange that their marriage should have led to my coming into this district, but the tragic side of it all about Cal – is still hazy and unreal to me."

"You never knowed him, did you?" Joel inquired.

"Never saw him in my life. He was only a name to me and not a very pleasant one. I came here tonight to try and get it more vivid in my mind the way it ended for him."

"Come up from Carloggas?"

"No; I haven't been home to tea. I waited around St. Dennis for an hour or two after the shop shut, and then rambled round the clay-works where you and Euan and Cal used to work. I'm not eager to get home tonight."

Joel noted the hard pout of her lips and, feeling self-conscious before the latent heat of her mood, edged forward and stood on the summit of the bank, peering down at the pool: a green, faintly glimmering surface cupped by the ragged dark cliffs of the quarry a hundred feet below.

"Your mother got some rum friends," he commented." Some of 'em coming to your place this evening, I s'pose?"

"Yes." She moved slowly up beside him through the thick wiry knots of heather. "Lela Skiddy and her mother, and Lela's aunt, Mrs Kessel, from Plymouth. A pretty loose woman, so I gather and she lives near the Barbican, where I was reared. I felt I couldn't bear the memories... I'd see it all again – that room where I suffered so much; just a bare room at the top of the stairs with the grubby little window on the bend, looking out over the smelly alleys. I've had enough nastiness lately without having those scenes burnt back into me again."

She was breathing in gusts, making sharp, confused gestures, her eyes darting mutinously around. Joel felt the bond strengthening with every new facet of her nature which she revealed to him. The ache of tenderness pierced him, deeper than he had ever known it as he watched this warm beauty, restless amid the still, twilit shapes. She touched him like a living, defiant flame arisen where death had struck, where coldness and horror breathed out from the pool.

"Must be tough on you," he muttered, "hanging round here this time o' night because you ha'n't got a home fit to go back to. I guessed the state o' things when I seen you outside Skiddys'."

"Yes – I was stupid to go there, only mother wanted to introduce me to Lela. We didn't hit it off, of course it got rather unpleasant, and when they all started telling bawdy tales about Cal I felt I had to get some fresh air. I wasn't much surprised, but I knew there must be some meaning in the breaking up of my Scilly Isles life, and that sort of thing didn't fit in with it."

Joel scanned the road southward, winding among a huddle of low refuse-heaps and visible as far as the railway bridge adjoining the quarry wharf where he had worked earlier that day. Near it was an old drying-shed with a broken stack; beyond the bridge the chimney of an engine-house jabbed up against the grim headstock of an aerial cableway that was used to lift stone from the quarry. There was little grandeur in the scene; the road seemed to twist into harsh squalor as it approach Lorraine's home.

"You must feel lonely over here," he said.

"No worse than at Hugh Town. A girl like me'd be lonely anywhere." She paused, buttoning her jacket, for the air was growing chill on this exposed ridge. "When I see these village girls clicking

211

about with their make-up on and hair-dos I wonder what they're thinking of – what they're trying to be. It's plain they're fretting and straining after something, but I haven't a clue to what it is." Her laugh rippled out, low and spontaneous.

Joel too now relaxed; he smiled reminiscently. "My old workmate George Bassett would say 'twas just swank wanting to climb on a pedestal so every-body'd see how smart they are."

"Well, I haven't had much chance to develop that. I've never had anything to be proud of. My mother, my home, Cal – how could I try to get on a pedestal against that background? I'd feel more like getting behind one to hide! Yet the shame of it all may have been good for me: it's kept me so real – always in touch with things that matter, things we've got to face." She swept her hand towards the veiled tarn. "Think what it means to me to be here, letting Cal's life and death burn into me! It's the same lesson I was learning in Plymouth when I was a kid, only so much clearer and deeper now, especially with you here."

Joel nodded slowly, moistening his lips. He scarcely knew how to answer her, but he did not feel distressed or impotent. This was a duel like his encounters with Marvran and Olive. There was no room for thrust and parry between him and Lorraine; they were too close, drawn in upon each other, already intimate. She was so eager and headlong, so unguarded, trusting him. Her words implied a personal bond beyond the association of Gwen with her return to Cornwall. She was seeking the clues of his male nature as frankly as Olive had done, yet the qualities of search and self-exposure were different in her, entirely wholesome. "You haven't heard much about me, I s'pose, apart from Gwen's wedding?" he asked.

"Not a great deal; but I knew you weren't on a pedestal as soon as I saw you!"

"'Tis true, I've never fitted in wi' the limelight stuff," he admitted. "I tried it back in me teens – got in a local football team but had to drop out after a year or two. I wasn't meant to be a mixer; 'twas the wrong world for me."

He had moved back a few paces, turning to face the lodge, and again Lorraine followed him.

"I'm the same – even worse than you, for I always loathed games." she said. "I'd seen too much of life in the raw: and the things respectable people did seemed so trivial. I wanted to escape into something that had meaning in it. At Plymouth when the slum life got a bit too crude, I used to dream of being a nun. Some of our neighbours were Catholics."

Joel stared, realising that aspects of the world she had known were alien to him. "You've growed out o' that now, I s'pose?" he said.

"Oh yes. I found a different sort of faith on St. Mary's."

It was going deeper, into their vitals, the full understanding. Joel's mind clouded for a moment. "But you didn't get married over there," he remarked.

She had been idly plucking the fern tips at the head of the path; her hand became very still amid the dusky foliage. She looked away from him. "No, I couldn't find anyone who was enough my own type for anything serious," she answered simply. "And of course they all knew I'd come from the slums, and my mother wasn't married. That didn't help."

There was a brief silence in which Joel's face hardened; the memories that fused him with her at this point were bitter. "A lot o' snobbishness about these days," he observed as he began descending the slope, through the trampled bracken. "I've run up against it too, me family being what they are. I daresay your mother've put me pretty much on Cal's level?"

Lorraine was somewhat agitated as she came down behind him, shadowy between the tall, faintly rocking fern clumps. "Hardly that: but it was through her I first heard of you. She'd seen us through Skiddys' window, of course, and started jeering about it as soon as she got home. 'You ought to have asked Joel Kruse to runoff with 'ee', she said, 'if you think you're so superior to me and Lela."

Joel turned to face her at the door of the lodge. There was tenseness in him now; his hands were clenched.

"Is that all she told you – that I was Gwen's brother?"

"Not quite," she answered, flushing slightly.

"Did she say she'd met me outside Olive Buzza's last March?"
"Yes."

"And that I went to phone for the doctor for Olive's father when he was dying that night?"
"Yes."

Joel felt his self-control slipping. "Did she lead you to think it meant anything?" he demanded.

Lorraine smiled, pausing a few yards off by the big square hole in the lodge wall that had once held a window-frame.

"She said you'd been there before. She asked the neighbour, and though the woman wouldn't admit anything definite, mother judged from her manner that her guess was right. But somehow I couldn't believe that..." Lorraine stooped to flick a tuft of bracken from her skirt, then added hesitantly as she straightened: "I've had it cleared up today by – that girl herself."

Joel frowned. "Olive? Where did you see she?"

"She came in the shop at St. Dennis and spoke about you."

"Told you I'd got to breaking point?"

"I don't know about that, only – that you didn't break."

"Were you glad to hear it?" he inquired.

"I'd have been glad to hear it of any man, knowing how that woman carried on with Cal. Seems she's mending her ways since he died. I hope it'll last."

The hot wave had swept over Joel and now receded; he felt more normal, ashamed of his crude, indelicate floundering. He stepped onto the threshold and set his hands on his hips.

"Well, so long's you don't think too bad o' me..." he remarked in a casual, deprecating tone.

"Of course I don't. We must all be tested somehow."

Lorraine moved forward, and they stood together in the doorway, peering into the hut. It was bare, except for slabs of fallen masonry lying about, and a stove with a rusty pipe sagging from the end wall. There was a close mouldy smell in the darkness; the atmosphere was oppressive and melancholy. Lorraine shivered.

"A bit morbid, isn't it?"

"Yes, I s'pose 'tis, 'specially when you think o' what was brought in here," he replied.

But she was thinking of Olive's confession, that desperate bid for a new image of married virtue, perversely gratified amid the associations of death. It drove her thoughts to rankness, and the obscure picture became almost palpable to her there on the shadowed floor. Joel sensed her recoil, the threat of the warped intimacy against which she struggled. He drew back into the open and glanced about, up into a starlit sky.

"Coming in pretty dark, now," he said with awkward persuasiveness. "Lonely bit o' road, too, between here and Carloggas. Would you-d'you mind if I go home that way, through Goonamarris? 'Twould be company for 'ee part o' the way."

Her quick flash of gratitude restored them to the clear, unflawed communion. "It's good of you – thanks," she murmured, stealing out among the bushes. "I don't expect we'll meet anyone: not that it matters, anyhow. There'll be talk enough, no doubt, before we're much older."

CHAPTER TWENTY-ONE

THE field behind Barrakellis farmhouse had been a scene of drowsy activity all the afternoon. Late June sunshine poured down on the harvesting of Digory's small hay crop, which had stood for several days in spindly stooks on the bleached stony soil.

Digory was being helped by five labourers, four of whom were usually at the farm during harvest: Euan, Fred Bullock and Jim Hooper, from Goonamarris, and Len Truscott, Veale's brother-in-law from Bloomdale on the Nanpean road. The fifth had never worked here before, though he was becoming a frequent visitor to the farm. This was Joel, who had come straight to Barrakellis from Slip quarry and taken his place with Len and Bullock, who were stationed on the field. He worked somewhat apart from them, gathering haycocks and strewn trusses at a higher point, but occasionally he went down to join them and assist in loading when Digory appeared with the empty wain. The heat had been intense and the men toiled in their shirt sleeves, their movements slow and sweat-heavy above the steel prongs that flashed amid the rustling hay. The sweet scent of dry grass and clover drugged the still air; birds were continually darting and singing overhead; bees and butterflies, persistent and inquisitive, scudded about the field, lingering by the hedge around the soft, flagging blaze of wild flowers.

When evening drew on the harvesters were still busy; by this time a welcome cool breeze had sprung up. Blowing from the west, it brought from the valley beyond Goonvean sand-dump the mellowed sound of a brass band. A tea for the Sunday School children was being held in a field at Trethosa, a mile away, and the band, which had led the march around the village lanes at four o'clock, was now seated on benches in the broad, sloping meadow. It was not visible from

Barrakellis, but as the men gathered in the hay they pictured the scene: the crowds of bare-limbed children and gaily-clad adults thronging the field and the road adjoining, patronising the fruiterers' and confectioners' stalls, the ice-cream and potato-chip vans, outside the chapel gates; chattering idly as they awaited the start of the sports and the final items of band music that would fade across the twilit dale. The reminder of normal village activities was poignant to Euan and Joel. They were so completely apart from the brisk surface routine, moving in massive tides of significance to which the everyday life of this rural community was alien. To Joel the faintly blaring sounds were like an echo from his past, a blunted mockery that could no longer pierce him. The band came from Bugle, and one of the trombones was being played by Eli Creba.

In the centre of the hayfield Len Truscott, a stout elderly man with a genial freckled face and ginger moustache, was lounging on his pitchfork. He jerked his head critically towards the farmyard, where from the wain drawn close to the rick, trusses of hay were being lifted by Digory and caught by Euan and Hooper, who proceeded to tread them firmly into the body of the stack.

"'Tisn't a bad looking rick, though Jim's doing the best part of it," commented Len in a quiet sing-song tone. "First time Euan tackled sich a job, 'a b'lieve: he been here on the field other years, though he never got the knack o' farm work – never seemed to know which was the right end of a pike, or how to hoist a bundle without letting it fall to pieces."

Bullock, tall and gaunt, with the dark oily appearance of a man who had spent much of his life attending to machinery, frowned as he stooped over a haycock three yards away. "No, Euan wasn't cut out for a farmer," he agreed, "but his worries have gived a twist to what was lackin'. First 'twas his father, then Lela, and now his mother: he've never been free to keep a hearty eye on his pitchfork."

Len straightened, gazing intently out over the downs towards the Kellas' cottage. "He seem to be lookin' Trethosa way a good bit this evening. His mother's out there to the tea, I s'pose, and he'll be minding how he used to go there ten year ago, wi' she and Bob buying his ice-cream cornets and chips, and great old strands o' liquorice or peppermint rock, whatever 'twas he was partial to. Can't be pleasant for'n to think now it all led up to such a split as this."

"'Tis a clean split, you can see. Euan ha'n't been down visiting his mother since the wedding, have 'a?"

"Don't think so; but I wouldn't expect no other wi' that woman. A bit o' flint in she, Fred – been growing on her ever since her man was killed. And when you think o' the hopes she had for that boy, you can sympathise with her – I do meself. He had the makings of a real clever chap when he was goin' Grammar School, while now – just look at 'n! Buried away here on the farm. All his makings is gone scat this last year or two."

Bullock nodded, fully facing Len and showing a large wart on his right cheek and false teeth gleaming under a long bare lip. "Scat enough," he assented. "Yet his workmates say he's happier now than he ever was."

"Ah, but before he had Lela Skiddy to reckon with. She'd be a tax on man's wits."

"Well, yes; and maybe that's why he've married a maid who can't tax him in that direction. There's a queer streak in Euan – like as if he's afraid of his own brains and want to forget he got any. I dunno exactly what's wrong wi' the chap, but there's a twist somewhere. You can hardly blame his mother for putting her foot down when he dashed her last hope of'n by marrying Zachy Kruse's daughter."

Bullock glanced warily at Joel, who was raking loose tufts of hay fifty yards further up the field, near the corner. He was obviously not listening to their talk; his back was towards them, and during his frequent pauses he stood looking dreamily up the moorland slope, past the abandoned clay-working, to Carloggas.

"Mrs Kella must be wishing Digory's missus had lived a bit longer," continued Bullock. "Gwen wouldn't have come here then and none o' this wouldn't have happened."

Len's blue eyes narrowed as he went to the nearest haycock and spat over it into the bristly stubble. "Yes, 'twas a shock that sister Bessie should die so young. We all expected her to last several years yet and get a bit o' water about her before the end. Ours is a dropsy-fied family: both our parents died with it, and grandfer too."

"Twasn't dropsy wi' she: she was thin as a rake when we was hay-making here last summer."

"True enough, Fred: I can't think why Bessie should have been so contrary as to have cancer. It struck quite a wrong note at the funeral

– everybody tongue-tied, for want of having nothing to compare it with. 'Dropsy again, poor soul – 'tis the family predicament,' we all wanted to say; but we couldn't."

"Well, one way or another, she's gone, and Digory do seem to be making the best o' things now he've shook off the Mannells. He and the young couple do get on brave an'well, and it must give him a family feeling in his old age – something he been in need of all along."

Len impaled the haycock aggressively. "That's another point where Bessie didn't toe the line," he remarked. "We Truscotts usually bring up a proper handful: I got six, as you know, and Gert up Karslake had twins the first time. But Bessie didn't produce somehow, though she and Digory both looked hearty enough to manage triplets."

"I wonder what Euan and Gwen'll manage?" observed Bullock, toeing the pitchfork that lay half buried in hay at his feet. "The marriage do seem decent enough – not what folks thought back in April, for all the hastiness of it. Gwen isn't showing any signs yet, so it couldn't have been a forced affair."

Len grunted but made no further response, and hearing the empty wain rattle across the farmyard, Bullock hastily seized the dropped tool in readiness for loading.

The waggon lurched through the gateway at the rear of the farm-house and with clattering boards and creaking wheels approached the middle of the field. The lower part had been cleared of stooks; more than half the enclosure was bare, looking like a patch of yellow skin from which bunches of hair and been shaved off. Veale walked jerkily at the horse's head, holding the bridle. He was a raw-boned, clumsy elderly man but robust and red-cheeked, wearing a trilby over his whitening hair – a typical small farmer in shabby corduroy breeches and leggings. His manner still showed something of the fierce, inarticulate humiliation he had suffered through his brief entanglement with Sue Mannell.

Joel too had noted the return of the wain, and came slowly down towards it, bearing a mass of hay on his raised pitchfork. The golden stalks trailed over his shoulders and his glistening bronzed arms, shadowing the damp sphinxish face from which the black eyes peered out, a little strained and uneasy, but with a deep inner peace and friendliness. He was a stranger to the other loaders, though they had both watched him play football in earlier years. They had no clue to the quiet, intense satisfaction which he obviously found in working with them in the field. They saw that he often gazed at the Mannell's cottage, the roof and chimney of which were just visible around the edge of some flat refuse-dumps; but it seemed natural to them that he should be fascinated by Cal's old home, and they read nothing more personal into his regard. The attachment between him and Lorraine was still a secret, not even declared openly to each other. He had walked up to Rostowrack Downs on several evenings during the past month, meeting Lorraine as she came back from work, and they had talked in the shelter of the bank or in the lodge. But the situation was becoming almost painful because of their forced evasions and the growing demand for intimacy.

Joel was as yet unable to take the full weight of passion. He had been weakened by the long attrition of his relationships with Marvran and Olive, and Lorraine was so different from either of them that he feared to repeat his old blunders, to disappoint her by crudely blundering into the lover's part. She was so rare, he was inhibited by his reverence for her. Thus there was a sense of deadlock, though it was superficial; neither he nor Lorraine doubted the final issue, but he needed a ripeness of mood in order to take it worthily, and had come here today hoping that the associations of the place would develop such a mood.

"Not many more loads now," he remarked with evident relief. "We'll finish the rick by seven o'clock or sooner."

"Gwen's getting early supper for us, isn't she?" Len inquired of Veale.

"Yes, roast pork'll be on the table as soon's we'm ready for it. First big cookery job she've tackled, this harvest supper, but she's doing brave, feeling quite homely about it, now 'tis for Joel too."

Joel smiled quietly as he tossed his load into the wain. "Gwen won't get flustered," he said.

Digory climbed into the waggon and adjusted the loose racks; the three men on the ground began carefully lifting the stooks to him. For a while the silence was broken only by the restless movements of the horse, the thrust and clang of the pitchforks, the soft crackle of hay, and the distant blurred strains of the band. The shadow of the rising load crept over the harvesters; Digory mounting higher on the trodden stems until the forks were directed towards him almost vertically.

When the crop of this area had been gathered, Bullock stepped back to the horse and led the animal on up the slope to the next group of haycocks. As the wain creaked to a standstill he turned abruptly to Joel, who had walked in the shade beside it with his hand on the rack.

"Big moves up around Roche lately, Joel," he observed in a tone of latent curiosity. "Have 'ee kept in touch with it?"

Joel edged out into the sunshine, carrying his pitchfork and staring moodily at the hay. "No, I don't go up there now." The reminder was somewhat distasteful to him, but the music of the band had already given a lighter touch to his memories of the old struggle: he spoke casually.

"Well," resumed Bullock as he approach a stook which had sagged in a flattish heap at the end of the row, "I hear your old house have been pulled down – nothing left of it, and some of the sand-burrow scooped up too; trucks and excavators busy for weeks shifting stone and gravel to make room for the pit to be digged back."

Joel shrugged, looking across at Len, who had followed behind the waggon and was mopping his face with a red handkerchief.

"Don't matter to me," he commented. "Me father said they'd started on it a week or two ago. I'm glad 'tis finished with."

"But 'tisn't only your home that's on the move," Bullock went on slyly. "Your old neighbours is hustling too same way Gwen've gone. There at the bungalow."

Joel's fork flashed suddenly into the snout of piled hay; he raised the load, his face hidden from Bullock. "That's no news to me, either," he said with dry reserve.

"Why, who do 'ee mean?" asked Len, halting by the next stook.

"Crebas' girl have got engaged to Cap'n Chegwidden's son," Bullock answered. "They Crebas was thick wi' your family, wasn't 'em Joel? Did 'ee know the maid well?"

Joel was not at the wain, releasing his fork as Digory pulled in the load. He frowned, but was really indifferent: the matter did not touch him vitally.

"No, didn't see much of her after she left school," he said. "She went down Falmouth for a year or more, and thought herself a cut above our party when she came back." He glanced around at Bullock, who was pitching in his load at the rear. "I heard about her going wi' Roy Chegwidden. As good a match as any, I s'pose."

The talk lapsed in the urgency of work, and the waggon was soon fully loaded. Bullock once more took the bridle, leading the horse in a broad semi-circle before beginning the descent of the slope to the farmyard. Digory stood knee-deep in hay, lounging on his fork and rocking with the lurching of the wain. To Joel and Len he became a tiny figure, outlined first against the pale blue sky and fluffy cumulus cloud, then against the white glare of sand-dumps on the horizon, and finally against the dark green wedge of the coppice and the cluster of elms around the farmhouse.

When the wain was near the bottom of the field a motor-cycle roared down past the end of the lane, a hundred yards to the east. Joel and Len caught a brief flickering glimpse of the machine as it began rattling up the northern hill to Goonamarris. Behind the rider sat a girl in a yellow frock and white linen hat. They swerved westward at the top of the hill, taking the road to Trethosa.

"Young couple going out tea, 'a s'pose," murmured Len.

Joel nodded and moved stolidly up towards the corner where more strewn wisps of the crop lay waiting to be raked into heaps. He was gazing at the Mannell's cottage.

Digory had noted something other than the passing of the motor-cycle. From his perch on the load he could see the whole length of the farm lane, and had observed, before the machine flashed by the gate, a man coming down towards the yard. He was tall and thin, wearing a grey flannel suit; he approached cautiously, glancing across the wire fence and the pasture to the bank of the clay-stream. As Bullock led the horse into the yard and brought the wain close to the rick, the man reached the big red gate in the lower wall and fumbled with the latch. The sound, breaking sharply as the wain grew silent, drew the attention of all four men in the yard, and they surveyed the intruder from varying levels: Euan and Hooper from the rick, Digory from the waggon, Bullock from a normal height. They all recognised him, though only Bullock had exchanged more than a casual greeting with him hitherto. It was Bullock who addressed him, now, lifting his brows in surprise.

"What 'ee doing down here, Charlie?"

Crago pushed open the gate and strolled in, scattering some

chickens that had been scratching amid the straw near the wall. He fingered his cigarette nervously, and his hollow face was screwed up irritably against the sun. "Need any help wi' the haymakin'?" he asked.

"No – nearly all the stooks is in and we'll soon top the rick," replied Digory in a brusque tone. He raised the first bundle to the stack, and Hooper, a round-shouldered, bristly man with a vacantly hanging face, bent forward to receive it.

"Was 'ee on your way out Trethosa?" Bullock inquired.

Charlie shook his head, scowling up the field at the two men who were busied among the small drifts of hay by the top hedge. They were not yet aware of his presence; their backs were towards him, and at that distance he did not perceive that one of them was Joel.

"Me and Olive called up Mannells' to see Sue," he explained uneasily. "But she was gone Plymouth wi' Mrs Skiddy; only the maid there and neither of us wanted to go indoors wi' that little bitch. Olive seen her in shop last month and it seems they had a bit o' fireworks. Anyhow, we come away again as soon's she told us Sue was gone."

Bullock removed his cap, mopped his bald sweating head, and asked: "Where's Olive?"

"Gone up Foxhole to catch the bus back home, so far's I know. I said I'd hang around and see if I could lend a hand, when I seen there was haymaking going on here."

The mention of Sue had darkened Veale's mood; he peered down at Crago rather sourly while lifting more hay. "Well, you needn't soil your flannels tonight, we can manage," he grunted.

Charlie was nettled by the repulse, but the root of his ill-temper clearly lay elsewhere. Euan, who watched him closely as he handled and trod the stooks, came nearest to understanding the queer, warped look of Charlie's face. He felt, moving amid the soft hay, that Charlie stood mentally on a similarly treacherous, inflammable foundation. Something strange and horrible was indeed happening in Crago's world. During recent weeks he had grown aware of shiftings in the depths of him, the slow dissolving of what he had thought solid ground, but which was proving no more than a fantastic cloud bred of an anaesthetic. It was as if he and Olive had taken some drug on the night of Cal's funeral, there in the hut by the flooded quarry, and lived since in dream-consciousness, remote and morbid. Its effect was now wearing off; cruel realities were glimpsed through the fog, jealousy and disgust awakening with sly malicious taps at nerves and brain. There had grown in them a dreary mood of cynicism, indifference masking the rage which swelled upon the knowledge that they had tricked themselves.

For several minutes there was silence between the men in the yard. Charlie lounged against the barn, watching the unloading of the waggon and occasionally glancing at the open back door of the farmhouse, only a dozen yards from the rick. He sometimes caught through the window a shadowy movement: Gwen was bustling about in the kitchen, attending to the roast and preparing the table for the harvest supper. Bullock lingered idly beside the horse, wishing to return to Joel and Len on the field, but suspicious of Charlie's motive and reluctant to miss any gossip that would throw light on the Crago's domestic affairs. A tenseness had fallen upon the scene; even Nature had become less genial. The breeze was growing gusty, whirling straws from the ground, and the shadow of the house lay dark across the enclosure, creeping up the rick so that only Euan and Hooper were now in the sunlight. The prongs of the fork glittered strangely, flashing up out of the shade as Digory raised the impaled heaps to the treaders.

The wain was almost empty when Euan gave a sudden start and straightened balancing himself amid the yielding bundles of hay. He had turned from the farmyard and was gazing across the lower part of the field towards the mica clay site, a hand guarding his eyes from the hair that blew untidily around his bare head. He became so absorbed that Digory had to call attention to the next truss he lifted. Euan turned slowly about, but still ignored the loaded fork, and Hooper stooped to pull in the tangled stalks. Euan was peering down at Charlie. "Looks like you were mistaken," he said.

Charlie had crushed the stump of his cigarette under his shoe; he stared up uncomprehendingly.

"Your wife hasn't gone up to catch the bus. She's coming across the field here."

Charlie's face grew pale, he moved out from the barn wall. "What? Olive coming?"

Hooper was now scanning the field, and nodded, mumbling into his moustache: "'Tis she, all right."

224

A curse escaped Crago; he staggered past the rick and through the gateway. He stood against the post, clutching the warm stone, a kind of stupor dulling his face as he saw who was approaching him. Olive was more than half-way across the hayfield; wearing the same halo hat and cream coloured frock she had worn when she bought her dress at Tamblyn's shop. She did not at first observe Charlie; she was surveying the upper part of the field, where Len and Joel were working, her eyes and cheeks puckered against the slant of sunshine. She too was obviously startled and smouldering, and when she glimpsed Charlie tense by the gate the depths of her old sensual derision of him were stirred, throwing a provocative insolence into her bearing. She was quite close before he greeted her.

"What the hell've 'ee come down here for?" he rasped. "Didn't I tell 'ee to go straight home?"

Olive smiled as she halted. "I think me and you ought to change places, Charlie."

"Eh?"

"Let me stay here with Joel while you go up and see what headway you can make with Cal's sister."

Charlie's hands wavered out from the post, slowly clenching; he blinked at her, nonplussed for a moment. "Joel Kruse?" he said dazedly.

"Yes – up there, look." She pointed. "Haven't you seen him? I saw 'twas he as I came across the field."

Crago's mood became more dangerous as he took the fresh shock. He glared up at Joel, who had clearly recognised Olive and was using his rake stiffly and jerkily, facing the sun and giving an occasional stealthy glance down past Len to the pair near the gateway.

"That bastard!" Charlie growled at length, in a tone with antagonism. "So that maggot's biting 'ee again, is it? You sneaked down hereafter him?"

"'Tis because of him in a way though I didn't know he was here when I decided to come down." Olive paused, her sweating freckled face growing bitter, malicious. "Did you see that motorbike go past here just now?"

"No; I was in the lane."

"It passed me on the road to Foxhole. Pity Joel didn't see who was riding it. He'd have got a shock too."

Charlie frowned as the association brought a flash of understanding to him. He was impatient to get the issue stripped of irrelevancies, releasing the naked heat, the brutal personal clash of their awakening.

"Roy Chegwidden and Marvran Creba?"

"Yes, on their way out to the band, I suppose. But you can guess what that did to me, right after finding Lorraine in possession at Cal's. The way Marvran looked at me – damned little snob – as if to say: 'So you didn't get him either!' It set me boiling, and I had to hit back somehow."

Charlie shrugged his thin shoulders, peering up over the hedge at the rick-top. Hooper was watching Olive furtively as he trod the hay, but Euan had moved to the lower end of the stack, near the ladder, and was gazing fixedly across at the doorway of the farm house. Gwen had just appeared on the threshold, and the pair seemed to fuse, silently regarding each other, isolating themselves from the squalid scene that was developing.

"You could ha' waited till I got home if you wanted another wrangle," cried Charlie, turning on the woman. "Not come here and make a fool o' yourself in front o' these fellows."

Olive met his eye steadily. "You always like to have everything done in a corner, don't you?" she jeered. "I'm glad this family party's going on: Joel and Euan and Gwen Kruse – they're all mixed up in the story."

"You'd better not stop here, anyhow. Go on home and wait."

"I shall do as I please," she answered, her plump hands tightened to fists as her passion flamed out against him.

Restraint snapped suddenly in Crago; his face reddened, he lunged forward with a threatening gesture. "You do what I tell 'ee! Clear off out o' the farm! Go out Trethosa tea wi' Marvran, if you're so innocent as you've pretended to be these last two months."

"I aren't in my innocent mood tonight, Charlie. I've been jolted out of it and you know who's top dog when I'm in this mood."

"I don't care a damn for any o' your moods. You got to go."

"You'll go before I do."

"We'll see about that."

Olive's laugh was brittle. "Seems you want to make a fool of yourself – trying to act the big bully."

Twenty One

"Another bloody word from you, and I'll... do something you'll be sorry for!"

Charlie's shrill, hysterical voice was borne up the field to Joel above the low, ironic booming of the band at Trethosa. He stood rigidly, gripping his rake, staring at the two poised figures as sickeningly familiar to him. He was shaken by the abrupt intrusion of this drama, fascinated as he watched the man and wife move closer to each other, crouching and menacing like mated beasts drawn instinctively by the recoil of their lust, the dark magnetism of combat.

CHAPTER TWENTY-TWO

LORRAINE stood in the claywork lane that wound westward from Carloggas hill towards the woods of Tregargus. The faded tints of her frock were further mellowed by the shadow of the dunes. This claywork had been abandoned at an early stage, as the deposits were poor. The two refuse sand-heaps running parallel from the pit, walling the lane, were nowhere more than fifty feet high; but being some hundred yards long they formed a screen behind which she could listen for the movements in the hayfield below or footsteps on the road. She had loitered in the lane for sometime, but heard only the band playing at the village tea, and the music irritated her. There was no sign that the harvesting was still in progress at Barrakellis: no rattle of a wain or shouts from the loaders. She supposed they had gone into the farmhouse for their supper, and waited with growing tension.

When the knock had come on the cottage door an hour ago she had hurried to open it, expecting to find Joel on the threshold. He had told her last week that he would be at the haymaking today, and she felt sure that, if he learnt from the harvesters that Sue was in Plymouth, he would call at her home before returning to Curyan. The irony of seeing Olive and Charlie on the doorstep had seemed the climax of a dark, ominous week in which the fate of others had shown itself again hostile and pitiless to her separate destiny. She had been unable to remain indoors for long after the Cragos left her. If Joel would not come to her she must go to him: she felt a strange convergence of events impelling her to action.

She understood why Joel hesitated. She knew there had been two other girls in his life during the past year, and neither of them had become his lover. He had mentioned little of Marvran to her, but she realised from Olive's hints in the drapery store that he had suffered frustration at Roche. He had matured spiritually through his attraction to Marvran and his recoil from Olive, but physically he was raw, unused, afraid and unsure of himself. She knew she had to help him in this, and the mood was now upon her, the compulsion in the knowledge that their whole future was at stake.

She had paused at the inner end of the dumps where the lane forked sharply south, and on the northern side a fenced enclosure sloped down like a beach in the lee of the dune. The small pit beyond was full of ice-blue water which glinted in the sunlight, the breeze ruffling its surface, making tiny wavelets that broke with a thin crest of foam against the grey rock. Leaning over the fence Lorraine gazed across the flooded pit to the earth-dump and Barrakellis – relic of a less successful attempt to find clay on the southern side of the valley, as not even sand had been forthcoming. It was a dark, gloomy pile, eighty feet high, matted with gorse and bramble, squatting like a bronze idol amid the white statuesque group of sand-heaps. The pit from which it had been thrown up was unique in the district, broad and shallow like a frying-pan, with soft slopes of crumbling brown soil. Lorraine could only glimpse the edge of it, but it depressed her, the symbol of earth without clay, upheaval without purgation, the mere waste of fate.

She thought of her mother in Plymouth; a heavy sense of degradation loomed within her until her desire ran wild in recoil, seizing on the memories of Joel as he stood and talked with her in the hut where Cal's body had lain. There lay the pledge of deliverance, of triumph over the death and the shallow pit of earthiness. But memory was not enough to break up the shadow; security was still beyond her grasp. She turned from the fence as Joel's name burst from her lips under the stress of her passion.

The loneliness was intolerable amid the heat and scent of summer, the pulsations of band music drifting in among the dunes, nagging cruelly with reminders of a bright texture of life in which she had no part. Sue was in Plymouth, and the vast overshadowing of evil blotted out the beauty and harmony of the June day. Without Joel to confirm her in the good of creation, everything seemed unreal except the sombre and obscene ripening of her childhood's nightmare in the slums. The very silence of the farm seemed to have a menace in it, and as she moved back towards the road she felt a desperate urge to visit the place where Joel had breathed and laboured during recent hours. When she drew level with the first big rut which rain had gashed down the side of the northern dump, she stepped into it and began climbing up, her shoes slipping down the loose stones.

Within a few minute she was on the broad flat summit, panting and perspiring, her hair fluttering in the wind. There was a stark, reckless defiance in her bearing as her eyes took in the lower part of the dale. Even had the harvesters been busy in the field and likely to observe her, she would not have cared. But the hayfield was empty, and the farm yard hidden by a gable of the house. She could just see the top of the rick but that too was deserted. The fields, the downs, the coppice: the whole scene was vague and dreamlike to her; even the grey scudding clouds and the declining sun now splashing the west more feebly beyond the hard white sand-peaks, made no impression of substance upon her senses. She was isolated, finding herself in a world where life frayed off into a monstrous personal microcosm; from here all natural phenomena appeared as tiny, remote fragments.

"Joel!" she murmured again with rousing anguish. "Joel, come to me!"

She had a deepening intuition that something was wrong at the farm. Although the men might only have gone indoors for supper, she felt that this was not the reason why the place seemed to be gripped in a paralysis. Her own mood was toned towards tragedy, and she had a presentiment that here, as in Plymouth, a sinister stroke of fate was threatening her.

Before she had been on the dump five minutes her apprehension was confirmed. A man suddenly entered the hayfield from the yard and hurried up the slope, stumbling and at times almost running over the stubble. He was dishevelled, bare-armed, in corduroy trousers and blue striped shirt. He carried no tool and was clearly not intending to resume work, if any remained to be done in the field. His erratic motion was that of one blindly heading away from a scene that had unnerved him. And as he came to the top hedge and climbed over it into the brake that stretched between the field and the refuse-dump, skirting the small earth-pit, Lorraine saw that it was Joel. She knew, too, that he was making towards her home, seeking her. But his obvious distress blunted the joy she would otherwise have felt at his approach. She moved nearer to the edge of the dune, watching him in fear and suspense, her feeling of relief blurred in dark curiosity.

Joel was close to the foot of the dump before he became aware of her presence. Glancing dazedly up as he started to pick his way among strewn boulders around the white glittering refuse to the lane, he glimpsed the now familiar figure on the brink of the gravel slope forty feet above him. He stopped, rigid, staring at her.

It was so like their first meeting on Rostowrack Downs, but lurid, here in the glaring sun, and this time she came down to him, breathless and distraught, over the face of the dump. The sand was hard and she slithered most of the way, her feet slipping at last amid the stones at the bottom. Joel put out his hand instinctively and steadied her, his fingers trembling on the fringe of her short sleeve. He helped her free of the rubble and soon they stood together on the turfed bank a few yards from the lane, which was an open cart-track between here and the road. Lorraine shrank a little from his drawn, shocked face, but the sight of his body, virile and unharmed, restored and sense of her basic security in him, While his hand still vibrated on her arm she broke the taut silence.

"I've been here waiting for you."

Joel frowned, uncomprehending. He looked more than ever like a wild young gypsy, the sweat streaming from his black hair and glistening on this half-bare chest and arms. His eyes were feverish with an inner struggle as he rallied towards the consolation.

"Have 'ee seen anything?" he asked presently in a thick, strained tone.

"No, but I guessed something had happened. Is it an accident – someone fallen off the rick or waggon?"

He shook his head, and she was confused by a sense of strangeness. He had been so quiet and stolid during their earlier meetings: now he was profoundly excited, beyond normal controls, incalculable.

"Nothing like that," he mumbled.

"Then what...?"

He jerked his arm, releasing her and looking agitatedly back at the field hedge.

"'Tis they Cragos," he muttered, forcing the words between grey, tight lips. "Charlie've just killed his wife, down there by the woods."

Lorraine's mood, dark though it had been, had not prepared her for this. Her eyes dilated.

"Olive?" she gasped.

"That's it." He was drawing his breath hard and painfully, fighting for a calm, impersonal approach to his narrative.

Lorraine stepped back into the lane where the cool shadows were creeping out. She raised a hand to her head, as though she felt dizzy. Her heavy chestnut hair was very warm; all her flesh was damp with sweat, yet under the groping hand her face was stiff and mask-like with the cold horror that gripped her mind.

"But they called at my place only about an hour ago," she protested.

"Yes, yes, Charlie told the fellows about that." He lurched forward into the shade beside her, his clayey hobnailed boots trampling the daisies and buttercups on the turf. "'Tis a ghastly link-up – my own past mixed in with it. Olive meant to go straight home from your place but she seen a girl she used to be jealous of; and it bit into her somewhere, so she had to come back and make trouble."

Lorraine edged westward again, drawn instinctively into the screen of the dunes which shut out the view of the farmstead, separating them from it. Joel followed her with a blind, unreasoning trust, vaguely grateful for the seclusion.

"What girl?" asked Lorraine, glancing sharply round at him. "Marvran Creba, I suppose?"

"That's it. I'll tell you all the story sometime. 'Twas nothing – not even a real friendship – but Olive thought that maid was in the way, keeping me off from her. And just after she left Carloggas Marvran passed her, on a motor-bike wi' the chap she's going to marry. Her father's playing in that band you can hear at Trethosa, so I expect they've gone there to listen. Anyhow, the sight o' Marvran put the devilish streak into Olive again, and both she and Charlie came out o' their dream and found they hated each other more than ever. When she got to the farm they started rowing right away, and it soon led to blows. Digory and Fred Bullock stepped in and parted 'em for the moment, and Olive flounced off down the lane. But we knew 'twasn't over: they was both determined to finish it this time. There wasn't much the fellows could do except tell Charlie to cool down. They let him go and he slunk off after her."

"And they – came to blows again?"

"Yes. She was waiting for him out by the clay stream, and 'twasn't long before we heard a scream from her. They was fighting there on the bank and he'd knocked her down over. The fall might not have hurt her much, but all the men except me and Euan hurried out, feeling something ugly was going on. When they got down to the stream she was lying half in the water and half amongst the ferns. Charlie was still kneeling on her, his hands round her throat. They pulled him away, but 'twas too late. He'd strangled her."

The silence was intense as Joel concluded his recital. He and Lorraine paused in the lane, looking out past the white ridges, across the clay-pit pool to the hump of downs westward. The red clouds of approaching sunset were floating up over the earth-dump so that the gorse bushes along its slopes seemed shaken by the wind against nebulous fires.

"You haven't seen her?" Loraine whispered.

"No. I only seen 'em start to fight in the field: that was sickening enough. I stayed wi' Gwen and Euan in the farmyard. Digory came back to tell us what they'd found, while Hooper went for the police and the doctor. The two, Len and Bullock, they're still down by the river, holding Charlie till the police come for him. I felt I had to get away before they arrived – and I couldn't go straight home."

"I know," said Lorraine quietly. Her gaze moved among the dandelions and mauve prickly teazels that pierced up from the fringe of gravel. "It's too cruel to you that this should happen there, of all places. I thought that day in the shop that there was something brittle about the new start those Cragos had made. It was too morbid to last long, and I suppose the reaction was... more violent because of the memory – Cal's funeral..."

The image returned to her, the threefold association of the lodge: Cal's drowned body, the Crago's perverted lust, Joel's face in the half-darkness burning with the true flame. The intimacy was rising in Lorraine, pulling free of the shock. Her tenderness for him was becoming also an appeal as her thought veered round to her own plight. They were somehow changed, loosened and fluid, and the restraints and embarrassments of conventional conduct no longer troubled them.

"I'm glad me and Gwen and Euan didn't see it happen," Joel continued, watching her. "'Twas a bad knock to 'em when Digory brought the news; but they got each other. It have upset me worse."

"It was bound to. But you'll soon get over it, Joel. That's the last cord slipped now – the last link that bound you to the old life."

Joel's face twitched convulsively, then a glow of fresh apprehension kindled in his eyes. "Yes, I see that – I see 'tis working to get me clear," he said. "But I need something to hold me right now under the shock. 'Tis like a bomb going off in the kiln, and I can't see yet what's blowed away or what's left, or where I am. Only I had to come up here, that's all I knowed. There was nowhere else but wi' you."

Lorraine stepped close to him, her emotion fuller than he had ever sensed it, stilling him into a direct fascination. "I'm not surprised you felt like that," she said tremulously. "We're both driven, Joel. You can't need me more than I need you tonight."

He said with an abrupt suppression: "Your mother's in Plymouth, isn't she?"

"Yes. Did the men tell you Mrs Skiddy's gone too?"

"Charlie mentioned it, and Euan told me afterwards while we was waiting in the yard. I s'pose they've gone up to see that Mrs Kessel?"

"I'm afraid so." Lorraine spoke with bitterness. She suddenly moved on, her underlip between her teeth, towards the end of the defile. Joel lagged behind this time, aware that they were heading into complete exposure, some fierce baptism that would awaken them from the nightmare. He trembled, peering at her beneath his cap and brushing from it and from his neck and shoulders the spatter of hayseeds and tufts of dry grass, as though any reminder of the harvesting was intolerable to him now that he was in transition, passing over to Lorraine's side of the crisis. She had soon reached the edge of the barrier and stood as on a frontier, her head and shoulders in sunlight, her body and limbs in the soft slanting shade of the dunes, and the water of the little lake shimmering behind her, between the wooden bars of the fence. The breeze stirred against her thin frock, showing the full, powerful mould of her breasts and thighs as she turned to him.

"Pity your mother's got in thick wi' that crew," he observed awkwardly. "Must make you feel pretty sick to be minded o' Plymouth."

"It isn't the memories."

He stopped short. "You don't mean she's gone there to live again?"

"Not yet, but she told me Thursday it won't be many weeks before she does. Then I'll be left alone here at the cottage."

There was a tense pause, Joel standing with hands on hips, frowning. He was surprised, but seemed to find the news agreeable; his tone and glance were challenging when he responded: "Well – don't that fit in wi' some o' your own plans?"

"I couldn't live there by myself for long."

"You know you won't have to."

"Mother thinks I shall, unless I go back to St. Mary's." Lorraine crept to the fence and leaned back against it, like a creature at bay. "I've been fearing something of this sort would develop, ever since Lela brought her aunt to our place. It was the slum life pulling again, just when mother was in the mood for it."

"So she's gone up today, to see the lodgings and make arrangements about shifting?"

"Yes."

Joel pondered, moistening his lips as he came forward into the sunlight and joined her at the fence. "A sudden turn," he admitted at length, "but I don't see why you need be sorry she's clearing out."

Lorraine put her hand vaguely on his fingers, which were fumbling with his belt. She hesitated, her eyes dark with disgust and humiliation.

"I hardly know how to tell you Joel, on top of this shock about Olive. But it's no good trying to gloss things over... The fact is Mother and Mrs Kessell are going into partnership."

"What some business?" He spoke with dull bewilderment, almost mechanically, his mind absorbing the thrill of her touch.

Lorraine looked round, watching a swallow flash over the pond, but there was no help or distraction for her in the tranquillity of the summer evening. She explained at once in rapid muttering undertones:

"It's through Hitler's threat to Danzig – at least, partly through that. If it leads to war, then Plymouth will soon be swarming with Service men again, a lot of 'em foreigners. And these fellows always seem to think there's only one sort o' place where they can get a real welcome. So Mother and Mrs Kessel want to show 'em some... kindness."

The first gleam of understanding smote Joel; he recoiled, but Lorraine's grip tightened on his hand, steadying him.

"You mean that couple are going to start a house for girls like Olive?"

"Yes. I hope those Skiddys don't blab the news around here. People'd say you've had to take a pretty steep drop, after Marvran Creba."

Joel's face twisted, becoming sullen, his eyes scowling past the earth-dump towards Trethosa. The band music still floated up the valley, but no longer in a level wave; it was frayed by the wind, flagging and swelling in broken chords.

"We can't help the talk," he said presently. "There's Cal, anyhow – and your mother's past. I've never worried much about that side of it."

They were near the fusion now, but Lorraine held off for a moment, releasing her hand.

"This is just the way I'd expect Mother to round off her life. She's growing more and more restless as she gets older. It may not be long before she falls out with Mrs Kessell and shifts off again. Goodness knows where she'll end. But I can't stop her or reason with her. I'm simply fed up – sick of the whole mess, and only want to cut clear – as you do."

She reached to him again and deliberately set her palms on his chest. The contact of her fingers with the hot flesh of his body made them both aware, startled by the deepening realisation of their relationship as lovers. Her eyes challenged him steadily, her mouth was twitching with the intense physical vibration, the latent sensuousness rising superb and unflawed from its long purgation.

"We've been brought to this point, Joel," she murmured in an altered, hungry tone. "Our clue – at Nanpean this is where it's led us. Things had to shape as they have tonight, and surely – you can't fail me now!"

"No – no. I've failed 'ee too long as 'tis ." He remained poised, his face glowing, dark and strange in the transfiguration of desire. She felt his heart swooping wildly, his muscles tightening, then quivering as the spasm leapt through him.

Suddenly his arm went round her, drawing her free of the fence. She pushed her hand back under his shirt until it fastened nakedly on his shoulder, near the neck, while her other arm wound about his collar, pressing his head forward.

"Lorraine," he said, choking.

"My own Joel – love me!" she whispered.

Her grasp tightened on the hard moist skin of his shoulder. He folded her more closely, whilst the quick heaving and yielding of her body became something vast and separate, dazing him with wonder and awe: a strange movement like an absolute tide pulling on him and lifting him. And then, blindingly sweet, the kiss came, her mouth gripping his like the soft, naked pulse of the deeper sheathed swell of her body. She was entirely his, focusing upon him and releasing him; the new life flooded them in all its complex affirmations. It had no colour in Joel's mind as yet, but was full of a grey beauty, like the faith that had made is possible. Joel had suffered too much spiritually to feel the mere natural response to this impact of passion. And he knew that Lorraine's response also was beyond the frontier. The shock of Olive's death had reminded them both that on the carnal side of the frontier human love was exposed to the dark and tragic movements of fate. They craved in every touch the assurance of that other, alien movement of predestination, in which their love was immune from such bludgeoning.

When they drew apart they were very quiet, almost shy, standing together by the fence. The scene around them looked different, remote. They were unconscious of the reddening clouds, the cuckoo calling from Tregargus, the cheeping of a yellowhammer behind the refuse-heap, the flutter of a whitethroat among the elms of the lane. They glanced at each other intimately, recognising that they were changed. Lorraine's beauty was even rarer now; her features were the same – roughly cast, broad and heavy – but the starkness was dissolved in the irradiation, the knowledge of her power and confidence. Their freedom was still warped and overshadowed by the sense of tragedy gripping the valley: they peered past the earth-dump, their minds forming brief, crumbling pictures of the group of men by the stream, guarding the dead body. They wanted to turn away, go even further from the contamination. But they lingered until the tumult of their awakening had slackened. Then Lorraine spoke.

"Now we can live it all down," she said with deep, triumphant satisfaction.

"Yes, we're ready," he replied, squeezing her hand hard. "It'll be a lonely road, I'm afraid – no real friends for us, except Gwen and Euan."

"I suppose not. But we'll be happy, I'm sure of it... Mother'll be vexed about us because you're Gwen's brother, and your people..."

"They'll take it as they've took Gwen's splicing: putting it on the only level they can understand."

"And thinking you've had to be content with second best," she added, her lips edging into a playful smile.

Joel shrugged indifferently. "That's their sense o' values," he said.

She slipped her arm through his, drawing him forward into the lane. "Mother won't be home till ten o'clock. We'd better go in and talk things over for an hour or two. There's so much to be planned before the storm breaks."

CHAPTER TWENTY-THREE

THE first day of war-time to break over Great Britain since 1918, was creeping inexorably towards the Isles of Scilly. The actual light reflected overhead was still below the horizon. The morning when it broke would reveal a clear sky beyond rough-edged clouds on the sea verge. In the half-light the clouds might have been mistaken for islands, and the islands for clouds. Towards the mainland there seemed to be black spires and towers low between the dark sea and the dark heavens: only by watching these closely for a few minutes until they changed shape was the illusion of solidity replaced by the sense of a phantasmagoric pageant treading the waters around the rim of the visible world.

At adjoining bedroom windows that overlooked the beach of Porth Cressa, two women were talking in low tones. Their faces were indistinguishable, but their heads and shoulders formed vague shapes above the white window frames. The absence of light in the bedrooms behind them was a grim reminder of the convulsion from Europe that had now shaken and pulled tragically at the roots of life even in this remote outpost, but the subject of their conversation showed that common gossip had not been submerged for ordinary folk.

Mrs Danning's voice, thick and sing-song from a throat swollen with goitre, fell upon the harsh slap of the incoming tide. "Have the honeymoon couple called on 'ee yet, Mrs Rescorla?"

The neighbour, taller and thinner than Mrs Danning, shook her head. "No; and I'm wondering if they will," she answered, her tone high-pitched but with the same characteristic island drawl. "Considering she lived here for years, 'twould only be civil to drop in

239

and say thank you. But as the memories of her mother can't be very savoury, she may prefer to keep clear o' the place."

"Folks stared their eyes out Saturday when they see her step off the boat wi' this chap – the weddin' ring shining on her finger. And they've took rooms in a hotel instead o' lodgings this time."

"Safest, no doubt," said Mrs Rescorla, glancing back towards the stairway Lorraine had climbed so often: first as an adolescent, shy and awkward, then with tired monotony on into her twenties, aloof, secretive, sometimes in tears.

"Well, I aren't surprised she've come here wi' what she picked up," resumed Mrs Danning. "Jist like thik maid to come back and show off, though she ha'n't chose a good time if she expect us to be much took up wi' such antics."

Mrs Rescorla sniffed, gazing seaward as a flash from Peninnis lighthouse swept across the bay, flicking the sombre coastline of Gugh and St. Agnes two miles to the south-west.

"Her match is nothing to brag about, I believe. I seen 'em down by the pier yesterday, looking up at the tea rooms where Lorraine parted from her mother last February. Big, hulking chap enough, but something rough in the man's looks. He seem real lost over here, too: Lorraine got to lead'n around like if he's half-baked. They hotel folks must be laughing to have such a fellow blundering about in their fine rooms."

The curtain rings rattled as Mrs Danning leaned further out over the lowered sash; her short arm made emphatic gestures.

"I s'pose she had to jump at the best she could git afore the men is all gone off to war," observed Mrs Danning contemptuously. "I never expected her to catch a dashing, high-spirited chap, wi' thik moody way she always had."

"Yes; and 'twasn't something she learnt here only," said Mrs Rescorla in a reminiscent tone. "I mind when she come here first – a big lout of a maid in short frocks. Too short they was and bright coloured woons – gaudy stuff picked up second hand in Plymouth, I 'spect – and you'd see 'em around the beach at all hours o' the day, or up around Garrison Hill or out on the cliffs where she'd sit for hours by herself. And the first spring she was here, afore she got thik shop job, she'd be over in the flower fields pickin' away wi' the best of 'em... And how she'd look at the flowers, huggin' the big bunches as if they was babies, and never thinkin' how much they'd fetch in the market. A sort o' tender way the maid had, what you couldn't help taking to if her mother was out o' sight."

"I admit she had a point in her favour that way," confessed Mrs Danning. "Nothin' greedy and graspin' about her."

"No more than our own island maids. I mind a very peculiar remark she made that spring, woon evenin' when she seed the flowers bein' packed down to ship across. 'Fancy these lovely flowers bein' sold,' she says, strokin' 'em so gentle as babies itself. 'It seem almost as bad as sellin' love, don't it?' Yes, that's what she said."

"She didn't seem to know the meanin' o' money – and more than woon have said as much," agreed Mrs Danning, also in a softened tone. "She always seemed to want to live free and wild – yet quite moral with it; not her mother's sort at all. She seemed to have a taste for beautiful things."

"She did; and that's what makes it all the queerer she should marry such a scarecrow as the man is... Not but what she had her contrarinesses. I've seen some of 'em in this house, and others have seen 'em outside. 'Twas said she was seen reading in the churchyard of a summer evening, loungin' against the palm trees and wi' the graves all round. She'd carry out the little Bible she brought from Plymouth and read un there. That was woon of her moods; and the woon she was in when she married this man, I should judge. There's a funeral look about'n, if you ask me."

Mrs Danning was silent for a minute, then she said with a shrug of impatience: "Well, the maid'll have to change her moods if her man isn't to turn as ugly as he looks. If he's spared in the war she'll have to handle her wage-packet very different from how she handled the flowers here... I wonder what her mother d'think o' the match."

"Judging by how she felt about Lorraine while they lived in this house..." Mrs Rescorla paused, and both women assumed attitudes of rigid attention, listening.

Footsteps were heard, clear and sharp on the road, then muffled, scraping on sand where the low dunes heaved up beyond the gardens. Two dark figures broke the grey mass of shadow, moving slowly past the row of cottages towards the cliff-path eastwards. Both were looking intently at the houses, and after a moment Mrs Danning exclaimed under her breath: "Here they come!"

The pair approached until they were within twenty yards of the watching women, and as the girl became aware of their presence she flinched, drawing the man's arm more tightly round her as if she felt a threat reaching out from behind those walls where she had known such heartache, loneliness and disgust.

It was Mrs Rescorla who first spoke, her greeting somewhat strained. "Good mornin' to 'ee!"

Joel and Lorraine halted near the garden wall, and Lorraine responded in a tone of confused emotional stress: "Well, Mrs Rescorla! And you too, Mrs Danning! Glad to find you still here."

Mrs Rescorla cleared her throat, her hand fluttering back in agitation to the bun of her white hair. "Surprised to see you here at Hugh Town again, Miss Lorraine and at such a time too. But I daresay you'm enjoying the circumstances."

"More than I enjoyed the ones that made me leave here, I must say. Still, I'm glad I did go over – and glad mother went."

Joel flushed as she nudged him, moving his feet clumsily in the sand. "She's Mrs Joel Kruse now," he said looking around at another swooping flash from the lighthouse. "We're settling in her brother's old home – got it all to ourselves."

"What's become of her mother?" asked Mrs Danning, grimly.

"Mother's gone to Plymouth for good, I believe," Lorraine replied with reserve.

"Wasn't she at the wedding?"

"No."

"Who gived 'ee away, then?" inquired Mrs Rescorla.

There was a touch of irony in Lorraine's smile as she answered. "An old friend or enemy of hers – neighbour called Veale my sister-in-law keeps house for. It was a very quiet wedding – no reception. We drove straight from church to the station. We'd had a wedding breakfast at Barrakellis – no guests except Gwen, Joel's sister, and her husband and Mr Veale. But we preferred it that way."

The warm, simple candour of both Joel and Lorraine marked their union as a genuine love match, and won Mrs Rescorla's sympathy. "You got as good a chance as most couples, I s'pose, now you'm free of your mother," she observed. "How long will 'ee be here on honeymoon?"

"Only a week. We go back Saturday morning."

"Well, you'm welcome to drop in for an hour any day, if you'd care to," said Mrs Rescorla.

"Thanks very much," responded Lorraine. "We'll see if we can manage it: though when I think of all I went through in there..."

"I understand."

Mrs Danning had now withdrawn from her window, and on noticing her absence Mrs Rescorla also edged back with a word of farewell and disappeared.

Joel and Lorraine moved stealthily, shadow-like, on across the isthmus, along the open fringe of the beach. The sea was washing in with a cold flutter of spume, the white froth sprawling over the shingle in sudden spurts from the great waters. The black tide was heaving in from the west where the light of peace remained undisturbed, and the daylight flowed in from the east where war had darkened the land. The reality and the symbol seemed to break confusedly together on these lonely shores.

The couple reached the base of the cliff path and began climbing slowly, still with arms around each other, forming a single smudge on the hillside. It was not the first time they had walked here; they had, in fact been strolling along the headland, out towards Porth Hellick, at that momentous hour yesterday when Chamberlain's tired voice was announcing Britain's declaration of war. They had known such a blow to be imminent, and were too awed by the burning joy of their new relationship to stagger or even to feel the need of fortitude. Quietly they had discussed the possible effects of the war upon their marriage: inconvenience, separation, material uncertainty. Having conquered their personal fate they were confronted by a wider fate, with its monstrous threat to the predestined pattern of their lives. But they possessed a core of security which neither personal nor national fate could disturb, and now they had tasted it in the flesh they were ready.

They walked in silence, Joel gazing steadily at the brightening coast, and the weird, terrifying seascape, with his moody absorption. Here as elsewhere he had no eye for detail. He would not observe any particular bird, tree or rock formation; he would merely note that there were birds, trees and rocks of some sort. Even the fantastic tropical luxuriance of natural beauty on the isles would impress him only as a vague background for the miraculous flowering of his own life. The palms, pittosporum and tamarisks meant no more to him than any odd-shaped claywork structure a half-finished tip-frame or dismantled, winding drum. He would not notice whether the puffins had yet shed their rainbow coloured beaks for the winter. He was unaware that puffins did shed their beaks – or even that the quaint little birds standing in solemn groups like dwarf penguins on outlying rocks were puffins at all. He had derived from Euan during recent months a rudimentary grasp of Christian mysticism, in which Nature is recognised as an instrument of Fate and repudiated. But the grey intensity which his love had fused with Lorraine's, when they had stumbled blindly to each other on that sombre harvest night two months ago, was now matured and coloured by the deepening warmth and richness of their union.

As he passed with Lorraine over the brow of the cliff and saw the frail loveliness of the isles, soft and dark amid the tides for miles all round, and the sky above the mainland reddening with sunrise, he was mentally seeing in perspective the strange workings of circumstances through which he and Gwen had finally achieved their release: Gwen entering smoothly, almost without hitch, upon her new inheritance, while he had plumbed depths of irony and bafflement that would always remain in his mind as a nightmare. The vision that had stirred so dimly in the squalid clay-pit cottage at Roche a year ago was now perfectly fulfilled; and he realised that it could have been fulfilled in no other way. He saw that the natural woman must be either as Marvran or as Olive, subtly defending herself or wantonly offering herself. Where there was no faith, love was fraudulent. Marvran would have defrauded him of that full self-exposure which would lead him on to possession; and Olive would have defrauded him of reverence, the sweetest spring of intimacy. Only Lorraine, the believer, could reveal to him the true allure of the woman as bride of election, in whom the redeemed soul flooded into the flesh, with faith controlling the thrill and the flame towering beyond Nature. All the material of his fate had been consumed in the flame, the scabs of the kiln burnt off, the leprous self obliterated...

Lorraine's voice broke quietly in upon his brooding. She had turned towards him, her dark broad face looking rosy and ethereal in the glow of the dawn.

"It'll be something of a strain to go in Mrs Rescorla's," she remarked. "But after all, I came here to feel the contrast... To see you sitting in that parlour, and then think how I used to sit in it less than six months ago..." She pointed to the signal tower on the rise ahead, now emerging from the appearance of a flat black shape, taking on roundness and clarity of detail. "Last February, there by that tower, that last wrangle between me and mother when she came over with the crazy news about Veale and your sister. It left me sick at heart, drained out. I remember how I felt as I looked out over the sea while she was raging, and after she'd gone back. How much has happened since then! It seems unbelievable."

"Yes, it certainly do," said Joel, releasing her as they halted on the path. "You couldn't guess what was happening up around Roche that week. 'Twas exactly then that things come to a crisis for me that terrible week when the kiln went freezing cold, when Marvran switched over to Roy Chegwidden and Olive pounced. And Gwen was getting hemmed in there at Barrakellis, afraid o' your brother. If she hadn't took the plunge and married..."

"Yes, I'm thankful to her – I can't help it, even though it meant such a tragedy and shame for me. It's like Euan says – things are dovetailed in a way we can't understand. The same event that's pre-destined for a believer may be part of the fate of someone who reacts to it without faith. Gwen's marriage was like that in its effect on Cal. But now it's linked up with our faith... I love the way Euan puts things, so strong and clear-cut."

"He's a man in a million," said Joel fervently. "I owe nearly as much to him as Gwen do, the way he's put me straight in my thinking. I was in a sort o' religious fog till he cut through it. And now you're getting to know him" – his lips twitched into a smile – "I might feel a bit scared. I'm so dull and clumsy beside him."

Lorraine remained serious, reaching for his hand as she gazed past the tower, northward towards Tresco.

"You're what I want, Joel," she answered in a low intense tone. "Anyone can see Euan's bound to Gwen heart and soul – even more secure now there's a baby coming... It was lovely to have them at the wedding on Saturday. I can't forget their faces: so glad for us, and so earnest, feeling the threat of the war as we did, knowing what it might mean, yet not really afraid. It hasn't caught 'em unprepared, though they probably haven't given much thought to such things, any more than we have."

Joel partly raised his cap, letting the breeze ruffle his short black hair.

"No, we haven't caught the general mood at all these past twelve months," he admitted. "I s'pose people'd say I've been selfish, wrapped up in me own affairs and not noticing anything outside. But as I've said before, it's like being in a kiln, the way I've growed up and got where I am. Penned in behind the walls and shutters, almost in the dark not even a window to look out of. Nothing to be seen but the hot clay: the air like a oven, getting thick wi' dust till you're half choked. That's what it been like for me."

Lorraine stepped in front of him and laid her hands on his shoulders. He felt the quiver of intimacy, the pride of the wife rousing in her; the big dark eyes searched him with complete reassurance.

"I know," she answered, her voice growing more passionate. "And you haven't been selfish, because you've been fighting to get out – where you could see the pattern of things – and fit in where you belonged. I've been the same, all through my childhood, almost exactly like you: the slums were a sort of kiln. And here on St. Mary's it was the loneliness, the feeling of being thrown out o' the kiln but not wanted... I was waiting for you all those years. And you were fighting through your fate, through the heat and slime of it, right down to the threat from Olive fighting through towards me. And if that Creba girl gave you a glimpse or foretaste of your true world, it doesn't spoil things, because you fought on past her when she, – when she thought the kiln was just a nice place to dance in. You needed someone who'd suffered and could understand. She taught you that, at least."

Joel's eyes were misty; he looked away from her, back towards the mainland. The great wave of colour was arching and kindling rapidly, and the flashes from Peninnis and Bishop Rock lighthouses had ceased.

"Yes – yes, 'tis true, she did," he said huskily. "I don't regret anything now. And I'm glad we've come here: nothing could bring home to me so vivid that I'm right outside the kiln. These islands" – he swept his arm slowly around – "I've never seen anything like it. I used to bike down to the coast sometimes when I was in the football team, but there wasn't any real sense o' freedom like there is here."

"I knew this touch would help you – that's why I suggested it," observed Lorraine, edging from the path and drawing him in upon the bumpy turfed ground towards the tower. "You're feeling now just what I felt when I came here first – the thrill of release. Still, I wouldn't like to settle here; I'm sure you'd get tired of it in time, as I did. The glimpse is helpful, but those clayworks… they have truths we need to keep in mind, truths we'd never learn on these flowery islands."

Joel pondered for a few moments, then nodded slowly.

"I see there's something in that," he said. "Nearer to real life somehow – 'specially now the war's come. Like Euan says, war puts the whole country in a sort o' kiln, shut in and stifled in the heat and dark. And like he says, what pattern comes out of it'll depend on people's faith."

Lorraine bowed her head in silent assent, the long brown hair blowing freely around it. They had soon reached the tower and turned, standing with their backs to it, facing the sunrise. They were the only humans visible on any of the islands, but wild life was abroad, flinging strange buoyant cries upon the mournful plash of the sea. Puffins were wheeling out from their breeding ground on Annet, three miles to the west; gulls and terns swooped over St. Mary's, passing like snowflakes above the shadowed land and the grey water. Down on the isthmus a few tufts of smoke were rising from the chimneys of Hugh Town.

The sunlight crept nearer, further west along the mainland, biting out the dusk from feverish cities and the dull, submissive countryside. It rippled among the sand-tips, then fanned out over the grey roofs of clay-dries until its seaward flash from Land's End struck the tower like a sundering blade, casting the broad warmth of peace upon the lonely watchers.

THE END

Other Works by Jack Clemo

A Different Drummer
A collection of thirty-six poems first published in 1986. These poems movingly and with optimism record aspects of his personal life in Cornwall and Dorset along with incidents in the lives of Holman Hunt, Virginia Woolf and others. 72 pages.
    Published by Tabb House in paperback. Price £2.99
    Distributed by Tor Mark Press. ISBN 0907 018 53 X

The Bouncing Hills
Dialect tales first published in Cornish Almanacks and light verse of more recent years together with a short glossary of Cornish dialect. 106 pages.
    Published by Dyllansow Truran in paperback. Price £1.99
    Distributed by Tor Mark Press. ISBN 0907566 38 3

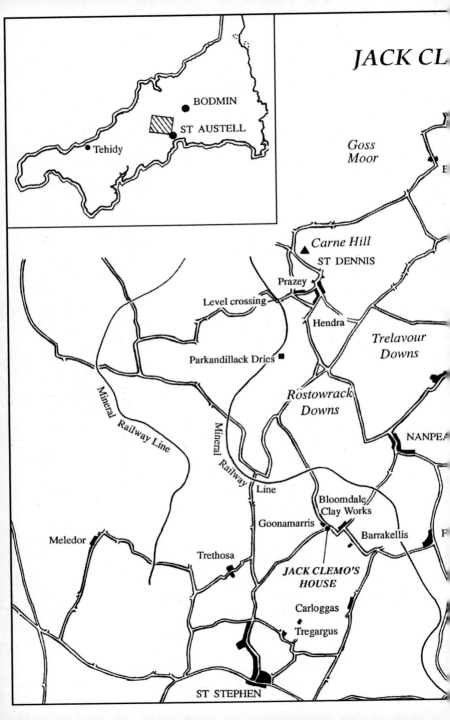

O'S CLAY COUNTRY

ROCHE

Roche Church

▲ Roche Rock

Carbis Dries

BODMIN

Tresayes

BUGLE

en

▲ *Hensbarrow Downs*

STENALEES

White Moor

▲ *Longstone Downs*

▲ *Watch Hill or Foxhole Beacon*

ST AUSTELL

| 1 | MILES | 2 | 3 |

R.D.P. delt Anno MM